THE VICIOUS CIRCLE

ALSO BY KATHERINE ST. JOHN

The Lion's Den

The Siren

THE
VICIOUS
CIRCLE

A NOVEL

KATHERINE
ST. JOHN

wm

WILLIAM MORROW

An Imprint of HarperCollinsPublishers

THE VICIOUS CIRCLE. Copyright © 2022 by Katherine St. John Inc. All rights reserved. Printed in the United States of America. No part of this book may be used or reproduced in any manner whatsoever without written permission except in the case of brief quotations embodied in critical articles and reviews. For information, address HarperCollins Publishers, 195 Broadway, New York, NY 10007.

HarperCollins books may be purchased for educational, business, or sales promotional use. For information, please email the Special Markets Department at SPsales@harpercollins.com.

FIRST EDITION

Designed by Kyle O'Brien
Art by EAKARAT BUANOI © Shutterstock, Inc.
and Chansom Pantip © Shutterstock, Inc.

Library of Congress Cataloging-in-Publication Data

Names: St. John, Katherine, 1979– author.
Title: The vicious circle : a novel / Katherine St. John.
Description: First edition. | New York : William Morrow,
an imprint of HarperCollinsPublishers, [2022]
Identifiers: LCCN 2021058514 | ISBN 9780063224056
(hardcover) | ISBN 9780063224063 (ebook)
Subjects: GSAFD: Suspense fiction.
Classification: LCC PS3619.T2484 V53 2022 | DDC 813/.6—dc23
LC record available at https://lccn.loc.gov/2021058514

ISBN 978-0-06-322405-6

22 23 24 25 26 LSC 10 9 8 7 6 5 4 3 2 1

For anyone who has ever felt inadequate.
You are perfect, just as you are.

KUBLA KHAN

Samuel Taylor Coleridge, 1816

In Xanadu did Kubla Khan
A stately pleasure-dome decree:
Where Alph, the sacred river, ran
Through caverns measureless to man
Down to a sunless sea. . . .

But oh! that deep romantic chasm which slanted
Down the green hill athwart a cedarn cover!
A savage place! as holy and enchanted
As e'er beneath a waning moon was haunted
By woman wailing for her demon-lover! . . .

That sunny dome! those caves of ice!
And all who heard should see them there,
And all should cry, Beware! Beware!
His flashing eyes, his floating hair!
Weave a circle round him thrice,
And close your eyes with holy dread,
For he on honey-dew hath fed,
And drunk the milk of Paradise.

THE VICIOUS CIRCLE

PROLOGUE

I have never been this far into the jungle. Never been this far from civilization, period. And suddenly, I feel as though I've made a terrible mistake.

Beyond the tangle of trees that line the banks of the narrow river, a flash of dazzling white catches my eye. The pit of my stomach hollows.

We must be nearly there now.

I squint past the strangler figs into the impenetrable forest as our canoe glides quietly through the murky water, my view obstructed by a choked patch of leafy bamboo.

"What did you see?" Lucas asks, casting a glance over his shoulder without interrupting the motion of his paddle.

I shrug, covering my apprehension with nonchalance. "Nothing."

I didn't think I'd ever lay eyes on Lucas Baranquilla again. Yet here he is, a dozen years later in a different country, just as irritatingly self-possessed as the last time we met.

He runs his fingers through his tousled dark hair, evaluating me with the slightest flick of his sharp eyes before turning back to the bow. I do appreciate that he's made no attempt to charm me. Though some recognition of the Herculean effort I exerted to come this far, this fast, at his behest, might have been nice. It's a long way from Manhattan to the Mexican jungle, and he has to recognize he's the last person I'd want to make the trip with.

Then again, maybe not.

Regardless, he's met my thorniness with cool tolerance, as though I'm a temperamental child with whom he must have patience—a requirement of his job, no doubt, seeing as he's my uncle's attorney, and, I suppose, mine now. God only knows what astronomical fee we're paying him. Not that he looks much like an attorney with his deep tan, ripped jeans, and faded red T-shirt. I see a hint of a tattoo on the inside of his muscle-bound bicep, too. It wasn't there last time I saw him, though I do remember another one clear as day.

I take a deep breath to wipe the thought from my mind, but the air is so thick it sticks in my lungs. Like the city in August if you swapped the trash smell for the aroma of damp soil and lush vegetation. I brush aside a strand of blond hair that's come loose from my ponytail and point, reaching for my high school Spanish. "La casa de mi . . ." My voice trails off as I fish in vain for the word for uncle.

I don't dare glance in Lucas's direction. Don't want to see him smirk at my almost certainly botched pronunciation, don't need him to translate for me.

Our river guide tilts his straw hat back on his head to peer up the hill where my finger points. "Sí, señora." The air whistles through the gap where his two front teeth should be.

I slap a mosquito that has settled on my thigh, leaving the smashed carcass in a halo of blood, then wipe my palm on my faded jean cutoffs, willing myself not to think about the consequences a mosquito bite can have in the tropics.

Unseen birds call to one another with unfamiliar songs as we navigate our canoe through swirling eddies beneath trees that reach toward one another across the water like long-lost lovers. Our guide points to what appears to be a bumpy log at the river's edge. "Cocodrilo," he says.

I inhale sharply, instinctively lifting my dripping paddle from the water.

"Crocodile," Lucas translates with a grin.

"Thanks, I got that," I return, eyeing the other logs floating in the river.

We glide around a bend and without warning we're dumped into a lagoon the size of a city block. I raise a hand to shade my eyes from the sudden glare of the sun, finally catching sight of the colossal villa that rises from the misty jungle like a wedding cake.

Xanadu sits in a clearing atop a hill, beyond a monumental fountain and a series of intricately terraced gardens that spill down to the water's edge, where a dock stretches into the lake. The reflection of the afternoon light on the ivory façade is so bright, I can't make out much detail beyond the wide columns and rows of arched windows at least three stories high, but the scope of the place is stunning.

"Damn." Lucas trails his paddle through the water as he stares up at the villa.

The pictures I googled of it online yesterday didn't take into account the juxtaposition with the landscape, didn't prepare me for the sheer size of the thing. It's not like this is the first time I've seen a palatial estate; though I grew up about as far from fancy as you can get, working as a model has put me squarely in the path of the world's wealthy for half my life at this point. My fiancé's parents have a house in Connecticut that must be at least fifteen thousand square feet, not to mention their Hamptons and Aspen homes. But this level of opulence, here of all places, is truly awe-inspiring.

I glance down at the square-cut diamond on my finger and the pit in my stomach deepens. Is he still my fiancé? God, it's been an awful year so far—and it's only January eighth. But I can't allow myself to dwell on that now.

I blink up at the riverside Babylon, half expecting the vision to shimmer and fade like a mirage. No wonder my uncle Paul—Shiva, I have to remember to call him here—named the place Xanadu. I carried a copy of the Coleridge poem in my wallet for years, though it was unnecessary: I can still recite the whole thing by heart, as could he the last time I saw him.

Eight years ago. It was Halloween, and I'd just turned twenty-one. I remember my party-girl roommates being dumbfounded that I'd willingly traded a night of costumed revelry for a lecture on spirituality at a Brooklyn theater. I didn't tell them who Paul Bentzen was to me. I shrank from the idea of anyone knowing he was my father's brother; didn't want to face the questions I couldn't answer about why we were estranged.

At least publicly, he was still Paul Bentzen then and at the height of his fame, before the bad press tarnished his shine, on tour promoting his latest book with a series of lectures at sold-out concert venues. *Living the Life You Deserve,* it was called. People lined up from all over the world to hear him talk about how to find stillness and true connection in an ever faster and more isolated world.

I listened to his lecture in a daze, just as transfixed by him as the seekers and believers in the audience. It was impossible not to be. He was in his late forties at the time, his tall frame draped in white linen, wavy silver-blond hair loose about his shoulders, ice-blue eyes flashing as he preached like a Viking Jesus about radical affirmation and the beauty of surrendering to God. My Russian Orthodox mother had dragged me to church for liturgy and dogma every Sunday until I left home at fourteen, and while I feared retribution for my many sins, never once did I feel my heart swell the way hers did gazing up at the stained-glass windows above the altar. But Paul's was a different God; an accessible God of love and light, of forgiveness and acceptance. It was no wonder he'd amassed a loyal following of millions with his books, podcasts, and workshops.

As I sat there with three hundred other lost souls listening to him speak, my heart ached with the realization of how much I'd missed him over the past decade. His sporadic visits between travels in far-flung locales had been the bright spots in my otherwise dingy childhood, his million-watt smile temporarily diffusing the gray clouds that always seemed to hang over our saltbox house. Even my reticent father seemed lighter when Paul was around. I remember falling asleep at night to the sound of their voices filtering through the thin walls as they sat at the kitchen table drinking coffee and debating religion, politics, and philosophy, quoting at one another from dog-eared esoteric tomes.

I listened in awe as Paul told me stories of tracking poachers in Kenya and recounted tales of being chased by wild boars in Indonesia and pirates off the coast of Sri Lanka. My dad couldn't deal with crowds or loud noises, but Paul took me to see the fireworks in DC on the Fourth of July and to the state fair in Raleigh, where he rode every ride with me and ate just as much cotton candy as I did. It was shortly after this experience I expressed to my mother that I wished he were my dad instead, and she slapped me across the face.

After Paul finished answering questions that evening in Brooklyn, I stood in line at the back of the auditorium with everyone else to get my copy signed. I hadn't seen him since my father's funeral, when I was eleven, and wasn't sure he'd know me, though our familial resemblance was stronger than ever. When he glanced up from the book he was signing to get my name, his eyes blazed with recognition and he broke into a radiant smile.

"Sveta!" he cried, standing abruptly. Bystanders looked on with interest as he leaned across the table to hug me, impervious to their stares. As we pulled apart, I found my eyes had misted and he was waving over a beautiful young woman with caramel skin and long raven hair, who couldn't have been more than ten years older than me. "I'm taking a break," he told her. She took me in with gleaming gray eyes, a hint of suspicion in her curiosity, and I recognized she was more than just his tour manager. "This is my niece, Sveta. My brother's daughter."

Her gaze softened and she gave me a warm smile. "Kali," she said, pulling me in to kiss me once on each cheek before enveloping me in a musky floral-scented hug. "So nice to meet you."

I don't remember exactly what Paul and I said in the quarter hour we spent sitting on a threadbare couch in the greenroom of the theater. I know he asked about my mother, who was still cleaning houses in South Florida and proud as ever. I recall being touched he'd followed my career and seen my latest spread in Italian *Vogue.* He encouraged me to continue writing poetry, asked whether I still remembered "Kubla Khan," and we recited it together. When Kali appeared in the doorway signaling our time was up, he invited me to meet him at the Plaza for dinner, but I had to catch a midnight flight to Japan for a job.

He reached out a couple of times after that, inviting me to visit the California retreat center he was operating before he exiled himself to this jungle in the wake of the accusations that tainted his name. Out of loyalty to my mother I never went. I still don't know why she cut him off after my father's death; her lips are sealed as tightly as a clamshell. She's not an easy woman, my mother. But she's also not a person who does things without reason, and she loves me like a mother bear loves her cubs: not softly, but biologically.

I'm so lost in thought that it takes me a moment to register the six-foot-high pile of sticks at the river's edge, a white shape barely visible atop it. My breath catches in my throat as I realize what I'm looking at.

My brilliant uncle, the bestselling author who inspired a spiritual awakening in so many, the last living member of my father's family, is wrapped inside that shroud. This pile of sticks on the bank of a river that snakes through the Lacandon Jungle is his funeral pyre.

Lucas looks from the pyre to me, his nearly black eyes creased with concern. Or perhaps he's simply squinting into the sun.

An unexpected wave of emotion crashes into my chest. I drop my damp forehead into my hands, staring past my knees to the muddy, dented metal bottom of the boat. I don't know what I'm so afraid of. I knew he was dead; I knew I was coming here for his funeral. But seeing his body wrapped in white gauze, so small in relation to this lake, this rain forest, that house—so vulnerable, about to be burned before my eyes . . . I didn't expect this.

I realize I'm sheltered. Out of touch, overly privileged. That is to say, American. We don't take care of our own dead anymore.

I vividly remember the uniformed pallbearers carrying my father's flag-draped casket from the hearse through the dappled shade of the orange and yellow sycamore trees to the grave site. After the funeral, I was tortured by dreams of his broken body tumbling onto the grass, his beloved face unrecognizable in the wake of the blast that killed him. I was a child, of course I was afraid of death. But I'm an adult now. I know intellectually that death is a natural part of the life cycle, and Paul of all people would understand this inherently.

Get it together, Sveta.

I won't be a coward. I will face this uncomfortable moment and live through it, as he instructed in *Surrender,* his first bestseller.

As we navigate past the pyre toward the dock, I force myself to raise my eyes and rest my gaze on the white gauze figure atop the pile of sticks. Blinking away the blur of unwanted tears, I grip the side of the canoe and bid my uncle farewell.

PART ONE

ROOTS

Is it not true that we define ourselves by the people
we're surrounded by and how they see us? If we are
praised, we believe we are worthy of praise. If we are
ridiculed, we believe we are worthy of ridicule. To end
this vicious cycle, we must develop an independent
sense of self-worth based in Divine Love.

—Paul Bentzen, *Living the Life You Deserve*

ONE

Nine Days Earlier

It was cold and only getting colder in the city; the temperature had been plummeting all day. Regardless, I'd been looking forward to wearing the gorgeous spaghetti-strap minidress covered in dime-size gold sequins that a designer friend had gifted me, and I was not to be deterred. I had just the right coat to bundle up in, too: a glamorous floor-length faux mink number that was like wearing a fur blanket and made me look like Veronica Lake, whom I've been told I favor. I even did a deep side part and wave like Veronica, completing the look with a pair of thigh-high black leather boots and red lipstick. It was New Year's Eve, after all. If not tonight, then when?

I felt a thrill of anticipation as I swanned down the bamboo stairs of the Tribeca loft I shared with my fiancé, stopping to pose in an exaggerated fashion for his benefit. He sat on the leather couch below watching a basketball game in a skinny black suit, looking good enough to eat, all clean shaven with his light brown hair slicked back like a dandy. I've always loved a man in a nice suit, and while every suit Chase Ayres owns is nice, this one was particularly dashing.

I cleared my throat and put on my best Russian accent, channeling my Soviet-born mother. "Dahlingk, I am veady to party."

Chase looked up, and I twirled to showcase my look. "Wow," he said.

The right word, but not exactly the delivery I'd been hoping for. "What?" I asked, tugging at the hem of my dress, suddenly self-conscious.

"You look hot. It's just . . . a lot, is all."

My heart sank. "You always want me to dress up more," I protested, clomping the rest of the way down the stairs. "And it's New Year's Eve."

"Yeah, but we're going to my brother's place for dinner. In Brooklyn Heights."

"And Becky's always wearing couture."

He stood and spun me toward the leather-bound mirror leaning against the wall. "But Becky doesn't look like you do in couture." He pressed himself into me from behind as he growled in my ear, sliding his hand up my skirt. "You wear that, every man in the room will wanna do the things only I get to do with you . . ."

"Jealous?" I teased.

"You know I love that ass." His face changed into something resembling a wince. "But you're always complaining my family doesn't respect you. And this getup—"

I shrugged him off. "Got it."

Dropping my coat over the iron railing, I flew up the stairs two at a time and stomped across our ivory bedroom rug in my boots, hoping the thought of the New York grime on the bottom of my shoes rubbing into the carpet made him as disgusted as I felt. He was right, though. I did want to be accepted by the people he cared about. The sophisticated gray wool wrap dress Chase's brother and his wife had given me for Christmas would be a better choice. But I was keeping the boots, damnit, and I'd wear my party dress beneath, for the club we planned on going to after—the club where we'd met, three years ago.

I'd never been much of a club girl, but it was fashion week, and I was there for the after-party of a show I'd walked. The space, called House Party, was designed to feel like a house, each room decorated differently, complete with a kitchen and bedrooms you could rent, ostensibly for parties, though I'd heard people used them more scandalously. I was in the "backyard" looking up at the twinkling lights masquerading as stars when I spied him leaning against the stone mantel of the "outdoor fireplace," scotch in hand, looking like he owned the place.

"It's the cockatoo," he said with an easy smile.

"You were at the show?" I asked, eyeing him. Damn, he was handsome.

He nodded. "Went to boarding school with Jared." Jared being the designer.

"Was he as fashionable then?" I asked.

"I do remember the day he showed up in a deconstructed uniform, held together with safety pins. I knew then he had it in him to design bird dresses for fancy ladies."

I laughed. "What was your favorite part?"

"The cockatoo, of course."

"Why's that? You into feathers?" I teased.

"It was the look in your eye. A little wild, like you might actually fly away."

"You must've been sitting close."

"Not close enough."

He held my gaze, and my heart fluttered. "Careful, I might take flight," I said.

"Where to?"

I bit my lip, emboldened by his obvious interest. "Where do you want to go?"

That easy smile again. The smile of a man for whom doors simply opened. "Wherever you're headed."

I looked up at the fake stars. "Somewhere with real stars."

"I have an idea."

We picked up a bottle of cabernet on the way to what turned out to be his office building, where we drank it straight from the bottle on a plastic lounger someone had dragged up to the roof. Beneath the scant stars visible above Manhattan, we traded witticisms and danced to music from our phones, laughing as we shared details about how opposite our upbringings had been. He was the Prince Charming to my Cinderella, only it didn't end at midnight. He kissed me as the sun rose over the city, and by the time I caught my breath, three years had passed.

We hadn't been back to House Party since, but when my friends invited us to meet up there to ring in the new year, I'd thought it might be fun to revisit the scene of the crime. I even went so far as to suggest a little light role-playing, in hopes of rekindling the flame between us that had dimmed since our engagement eight months ago. Hence my desire to look sexy and a little wild—like a bird that might fly away.

But first, wool.

"Okay, I'm ready," I called as I descended the stairs, fastening the tie of the gray wrap dress over my sequins. "Better?" I asked, gesturing to my outfit. "It's what they gave me for Christmas."

"Perfect."

I strode across the stainless steel kitchen and swung open the refrigerator, pulling out the Veuve I'd picked up earlier.

His eyes flicked to the bottle in my hand. "Is that what we're bringing?"

"Yeah, I figured champagne was appropriate."

He bit his lip.

"What?" I asked.

"Nothing," he said.

"Then why is your face all pinched?"

"It's just—they're not gonna drink that."

"What? Why?" I asked.

"They're connoisseurs." He rubbed his temples, frustrated. "You know this."

"Right." I squinted at him, confused. "I distinctly remember your brother saying anything under fifty dollars was undrinkable. This was over fifty bucks."

"It's not the cost, it's a taste thing."

"It tastes good enough they sell it in practically every liquor store in the city."

"Exactly." He sighed and checked his watch, making a mental calculation. "No time to stop. It'll be fine."

"Brock and Becky's lives are one big Rich People Problem," I remarked as I sashayed toward the door. "It'll be good for them to drink the nectar of the populace."

Chase's silence in the elevator told me my attempt at levity had fallen flat. It was true, though, except the bit about fifty-dollar champagne being the nectar of the populace, obviously. My hardworking mother would have a heart attack if she knew I'd wasted fifty dollars on champagne. Actually, I take that back. If she knew it was for Chase's family, she'd be fine with it. The Ayreses could do no wrong in her eyes, though they'd never made an effort to so much as meet her. This did nothing to dampen her adoration of Chase, who'd charmed her thoroughly every time she was in town. The day I married my Prince Charming and she no longer had to be so worried about me would be the best day of her life.

I hoped it wouldn't also be the first time she laid eyes on my soon-to-be in-laws. She hated to travel during the holidays, so she normally came to visit in October for my birthday, and Chase's family had been full of excuses every time I'd invited them to meet her during these trips. So when she canceled her birthday trip last-minute this year, I insisted she come for Thanksgiving, knowing they would have to invite her to dinner if she was in town. Unfortunately, she canceled that visit, too, so they were yet to meet.

Outside, delicate flakes of snow were just beginning to fall. I tilted my head back and stuck out my tongue. My breath fogged in the night and pinpricks of ice caressed my face. I felt alive. Chase signaled the black Suburban idling at the curb a few yards up the cobblestone street.

I placed a gloved hand on the sleeve of his cashmere overcoat as the car rolled slowly toward us, knowing I needed to speak up before we got in. Chase was a stickler for not airing your dirty laundry in front of chauffeurs. "Sorry," I said sincerely. "I guess I just get defensive around the subject of your brother because of our history."

Our history being that Brock told Chase I was just after his money and he'd be sorry for marrying me. After which, to his credit, Chase didn't speak to him for nearly a month. I was supposed to have forgiven and forgotten like Chase had, but it's been a struggle, to say the least.

"It's okay." He kissed me, his lips warm on mine. "Their lives *are* one big Rich People Problem." He chuckled. "You're so right."

He took my hand and together we dove into the dark serenity of the Suburban.

TWO

Across the river, the lights of lower Manhattan twinkled gold and silver through the thick white flakes like a bewitched snow globe. The scene was almost beautiful enough to make up for the knot of anxiety that had formed in the pit of my stomach right on schedule, the moment we walked into Brock and Becky's penthouse.

But tonight was going to be different. Tonight, I wouldn't offend the hosts by telling them I'd fallen in love with their dining room table when I'd seen it at Pottery Barn (it was *not* from Pottery Barn—nothing here was). I wouldn't comment that I'd heard the schools in this area were great (they weren't nearly as great as the sixty-five-thousand-dollar-a-year private school their kindergartner attended, which was apparently a bargain). I wouldn't be the butt of jokes after mispronouncing some word everyone else had no trouble with (who knew the *p* in "ophthalmologist" sounded like an *f*?). And I certainly wouldn't hand them an offensive bottle of Veuve Clicquot. No, we'd left that in the car.

Brock and Becky's apartment was stunning. A large corner unit on the nineteenth floor of a brand-spanking-new building that soared above the surrounding brownstones like a spaceship parked at the river's edge, it had an open floor plan, walls of glass, and an aerodynamically curved balcony complete with a firepit. The Wallace-Ayreses' taste was more contemporary than mine—modern art and oddly patterned chunky chairs atop a bold rug Brock had eagerly divulged cost more than most cars—but the bones and view were so extraordinary, it didn't much matter.

We were the first to arrive. I stood barefoot at the window gazing out at the night, wishing it were warm enough to enjoy the balcony. Over the jazz that filtered through the speakers, I could hear Brock at the bar waxing poetic about the exclusive small-batch whiskey he and Chase were drinking. A uniformed chef and two servers worked silently in the sleek kitchen while somewhere in the depths of the apartment the nanny put the baby and the five-year-old to bed. Becky was yet to appear.

Growing up an only child, I'd always wished for a sister and hoped that maybe someday I'd gain one through marriage. I was optimistic about Becky at first: unlike her husband, she was always nice to me. So I tried with her, I really did. I perused her Instagram page for what we had in common and dropped it into conversation ("I love Pilates! Have you tried Barre-lates? We should go together!"). When we went on a ski vacation with his family, I abandoned my snowboard to keep her company skiing blues and greens while the guys hit the double black diamonds that called my name. But she never returned the effort. In the three years Chase and I have been together, she and I still haven't even traded phone numbers. In fact, I don't think she's ever asked me a single question about my life—though I could write a thesis on The Problems They've Encountered Building Their Beach House or The Reasons They Fired Their Last Nanny.

"Dom?" Chase proffered a glass of bubbly with a wink.

"Thank you, darlingk, don't mind if I do." The Russian accent again, a sure sign I was uncomfortable. I gulped down half the glass, leaving my esophagus burning.

The click of heels on the hardwood drew my attention to Becky, carefully treading down the hallway toward us in gorgeous four-inch black-and-green snakeskin Louboutins. "I just buzzed the Thompsons up," she announced.

Her petite frame was wrapped in a skintight black dress with a deeply plunging neckline complemented by emerald earrings that dangled below her chin-length beige-blond hair, bringing out her round green eyes. Her husband let out a low whistle, the response I'd been hoping for from his brother earlier in the evening.

"I know, I know," she said. "We're staying in, it's silly. But it's New Year's Eve!"

"You look beautiful," I said, starting across the living room to embrace her, but the elevator dinged before I could reach her, and she moved beyond the fogged glass partition that concealed the entry.

Unsure what to do with myself, I glanced over at Chase and Brock, perusing the appetizer spread on the dining room table while talking in hushed tones. Brock was four years older and two inches shorter, but otherwise they looked so much alike they were practically twins, with their black suits, slicked-back hair, and perfectly shined shoes. Shoes. I'd taken mine off because they normally had a rule about it, but—I looked around—*was I the only one not wearing shoes?*

I slipped into the entryway to grab my shoes and found Becky greeting a couple who looked like they'd walked off the cover of *Yachting* magazine, the winter issue. They were tan and blond and vaguely sporty looking, Barbie in a navy-and-white dress I recognized as last-season Chanel, her Ken in a collared shirt that peeked out from beneath his cashmere sweater.

"Leave those gorgeous shoes on, it's fine," Becky said to Barbie. I brushed her hip as I reached to grab my discarded boots, causing her to gasp and spin around. "You scared me!" She laughed. "I didn't see you there."

I smiled. "Just gonna slip my boots back on."

"Don't bother," she returned with a dismissive wave of her hand. "You're so tall you dwarf us."

I prickled, covering with a hollow laugh. I wish people knew just how many times tall people are made to feel guilty for being tall. Like it's our fault. In school, the kids called me Skeletor after I shot up ten inches between seventh and eighth grade without gaining an ounce of curve, and none of the boys would dance with me because I towered over them. I hate to admit that it still gives me pleasure to think of the girls who used to whisper behind my back now flipping through *Cosmopolitan* magazine and seeing me in a perfume ad. Yes, I'm grateful for my height because it gave me the career that was my ticket out of nowheresville; still, I've always envied the shorter girls who make me feel like Godzilla.

Regardless, in the interest of social grace I obediently deserted my shoes and extended my hand to Barbie. "Hi, I'm Sveta."

"Sveta's Brock's brother's girlfriend," Becky explained.

"Fiancée." I smiled, displaying the three-carat stunner on my finger. Somehow his family always failed to make this distinction, as though if they just ignored it long enough, the ring might disappear.

"Sveta," her husband mulled, looking me over. "Short for Svetlana?"

I nodded, and he proudly disgorged a halting string of consonants from his throat.

I gave him an apologetic smile. "Sorry, I don't speak Russian."

"No?" His face said he thought I was lying. "With a name like that I figured—but maybe you're Czech? Or Croatian?"

"No, you're right—my mother is from Russia," I said. "But I never learned the language."

"Why not?" he asked.

His wife crossed her arms, impatient for the conversation to be over, so I took my time to reply. "My mom had a hard life growing up there. Her parents died when she was a kid—I'm actually named for her mother. But my father was American, and she wanted me to be American, so she refused to speak Russian with me. Wanted me to belong, I guess."

"A shame," he said. "It's a beautiful language."

"Beautiful" isn't exactly the adjective I would use to describe Russian, but at least he was being nice. "How do you know Russian?" I asked.

"He doesn't," Barbie answered with a tight smile before turning and walking away with Becky on her heels, entreating her to try the hors d'oeuvres.

Ken gestured to his wife's back as he leaned in, whispering, "My ex is Russian. She can get a little touchy about it."

BY THE TIME WE SAT down to dinner I'd lost track of how often my glass had been refilled, and the knot in my stomach had somewhat unwound. The elegant wood dining table was tastefully bedecked with delicate white flowers and airy greenery and set for eleven, with five on one side and six on the other, as one of the men's wives had come down with a fever that afternoon. I was of course the sacrificial sixth seat on the end.

"This silver is exquisite," enthused a busty woman in a fur wrap who was married to a reedy bald man. The many diamonds on her fingers sparkled in the light cast by the two ornate candelabras as she inspected a fork. "It's so old school."

"Thank you, Carla," Becky answered. "It was my grandmother's. I never get to use it."

Becky's grandmother was also from North Carolina, though a different sort of North Carolina from me.

"It makes me think," Carla went on, "maybe we should use real silver at the fundraiser next month. Did I tell you the Watersons just committed twenty-five cases of pinot from their winery in Napa?"

"Too bad I won't be able to enjoy it." Brock's Yale rowing teammate Teddy brandished his empty wineglass in the direction of the server, who immediately refilled it. "Sobriety starts tomorrow," he groused with a resentful glance across the table at his wife, who I noticed had not touched her own wine. "Li Min thinks I drink too much."

A split second of sheer loathing flashed across Li Min's pretty face before she covered it with a smile. "Only for January," she clarified lightly. "So we'll be finished in time for the fundraiser. And we're both doing it."

"Whole Thirty?" Brock guessed.

Teddy shrugged as he drained half his glass in one swig. "She's been reading some self-help book about how you can find happiness if you just take all the fun out of everything. Makes no fucking sense."

"It's called the Reset," Li Min said calmly. The knot in my stomach grew to the size of a baseball with the recognition of the diet my uncle Paul had pioneered. "It's about getting rid of impurities in the body to jump-start your life."

"Oh! I did that years ago," Barbie said. "There's a guided meditation part, too, right? Like, videos online," she explained to the table. "With really beautiful people telling you to let go of past trauma and embrace your true self. Some famous self-help guy started it."

"Paul Bentzen," Li Min confirmed.

Her husband recoiled. "You didn't tell me there were videos. That's not happening."

Brock furrowed his brow, trying to place the name. "Isn't Paul Bentzen the one that got me-too'd a while back?"

"I think it was some kind of sex thing," Carla chimed in, stroking her fur wrap.

"Great, we're doing the rapist diet," Teddy snorted.

I shot Chase a glance, anger simmering beneath my skin. He knew Paul was my uncle, but Brock and Becky didn't. I'd never mentioned it because of the rumors currently being discussed, regardless of their falsity.

"Seriously," Carla said. "I don't remember exactly, but I think he raped one of his followers, like, in front of people. It was really crazy."

I couldn't hold my tongue any longer. "That's not true," I blurted.

All heads swiveled toward me.

"He didn't rape anyone," I continued. "He wasn't even there when the alleged incident happened."

"How do you know?" Carla asked.

"He's my uncle," I said as evenly as I could muster. I was hyper-aware this revelation would only further stigmatize me in the eyes of Brock and Becky, but if I couldn't stand up for my own blood, then who was I?

Becky's silver fork clattered to her plate. "Oh my God," she exclaimed. "Paul Bentzen is your uncle?"

"And he didn't rape anyone," I confirmed. I hadn't heard it from his lips, of course, but after years of not speaking to him, my mother had called him at the time to hear his side of the story, which she relayed to me. "There was a ritual ceremony a participant sued over, claiming she was uncomfortable. It settled out of court because she'd signed off on it and was free to leave at any time but chose to stay and participate. He was devastated that his practices could have caused anyone psychological harm and closed his California retreat center over it. Then later it came out that she'd sued multiple companies for various things under different aliases."

"What was the ceremony?" Carla asked.

"What's he like?" Li Min overlapped.

"He's wonderful," I answered honestly. "Big heart, genuinely interested in people . . ."

"So what happened to him after the—I mean, where is he now?" Carla asked.

"He's retired from public life." I didn't feel the need to tell them that I didn't know much else, as I hadn't actually seen him in years. "He lives at his retreat center in the jungle with his wife."

"Who's his—"

"So, I think congratulations are in order," Brock interrupted Li Min, evidently tired of this line of conversation. He clapped Chase on the back and looked to me with a wolfish smile, raising his wineglass. "Two years from tonight, my little brother will be a married man."

"One year," I said, forcing a smile. I'd wanted nothing more than a beach wedding this coming summer, but had acquiesced to Chase's mother's insistence that we marry in her church in Connecticut next New Year's Eve, hoping it would make her more receptive to me. So far, no luck.

"Mother changed it," Chase mumbled, not meeting my eye.

I stared at him, suddenly claustrophobic in my stupid wool dress, the effort to stay cool sending beads of perspiration trickling down my back.

"Renovations on the Aspen house won't be finished until next fall, and she wants to spend the holidays there next year," Brock explained. "You know Mother and her houses."

I wanted to scream. Brock had surely known I was unaware of the change and had wanted to jab me. But why hadn't Chase told me?

I stared at his patrician profile, willing him to look at me, but he didn't turn, instead raising his glass with a flawless smile. "To Sveta, my beautiful bride."

I mechanically raised my glass and pasted on a smile, the knot in my stomach now a bowling ball. But I couldn't let Brock see he'd gutted me, wouldn't let him win.

I noticed a rash creeping up Chase's neck toward his hairline. So he was as upset as I was, though for different reasons. Good.

"Where's the wedding?" Carla asked.

"Saint Luke's," I said, holding on to my composure by a straw.

"With a reception at the country club." Brock grinned. "Just like ours."

"Aw, I remember your wedding!" Li Min enthused.

"Your dress was so gorgeous," Barbie added, looking at Becky.

I fumed as the rest of the table set off on a tangent about the elegance of Brock and Becky's wedding.

Chase leaned in, his voice low in my ear. "You okay?"

I grabbed my wineglass and stood, turning abruptly away from the table to hide the fury written on my face as I beelined for the entryway, where I grabbed my purse and shoes. I could feel Chase's eyes on my back as I ducked into the over-wallpapered powder room and shut the door firmly behind me.

I white-knuckled the edge of the vanity and let out a silent string of expletives to my countenance in the mirror, unsure whether I was angrier that he'd allowed his mother to delay our marriage by a year, or that he'd put me in the position to hear about it from Brock—in public, no less. It wasn't fair. I tried so hard to fit in with his family, but it was never enough. I was never enough—would never *be* enough. I wasn't a blue blood, I wasn't educated, I wasn't wealthy. I was the kind of girl he was supposed to have a fling with, not marry. So *of course* his family was making it as hard as possible for us to become husband and wife.

But I wasn't about to let them win.

Screw him. Screw all of them. No way was I sitting through the rest of dinner. I had to get out of there.

I peeled off the stupid wool wrap to reveal my sexy minidress and pulled on my gorgeous boots, prototypes for next year's collection that were more expensive, I was sure, than any of the designer shoes all the other women were wearing. Not that I cared, but expensive clothes were armor in a room with Brock and Becky's friends, and I needed the strongest defense possible to get out of there without letting my emotion get the best of me.

I retouched my makeup in the mirror as I racked my brain for the best exit strategy. I could literally just walk out without a word. Chase deserved it. But I didn't want Brock to know he'd gotten between us.

I called up my catwalk confidence to exit the bathroom with my phone in hand and strode over to the end of the table, where I stood glittering like a disco ball in the candlelight. They wanted a vapid, bitchy model, let them have a vapid, bitchy model. I made sure I could feel everyone's eyes on me before I looked up from my phone and fixed my eyes on Chase. "Babe"—I ran my fingers through my hair, displaying the long arrow tattoo that ran down the inside of my arm—"we've gotta go."

"Oh," Chase said, clearly unsure how to respond. "Right. Can't we—? Do we have to go now?"

"I was having so much fun, I didn't realize what time it was," I said without smiling. "We're already late."

"Right, right." Recognizing he needed to go along with me if he didn't want a scene, Chase pushed his chair back abruptly and stood. "I'm so sorry to take off like this," he said to Brock and Becky. I leaned over and left a red lipstick stain on Becky's cheek, fully aware I was exposing a scandalous amount of cleavage to the opposite side of the table, then straightened up and blew them all a kiss. "Happy New Year." I beamed.

I snaked my arm around Chase's waist, relishing the fact that the tiger tattoo on my back was glaring at them through the straps of my dress as we exited.

THREE

What the hell?" I demanded the minute the elevator doors closed. His fingers flew over the keyboard of his phone. "I'm texting the driver," he said without looking up.

I stared daggers into him. "Two years?"

His shoulders sagged as he met my eye. "I'm sorry. I was gonna tell you."

"When?"

"I meant to tell you this week, but I knew you'd react like this."

I fought back tears. "As I have every right to!"

"You know my mom, she's a steamroller. I didn't have any part in it—"

"But you didn't stop it."

"I said I'm sorry!" He rubbed his temples. "My head is pounding. Can we please just skip the yelling and get to the part where you understand this is for the best?" he implored.

It made my blood boil that he was right: my pattern was to blow a gasket, then, in the interest of preserving the peace, roll over and apologize. But this was too important—and I'd had too much Dom—to preserve the peace tonight.

"You realize she's only doing this to drive us apart," I pressed.

"Clearly it's working," he muttered.

"Because you're letting her have her way!"

"She's my mother, Sveta. She's not some monster. And she's paying for it."

"Which is totally unnecessary," I pointed out. "We can pay for it. Hell, I'll get married at city hall if you don't want to spend money on a wedding. I'd rather that, actually. You know I only agreed to this fancy wedding because it's what she wants. And now she's throwing it back in my face."

The elevator doors opened into the chic, clublike lobby, empty save the doorman, and Chase strode purposefully across the terrazzo tile toward the double glass doors. I scurried after him out into the snow, where our Suburban idled at the curb.

The driver held the car door open for us and we dove into the back. "She's picked the venue, she's picked the date—next thing I know she'll be choosing my dress," I whispered urgently. "Then she'll be naming our children and deciding which schools they attend."

"Sveta." He shot me a warning glance as the chauffeur climbed into the driver's seat. But to hell with decorum, there was no way I was shutting up this time.

"This is our wedding," I continued. "Not hers."

He cut his eyes to the driver, the corner of his mouth down-turned.

"I don't give a damn," I snapped, surprised by my own audacity. The train had left the station and there didn't seem to be any slowing it. "We have to talk about this."

"Can you at least stop cursing," he hissed.

"Jesus *fucking* Christ," I groaned.

He set his mouth in a hard line and breathed deeply through his nose. "You're drunk."

"I'm not drunk," I retorted. But that was a lie. I took a deep breath, suppressing my outrage. "Fine, you're right. I drank too much trying to be comfortable around those people." I sighed. He nodded.

I took his hand. "Can't we just elope?" I asked more gently. "Go somewhere romantic, just the two of us? Or we can get married in Vegas for all I care. I feel like this wedding is tearing us apart. I just want to be us again."

He shifted his gaze to me, his eyes tired. "My family is my family," he said quietly. "It's never going to be just us." He rubbed his temples and looked out the window again. We were on the bridge now, steel supports blurring as we sped past. "I just wish you could get along with them."

"I really am trying," I said, indignant. "I agreed to the church, when you know it's not what I wanted." The anger I'd dampened flared. "Not to mention, I gave up my career when we got engaged because your mom didn't approve—"

"Your modeling career was going to be over soon anyway, and we agreed I make so much money it didn't make sense for you to go back to pounding the pavement for castings." He popped his knuckles. "I'm trying to give you a great life. Can't you see that?"

"Trying to give me?" I blinked at him. "I thought we were building a great life together."

"Jesus, semantics! Why does this have to be so hard?"

Tears rolled down my cheeks. "You mean why can't I just fall in line and become the person your family wishes I were?"

"You're right, okay?" He threw his hands up. "My family said you weren't marriage material. *But I proposed anyway.* I didn't listen. I'm not the bad guy here. I'm just trying to make everybody happy, and it's killing me."

My throat constricted, holding in the sobs I couldn't let out in front of him. Blinking back tears, I stared at the gorgeous diamond on my finger, wondering how it had done so much damage to our relationship.

"Do you still love me?" I asked.

"Of course," he muttered. But he was looking out the window again.

Not exactly the profession of undying love I was hoping for. "Do you still want to marry me?" I pressed.

He met my gaze, his eyes unreadable in the dark. "Do you still want to marry me?"

Did I? I'd been so giddy when he'd dropped to his knee on the beach in Hawaii back in May, but now our impending nuptials just filled me with dread. And what about after? Did I really think his family would welcome me with open arms once we'd said "I do"?

"I don't know," I admitted, my voice barely audible. "I think we could use some space to figure things out."

It felt like hours passed before he nodded. "If that's what you want. I can go to my parents', I guess."

That was the last thing I wanted. "No," I said. "I'll go."

I wiped my eyes and tried to still my breath, feeling as though I'd just jumped off a bridge with no idea what was beneath. I had to get out of the car. "Driver, can you pull over here, please?"

"Where are you going?" Chase asked as the Suburban rolled to a stop at the curb.

"I don't know," I said, grabbing the Veuve from beneath the seat. I had a feeling I was going to need it. "Happy New Year."

And with that, I flung open the door and stumbled out into the falling snow.

FOUR

"Welcome to the Mandala." The woman in the video was as beautiful as her voice was soothing, with glowing ebony skin and large, mesmerizing eyes that seemed to reach through the computer screen. "I'm Ruby, and I'll be your guide for video six in our complimentary series on embracing your true self. Now close your eyes, taking a moment to center."

I did as instructed, though I'd be a liar if I said I was anywhere close to centered. I'd been living on my modeling mentor Tara and her wife Roz's couch for a full week, and I was just as much of a mess as when I'd shown up: angry and righteous, sad and lonely. The idea of breaking off the engagement shriveled my heart, while the thought of waiting a full two years for the wedding filled me with fury.

In search of guidance, I'd located Paul's videos on YouTube, sifting through hours of footage of his lectures on diffusing spiritual blocks and processing pain to find morsels of advice relevant to my situation. A few of the videos I'd seen before, but most were new to me, though they weren't recent—the latest was posted over four years ago.

The newer videos, like the one I was watching now, were of different people—all of them remarkably good looking, as the woman at Brock and Becky's had noted. These free videos linked to a website where you could pay for virtual courses on topics like "Healing Childhood Trauma," "Creating Healthy Habits," and "Awakening Erotic Energy." I preferred Paul's videos, which were less esoteric, but it seemed he had stopped creating content when he retired from public life.

"Take a deep breath in, imagining you are breathing in bright white light," said the woman on the screen. "Hold it, allowing the light to heal you. Good, now let it out."

Next to me on the couch, my phone suddenly blared "I Love It" at top volume. My heart stopped. That was Chase's ring. Neither of us had yet contacted the other.

I palmed the phone and stared at the picture of us kissing atop the Eiffel Tower during Paris fashion week the first year we were together. Should I answer? What did he want? What did I want?

"Can you paint my nails?"

I looked up to see Tara and Roz's four-year-old looking at me with puppy-dog eyes from behind a mop of unruly curls. The phone stopped ringing. I snapped the laptop shut.

"If your mommies say it's okay," I returned with a smile.

"It's okay," she assured me, her cherubic face serious. "I'm a big girl."

I scooped her up and carried her into the black-and-white-tiled kitchen, where incense curled from a stick shoved into the windowsill above the sink.

Tara was at the table before a scale and a pile of sticky, fragrant marijuana, carefully measuring and packaging it. She was ten years older than me, her long dark hair now streaked with a skunk stripe of silver in the front that served only to make her angular face and midnight-blue eyes that much more striking. In her day, Tara had walked catwalks across the world, putting away enough money to retire at thirty-five, so that she was now free to focus on her true passion, helping the citizens of New York cope with their stressful lives through curated CBD-heavy strains of marijuana. At the moment, that included me.

"Chase just called," I said as I set Rain on the granite countertop.

Tara's head snapped up. "Did you talk to him?"

"Wait, what?" Roz came running in from the front room, her overalls splattered with paint the same blue as the paintbrush in her hand.

Roz was Puerto Rican, with curly hair and big brown eyes that matched her daughter's. "What did he say?"

I pulled my phone from my pocket and looked at it. "I didn't pick up and he didn't leave a message."

"Good for you, not picking up." Roz balanced the paintbrush on the edge of the sink and poured coffee into a mug that read, "You don't scare me, I'm a SOCIAL WORKER."

"I don't know what to say to him. But I am gonna have to go over there and get my stuff at some point." I sighed. "I can't live in Tara's clothes forever. Or sleep on your couch."

"You can stay here as long as you want," Tara said.

My phone rang and they both stared at me. "Is it him?" Tara asked.

I knew from the ring it wasn't him but checked the screen anyway. "It's a 415 number."

"San Francisco," Roz said.

"Hello?" I answered, expecting to tell a telemarketer to take me off their call list.

"Is Svetlana Bentzen available?" A woman's voice. Clipped, professional. No one who knew me used my full name.

"That's me."

"I'm calling from the law offices of Baranquilla Hall Webster. I have Mr. Baranquilla for you."

Baranquilla. The name set off alarm bells, but surely there was more than one Baranquilla family in the world. I frowned. "What is this concerning?"

"Mr. Baranquilla has that information. Please hold."

Elevator music replaced the sound of her voice and my stomach dropped as I tried to come up with a reason some lawyer might be calling me.

"This is Lucas." I was too stunned to respond. "Hello?"

"Lucas?" I breathed.

"Hi, Sveta." His voice was lower than it had been when I last spoke to him, more mature. But then, more than a decade had passed. "I'm sorry, my assistant didn't tell me she'd gotten you on the line."

His assistant. Lucas was an attorney now, with an assistant. In my mind I dressed the brooding surfer I'd known when I was eighteen in a suit and gave him facial hair, but still I couldn't quite put the picture together.

"Why are you calling me?" I asked.

I may have been a touch defensive, but rightfully so.

"I apologize for calling out of the blue. It's about your uncle Paul."

I paused, thrown. "What about him?"

"I'm the presumed executor of his estate," he explained. "I'm sorry to have to be the one to tell you this, but . . . he passed away last night."

The world tilted. I inhaled sharply. "Oh my God. How?"

I was vaguely aware of Roz sliding a chair behind me and Tara helping me to sit in it.

"He was ill for a long time, but . . ." His voice trailed off.

"But what?"

"I don't yet know the details." He hesitated, perhaps expecting me to say something, but I was in too much shock to think straight. "I'm really sorry," he added.

"Okay," I said, replaying his words in my head while trying to dredge up what I should ask. "Is there going to be a funeral?" I wasn't even sure exactly where Paul lived. Had lived. Somewhere in the jungle in Central America. "Who do I talk to? Do you have Kali's number?"

"Yes, I'll help you with all of that. But . . . there are some things we should discuss," he said. "You're named as beneficiary."

Outside the window, a cloud passed over the sun, darkening the kitchen.

"Of what?" I asked.

"His estate. All of it."

My breath caught. But this had to be some kind of sick joke. Sure, I'd been close with my uncle when I was a child, but I'd seen him only once since my father died when I was eleven. "What about Kali?"

"In the will, you're named as sole beneficiary."

It didn't make any sense. Kali was his wife. My thoughts reeled back to the lunch I'd had with her a few weeks ago, mining our conversation for clues, but I came up empty handed. "But why?"

"I don't know," he said.

"What's in the estate?"

"There are a lot of assets. It's complicated because of the business— we'll need to sit down and go over everything. There's a TOD account, too, it looks like. Two, actually. One's a brokerage account and the other's savings, in the Caymans."

My body suddenly felt as though it were full of helium. "TOD?"

"Transfer on death. Means the accounts are yours without probate, once the death certificate has been furnished."

My head spun. The whole thing sounded crazy. Why name me as the beneficiary, why not Kali? The idea of inheriting his estate and what that meant, if there wasn't some mistake, was too overwhelming to consider. Surely there was a mistake. And why was Lucas Baranquilla calling to tell me? I remembered his father had been friends with my father, but the pieces still didn't quite fit. "Why are you the executor of his will?"

"My dad was Paul's attorney until he passed away last year, and I took over," he said. "They knew each other for a long time. They were roommates with your dad years ago."

"I'm sorry you lost your dad," I said.

"Thanks," he said. "I appreciate that. Anyway, you should know that Paul's funeral is tomorrow evening. I know it's fast. Mexican law requires that the body be interred within forty-eight hours."

"Tomorrow evening?" That would mean I needed to get on a plane now, basically. "I mean, I'd love to be there, of course, but that's really soon. And you said Mexico?"

"That's right. At his retreat center, Xanadu. Kali has requested you come, if you can."

"You spoke to her?" I asked.

"No, but her attorney relayed the message."

Xanadu. My heart tugged, remembering Paul's favorite poem. "Where exactly is it?"

"In the state of Chiapas, near the Guatemalan border. It's not easy to get to, but . . . I know how much he cared about you. I think he would've wanted you to be there."

I balked. That was a long way. But I felt terrible thinking of Paul's multiple invitations to visit over the years, which I'd always declined. As much as I'd yearned to see him again, I'd begged off with excuses about being busy with work, telling myself I couldn't go out of respect for my mother's wishes, even though she hadn't actually mentioned Paul in years. In fact, the last time we'd talked about him had been shortly after he was sued. I remembered being surprised by how much it angered her. "Paul never hurt a person," she'd said, her voice edged with emotion.

Truthfully, it wasn't only because of my mother that I'd never visited. I'd been intimidated by the idea of a bunch of mystic hippies who'd devoted their lives to the greater good. I was sure they'd think me shallow and inconsequential, my priorities all wrong. And if I was really honest, I worried I'd think those things of myself, too. But Kali had been the opposite of judgmental when we met for lunch last month.

What a grim coincidence that after all this time, Paul and I had arranged to meet in the city mere weeks ago. I'd been disappointed he was unable to come at the last minute, but grateful for the opportunity to get to know Kali better when she showed up in his place, and I'd promised I would come to see them at Xanadu soon.

Now Paul was gone, and we'd never reconnect.

I was heartbroken I'd missed my opportunity to visit when he was alive; going now to bid farewell to him with the people he loved was the least I could do. If someone dies and leaves you their entire estate, you go to the funeral, no matter how difficult the journey. But Kali . . .

"You're sure Kali wants me there?" I asked. We'd gotten along well when we'd met for lunch, but would she really want to see me when I'd just inherited everything she'd likely assumed would be hers?

"Her attorney assured me she does."

Confirmation that she was a bigger person than I was. For the first time since New Year's Eve, a tingle of excitement buzzed in my chest. "Okay then. I'll go."

"I can make the arrangements."

"I can make my own arrangements, thanks." I bristled. "Just send me the address."

"There's no address. It's in the Lacandon Jungle." I heard the riffling of papers. "Requires a helicopter and boat. Probably best if I do it, if you don't mind. I'll just need your passport number. You can fly tonight?"

"I can go, yes." Shit, my passport was at Chase's, along with all my other stuff. "But I don't have my passport on me right now. I'll have to call you back. At this number?"

"Please. The sooner the better."

"Thanks." I hung up the phone and met Tara's and Roz's concerned eyes.

"Who was that?" Roz asked.

"What happened?" Tara overlapped.

"That was the guy I lost my virginity to, calling to tell me my uncle Paul died," I said, shaking my head in disbelief. "An illness."

"I'm so sorry," Roz said, putting her arms around me.

"I remember you got an email from your uncle when we were at the harvest festival at Riri's school in the fall," Tara recalled. "You were supposed to meet up with him in December, right?"

"Yeah," I confirmed. "We'd planned to get together when he was in town, but he couldn't make it, so I had lunch with his wife instead."

"What's she like?" Roz asked.

I shrugged. "Gorgeous. Very—I don't know, spiritual? But cool. In her thirties."

"But he was older, right?"

I nodded. "Yeah. They went together, though. They had that same ethereal thing about them. Just really calm, grounded . . ." I sighed. "I have to go to my apartment and get my passport. The funeral's tomorrow, somewhere in Mexico."

I glanced up at the clock above Tara's head. Eleven forty-five A.M. And it was a Friday, which meant Chase was likely working from home. I was not prepared for this.

"Do you want one of us to come with you?" Roz asked.

"No, it's okay." I sighed. "I have to face him at some point, it might as well be now." I took out my phone to text him and found my hands were shaking.

"Take a breath," Roz said, her eyes sympathetic. "You've just had a shock. The passport can wait five minutes."

Tara rose and the two of them enveloped me in a group hug, Rain wrapping herself around my legs. In the safety of their arms, I let the sobs escape from my chest.

FIVE

One Month Earlier

Paul had planned to stay at the Plaza, so we'd arranged to meet nearby at a trendy midtown vegan restaurant known for their homemade kombucha and assortment of locavore fare, where the servers wore pin-striped overalls and white newsboy caps, and the tables and bar were made from recycled wood and brass.

I was expecting Paul alone, as he hadn't mentioned Kali in any of our correspondence, but when I gave the tattooed and pierced hostess my name, she led me to a table for two in front of the window, where I was surprised to find Kali looking over the menu. It took me a moment to place who she was—I'd met her only that one time eight years before—but she hadn't aged a day. She was dressed for the chilly December weather in a fitted scoop-neck cream cashmere sweater with jeans that accentuated her figure and tall tan boots, her long onyx locks loose about her shoulders.

As she stood to embrace me, I caught a whiff of a sweet and musky perfume. "Svetlana," she said, her gray eyes locking on mine. "It's so good to see you." She had a regal bearing and the slight, unplaceable accent of a global citizen who speaks multiple languages.

"Call me Sveta," I replied.

"Sveta." She squeezed my hand, then settled into her chair with her back to the window.

"Where's Paul?" I asked, sitting tentatively across from her.

"He's so sorry he couldn't make it," she said, holding my gaze. "He very much wanted to see you, but wasn't feeling well and decided last minute he wasn't up to the journey. So you have me instead." A cloud passed over her placid face. "He hated that he couldn't come along."

"I hope he's okay," I said expectantly, but she only gave a slight nod, apparently disinclined to comment further. "What are you in town for?"

"Taking care of a few business things. And truthfully, I just love to visit the city at Christmas." She smiled. "It never really feels like Christmas in the jungle. I've got my fingers crossed for snow."

"You may get it," I said, looking out the window at the leaden skies.

As she fingered one of many gold pendants that dangled from her neck, it was impossible not to notice she wasn't wearing a bra. "Your eyes are striking," she said, evaluating me from behind a thick fringe of lashes. "Glacier blue with that royal iris, just like Shiva's. No wonder you've had such a successful career as a model."

"Thank you," I said, self-conscious, "but I don't know how successful it was."

"Oh, please," she said good-naturedly. "When I was younger I knew lots of girls who called themselves models, and none of them were half as successful as you. Your face was on a billboard in Times Square!"

"That was a long time ago. And trust me, it was not as lucrative as you'd think."

"Regardless, it's pretty awesome," she said. "And the designers you've worked with . . . I bet you've gotten to wear some incredible clothes. That feather dress for Jared Cott?"

I smiled, remembering the cockatoo dress I'd worn in Jared's show the night I met Chase, which I'd also worn in an ad that ran in all the big magazines at the time.

"Shiva's always followed your career," she continued. "And I'm right there looking over his shoulder, explaining who all the designers are."

We both laughed. "Yeah, he's never struck me as the type to be into fashion," I said. "But then, I wouldn't have guessed you were, either."

"Just because fashion isn't a part of my life anymore doesn't mean I can't appreciate the artistry of it," she said. "We're both very proud of you."

"Thank you," I said again.

Her steady, open gaze settled on me, leaving me flustered and acutely aware of how infrequently I locked eyes with anyone for longer than a brief moment. Even in bed, Chase and I didn't look at each other that openly. But no one did—did they? Besides children, of course. Not in New York, anyway.

The server, a pale man with a handlebar mustache, came over to take our order, and Kali shifted her stare to him. His face turned red as an apple as he wrote down her order. So I wasn't the only one hot under the intensity of her gaze.

"So, how did you and my uncle meet?" I asked once he'd departed.

"In an ashram in India." She smiled, remembering. "He was already famous, but I didn't know who he was. All I saw was this beautiful spirit— and those eyes, the same ones you have. We had an immediate connection. But it was a silent retreat, so we meditated together for a full ten days before we ever spoke." She shook her head with a laugh. "I have to admit, though, I was pretty distracted by him. I don't know how much inner peace I cultivated on that retreat."

"Is India where you grew up?" I asked, still trying to place her accent.

"My mom's people are Indian, so I spent a lot of time there, but we lived all over the place. My parents were missionaries—Africa, Central and South America, Southeast Asia—you name it, we lived there."

"That's so cool," I said.

"It was and it wasn't," she confided. "I mean, I did love the travel and seeing all the different places, meeting all different types of people. You must have gotten to do that, too, with modeling?"

"That was my favorite thing about it," I confirmed.

"My parents' rules were pretty strict, though. I guess all teenagers have issues with their parents, but I didn't speak to mine for a long time after I left home. Our relationship was something I really had to work on healing."

I nodded, sympathetic. "But you ended up living a very spiritual life."

She shrugged. "I always felt the calling, but I fought it. I think that's why I was so resistant to my parents. I wanted to be normal, to live in the material world—and I did, I mean I spent my early twenties doing all the things I hadn't been allowed to do as a girl."

"Like what?" I asked, intrigued. Kali was turning out to be much more down to earth than I'd assumed she'd be.

"Oh, you know. Sex, drugs, and rock 'n' roll." She winked.

I laughed. "So what brought you back to spirituality?"

"All that was fun at first, but after a while I felt this gnawing emptiness inside. I'd take drugs just to feel something. One night I was in a friend's car, coming home from a party in the rain. There was a car stopped on the road with no lights on, and we didn't see it. My friend swerved at the last minute and our car flipped. He didn't make it."

My hand flew to my mouth. "Oh my God, I'm so sorry."

"I came full circle after that, though my beliefs are different from what I was raised with. It's been a journey for sure, but I am happier and more fulfilled now than I ever imagined possible." She reached across the table and took my hand in hers. "But enough about me, I want to hear about you."

While we waited for our food, she asked about my life with such genuine warmth that I found myself compelled to open up to her, telling her not only about Chase, but about his mother and all our problems. She listened intently, her changeable eyes absorbing my pain without judgment, as if she could see straight to my soul. Her attentiveness made me realize how long it had been since anyone had *really* listened to me. But maybe that was my fault, for not speaking up more often.

When I was finished, she thought for a moment, and then said slowly, "You doubt yourself because that's what you've been conditioned to do. But your inner strength is there inside, waiting for you. Everything you need"—she tapped the tangle of necklaces on her chest with her clean, bare nails—"is right here within you."

I wasn't totally sure what that meant in the context of the dirty laundry I'd dumped on the table, but she was certainly right that a career in fashion had conditioned me to doubt myself. I had the sense she truly believed that my future could be anything I wanted it to be—something I hadn't felt for a long time.

"You need to come see us," Kali said, shaking her head. "Shiva hasn't done enough for you. We have our family at Xanadu, but you're his blood. He—"

My ears pricked up. "Xanadu?" He'd invited me to visit the place in the jungle a handful of times, but this was the first time I'd heard the name.

"Our piece of paradise." Her eyes danced. "Sveta, you've never seen anything like it."

"A stately pleasure dome?" I quoted. "Where the sacred river runs?"

Her smile lit up the room. "Down to a sunless sea." She grasped my hand. "You have to come. Promise you'll come."

"Yes." I nodded wildly, suddenly overcome with the desire to visit my uncle and his enchanting—wife? Girlfriend? A simple gold band encircled her ring finger. So they must have married at some point. How lucky, I felt, to stumble upon this winsome branch of my family tree.

The loss of my career combined with the chasm that had opened between Chase and me since we'd become engaged had left me feeling adrift lately, and Kali certainly seemed more grounded than anyone I knew. Maybe some time at a spiritual retreat in the jungle was just what I needed.

"How many of you live at Xanadu?" I asked.

"There are about seventy-five of us," she said. "Though we have rooms for visitors as well."

"And what do you do out there in the jungle?" I asked, intrigued.

She laughed. "So much. We share all the household activities like cooking, cleaning, gardening. We meditate, of course, and do a lot of physical activity—swimming, yoga, dance. Some of us are painters or musicians. We practice both group and individual therapy. We're focused on finding personal freedom and living our best lives, while helping others to do the same."

"That sounds wonderful," I breathed.

"It is." She glowed from within as she spoke. "It's a more natural, healthy way to live. I see so much loneliness here." She gestured to the restaurant. "Everyone on their phones, no one meeting eyes or holding space for one another. We may be deep in the jungle at Xanadu, but we are never lonely."

"What do you do if you get sick?" I asked.

"The forest is full of herbal remedies. Though we're rarely ill. When your vibration hits a certain level, you're no longer susceptible to the diseases that plague humanity."

"But I thought Uncle Pa—Shiva was sick," I said. "I mean, that's why he couldn't come today, right?"

Again the dark cloud passed over her face. "His dis-ease is something else," she said, turmoil swirling behind her luminous eyes. "Metaphysical, I'm afraid. He—" She broke off, looking, for the first time since we'd sat down, unsure of herself. "It's why I wanted to meet you. I'm worried about him, to be honest. He's withdrawn more and more the past few months."

"I'm sorry," I said. I had no idea what else to say to this. I hardly knew the man as an adult, and I certainly wasn't the right person to counsel her on matters of the heart. Also, I wasn't entirely sure what she meant by his illness being metaphysical. Was that even possible? It sounded medieval, like something that would be cured by bloodletting or an alchemist. "I'm not sure how I can help, though."

"He has visions," she went on, "terrible visions. And he's started to say things about people plotting against him."

"What people?" I asked, disturbed.

"Members of the Mandala, our council. Even me."

"The Mandala?"

"Our group. It means circle." Her gray eyes were so vulnerable, I felt the urge to wrap her in a hug. "He hasn't reached out to you?"

"No."

"Has your mother spoken to him lately?"

"My mom?" I drew back, confused. "No, not that I'm aware. I mean, they haven't talked in years. They're not friendly."

"Oh." She tucked a strand of silky hair behind her ear. "I just wondered, with your family history . . ." Her voice trailed off.

I stared at her, at a loss. "What history?"

"I know it must be hard for you to talk about," she said gently. "I'm just worried he's depressed. I've never seen him like this. With your father's suicide, I . . ."

A bomb went off in my head, taking with it all the noise of the restaurant. All I could hear was a high-pitched whining as I gaped at her, shaken to my core.

"Oh, Sveta," she cried, taking both my hands in hers. "Did you not know?"

But I had no words.

"How stupid of me. Though you were so young, it makes sense—" Her face crumpled into a mask of sympathy mixed with something else—disbelief? Scorn? "But you're a grown woman, have they kept it from you this long?"

Her shock wasn't unwarranted. I fumbled for my orange cardamom kombucha, drinking until half the glass was gone. "I was told he died fighting in Afghanistan," I said finally. "Soldiers carried his casket. It was draped with a flag."

"I'm so sorry," she said.

How could my mom have kept this from me?

But I was only eleven. Surely she'd only lied to me to protect me. She must have been in so much pain. After years of my struggling to understand why she'd cut Paul out of our lives, suddenly her reason became clear. One of the things I remembered from *Surrender* was that he believed in radical honesty. No little white lies, no untruths to protect someone from the fact that you thought that dress was unflattering or their father had killed himself. Paul must have wanted to tell me the truth, and my mother wanted to protect me.

As devastated as I was by Kali's revelation, at least this explanation made sense. Though it left me with only more questions.

After lunch, I wandered through the park, impervious to the cold. Leaves crunched underfoot as I trod the asphalt paths beneath the bare red oak trees, replaying scenes from my childhood through the lens of what I'd just learned about my father's death. I was both infuriated and more mystified than ever by my forever stoic mother, who took the punches life doled out without complaint, always with her head held high.

I'd learned over the years that small but mighty Irina Bentzen was not the person to call when I was feeling sorry for myself. When the kids in junior high made fun of me because, due to our meager income, I had no choice but to wear the same clothes in close rotation, she pointed out that I was lucky to have clothes to rotate. She had not been so lucky back in Russia, she assured me. Complaint was weakness to her, and weakness was not acceptable. "Do you have two eyes?" she'd scoff. "All your fingers and toes? Food in your belly and a roof to keep you warm at night? You have no problem."

Her father had left when she was two, and after her mom died in an accident when she was nine, she'd been raised by relatives who, unhappy about having another child to feed, neglected her. So when a school friend of hers who'd gone to America as a mail-order bride called to ask if she'd be open to marrying her new husband's army friend sight unseen, she saw the opportunity as a blessing from God. The friend accurately described my father as kind and shy, and I'm certain that even if eighteen-year-old Irina had known what trials lay ahead for her in America, she would still have taken that transatlantic flight without looking back.

So, as much as I wanted to demand answers from her, ultimately I thought better of it. Not only because I would have to admit to having had lunch with Paul's wife, but because she'd chosen not to tell me and I'd learned to respect her decisions, whether or not I thought they were the right ones.

I was no stranger to withholding details. Like how I'd told Chase that my parents met at a dance when my father was stationed in Russia.

It wasn't that I was worried he'd be put off by my parents' origin story or say something to his family that would make them think even less of me than they already did—he didn't want that, either. No, the real reason was that with Chase I was allowed to be someone else. Someone who grew up poor, yes, but romantically, not tragically so. With Chase, I spoke about my past with pluck and charm, told the kind of tales he could see himself relaying to his grandchildren one day about my rags-to-riches story. After repeating it enough, I began to think that the rosier version I told Chase was true.

But Kali had reminded me in no uncertain terms that it wasn't.

SIX

It wasn't until a month later, in the Uber on the way to pick up my passport from Chase's, that I worked up the courage to call my mom and talk to her about what Kali had told me. I knew we wouldn't have time to hash it all out, but she deserved to know Paul had died, and should at least be aware I was going to his funeral. However, she didn't answer, and I didn't want to leave that information on her voice mail, so I just asked her to call me as soon as she could.

After the car dropped me off in front of the apartment I technically still shared with my fiancé, I hunched against the freezing wind, checking my phone again to see whether he'd responded to the text I sent an hour ago. Nothing. I pulled off my glove and typed with fingers so cold I could hardly control them:

Not sure if you got my text. Have to go out of town tonight.
I'm outside the loft, about to come up and grab a few things.
Hope that's okay.

I waited a minute and when there was still no response, keyed the entry code and pushed open the glass door.

I rode the elevator to the fifth floor and stood in front of 5B, my heart in my throat as I rapped on the door. All was quiet. I knocked again, then inserted my key in the lock and pushed inside.

The apartment was dark, the heavy velvet drapes pulled across the floor-to-ceiling windows. "Chase? Are you home?" I called out.

Standing in the entry hall, a strange feeling came over me, as though I was looking through a window into my life. My heart tugged with a yearning to return to normal. I hung my coat on the rack and riffled through the jumble of mail on the entry table, throwing everything with my name on it into my oversize shoulder bag. "Chase?" I called again, wandering into the kitchen.

Dishes were piled in and around the sink and an empty pizza box sat on the stainless steel kitchen counter next to a depleted bottle of wine, a couple of disposable coffee cups, and a plastic bag of what appeared to be empty takeout boxes. I hated the fact that seeing the usually fastidious Chase's mess made me feel better. Perhaps he'd missed me after all. Though upon closer inspection, one of the coffee cups did have a pink lipstick stain on it.

Feeling like an intruder in my own home, I crept up the stairs and flipped on the bedroom light. The normally spotless room looked like a tornado had hit it. Candy wrappers and water bottles crowded the bedside table; clothes and shoes littered the floor. I started as Chase sat up from the pile of bedclothes bare-chested and blinking in the light, his hair at odd angles.

"I texted," I blurted at the same time he said:

"What are you doing here?"

We stared at each other.

"I'm sorry to wake you." I did my best to sound normal, but my throat was so tight I could hardly speak. "I have to go out of town tonight, so I came by to get some things."

He grabbed a vial of Tylenol from the bedside table and downed two with the end of a bottle of water. "You should've called."

"I texted," I repeated. "Are you okay?"

He glared at me. "My fiancée left me, you may remember."

"I didn't leave you, I just needed some time."

He slumped off the platform bed and pulled on a pair of jeans. "Well? Have you had enough time?"

"Have you?" I asked.

"I just don't want to fight anymore," he groaned.

"Then change the wedding date back," I said, my voice more exasperated than I intended it to be.

He crossed his arms. "Is that an ultimatum?"

Apparently, a week had not been sufficient time to sort out our differences. "You know it's representative of a lot of other things."

"I just don't understand why it's so bad that I want to make my mother happy."

I studied him. "Because you're putting her happiness above mine."

"But it's also for you. She'll respect you more if we do it her way."

"Will she, though?" I sighed. "We're going in circles. Let's stop. We can talk about it again when I get back."

"Where are you going?"

"Mexico."

"Mexico?" he asked, as though I'd told him I was about to bungee jump off the Empire State Building.

I'd almost forgotten Chase wouldn't go to Mexico because of fears about violence. "My uncle died, and the funeral is there."

"Paul?"

I nodded.

Though he'd never met my uncle, Chase looked as shocked as I felt. "How did he die?"

"An illness, apparently. Don't say anything to anyone, it hasn't been reported yet."

"And you're going to the funeral? Why?"

"To say goodbye," I returned. "Because he was my uncle and I loved him."

He held his hands up. "Sorry, I didn't think you were that close."

"We were when I was a kid," I said. "Just because I didn't see him regularly doesn't mean I didn't love him. And he . . ." The words were on the tip of my tongue, but I held them back.

"He what?"

I sighed again. It was pointless keeping it from him. He'd find out soon enough. "Apparently I'm his beneficiary."

"What?" He gaped at me. "Did he have no will? Were you the next of kin?"

"No, he had a will. And he was married. But he named me as sole beneficiary, for some unknown reason."

"Alexa," Chase called, pointing his voice at the speaker on the circular side table next to the Eames chair in the corner, barely visible beneath a pile of discarded clothes. "What's the net worth of Paul Bentzen?"

"Paul Bentzen is a self-help author and motivational speaker," the soothing robotic voice answered. "His net worth is estimated to be one hundred eighty million dollars."

Chase and I stared at each other, stunned. "Shit," he said, laughing.

I couldn't feel my legs. "That can't be right."

"If it's off, it's not gonna be off by that much," he returned, grabbing me by the shoulders. "You're rich."

I couldn't wrap my head around it. A hundred and eighty million dollars? "How the hell did he make that much money? He was a writer."

"And motivational speaker who did workshops all over the world that they charged God only knows what for," he added. "And he had that vitamin company, didn't he?"

I nodded, vaguely recalling something about natural energy supplements.

"Well, damn." He grinned. "You're now richer than everyone in my family."

I furrowed my brow. "Not yet."

He laughed, shaking his head. "Why didn't you lead with this? This changes everything. They'll have to respect you now."

I stared at him, dubious. "Because I'm rich?"

He sighed. "They'll know you're not after me for my money. You know how they are. This is going to make things so much easier."

He hugged me, the familiar feeling of his arms around me like a worn pair of jeans.

"We don't have to prove anything anymore," he went on. "We can get married wherever you want now and pay for it ourselves. We can buy our own apartment, not live in theirs. We can do whatever we want!"

My head spun. "But we could have done that before," I protested, pulling back to look at him. "You make plenty of money. We don't need theirs. We never have. And it's not all about money."

"You're so sweet, thinking it's not all about money. I love that about you." He cupped my face in his hands and kissed me.

I leaned into the kiss, thawing beneath his touch, immediately nostalgic for the security of our future together. It was so tempting to give in and let everything go back to the way it was before, get back on the train to a dependable destiny.

He unbuttoned my jeans, pulling me toward the bed. But my mind stepped in, reminding me that we had very real problems that couldn't be solved in bed, and if I went to bed with him, we'd end up right back where we started without solving any of those problems.

"Chase." I drew back, rebuttoning my jeans. "I have a plane to catch." I started for the closet. "I have to pack."

"I can help." He shook his head in disbelief, laughing. "One hundred eighty million dollars. Incredible."

"We'll see," I said. I was wary of his unbridled enthusiasm over my presumed inheritance but didn't have time to get into it with him, so I kept my mouth shut as we quickly located what I would need in Mexico. I'd face our issues when I returned.

SEVEN

The Mexico City airport was boxy and punctured with round windows that let in light from all angles, like a giant cheese grater.

I'd had about three hours of sleep when my red-eye flight landed at five in the morning, which left me ill-prepared for the shit show that getting through customs and from one terminal to the other proved to be. Four long hours loomed before my connecting flight, though, so I wasn't short on time. Finding all the seats at my gate occupied, I settled on the cold terrazzo floor against the exterior wall and dozed fitfully on top of my backpack with my sunglasses on until the alarm I'd set on my phone buzzed.

I sat up, bleary eyed, to a forest of legs. The throngs of passengers had multiplied in the hours I'd been on the ground; the airport was overrun with people moving in different directions.

"Hi."

Annoyed some guy thought this would be a good time to chat, I turned. My jaw dropped as my gaze landed on none other than Lucas Baranquilla, sitting on the floor next to me.

He was just as maddeningly good looking as I'd remembered him: tan skin and thick wavy dark hair, a five o'clock shadow, and those inscrutable, nearly black eyes. He was sharper edged than he had been at twenty, his formerly straight nose now slightly crooked and sporting a small bump, his full lips outlined by his scruff. He was tall and athletic, muscled broad shoulders visible through his worn red T-shirt, and his body had filled out from the malleable form of a boy into the hardened build of a man.

"What are you doing here?" I blurted.

The corner of his mouth lifted as he took in my surely rumpled appearance. "Watching you sleep."

I pulled off my sunglasses and shoved them into my bag. "You didn't tell me you were coming."

He evaluated me as though aware his reply would rub me the wrong way. "Because I knew you'd tell me not to. Sometimes it's better to ask for forgiveness than permission."

"I hope you don't apply that to dating," I snipped. He laughed, and I saw his eyes briefly flick to my ring as I ran my fingers through my hair. "Still doesn't explain why you're here, though."

He hesitated, a shadow falling over his face. "I don't think you should go alone."

"I've traveled alone all over the world." I crossed my arms. "Been more places than you have, I'm sure."

"I don't know about that," he challenged. "I've been a few places since I last saw you." He laid a gentle hand on my forearm and I stared at it, not willing to meet his gaze. "Hey, I'm sorry about the way things—"

"I don't want to talk about it." I cut him off, shrugging his hand from my arm without meeting his eye.

"It was my fault. I—"

"I told you, I don't want to hear it." I zipped my bag and reinforced all my defenses to finally look at him, my face hard. "I don't care."

He raised his hands in defeat. "Okay."

A dull pain throbbed in my head. "I need coffee," I grumbled.

"Me, too."

He rose and extended his hand to me, but I ignored it and stood on my own, stretching my stiff knees and rolling my ankles. Pins and needles pricked my feet.

I'd forgotten how tall he was. He had a good four or five inches on me, and I was five foot ten. For some reason in my caffeine-deprived state I found this annoying, as though it somehow undermined my strength. It was, however, useful for keeping track of him as we threaded our way through the crush of weary and rushed travelers to the coffee shop a few gates down.

"It's not about the travel," he said as we parked ourselves at the back of the long line. "I know you can travel alone. It's everything else." I could see the gears in his mind turning as he tried to figure out how to say whatever he was going to say next. "You know Paul and Kali were married?"

Apparently Kali hadn't mentioned our lunch to him. "So?"

"Not legally married," he went on. My ears perked up. "It was a spiritual ceremony, and in Mexico you have to do a certain legal ceremony for it to be legally binding. But I'm sure Kali's disappointed he gave you everything."

"Honestly, I was surprised she even wanted me to come." He nodded, and I could tell there was more he wanted to say. "What?" I asked.

He paused. "I worry she'll drag her feet on filing the death certificate," he finally said. "Probate can't happen without it, and there's a somewhat involved process for getting it approved by the US. I got the feeling talking to her attorney yesterday that following laws and protocols may not be high up on their list."

A metallic announcement came over the loudspeaker in Spanish too rapid for me to catch. "Our flight's boarding in ten minutes from gate seventy-two," Lucas translated.

"You're . . . Argentine, right?" I asked, though I remembered clearly that he was.

"My dad was," he returned.

"How well did you know my uncle?" I asked.

"I've known him since I was a kid. Saw him rarely in the past decade but reconnected with him when he came to my dad's funeral. He was sick. Cancer."

I cocked my head, surprised Kali hadn't mentioned it at our lunch. "For how long?"

"I don't know, but he wasn't doing well."

"Alexa said his fortune was estimated to be"—I lowered my voice to a whisper—"one hundred eighty million."

"Who's Alexa?" he asked, confused.

"AI. The Amazon speaker."

He raised his brows, amused. "Right. Well, I don't know the exact number, but with the property and business, that sounds about right."

The confirmation of the mind-boggling amount made me light-headed.

"So, what *exactly* am I inheriting?" I asked.

"Everything that was his is yours. His house in the Bay Area, his shares in the Mandala Corporation, his brokerage, retirement, and bank accounts, personalty—all of it."

"Personalty?"

"Personal effects. Like watches or cars or paintings or whatever."

"And what's in the accounts?" I asked.

"I don't know. We need the death certificate to be allowed access, which is why—"

"Why you're so hung up on it. Got it." It was beginning to make sense.

"I wish I knew more, but I'm as in the dark as you are." He must have read the incredulity on my face because he continued, "I promise, I'm not keeping any information from you. Whatever I learn, you'll be the first to know."

I nodded. "I'd appreciate that. How does this all work—the process, I mean? I've never been through anything like this."

"Normally a family member is the executor of the estate, but he appointed my dad—then me last year, after my dad passed—because he realized this would all come as a shock to you, and it could be a fraught situation with Kali. Basically, I file the death certificate with the court to open probate, at which point we're allowed to establish an account for his estate with his money—to pay creditors, funeral expenses, that kind of thing. You'll immediately get access to the transfer-on-death accounts, and the rest of the estate will go through probate, which generally takes a couple of months but can take longer if it's complicated."

We were finally at the front of the line. There wasn't time to get my usual iced latte, so I ordered a drip coffee over ice, which I drained as we hurried down the crowded hallway to our gate, where our flight was nearly finished boarding. Through the steel door and down a flight of stairs into the warm sun we jogged, across the tarmac and up the airstair into the stifling tin can.

The ceiling was so low that neither Lucas nor I could stand straight as we made our way down the aisle and took our seats, two rows apart. I was glad we weren't seated together; I needed time to process everything he'd told me.

When I took out my phone to turn it to airplane mode before take-off, I saw my mom had finally called me back. She'd left a message, but visual voice mail wasn't working, and just as I raised the phone to my ear to hear her message, the flight attendant came by, asking me to power it off. Frustrated, I obeyed.

I felt the engine of the plane rumble to life beneath me and closed my eyes, slipping into a dreamless sleep.

Ninety minutes later, I awakened to the jolt of the aircraft wheels touching ground.

We deplaned to a significantly balmier climate in Palenque, near the Guatemalan border. Waves of heat rose from the lone airstrip and industrious plants sprouted from the cracks in the pavement. The constant drone of the insects humming sounded conspicuously like Mother Nature laughing at the attempts of mankind to dominate her. I collected my small roller suitcase from the single luggage belt in the terminal and ate a Snickers bar from the vending machine—something I never would have done during my modeling years.

I was grateful Lucas didn't try to make small talk as we trekked across the scorching pavement to the helicopter waiting for us, a rickety lime-green thing that resembled a dragonfly. Just the sight of it made me jittery. The stocky pilot mopped his brow with a handkerchief he stuffed into the back pocket of his jeans as he extended a hand to each of us, introducing himself as José. Lucas bantered in Spanish with him while they loaded our bags into the luggage compartment in the back, then opened the front passenger-side door for me.

"It's okay," I said. "You can take it."

I climbed into the back and untangled the curly cord of the head-phones that hung from the roof, placing them over my ears with a silent prayer. The blades began to thrum faster and faster until we lifted off the ground with a slight sway and rose up into the milky blue sky.

Over a patchwork of verdant fields and villages too small to be called towns we flew, the mountains on the horizon transforming from blue to green as we drew closer. Through the smudged window I watched grass-lands quickly turn to dense forests that climbed the hills and blanketed the mountains with a canopy so thick as to obscure everything beneath.

"Parque Natural Montes Azules." The pilot's voice was barely audible over the headset.

He said something else in Spanish I couldn't catch, and Lucas trans-lated, "Part of the second-largest extension of rain forest in the Americas, after the Amazon in Brazil."

As the last settlement faded from view and we soared over the impen-etrable rain forest, I couldn't help but think of Marlow and Kurtz and wonder just what the hell I'd gotten myself into.

PART TWO

CONNECTION

Here's something that may come as a surprise to many of us: We don't have to participate in harmful relationships. For when we release the connections that were holding us back and replace them with connections to those who support and encourage us, we begin to raise our vibration. And when we raise our vibration, suddenly the universe opens up for us and anything is possible.

—Paul Bentzen, *Connection*

EIGHT

Day One

The glassy lake reflects the late afternoon sky like liquid mercury.
As our little boat draws closer to land, I notice a man sitting at
the end of the pier with his back to the stately villa that rises from the
jungle, his feet dangling into the water. He's Latino, about my age and
dressed in loose white clothing, his neck and arms fully covered in tattoos. He smiles and offers me his hand when the side of our canoe strikes
the wooden pylons with a hollow clank, the strength in his arms at odds
with his diminutive size as he easily hoists me onto the dock.

"You must be Svetlana," he says. He wraps me in a hug, which I
awkwardly return, then pulls back to study my face. "You look so much
like Shiva."

"We both favor his father—my grandfather—I'm told."

He shifts his gaze to Lucas, who clambers onto the dock behind me
with his backpack on his shoulders, dragging my bag up behind him.
"And is this your fiancé?"

I shoot an accusatory glance at Lucas, who'd neglected to mention he
hadn't told anyone he was coming.

"Lucas Baranquilla." Lucas extends his hand. "Paul's attorney."

The guy's smile fades as he appraises Lucas, clearly unsure what to
do about his unannounced presence. "We didn't know to expect you,"
he says.

"My dad was very close with Paul for forty years. He passed away recently, so I've come to pay his respects. I'm sorry I didn't let anyone know. It all happened so fast. I hope you can accommodate me."

The man's expression softens and he nods. "I'm sure Kali will be happy to see you." He hefts my bag and exchanges a few words of rapid Spanish with our river guide, who departs with a wave. "How was the journey?"

"Long," I answer as we walk over the wooden planks toward the shore.

"It's a lot," he concurs. "But once you're here, it's—" He sweeps his arm across the landscape. "It's pretty awesome, right?"

"Yeah," Lucas agrees, tilting his head back to take in the view of the imposing house.

"Wait'll you see the rest of the property," the man says.

I nod, though I don't know how much we'll be able to see in the brief time we're here. Lucas booked our tickets with a twenty-four-hour turnaround, which seems entirely too short after the arduous journey.

I cast a glance from the forbidding forest to the funeral pyre on the river's edge and shudder. "I didn't catch your name," I say.

"Aguilar."

"Aguilar," I repeat.

"It means eagle," he explains. "We all get new names here. It helps us let go of the past and become the fullest expression of our true selves." I nod, internally rolling my eyes. "'Aguilar' honors my Guatemalan roots and also my spirit animal. I was in a gang when I was young, so it was important to release the negative energy of my old name."

He flashes a disarming smile that makes me chide myself for being so narrow-minded as he points to the flower bed next to me. I jump back from a huge iguana half-hidden behind a bush, staring at us with eyes like mothballs. "He's huge," I breathe.

"She doesn't bite." He chuckles. "Waka's lived around here so long, she's almost a pet."

As we make our way up the stone path between hanging clusters of colorful flowers, I spy statues of Buddha, Shiva, and other gods I don't recognize nestled among the African violets and birds-of-paradise in the immaculately tended beds, but don't see people anywhere.

"Where is everyone?" I ask, surveying the deserted grounds.

He points in the general direction of the forest to the right of the house. "Meditation. But Kali's waiting for you at the house." He watches Lucas check his phone for service. "You won't find service out here. Xanadu is a tech-free zone. It keeps the energy field pure."

I feel a swirl of unease in my stomach as Lucas frowns and tucks his phone into the front pocket of his jeans.

"We do have internet in the tech room," Aguilar continues. "Which is where all technology must stay. You can store your devices there."

Okay, fine. A twenty-four-hour digital detox will probably do me good.

When we reach the top of the hill, Aguilar gestures to the fountain in front of the villa, where two life-size golden jaguars rise from the water poised for a fight, jets spurting from their snarling mouths. "Jaguars were worshiped as gods by the Mayans, rulers of the underworld and symbols of power and vision." He indicates the bigger of the two. "Xibalbá is the night sun, god of prophecy and war. Ix-Chel is the moon goddess, the goddess of birth and medicine. They replaced the statue of Menendez that was here when we moved in."

"Who's Menendez?" I ask.

"Tito Menendez was the cartel leader who built Xanadu in 2005, but he only lived in it for a year before he was killed in a raid."

My mind reels. "Wait, this was a drug lord's place?"

Aguilar nods. "Crazy, right?"

"And he was killed—here?" Lucas asks.

"He and twenty-three others," Aguilar confirms. "The cartel collapsed after that, and the place sat empty until Shiva bought it from the government for pennies ten years ago. Took three years to restore and rebuild."

I'm speechless. I don't believe in ghosts, but to build a spiritual retreat center on the grounds of a mass killing? Not to mention the part about it being built as a drug lord's lair? It seems ill-advised, at the very least. Talk about bad juju.

Aguilar must catch the glance Lucas and I exchange because he continues, "Shiva and Kali did extensive energy cleansing and asked any unfriendly spirits to move on."

"And did they?" I ask, picturing a cartel member floating facedown in the sparkling fountain, his blood slowly turning the water red.

"Most of them. We still get a disruption now and then, but it's healthy for tula—balance."

O-kay.

I raise my eyes to the formidable villa as we follow Aguilar toward it. Beyond a bed of ferns and spiky orange flowers, covered stone walkways with arched openings run along the ground floor, accentuated by intricately carved friezes that snake around the vaulted windows and up the columns. Angels and demons, jaguars and birds, gods and gargoyles are frozen in exuberant tumult, the sharp shadows of the slanted afternoon light creating the illusion of movement as we ascend the ivory marble steps to the domed portico.

I turn my attention to the oversize double doors, covered in sinuous bronze vines that coil around the letters *T* and *M*. Aguilar fingers the letters. "We didn't have to change these. 'Tito Menendez' and 'The Mandala' have the same initials. One of the signs this was the right place for us."

Or an odd and somewhat macabre coincidence.

Aguilar pushes open the door and we follow him into a soaring foyer with an elaborate white-and-gold-tiled mandala floor and mirror-image curved ivory marble staircases that ascend to an open balcony. The ceiling is again domed and features detailed depictions of a discordant mixture of Christian saints, Buddhas, and Hindu gods frolicking and copulating joyfully in the sunlight that streams through the cut-glass windows in prisms and rainbows. The effect is dizzying.

"Jesus," I exhale.

". . . and Buddha and Krishna," Lucas mutters.

"Yes." Aguilar grins. "Follow me."

He starts up the staircase on the right and I trail behind, holding on to the gold railing so I can lean my head back to take in the spectacle. *Is this place part of my inheritance, too?* The thought is overwhelming.

Off the landing is another staircase that leads up to a third floor, and beyond that, a sitting room with a Moroccan flair that transforms the gaudy style of the mansion into the exotic. Brass pendant lights dangle from the high beamed ceiling above low-slung couches and leafy potted plants while gauzy curtains flutter in the breeze.

On either side of the landing extend wide hallways lined with hand-woven Turkish rugs. "Kali's quarters are upstairs." Aguilar gestures to the staircase as he moves down the hallway to the right, past simple sun-lit bedrooms that hold a combination of twin and bunk beds.

It strikes me as odd that he refers to the top floor as Kali's quarters without making any mention of my uncle. "My uncle lived with Kali upstairs?" I ask.

"Sometimes," he says. "But he increasingly retreated to his own quarters as he prepared to take leave of his body."

The phrase is jarring, evoking an image of Zeus dropping his animal disguise to return to Mount Olympus after ravaging some poor woman. But if Paul's faith was as strong as it seems to have been, I suppose it makes sense that he would have believed in the afterlife and prepared for death when he knew the end was near.

Aguilar strides to the large window at the end of the hallway and points. "Just there." I peer past a giant piano-shaped pool—surely a left-over from the cartel days—to a path that leads up an incline into the rain forest, but fail to see what he's pointing at. "Higher," he says.

I lift my gaze and begin to make out the shape of a multisided wood structure perched among the trees. It's only a stone's throw away, but far enough beyond the shadow of the villa that it maintains its own privacy and view. It's also built in an entirely different style from the main building: less drug lord's marble trophy, more eco-luxury tree house. It looks far more like a place I would have expected Paul to live, and immediately I wish I were staying there.

But Aguilar enters the final room on the jungle-facing side of the hallway and drops my bag. "This'll be your room."

It's a square room with a window framed by sheer curtains, centered around a rug with a mostly red design. Four twin beds with ivory linens line the walls, each with its own two-drawer bedside table topped with a potted orchid. Lucas releases his bag to the floor with a thunk. "Any bed?" he asks.

"I think he means this is my room," I say, turning to Aguilar. "Right?"

"This is the only guest room available right now," Aguilar returns with an apologetic smile.

Fucking perfect.

"The bathroom is through that door." He indicates a partially open door on the wall to the left. "You'll share with Blaze, Luna, Amber, and Clef. They're in the room next door."

"Hi, guys." As if on cue, the bathroom door flies open, and a rangy man with shoulder-length brown hair comes through, his palm raised in salutation. "I'm Blaze. Welcome." Blaze is probably about forty-five, with a scruffy beard, bright blue eyes, and the weathered tan of someone who's spent a lot of time in the sun.

"Thanks," I say, taking his outstretched hand.

"If you guys need anything while you're here, we're right next door." He flashes a smile. "Sorry for the in and out, but I've gotta get back to the kuti. See you down there?"

"We'll be down soon," Aguilar replies.

Blaze tips an imaginary hat, only strengthening his striking resemblance to Crocodile Dundee, and with that he's gone through the bathroom door as quickly as he appeared.

"I'm gonna let Kali know you're here," Aguilar says. "You can wash up while you wait."

As he exits, I notice the doorframe holds no door. I stick my head into the hallway and glance up and down, confirming that none of the other rooms have doors, either. Odd.

"What?" Lucas asks. As he leans past me to see what I'm looking at, I catch the scent of something faintly woodsy and masculine.

"No doors," I say, quickly stepping away from him.

Lucas rolls his eyes. "Communes. Everybody's gotta overshare." Responding to my quizzical look, he continues, "I lived in one when I was a teenager."

"You did?" I ask, surprised. I'm sure he never mentioned that when we first met. "With your parents?"

"My mom." I notice that the corner of his mouth turns down slightly at the mention of her. He ambles into the spacious marble and gold bathroom, which fortunately does have a door, and washes his hands in the sink, looking at me through the mirror as I do the same at the matching sink. "She and my dad got divorced when I was twelve, and she took me and my sister to live with a bunch of hippies in the foothills of the Sierras."

"Why?"

"Good question," he answers dryly. "I don't know. She was always more religious than my dad, but after they divorced, she kinda went off the deep end with it, wanted to devote her life to God, live more 'naturally.' She sold candles she made at the farmers' market outside of Oakland and met the leader of the group there—before I knew it I was living in a bunk room with fifty other kids."

"Where was your dad?" I ask.

"In Argentina taking care of his dying mother. Had a hell of a time finding us when he got back."

"Wow." I dry my hands and lean against the counter facing the Jacuzzi and gold-rimmed shower as Lucas splashes his face with water. I'm annoyed he's here, but in two days' time I'll never see him again, and never having met anyone who grew up in an actual commune, I *am* curious. "What was that like, living in a commune?"

"I mean, I was a kid, so at first I thought it was awesome. There were giant flowers painted on the side of our house, everyone skinny-dipped in the lake, and we homeschooled, which basically meant the older kids who were supposed to be teaching us let us run wild while they smoked weed behind the schoolhouse."

"What were the adults doing?"

"Gardening, cooking, making the herbal remedies they sold," he says, shrugging. "Traveling to spread the word of God."

"So it was a religious group?" I ask.

"Yeah." He abruptly turns and withdraws to the bedroom.

"What changed?" I ask, following him.

He peers at me from beneath his brow. "What?"

"You said you thought it was great *at first*. What changed?"

He sighs. "The religious shit. It was a lot. Their beliefs were pretty . . . unhealthy. It really fucked me up for a while. But I'm past it now. And I'd rather just leave it in the past."

Yeah, no. He's about as past it as I am past Chase's family thinking I'm a gold digger. But I hold up my hands in surrender. "Okay." I go to the window and gaze down at the pool, changing the subject. "Is this place part of my inheritance, too?"

He nods. "Paul owned all the shares in the Mandala Corporation, which owns Xanadu, and they all go to you, so yes."

I stare at him, not fully understanding. "But where does the money come from? In the corporation, I mean."

"These days they're not doing live seminars anymore, but they still have pretty significant online sales, and also the royalties on Paul's books and videos."

We hear a cough and spin to see Aguilar standing in the doorway. "Kali's ready for you."

I immediately worry how much he heard of our conversation, but if he caught any of it, he doesn't let on. Still, as we follow him from the room, I feel unease creeping into my periphery, like a vignette darkening the edges of a photograph.

NINE

Lucas and I trail Aguilar up the staircase off the second-level sitting room to a set of elaborately carved wood double doors, where he stops abruptly and spins to face us. "No sudden movements," he says.

Before I can ask what he means, he's swung the doors open to reveal Kali, luminous in a white dress on a dark green velvet couch beneath a lazily turning ceiling fan, gently stroking the massive head of a full-grown jaguar.

I freeze.

Every muscle in my body tenses as the jaguar evaluates us with vigilant golden eyes, black rosettes rippling with its breath.

Out of the corner of my eye I see that Lucas is as rigid as I am.

"Sveta," Kali calls warmly. "Welcome. I'm so glad you could come." She switches her focus to Lucas, her eyes unreadable. "And Lucas, is it?"

"That's right," he answers.

"We weren't aware you'd be joining us." She breaks into a smile that could melt the polar ice caps. "But we're glad to have you."

"Thank you for your hospitality," he says.

"My pleasure," she returns.

The jaguar emits a low rumbling noise, and I involuntarily gasp.

Kali's laugh is breathy and musical. "That's a purr. You'd know if it were a growl," she says, stroking the animal's head fondly. "Ix-Chel has been with us since she was a baby. And she's very well fed, aren't you, darling?" She fingers the studded collar around Ix-Chel's neck. "She's also wearing a shock collar. It's Xibalbá you have to worry about."

I scan the room for another cat, my heart in my throat.

"My God." Kali's eyes widen. "He's in his pen. I would never bring him up here. Have a little faith." She waves at the two velvet chairs across from her. "Come, sit, I know you've had a long trip."

Sage smoke curls in thick wisps from a polished brass Ganesh incense holder on the heavy coffee table. Neither of us moves.

Kali casts a look at Aguilar, and he grabs a heavy chain-link leash from beside the couch, latching it to Ix-Chel's collar. "I'm so used to her I forget how ferocious she looks," she says as the jaguar slinks off the couch and obediently trails Aguilar through the French doors at the back of the room, onto a covered deck that faces the endless jungle.

Once Aguilar has shut the doors behind them, Kali rises from the couch and extends her arms, fixing me with her magnetic gaze. "Come, come." I go to her, and she embraces me, kissing me once on each cheek, her gunmetal eyes gleaming with tears. "I wish you could have visited before this happened, but I'm happy you're here now."

Her feather-light voice combined with the scent of sage and the adrenaline still swirling in my veins leaves me light-headed. "Me, too," I manage, relieved that under the circumstances, she still seems glad to see me.

"And Lucas." She switches her gaze to Lucas, standing on her toes to kiss him sensuously on each cheek. The sight of his massive hand on her bare back brings back an uninvited flash of memory of those hands on my back, among other places.

"I know Paul was very fond of your father," Kali says as she pulls away. Her eyes soften, scanning our periphery. "I can see you're tired." She takes the bunch of burning sage from the bronze Ganesh and waves it around us, muttering something under her breath. When she's finished, she contemplates us again. "Much better," she pronounces, returning the sage to its holder.

She gestures for us to take a seat on the chairs facing her couch, beneath a life-size oil painting of copulating gods with jaguar heads atop human bodies. "Please." She follows my gaze to the painting as we sit. "Beautiful, isn't it? The Mayans depicted a number of their gods this way. The tribe that lived on this land would sacrifice a virgin once a year, feeding her beating heart to a jaguar as an offering to the jaguar gods to stave off war and famine."

I gape at her, disturbed.

"Really," Lucas says with more than a hint of disbelief. "I studied the Mayans in school, and no one ever mentioned that."

Her smile is enigmatic. "It's not widely known."

A tall Asian guy with high cheekbones emerges through an archway that opens into a kitchenette and dining area. He's carrying a tray that holds an ornate china teapot with matching teacups and saucers.

"Thank you, Hikari," Kali says as he pours the tea and hands us each a cup before slipping quietly out of the room. "I know hot tea in the Mexican jungle may seem strange," she goes on, as if that's the strangest thing about this meeting. "But my parents were Indian and English, I can't help myself."

Steam curls from my cup as I inhale the floral aroma of the amber liquid. "It smells delicious," I say.

She smiles. "We make it here. We have a huge variety of herbs in our gardens."

I blow on it and take a tentative sip. It's simultaneously sweet and earthy, like honeysuckle and moss. I sneak a glance at Lucas, who hasn't even bothered with the pretense of raising his cup. I look at his cup pointedly, encouraging him to be polite. His jaw tightens, but he raises the cup and drinks.

"So, what happened?" I ask, unable to hold it in any longer. "To Paul?"

"Follow me," she says, suddenly rising. "You can bring your tea."

It's strange, when I met Kali in New York a few weeks ago, she'd seemed so down to earth. But here she's a different person, her power palpable. I don't quite know what to make of it.

Lucas and I follow Kali through another set of French doors onto the broad balcony on the front corner of the house. The heat of the day has dissipated and the faintest breeze caresses my skin as we stand at the stone balustrade above the gardens that spill down the hill to the dark waters of the lake. A mist hovers over its glassy surface as the sun sinks beneath the impregnable jungle on the far bank. Nothing but forest, as far as the eye can see.

Kali lowers her voice to an almost imperceptible level, her face serious. "I'm going to tell you the truth, but this information doesn't go beyond us. Do you understand?"

Lucas and I nod, leaning closer to hear.

"No one knows this. They can't; it would destroy everything he worked so hard for." She bites her lip as though reluctant to continue, then takes a deep breath and looks deeply into each of our faces in turn. "He was ill. He'd been ill for a while." She focuses her gaze on me. "When I mentioned it in December, it had already been going on for some time."

I feel Lucas's brisk glance—I still haven't mentioned our meeting to him—but ignore it.

"He'd grown skinny," Kali continues sadly, "his eyes had lost their sparkle, he was tired all the time. I begged him to see someone, but he wouldn't let any of our shamans near him. He believed this was what was meant to be and asked me to accept it as he had. What the others say is true: he took leave of his body. But it was illness that killed him."

Lucas squints at her, as confused as I am. "He had cancer," he says. "And he did see someone. He told me he was receiving chemo in the States."

"Western medicine is a Band-Aid," Kali says dismissively. "It addresses the symptom, not the cause of illness."

"What do you mean?" I ask.

"Our physical state reflects our spiritual state," she explains patiently. "If your vibration is high enough, you're not vulnerable to disease. We never have illness at Xanadu because everything we do here raises our vibration. The deterioration of Shiva's health exposed the cracks in his spiritual purity; therefore he chose to believe the Divine was simply calling him home. He handed the reins to me and instructed me what to say to his students to maintain continuity."

I don't follow this logic, but before I can pin down what question to ask, she reaches out and squeezes my hand, her eyes again welling with tears. "But you're his family, you deserve to know the truth. I want you to understand that he'd made peace with physical death—that, no matter how painful it may be for those of us left behind, this is what he wanted." She takes a deep breath, stilling her trembling lip. "I'm sorry. I'm trying to be strong for everyone and I celebrate the freedom of his spirit, but I miss him."

Glad to catch a glimpse of the Kali I met in New York, I reach out and wrap her in a hug, which she returns gratefully. She may be a priest-ess or whatever, but the poor woman is only human, and she's just lost her husband.

"So, what will the death certificate say?" Lucas asks, unmoved.

"Natural causes." She wipes away a tear as we release each other. "And I have to ask you to uphold that. If the media were to find out he'd been ill, they'd have a field day."

Lucas looks dubious. "And the request for issuance of death certificate has been filed?"

"Not yet," Kali says. "We haven't had an opportunity to take the forms into town. It's a long way, as you saw."

"Once the death certificate is issued, it still has to go through the US consulate to get the probate process started," he returns. "So we shouldn't waste time."

"You really don't need to worry about this," Kali says calmly. "It will all be taken care of. You have my word."

Lucas finally nods. "I can drop the forms on our way to the airport tomorrow."

"Thank you," she says, gliding to the door. "We should go now.

They'll be waiting for us. Please change into the clothes left on your beds. I'll be down in just a minute, and we can walk over together."

Inside, Hikari takes my empty cup. As he leads us toward the exit, I can see Ix-Chel through the glass doors on the opposite side of the room prowling back and forth, muscles rippling beneath her spotted coat. I have to remind myself that the rumbling I hear is a purr, not a growl.

TEN

As Lucas and I descend the wide wooden staircase to the deserted second floor, it strikes me just how far from home I am. "That was intense," I whisper, once we're far enough from Kali's lair.

"She was trying to intimidate us," he says.

"It worked." I shudder, picturing Ix-Chel's vigilant gaze. But then I think of Kali, her eyes shining with tears, and my heart swells with compassion for her. Perhaps I'm saddling the experience with my own preconceptions. Perhaps the jaguar is simply a beloved pet, helping her through a hard time.

But Lucas has other ideas.

"All that stuff about being so enlightened they don't get sick?" he continues, shaking his head. "*Of course* they don't have a lot of illness here, it's a closed environment. It has nothing to do with how enlightened they are."

"Yeah, I'm with you, it's all a bit weird," I agree, "but we're here for only one night, so what does it matter?"

It is also a little weird that after hearing nothing from her in the eight years she was with Paul, we had lunch only a month ago, and now I'm here in her home. But it can only be coincidence, right? She couldn't possibly have known what the future would hold. Could she? No. She certainly has a powerful presence, but I'm not about to start believing Kali's an actual prophet.

I slip through the door to our room and immediately my stomach drops. Our bags are gone. Lucas throws his hands up. "Seriously?"

I lift the blanket to look beneath the bed as he pushes open the bathroom door and glances around. "We shouldn't have left them," he groans, agitated. He extracts his phone from the pocket of his jeans and checks the display, then turns it off. "This thing is useless," he laments.

"You know they're gonna ask you for that," I say.

"My work phone is still in my bag, hopefully they'll think it's my only phone," he mutters, shoving it under the mattress. "I can't believe they took our stuff."

"I'm sure there's an explanation," I say, trying to put on a good face, though in truth I'm as disturbed as he is. "Let's just get dressed. We'll ask Kali when she comes down."

"She's like a cobra, staring into your eyes, ready to strike at any moment," he grumbles.

"O-kay," I say, confounded by the intensity of his hostility toward her. "I'm annoyed about the bags, too, but Kali's been nothing but kind to us, especially under the circumstances."

He glowers at me as I grab the white dress laid out on the bed and take it into the bathroom, shutting the door behind me. In the gold-edged mirror I see I'm a mess, my eyes bloodshot with dark circles beneath from lack of sleep, my tangled hair coming loose from its messy ponytail. Over the years I can't say I haven't dreamed of bumping into Lucas, but in my fantasies I am red-carpet ready on the arm of a dashing man, surrounded by my fanciest friends. Not sleep deprived and makeup-free, my troubled mind swimming with my questionable life decisions. And he isn't such a dick.

Not that it matters.

I shed my clothes and quickly take a whore's bath in the sink, then step into the soft linen dress, identical to Kali's. I feel my shoulders drop the moment I put it on. It's the most comfortable thing I've ever worn, and I have to say it looks fantastic on me. Honestly, with its flowing silhouette, deep V in the front, and open back, it's the kind of dress that looks fantastic on everyone, but I do appreciate the way it displays the entire tiger on my back. My black thong, however, is fully visible through the thin fabric, so I shed it and let down my hair, then stuff my clothes into the cabinet beneath the sink in hopes they won't be confiscated.

In the bedroom, I find Lucas wearing the same white linen drawstring pants and collarless shirt as Aguilar and Hikari, with both the sleeves and pant legs rolled up. I give him a quizzical look. "It was all a little short," he explains. "This looks better than the alternative, trust me."

"At least you're tan," I return. "I look like a ghost in this."

He sizes me up with a slight smile. "Exactly what I was thinking."

I roll my neck out, feeling more relaxed now that I'm out of my travel clothes. Lighter, though I can't explain it.

"I'm sorry I was a dick about Kali," he says. I look up at him, surprised by the quick about-face. "I'm on edge because I haven't slept, and Paul was important to my dad. I'm not trying to make excuses . . . I just want everything to go smoothly."

"That's all?" I ask. "You seemed really upset by her. Is there anything else you're keeping from me?"

"That's all. I promise."

"Okay." I acquiesce. "Let's just . . . get through this. It's one day."

He nods.

I open the top drawer of the bedside table and take out three of Paul's books: *Surrender, Living the Life You Deserve,* and *The End of Illness.* I read to him from the back of the last one: "'Decrease stress and release negative energy to boost your immunity and live the *healthy* life you deserve.' That's what Kali was talking about."

"It's a theme," he confirms. "Clearing your energy to attain the different facets of the life you deserve. But then, you probably know that."

"I've read *Surrender* and *Connection,*" I offer. "And part of *Living the Life You Deserve,* before one of my roommates stole it."

"I read those, too," he replies. "And *Anusara.*" He sifts through the top drawer of the bedside table next to mine, producing a copy of *Anusara.*

"Isn't that a type of yoga?" I ask.

"Yeah," he says, "but it means 'to be in the flow of grace.' It's all about opening up to Divine Will to find your calling." He cocks his head, considering me. "I figured as his niece, you'd be familiar with all this stuff."

"Honestly, I haven't really seen him since I was a kid," I say. "He and my mom didn't get along—don't ask me why, I have no idea. So yeah, you probably know more about this stuff than I do."

He shrugs. "I dated a yoga instructor for a while who followed his ideology, and she got me into his books. I was curious anyway because he and my dad were friends. I mean, they're good, if you're into that sort of thing."

"And you are?"

"To a degree. Not this degree." He waves his hand around, indicating Xanadu. "Honestly, people who act all woo-woo spiritual kinda get on my nerves."

I raise an eyebrow. "Because of the group you were in with your mom?"

His gaze could cut through ice, but the corner of his mouth lifts. "You sound like my therapist."

"You go to therapy?" I comment, impressed.

He sighs. "I'm trying."

"Trying to do what?"

"You ask a lot of questions."

He tosses the book onto his bed and a glossy pamphlet falls out, featuring the outline of a glowing person with each of his chakras represented by a circle of the corresponding color. I pick it up. "Spin the wheel to elevate your consciousness," I read, raising my brows. "Mandala Enrollment Opportunities, 2017."

"Twenty seventeen . . . I think that was the year before the woman made those allegations and Paul sold the California retreat center," Lucas muses. "Which would have been the last year they offered in-person classes."

He looks over my shoulder as I unfold the pamphlet. Inside, a number of courses are listed within colored boxes in rainbow order, red to violet. An introduction at the top reads:

The Mandala offers a structured path for seekers of Enlighten-ment, specifically designed to bring about positive personal trans-formation. Each course is aligned with a corresponding chakra and builds upon the knowledge gained in previous courses to clear energy blockages and empower you to live the connected life you were always meant to live! *A schedule of seminar locations and times can be found on our website.*

The first box is red and labeled "Root Chakra," with three courses listed:

- Know Yourself (To know yourself is to know the Divine!)
- Reclaim Your Life (Let go of fear to realize your full potential!)
- Finding Freedom in Commitment (Free yourself to commit to your personal growth!)

The second box is orange and labeled "Sacral Chakra," with another three courses listed:

- Respecting the Body (Your body is the Temple of the Divine!)
- Opening to Change (Release restrictive beliefs to become your best self!)
- Go with the Flow (Surrender to Divine Will to find joy!)

The third is yellow and labeled "Solar Plexus Chakra," with an addi-tional three courses, but before I can read it, we're interrupted by Kali, flanked by a jacked white guy who resembles Superman and a beautiful Black woman with thick box braids, who I recognize from the videos.

Jesus. The people I've come across at Xanadu thus far would give the models I've worked with over the years a run for their money.

"The dress suits you," Kali says with a smile. "This is Ruby and Rex." They bow to us, and we awkwardly return the gesture. "Are you ready?"

"We are." I drop the pamphlet onto my bed and glance down at their feet to see they're all wearing huarache sandals. "Should we wear the shoes we arrived in?"

"We have sandals you can borrow downstairs," Ruby says.

"Great," I reply, smiling. "Because my running shoes wouldn't look so good with this dress."

Kali takes my elbow as we exit the room. "I'm so glad you're here," she says again, giving my arm a squeeze.

"What happened to our bags?" Lucas asks as he follows behind us, Rex and Ruby bringing up the rear.

"They're in storage," Rex replies casually. "You won't need them while you're here. We provide everything you need."

"But I need my computer," Lucas protests.

"And it's completely safe in the tech room," Rex returns. "You can use it there."

"I'm sorry if Aguilar didn't tell you," Kali apologizes. "He was certainly meant to." She stops at the top of the grand staircase, regarding us with compassion. "I know it may seem strange, but I promise it's for the greater good. We're a family here, we take care of each other. Some of us are recovering from addiction or abuse suffered in the outside world, and pills left on the counter could be a temptation that sets someone back months; even something as simple as seeing street clothes can be triggering. Others are in hiding from the press or political rivals who want them dead, so we can't have photography of any kind. This is a safe space, and its integrity has to be protected."

I nod. That makes sense, I guess.

When we reach the bottom of the stairs, she leads us toward the back of the house and down a marble hallway lit by gold sconces that runs directly beneath the hall where our room is located. I glance at the framed lithographs of plants that line the walls as we pass by offices, a number of what appear to be massage rooms, a couple of bedrooms, and finally a laundry and mudroom. On the inside wall are six industrial-size washers and as many dryers, and on the back wall is a door to the outside.

Kali opens a cabinet to our right to reveal rows and rows of sandals with sizes listed below them. "What size are you?"

"Nine," I say, so accustomed to lying that the number slips off my tongue. But this is not a fitting for a client who wants to show their shoes in the smallest possible size to make them look feminine. "Sorry, ten," I correct myself. Then, unnecessarily, "I have big feet."

"Thirteen." Lucas grins. "I have even bigger feet."

Ruby spritzes us with a rosemary-scented herbal remedy meant to ward off bugs, and we file out the back door into the balmy evening. The sun has sunk beneath the trees on the opposite side of the lake, leaving the sky lavender in its wake. We follow a stone walkway past the pool and tree house and across a trickling stream, beyond which the path turns to packed dirt the color of espresso and winds up a hill into the dense, dark forest. The emergent layer must reach two hundred feet toward the sky, obscured from my view by a canopy so thick that hardly any daylight reaches the forest floor. I've never felt so small or so enveloped by nature.

An image of the crocodile we saw in the river comes to mind, and I wonder what other dangers lurk beyond the fat trees, snaking vines, and overgrown ferns.

The faint sound of drums and chanting grows louder as we draw closer to a large wooden structure with a steeply sloped thatched roof, hidden among the trees.

We ascend a wet wooden staircase to the open-air building, which appears to be roughly hexagonal, stopping beneath an attached portico to shed our shoes and store them in the wall of cubbyholes while Ruby pours each of us a small cup of steaming tea from an orange drink dispenser. Hot tea is the last thing I want to drink in this humid environment, but she whispers that it's "for the ceremony," as she presses the ceramic cup into my hands. Without my sandals I can feel the vibration of the chanting through the wood floor as Lucas and I follow Kali, Ruby, and Rex inside.

Surrounded on all sides by the quickly darkening jungle, the room glows with the flickering light of candles and globe lights strung from the ceiling. About seventy-five people dressed in the same white linen we wear sit on floor cushions facing a raised platform at the far end of the space, where Blaze and a small brown-haired woman are seated on the stairs playing bongos while a man between them strums a sitar. The walls are made of screens, but the air is heavy with the almost carnal scent of incense mixed with earth, plants, and human bodies.

As Kali threads her way through the center of the group trailed by Rex and Ruby, the chanting turns to the universal "Om," and the music ceases. Lucas and I hover at the back of the room, unsure what to do with ourselves, but Kali beckons us forward. All eyes are on us as we make our way up the three steps to join her on the platform. At the top, she turns and faces the crowd, a hand on each of our backs.

She waits for the room to go quiet before she speaks. "This is Shiva's niece, Sveta," she announces. "And Lucas, whose father was close with Shiva for many years. They've come a long way to be here today. Please give them a warm Mandala welcome."

"Namaste," the crowd calls in unison, bowing to us with prayer hands.

"Let us drink to their health," Kali instructs, holding aloft her cup.

Everyone raises their cup, then drinks, and we mirror the gesture. This tea is thicker and stronger than what I drank earlier, with an aftertaste like licorice. I cover a grimace as it goes down.

Kali gestures for us to take the two empty cushions between Rex and Ruby, and we comply. Standing on the candlelit stage she is resplendent, looking down upon us like a goddess from a pedestal.

"This evening we celebrate the earthly life of our guru Shiva, and his freedom from the bonds of embodiment," she begins. "While we are grieving the loss of his counsel, it's important to remember that we are the fortunate, tasked with bearing witness to the messages he received while he walked among us; we are the chosen, charged with the noble duty of passing on these messages. We will continue to strengthen our bodies, purify our minds, and liberate our souls so that we can be of service to mankind."

In a gesture reminiscent of communion, she again lifts her cup in both hands and drinks from it, and everyone follows suit. Lucas and I exchange a quick glance, then raise our own cups to our lips.

Kali brings her hands together at her heart and chants, "Om," the sound growing as the rest of the room joins in while a freckled brunette sweeps some kind of mallet through a huge bronze bowl, creating a dome of resonance. I clasp my own hands in prayer like the others, feeling my resistance crumble as the sound reverberates through my body. After each chant of "Om," everyone drinks the pungent tea, and I do the same. Once our cups are empty, Kali begins a Sanskrit mantra and the group follows, their voices swelling together in powerful tones closer to an incantation than a song.

As the chanting continues, I feel the burden that's weighed on me since New Year's begin to dissolve. The uncertainty that seemed so daunting turns auspicious; the future seems full, not of apprehension but of possibility. My heart swells with compassion for Chase, struggling to make both his mother and me happy, and I'm overcome with the desire to hug him and tell him I forgive him.

As the sitar soars above the voices and my heart beats in rhythm with the drums, I have the strangest sensation of levity, as though I'm crowd surfing, supported by the chorus of voices, buoyed by a deep sense of connection to my fellow humans. I'm flooded with love for my brave mother, raising a child alone after losing my father, whose mental health struggles must have been a weight for both of them. I feel a surge of affection for Kali, trying to remain strong in the wake of her partner's untimely death. I see how important this place is to her, these people. And I'm struck by how happy they seem, how grounded. I feel it, too, the synchronicity, the pulse of the universe in the throbbing music. This must be the connection they speak of.

Even Lucas nods his head to the music, and I feel a rush of warmth as our eyes meet.

In a flash, I'm an eighteen-year-old virgin again, walking through a park with a handsome boy. Even after all this time, my chest tightens at the memory. But Lucas doesn't know he hurt me. He was only twenty, making the same kind of self-centered decisions I was at the time. As the music pulses around me and the sounds of the night jungle swell outside, my grievances seem small and inconsequential. We've both grown in the past decade. Perhaps we can be friends now. I'd like that, I think.

ELEVEN

I first met Lucas Baranquilla twelve years ago, on my eighteenth birthday.

By chance, he and his father were in the city visiting relatives at the same time my mom was in town for my birthday, and they saw one another's Facebook posts and decided to meet up. I'd never heard of the Baranquillas before that, though I did vaguely recognize Mr. Baranquilla when I met him, from my dad's funeral.

My mom had been living in Miami for three years at that point—she'd packed up and left North Carolina just months after I'd departed for New York when I was fourteen—but she came to visit me frequently back then. She never stayed with me, though, preferring a room at whatever hotel was offering special rates to the couch in the compact two-bedroom apartment I shared with three other girls.

It was a rainy October night and we'd just been seated at her favorite cozy Italian joint in the Village when I glanced up from my menu to see her sapphire eyes clouded with worry.

"Uh-oh," I said. "What's up?"

She tucked a strand of dark hair behind her ear. "I know we have plans tomorrow for your birthday." She'd come to the United States without knowing a word of English, but after marrying my father she studied the language with laser focus until she was fluent, though her accent was still thick. "But I have a small problem. A friend of your father's called me today. He's in town, and I must see him tomorrow."

"Why?" I asked, annoyed she was prioritizing this man over me on my birthday. "Can't you see him some other time?"

"Tomorrow is his last day before he returns to California."

I sighed. The leaves were in peak color, and I'd planned to take her for lunch at a restaurant on the lake in Central Park so that we could enjoy the display. "So, no lunch?"

"I'm so sorry, solnyshka." Hearing the Russian term of endearment she'd used with me when I was younger, I knew she really was sorry. "But we can go the next day."

"Okay."

I could tell she was relieved I hadn't put up a fight. "How about tonight, you stay at my hotel with me, and we watch a movie in bed?"

This was our custom every time she was in town, and I agreed.

It wasn't until we were about to start the movie that she informed me my dad's friend would be bringing his twenty-year-old son, whom I would need to entertain while she and his father talked "business"—what business, she wouldn't specify.

"But Mom, it's my birthday," I complained.

"Please," she said.

I don't know that I'd ever heard my mom say "please" before. She was a direct person, reserved and proud to boot, her fine features and flirty dresses camouflage for her stalwart personality, and pleading wasn't in her repertoire.

To the best of my knowledge, she hadn't dated since my father's death, though I couldn't fathom why. A woman as beautiful as she was, with a rare laugh that tinkled like a wind chime on a breezy afternoon, could have easily bagged a businessman with a boat and a house on the bay. I didn't know what her dreams were as a girl—she thought of dreams as frivolous and never talked of such things—but surely she'd aspired to more than scrubbing other people's toilets. Or maybe that was just my American upbringing speaking, because anytime I mentioned it, she clucked her tongue disapprovingly and told me there was nothing wrong with an honest day's work.

Now I felt a pang of compassion. "Okay," I said. Then I added, with more than a hint of sarcasm, "He'd better be cute."

She squeezed my hand with a grateful smile.

Regardless, I had no expectations when we went down to the lobby to meet them the next morning. I'd resigned myself to the circumstances, assured by my mother that I'd be finished with my hosting duties in plenty of time to go out with my friends for my birthday. So I was pleasantly surprised when my mom pointed out the Baranquillas striding through the revolving door.

I lie. I was thrilled.

Lucas was tall and tan, with an athlete's body, his moody dark eyes fringed with long lashes, his wavy, almost black hair long enough to tuck behind his ears. He wore ripped gray jeans and a black hoodie, with a scowl that said he had also been dragged here against his wishes.

His father was probably ten years older than my mother, which made sense because she'd been only twenty-two when she had me. He was dressed in a button-down and slacks, paired with leather shoes and a watch I could tell were expensive, and had the same height and broad shoulders as his son, though his thick hair was mostly gray and his face more narrow.

My mother waved to them with a bright smile. I noticed she'd taken extra care getting ready that morning, curling her hair and selecting a lilac sweater that complemented her pale skin, and wondered briefly whether she and Mr. Baranquilla were involved romantically. Though surely not, if he'd been a friend of my dad's.

As they approached, the father extended a hand to me and I shook it. "I'm Lucas Baranquilla," he said in a manner more formal than I was used to, with an accent I couldn't place. "And this is my son, Lucas Jr."

I was relieved to see that the son's scowl had dissipated. "Hi," he said.

A waft of floral perfume enveloped me as my mom leaned past to give Mr. Baranquilla an overly warm hug that he awkwardly returned. "Irina," he said. "You look beautiful, as always."

It was strange to see her like this. I was reminded of how young she was and felt another pang of sympathy for her. "Sveta will show Lucas the park," she said.

We hadn't discussed this, but it seemed like as good an idea as any. "Is that good with you?" I asked him.

"Sure," he agreed.

Outside, the day was bright and crisp, the streets of midtown bustling with Saturday shoppers and brunchers.

Lucas and I walked side by side for a full block before either of us spoke. "So you live here?" he finally asked.

"Yeah." I glanced over at him.

"That's cool," he said. "I'd love to live here someday."

"California's pretty cool, too, though," I said. "Do you surf?"

That elicited a smile. "Yeah. I guess I'm a cliché that way. But the water's freezing up where me and my dad live, so it's not what you imagine."

"Nothing's ever what you imagine," I commented.

He studied me. "True." There was something pensive about him, a depth behind his eyes that most boys his age didn't have, and it made me want to know more.

"You any good?" I asked. "At surfing."

He shrugged. "I've won contests here and there. I wanted to try to do it professionally, but my dad insisted I go to college."

That statement alone spoke volumes about how different our upbringings had been, but I didn't hold it against him. I could tell he wasn't trying to lord it over me like some people did. "Where do you go?" I asked.

"Stanford."

"You're a sophomore or junior?" I asked, remembering my mom had said he was twenty.

But he shook his head. "I just started."

"Oh. Did you take a gap year or something?"

"Something like that."

I could tell there was more to that story, but he didn't elaborate, and it felt rude to pry.

"I want to go to college someday," I offered.

"Why wouldn't you?" he asked.

"It's hard to justify the expense when I'm not even sure what I want to do. And I'm working so much right now, I can't really turn down the money. I figure maybe if I work a few years more and save up, then I'll be able to afford it. I do have my GED."

"I get that." Our arms brushed as I sidestepped a giant inflatable orange pumpkin, and he caught my eye, holding my gaze a moment too long. My insides did a somersault. "My dad told me you're a model. Is that fun?"

I shrugged. "I like it. But it's not as glamorous as it looks."

"Nothing's ever what you imagine, right?" He echoed my earlier statement, and I smiled.

In the park, the cool fire of fall had just begun to turn the tips of the trees yellow and red, and though it was warm enough that we both shed our sweaters, the breeze that sent leaves twirling down from the towering elms had an invigorating chill to it. We climbed to the top of a giant boulder, where we talked about our favorite far-flung locales, thrilled to discover some of them matched. Lucas told me about the band he played in, and I regaled him with tales of my crazy roommates' antics.

When he mentioned he was hungry and I checked my watch, I was surprised to find that over two hours had passed. "I have a reservation for me and my mom that I forgot to cancel," I offered. "It's close by."

"Perfect, let's do it," he said.

But when we reached the boathouse restaurant, he stopped. "What?" I asked.

"Nothing, it's just—" His frown deepened. "I came here with my mom, a long time ago. It brings back memories, is all."

Whatever memories it brought back were clearly upsetting. "Did your mom . . . pass away?" I asked gently.

"Might as well have."

As with the gap year before college, I could tell there was more to this story, but his expression didn't invite questions. "Do you want to go somewhere else?" I asked.

He shook his head. "It's fine."

It clearly wasn't fine, but it wasn't my place to push, and anyway, I was hungry, so we followed the hostess to a shaded white-tableclothed table overlooking the lake. "Happy birthday, Svetlana," she said as she handed us our menus.

"Thank you," I replied, blushing.

Once she'd departed, Lucas raised his brows at me. "You didn't tell me it was your birthday."

I shrugged. "You didn't ask."

"And you're stuck entertaining some random guy . . ."

I laughed. "I don't mind."

"Good," he said. Our eyes caught and a shower of sparks fizzed inside me. "You're not what I expected."

From the way he said it, I knew it was a compliment. "You, either," I said.

"How old are you turning?"

"Eighteen."

He stared at me. "Wow."

"What?"

"I just would've guessed you were older."

"I'm not that young," I protested. "I'm only two years younger than you."

"You're just . . . mature, is all."

I snorted. "Get to know me better."

"I'd like that," he said, and the sparks inside me caught fire. "Do you have plans tonight?"

"I'm meeting some girlfriends for dinner, then we're going to a club." I gathered my courage. "You're welcome to come if you're not busy," I offered in what I hoped was a casual tone.

The whole world stopped as he took me in, his eyes glinting in the sunlight off the lake. "Yeah," he said finally, the corner of his mouth quirking up. "Sounds good."

LUCAS TURNED UP AT THE swanky sushi place looking devastating in a white button-down and fitted jeans. My girlfriends eyed him thirstily throughout dinner, making suggestive comments that embarrassed the hell out of me, but he handled their innuendo and bawdy humor like a pro, which of course only made me like him more.

Girls whose parents allowed them to drop out of high school and move to New York in order to pursue a career in modeling tended to be wilder and brasher than the average American schoolgirl. These were girls who had developed the thick skin that comes with daily rejection before they could even vote, cultivated the street sense it takes to persevere in the concrete jungle before obtaining their GEDs. They wouldn't all survive it by a long stretch. Some went home after a few weeks or months, scarred by the cutthroat nature of the fashion business; others developed drug habits or eating disorders, or worse.

Yes, fashion was an ugly business, but if you could make it, you could have the kind of glamorous life most people only ever gawked at in magazines or on reality television shows. To the ones who stayed, the gamble was worth it.

By the time we left dinner, we were all good and tipsy, impervious to the nip in the air as we pranced down the busy streets of Manhattan in our barely there dresses as if we thought we were in a music video. The chemistry between Lucas and me had reached electrical status, my whole body twinkling like the lights of the city every time we touched, which we did with increasing frequency.

In the cavelike club, my friends beelined for the bar while the two of us lingered in a dark corner, savoring the closeness required to hear each other above the music. It didn't matter what we were talking about. My chest grazed his as I stood on my toes to reach his ear, his shoulder brushed mine, our fingers intertwined. Our lips met and booming fire-works went off inside me.

When our kissing threatened to become indecent, he took my hand and led me through the flashing blue and pink lights onto the dance floor, vibrating with bass. His sleeves were rolled up, his shirt unbuttoned just enough that I could see his breastbone glistening with sweat in the rotat-ing colored lights as our bodies moved in sync. He was a fantastic dancer, confident on his feet, his touch so light I craved more.

If he can move like this on a dance floor, what would he be like in bed?

Amazing, most likely. But what about me? He clearly had more ex-perience than me, seeing as I had none. None at all. I was a virgin, which was something I'd been wanting to change for a while. But what if I was terrible? What if it hurt and I couldn't go through with it?

Suddenly I was nervous, my longing for him tied up with perfor-mance anxiety. Liquid courage was what I needed.

Tequila burned down my throat, followed by the sharp tang of lime. Champagne bubbled over my tongue. More tequila, no need for lime this time. His dark eyes locked on mine; the world went topsy-turvy, the light of the disco ball sliding over our skin as we kissed.

I AWOKE TO THE SOUND of the air conditioner clicking on.

Where was I?

Groggy, I raised my head to see a plush hotel room, lit only by the slivers of daylight that bled through the edges of the blackout curtains. I was alone in bed, tangled up in the sheet in nothing but my peach lace panties.

I grabbed my phone off the bedside table and checked the time: 8:43 A.M.

Where was Lucas? What had happened?

I remembered dancing, kissing, shots, the girls giving us shit for making out, more shots . . . but when did we leave? Or did I leave alone?

And which of us rented this hotel room? I hoped it wasn't me. I definitely could not afford this hotel.

Regardless, I'd very obviously overdone it.

Silently cursing my freshly eighteen-year-old self, I dragged my sorry ass out of bed and padded into the bathroom. My reflection in the mirror wasn't half as bad as I expected it to be. I'd apparently washed off my makeup, at least, and dropped my jewelry in the empty soap dish next to the sink. No signs I'd been sick, either, thank God.

I flipped on the shower and let the water warm while I brushed my teeth, then stripped off my underwear and inspected it for signs I'd done the deed. Not that I felt any soreness down there—and everyone had told me I'd be sore after. The pristine panties only confirmed what I already knew.

As I stepped into the white-and-gray marble shower, I noticed the minidress I'd been wearing last night balled in the corner, soaking wet. The memory of peeling it off beneath the stream of water flashed before my eyes. Lucas unzipping me, smiling, drunk but not as drunk as I was.

So he'd been here with me, and I'd stripped in front of him in the shower, then we . . . hadn't had sex? It seemed odd. Had I done something or said something that sent him running?

Dispirited, I cut off the water and dried myself with a plush white bath towel, wrapping it around me as I stepped into the bedroom.

"Hi."

I jumped and yelped, spinning to see Lucas setting up breakfast on the table at the far end of the room. "Oh my God, you scared the shit out of me," I breathed.

He laughed. "I just went down to pick up croissants and coffee for us."

He held out an iced latte and I gaped at it. "How did you know my drink?"

"You were very adamant last night that this morning I should bring you an iced almond milk latte."

"Oh God, what else did I say?" I asked, tentatively crossing to him.

He grinned. "I'll never tell."

I used the hand that wasn't holding my towel in place to cover my face. "How'd we get this hotel room?" I asked.

"It's mine," he said. "My dad's on the next floor."

"You gave me a shower?" I asked. "I remember you helping me out of the dress, but not much else."

"You showered," he confirmed, his deep brown eyes dancing. "I think you were trying to sober up enough that we could have sex."

"But we didn't," I said.

He shook his head. "I didn't think you were in any position to be making decisions, and I didn't want you to regret it."

"I appreciate that," I said, closing the distance between us. I pressed my knee between his. "What time do you have to leave?"

He bent his head toward mine. "I have about two hours."

"I'm not drunk anymore." I released the towel.

He inhaled sharply, gazing down at my naked body. I grabbed his hand and pulled him to the bed. We worked fast to unbutton his shirt and pants, our desire growing stronger with every touch. He kissed me gently as he laid me on the pillows, wearing nothing but his boxer briefs, his soft lips lighting a trail of sparks all the way down my torso as I moaned with pleasure. It was finally happening, and it felt better than I'd ever imagined.

The surprise of his tongue between my legs set my whole body on fire, waves of pleasure radiating from my center until I shuddered far too soon. He smiled and pushed his boxers down, reaching for a condom.

"That was incredible," I panted.

"I know it can be painful your first time," he said, opening the foil, "so I wanted to give you pleasure first."

"I told you I'm a virgin?"

He nodded. "I'll be slow, okay? Let me know if you want me to stop." He sat up to slide on the condom. "Are you sure you want to?" he asked.

"Yes, I want to." *Desperately.*

I reached for him and he lowered himself on top of me, tenderly kissing me as he pressed slowly into me. The pain was bright and sharp. He stopped, checking on me, his tenderness only turning me on further. "Keep going, I'm okay," I said.

It only took a few minutes for pleasure to edge out the pain, our breath falling into sync as our bodies found their rhythm.

Afterward, as I lay in his arms feeling his chest rise and fall, I felt a bittersweet aching for him flood through me, an unquenchable thirst to know him, to hold him, to be with him. I'd never been in love before, but I thought this might be what it felt like. I wanted to tell him how fortunate I felt to have met him, to ask him when we'd see each other again, if perhaps he might like to change his flight today and stay for a while. But he wasn't saying any of those things, and I didn't want to come off as needy.

I traced the thin outline of the circle tattooed between his navel and his pubic bone with my fingernail. "What's this?" I asked.

"The circle of life," he replied.

"I like it," I said.

He kissed the top of my head.

We didn't have much time before he had to leave, so we dressed and drank our coffee together on the balcony in the warm morning sun. "I wish we had another day," I said.

"Me, too," he said, but he didn't elaborate, and I wondered briefly whether my feelings might be bigger than his.

But the way he looked at me when we said goodbye in the doorway of his suite told me the past twenty-four hours had meant just as much to him as they had to me.

I spent the rest of the day with my mom on cloud nine. I was still smiling when I hadn't heard from him the next day, figuring he'd had a long flight back to San Francisco and a time change to contend with. I composed a text to him, then deleted it, unsure what to say. Over and over again I repeated this process, never hitting Send. If he wasn't texting me, there had to be a reason, right?

I gave it another day, and another, my happiness souring with every passing hour.

After a week, I caved and looked up his Facebook profile. But there was no Facebook profile. No other social media that I could find, either. Perhaps they were under a nickname, I figured, disappointed.

I waited another three days before I finally texted him:

Hey there, you make it back to SF ok?

He never wrote back.

TWELVE

The musicians bring their instruments into the unison of one harmonious chord that recedes until it ceases altogether, the sounds of the night jungle rushing in to fill the silence. Next to me, Ruby wipes tears from her cheeks, taking deep breaths. She catches me looking at her and quickly pulls herself together.

Kali stands, and the musicians follow her through the crowd and out the door, where they gather their shoes before descending into the forest. My body still hums with the residue of the music as we all follow suit, quietly filing into the anteroom to slip on our shoes, then down the stairs onto the packed wet dirt of the jungle path, lit with tiki torches that throw flickering shadows into the undergrowth.

I walk the jungle path next to Lucas, the humid air soft on my skin as the line of ghostlike figures trickles out of the woods and down the hill toward the lake. We follow the trail along the terraced garden to the water's edge, toward where my uncle's body lies shrouded atop the funeral pyre, amid a circle of torches.

The strike of a gong echoes over the water and Kali faces the crowd, flanked by Rex, Ruby, Aguilar, and Hikari. "Tonight we bid farewell to the body of our beloved Shiva. With this fire we release his spirit."

She extends her arms to her sides, her ring fingers touching her thumbs as she intones a mantra in Sanskrit, her voice rising and falling with the melodic syllables.

When she's finished, the gong rings again and Hikari passes her a clay pot that, from the way she holds it, must be heavy. The drums take up a ponderous rhythm and the sitar starts in with a haunting melody, followed by a honeyed, plaintive voice that floats over the water like a siren's call. I crane my neck to see that the singer is Ruby, her face again wet with tears in the flickering firelight.

Chills run up my spine as Kali circles the funeral pyre holding the pot. When she returns, Hikari pierces the clay with a sharp rod that sends water gushing over her. Then she places the pot on the ground and stomps on it, smashing it to pieces. The gong rings again and Kali holds a torch to the base of the pyre. Gray smoke billows for a moment before the wood crackles and ignites. I blink back tears as Kali lights little fires all along the rim of the pyre until the entire structure is ablaze, then steps back to watch the hungry orange flames lick the wood.

Blaze grabs a torch and holds it alight. "Ram nam sit hair," he cries, his eyes alive in the firelight.

"Ram nam sit hair," the others join in. "Ram nam sit hair, ram nam sit hair."

Chanting with growing fervor, they circle the pyre as the blaze intensifies, their swaying forms sending irregular shadows dancing into the night.

"It's a variation on a Hindu burial ritual," Lucas whispers into my hair.

"How do you know?" I ask.

"I visited Varanasi in India, on the banks of the Ganges, where hundreds of funeral rites are performed every day. It was . . ." He shakes his head. "I've never experienced anything like it."

The fire sizzles and I flinch at my first whiff of something sulfurous and acrid. I cover my mouth and nose with my hands, but it's not enough to block out the pungent smell of burning flesh, so thick it's almost a taste. I think I'm going to be sick. I back away from the fire, but the steaky, putrid stench follows me, permeating everything. It's too much. I'm suddenly claustrophobic, trapped by the fetid odor of death. Unable to breathe, I stumble out of the circle of light and run for the villa.

My sandals slap the stones as I bolt up the hill in the dark, panting and choking on tears. In front of the house the fountain glows like a beacon, the spouts from the open mouths of the golden jaguars spilling perpetually into the incandescent pool beneath.

Lucas catches me as I near the top of the incline. "Are you okay?"

I shake my head vehemently, refusing to look at him. "What do you think?"

The air must be cleaner up here a hundred yards away from the pyre, but I can still smell the stink of burned meat on my clothes, my skin, my hair.

"It's intense," he sympathizes.

Through my distress, I nearly laugh at the absurdity of the word, of any word, to describe what I'm feeling. Words are so small in the face of something so huge, so all-encompassing.

He grabs my hand and pulls me toward the fountain. "Come on."

"What are you doing?" I resist.

But he has my hand clenched firmly in his as he kicks off his shoes and steps up onto the marble lip of the fountain, pulling me with him. I have no choice but to shed my own shoes and follow him over the edge, into the water with a splash. The pool is waist deep and nearly as warm as the air, a welcome relief from the smell of smoke and death below.

He releases my hand as he dives under, and I follow suit, my dress billowing around me in the chlorinated water. I come up only long enough to fill my lungs, then sink beneath the surface again, raking my fingers through my swirling hair and rubbing my face with my hands to purge my skin of the stench. I emerge refreshed to see Lucas standing beneath one of the jaguar's spouts, his head tossed back, eyes closed. His white linen clothes are completely translucent and matted to his skin, outlining every muscle in his toned body, like the cover of the kind of steamy romance novel you have to hide on the train.

I rip my gaze away and swim to the other jaguar. With my eyes closed, I stand under it, allowing the powerful flow to massage my back.

"Better?"

I open my eyes to see him swimming toward me and, realizing that if his clothes are nearly transparent mine must be also, sink into the water. "Yes," I say. "Thank you. I wasn't mentally prepared, I guess."

"I don't think you could've been," he replies, his eyes glistening in the light off the water. "We don't have any framework to process something like that. Culturally, I mean."

"I was thinking the same thing when we first saw the pyre this afternoon," I agree. "Our lives are so sanitized, so detached from nature and the life cycle." I realize as I say it how silly I sound. How privileged. "I mean, I'm one to talk, I couldn't last five minutes down there, and I'm not saying we should start burning our dead on the banks of the Hudson, but . . ." I shake my head. What *am* I trying to say?

He regards me seriously, his gaze soft. "You can't blame yourself for the culture you were born into. But you're right. In the Western world we turn away from anything unpleasant, which gives us fewer opportunities for growth."

I nod, feeling as though I've failed at being a worthy human. "We outsource everything uncomfortable so that we can focus on ourselves. It's terrible."

He shrugs. "It's practical. We don't bury people in our rivers for more reasons than we just don't want to."

"Right." I sigh. How is he so grounded when my head is spinning like a tornado? "Of course. I just . . . I want to live more deeply, I guess," I confess. "I don't want to be the kind of person who runs away from a funeral pyre."

He gives me a knowing smile. "You want to live deep and suck out all the marrow of life?"

"A modern-day Thoreau," I confirm, demonstrating I know the quote, then immediately feeling gross for needing to demonstrate I know the quote. And why am I confessing all this to Lucas, of all people?

"Running away from a funeral pyre has nothing to do with living more deeply," he says sincerely. "I mean, Thoreau was a transcendentalist, after all; he was more interested in empirical thinking than the physical world. He might very well have done the same."

His steady gaze makes me feel even more off-kilter than the fact that I'm not totally sure what empirical thinking is.

I slosh to the edge of the fountain and hoist myself over the lip, my soaked dress dripping everywhere, to see Aguilar coming up the walkway, backlit by the blaze from the fire down below.

"Are you guys okay?" he calls as he approaches.

"Yeah," Lucas responds from behind me. "We were having some trouble with the smell."

"It's powerful," Aguilar agrees.

"That's one way of putting it," I mutter, wringing out my dress.

"I'll leave towels outside the door," he says, pointing at the main entrance. "Everyone is coming up shortly, then we'll meet in the dining room for the feast."

How the hell anyone can want to eat after roasting a human being is beyond me, but I nod. "Thank you."

He continues toward the villa and I squeeze more water out of the bottom of my dress as Lucas climbs out of the fountain. "Is that your spirit animal?"

"What?"

He indicates my back. "The tiger."

I can't ever tell whether he's messing with me or serious. "Yeah, maybe."

"I think definitely."

I point to the mass of dark ink on his chest and arm I can make out beneath his wet shirt. "What's that?"

"It's an Amazonian depiction of the ocean—homage to my dad's roots."

"And your love of surfing?"

"Yeah." He holds my gaze. "You remembered."

I look away first, focusing on the waxing moon that rises from the tree line on the far side of the lake, bathing the scene in silvery light. "Were you close with your dad?" I ask.

He nods. The distant sound of chanting echoes over the water.

"How did he die, if you don't mind my asking?" I ask.

"Heart attack."

"I'm so sorry."

"Thanks." He wrings out his shirt. "It's been tough, but I'm getting through it."

I smile. "With therapy?"

"You know it."

We slosh across the pavers and up the marble steps to the grand front entrance, where Aguilar has left two white towels in a woven basket just outside the ornate bronze door. I wrap mine around my dress while Lucas fixes the other around his waist, shedding his soaked pants beneath.

We push open the heavy doors to find a handful of Mandala members working to transform the giant dining room to the left of the domed foyer into a banquet hall, complete with flowers and candles. A few of them look up and smile curiously, perplexed by our soggy state as we scurry, dripping, across the intricately tiled circle and up the marble staircase.

"You can shower first," Lucas says when we finally reach our room at the end of the long hall. "I'll see if I can find us some dry clothes."

I nod and step into the gold and ivory bathroom, where I spot a fresh set of white linen garments for each of us neatly folded on the countertop between the sinks. "Found them," I call.

Standing under the torrent of warm water in the marble shower, I feel all the anxiety that had been buried under the intensity of the past few hours come rushing back. Kali was welcoming enough today, but she can't possibly really be fine with me inheriting everything, no matter how enlightened she is. And what's the real reason Lucas escorted me down here? Does he know something he's not sharing with me? He said he's told me everything, but I can't shake the nagging feeling that's not quite true.

I search my gut for who to trust, but my inner compass is going haywire, and I feel adrift, bumping up against my past. My memories of Paul are all tied up with who I was as a child, my memories of Lucas intertwined with the girl I was at eighteen, and I can't help wondering if that child and that girl would be disappointed in the woman I've become. Or haven't become.

Aware that time is slipping away, I reluctantly cut the water, towel off, and step into the dry dress, identical to the one I discarded.

In the bedroom, I find Lucas sitting on his bed shirtless, flipping through the bedside copy of *Surrender*.

"All yours," I say.

"Thanks."

I step out of his way as he rises and moves toward the bathroom, gripping his towel in one hand while sweeping his hair out of his eyes with the other. As he passes, I catch a glimpse of the circle tattoo beneath his navel peeking out from under the towel, and an uninvited heat wave shimmers through my body. The door clicks shut behind him, and I lie down on my bed staring up at the ceiling, frustrated by the undeniable pull I still feel toward him.

No. I stop myself. I'm being ridiculous. I don't want Lucas. Of course I don't want Lucas. I'm engaged! And I don't even know Lucas—not really. We had a one-night stand. Years ago. That's all it was, regardless of how it felt at the time. I've long since moved on. I'm just inappropriately lustful for some reason tonight, and he's in my line of sight.

I call to mind the softness of Chase's lips on mine just yesterday, picture his blue eyes, his aquiline nose. His beautiful shirts. He really does have incredible taste. So what if he insists on wearing a collared shirt to a rock concert? Opposites attract. Where I'm casual, he's formal; where I'm flighty, he's solid; where my family has no roots, his dates back to landed gentry.

And therein lies the problem: all my thoughts of him right now are tied up with my inability to fit in with his family. Lately I feel like I've been trying so hard to go along with what they want that I've forgotten what I want.

I know I'm not the easiest person to love. As much as I've altered my life to accommodate his, I still have hard edges; I'm challenging, defensive, impulsive. There was a time when Chase found my imperfections charming—appealing, even—but since our engagement, it's like every part of me needs to be polished in the effort of molding me into an Ayres wife.

Now here I am with one foot in and one foot out of the relationship, paralyzed with doubt and terrified I'll end up like one of Becky's friends: maintaining my relevance by keeping up my appearance, but scared to leave him, for fear of discarding what could be my one chance at love, without which I'll end up alone.

I open the copy of *Anusara* on my bedside table and flip through the pages, landing on a chapter titled "Everything You Need Is Within You." Perfect.

Everything you need is within you because the Divine resides inside you. Only once you realize this will you experience true freedom. You alone have the power to transform your life; it is your choice to live an existence that is full of bliss or sorrow. To know your Self is to know the Divine.

Well, if that's not fitting, I don't know what is. Though the idea that knowing myself will give me freedom isn't totally comforting right now, considering I'm having so much trouble deciding what I want.

"I think they figured out my size." Lucas emerges from the bathroom in white linen that does indeed fit him better this time. He holds up my engagement ring. "Found this by the sink."

"Oh." Unaware I'd even taken it off, I slip it back on my finger.

"When's the wedding?" Lucas asks.

I stare at the sparkly thing that used to make me so giddy. "Two years," I reply.

His eyebrows shoot up. "That's a long time."

"Not my choice," I say. Then, unable to stop myself, "I don't really have any say."

He sticks his hand under his mattress and feels for his phone. "Still there," he reports. "Shockingly." Sitting on the mosaic scarlet rug, he stretches a leg out in front of him and reaches for his toes. "Don't brides call all the shots? Bridezilla and all that?"

"Not all women are stereotypes," I shoot back.

"So you don't want to have a say?"

"No, I do." I spin the rock toward the inside of my palm and close my hand around it. "But my fiancé's family is very particular."

He snorts and switches legs. "If I ever get married, my wife will have all the say. I have enough sense to know I have no sense about that stuff."

Unable to watch someone stretch without joining in, I move down to the rug and assume butterfly pose with my feet together, knees apart. "What if your bride has no sense, either?" I ask.

"Then I guess we'll just have to elope," he says. "Actually, if I did have any say, that's what I'd say."

I sigh, feeling my spine unkink as I lie back and stretch my arms above my head, staring up at the wide blades of the fan turning slowly above. Eloping sounds like heaven. To be so in love that you don't even need anyone else there; all you need is each other? So romantic. If only Chase felt that way. "Where would you elope to?" I ask.

"A beach somewhere," he answers without missing a beat. "So I could surf after, obviously."

"Obviously." I glance up just in time to catch a soft expression in his eyes as he looks at me. "So, who's the lucky girl?" I ask, averting my gaze.

"No girl."

"Why not?"

He shrugs. "I'm too picky, I guess."

Too picky for me, apparently. I laugh to cover the twinge of regret. I wonder what was wrong with me, what I did to make him never call me again?

It doesn't matter, I remind myself. *It wasn't meant to be. And now I have Chase.*

"So what are you looking for?" I ask. "I have plenty of single friends."

"I remember them." He laughs. "Definitely not my type." He lies on his back and bends his knees to one side. "I don't know. Someone I can be myself with, I guess. Who doesn't try to change me."

His words hit me like a punch to the gut. "But what if you need to change?" I ask. "To grow, I mean."

"Those are two different things." His gaze is thoughtful. "Supporting your desire for personal growth is different from asking you to change."

Everything in me wants to protest, but I can't. He's right. I know instinctively by the sinking emptiness in my chest.

"So, what do girls try to change about you?" I ask.

"Depends on the girl." He sits up and runs his fingers through his thick waves. "The movies I watch aren't intellectual enough or my friends aren't cool enough. I surf too much. Yoga girl wanted me to become vegan and stop using deodorant. I dated this corporate chick who was on me to take up golf, for networking purposes. Everything was about achievement to her. She'd check her Fitbit after sex to see how many calories she'd burned."

I guffaw. "That's intense."

"Yeah." He leans back on his elbow to gaze at me with those deep brown eyes, and I try not to look at the tattoo snaking down his bulging biceps. I'm a fool for tattoos, though Chase doesn't have any. I've tried to convince him to get one, but he refuses.

So maybe he's not the only one in the relationship trying to change the other person.

"What?" I ask when he doesn't stop staring.

"It's good to see you," he says.

I trace the movement of the fan blades as they go around without answering.

"I didn't know what you'd be like now," he goes on. "People change. I was worried you'd be high maintenance."

"Because of my career?"

"And I read about your engagement online," he admits. "Seemed fancy."

I hate that the thought of him looking me up makes my stomach flip. "It is."

"But you're not," he says. Out of the corner of my eye, I can see him still gazing at me openly. "You're the same girl I met all those years ago."

"I mean, not totally," I say. "I like to think I've matured a little." I allow myself to look over at him. "And I'm not a virgin anymore."

He smiles. "I was there, you may remember."

The shared memory hangs between us like forbidden fruit, sending heat creeping up my neck.

"Dinner's ready."

I jump at the unexpected voice and look up to see Aguilar standing in the doorway, watching us.

How long has he been there?

I scramble to my feet, relieved to be saved from the dangerous direction the conversation was headed in, and follow Aguilar toward the sound of chatter filtering up the stairs.

THIRTEEN

Kali's face is radiant in the abundant candlelight, enhanced by the wreath of white flowers in her hair. She stands at the head of our table in the front of the dining room, flanked on one side by Aguilar, Rex, Ruby, and me, and on the other by Hikari, Lucas, Blaze, and the freckled brunette who was playing the bronze bowl in the meditation chamber earlier. The rest of the group is scattered among wood tables of about twelve each, adorned with bright jungle flowers and lit by candles in mason jars, while crystal chandeliers burn softly overhead.

"Shiva accomplished so much while bodied," Kali says. "But I know his greatest joy was the Mandala, and what we have created here at Xanadu. He loved each of you like he loved himself, and he will always be within you. He is not gone; he has simply shed his human form."

She raises her gold-leafed teacup and everyone follows suit, as they did in the meditation studio. "May his light shine from within each of us."

The earthy, warm liquid coats my tongue, a more medicinal than herbal taste.

"On his last day, Shiva called me to him and told me the time had come for me to lead, and I humbly accepted his charge." Kali goes on.

I can't help but wonder: If he asked her to lead, why didn't he will her the Mandala? Why give it to me? It's incongruous. Her piercing gaze lands on me, and for a moment I'm possessed by the absurd fear that she can read my mind as she continues, "I vow to channel his spirit and continue his work here. Namaste."

"Namaste," everyone replies in sync.

Immediately the sound of plates and utensils clattering fills the banquet hall as everyone loads their plates with the falafel, chickpea za'atar, zucchini fritters, rice, roasted green beans, and grilled red peppers that line the centers of the tables.

Scanning the warmly lit room, I notice that while ethnically diverse, most of the group are on the younger end of the spectrum, though there are a handful who appear older. There seems to be an even ratio of men and women, and I'm once again struck by how attractive everyone is—and how well groomed, for living in the middle of a jungle. They're all fit, their skin glowing, their nails clean and manicured—and while I do notice the odd wary glance in my direction, each time it's so quickly replaced with a smile that I doubt whether I saw it at all.

Lucas turns to Blaze, seated next to him. "You're Blaze, right?" he asks.

Blaze nods. "I knew your father—not well, but I met him through Shiva a few times, many years ago. He was a good man."

Lucas's face grows somber. "Thanks, man. He was."

"Hi, I'm Luna." The brunette on the other side of Blaze leans around him to extend her hand to Lucas and then me. "Welcome."

"Thank you," I say, cutting into a grilled red pepper.

"How long have you guys been living at Xanadu?" I ask, looking from Blaze to Luna to Ruby, who sits next to me.

"I've been here about four years," Ruby answers.

"Me, too," Luna chimes in.

"But Blaze has been here longer than any of us," Ruby adds.

"Eight for me," Blaze confirms. "I met Shiva when he hired me as contractor for the California Mandala Center outside of Sonoma—man, twelve, thirteen years ago? I helped him find this place. It was run-down and overgrown, but we both fell in love with it, and he got it for a steal because of its history. I was the first to live down here because I oversaw the remodel with a local crew."

"I visited the California center a few times with my dad," Lucas says. "It's a spa now, right?"

Blaze nods. "The Golden Bell."

"Does everyone from California live here now?" I ask.

"No," Ruby says. "The California place was bigger and run more like a traditional retreat center. We were always teaching seminars, and there were a lot more people in and out. Xanadu was built as a live-in center for christened members of the Mandala, where we could live like a family."

"Christened members?" I ask.

"It means you've cycled through the Wheel and gotten your Mandala name," Luna pipes up.

"The Wheel is the training and development program," Ruby clarifies. "The classes are all color coded and linked to the chakras, which is why it's called the Wheel. You have to complete the Crown Chakra level to be christened with your Mandala name."

"Ah," I say, exchanging a glance with Lucas. "I think I saw a pamphlet for that in my room earlier."

"Did you?" Ruby asks, surprised.

"It was from 2017," Lucas adds.

She nods. "That was the last year we did in-person classes. Once we moved down here, everything went online."

As the evening progresses, I feel a lightening sensation in my body similar to what I felt during the chanting session, like a warm internal glow. The people are all friendly, and I enjoy listening to their stories about my uncle and answering their questions about what he was like when I was a child. I would normally be suspicious of such unanimous veneration, especially of a religious—or as they call themselves, sacred—organization, but the peace they've found here seems so genuine that they must be doing something right.

Regardless, by the time Kali invites us into the lounge for music after dinner, I'm so overtired that I attempt to beg off. Luna, however, will have none of it. "You have to come," she insists, looping her arm through mine, her olive-green eyes serious. "Just for a bit. I promise it'll be fun."

I acquiesce, allowing myself to be carried with the stream into the sunken living room, which, like the rest of the villa, is decorated in a vaguely Moroccan style, though the color scheme is lighter. A grand piano stands near the entrance, and the arched French doors along the back wall are flung open to the thrumming concert of insects and animals outside, invisible in the vast darkness beyond the globe lights strung over the pool deck. Brass pendants dangle from the soaring ceiling, casting mosaic shadows across the cream trellis rug and the low-slung couches, arranged in a roughly circular configuration.

Kali settles into the corner of one of the ivory couches against a pale gold cushion, and the group fills in around her, reclining on pillows and draping themselves across the furniture, all jockeying to be closer to her. One girl hands her a cup of tea while another rubs her shoulders. Luna plants the two of us on a love seat, and Lucas sits on the floor nearby. Someone takes up the bongos and begins tapping a rhythm that gets heads nodding, and before long Rex is strumming a guitar, his square jaw outlined in the flickering candlelight.

I must have pushed through extreme exhaustion into delirium, because I feel a surge of energy as the music heats up, and before long, I'm smacking a tambourine with the best of them. It's all a bit surreal, as though I've stumbled into a scarcely credible scene from a movie, and I find myself wondering if I shouldn't postpone my flight and stay a few more days.

The night continues song after song, guitar to piano and back again, classic rock and folk, a celebration of my uncle's favorites, I'm told. He was an adept pianist. We didn't have a piano when I was a child, so I'd never heard him play until he came to visit once when I was about eight and took my mom and me to lunch at the fancy hotel where he was staying. My dad wasn't there—which, I hated to admit, made the visit that much more fun. As much as I loved my dad, he was all dark clouds and mood swings and walking on eggshells, while Paul was sunshine and rainbows and swinging me in circles. I looked forward to his visits like Christmas morning.

I remember a shiny ebony grand piano stood in the ornate lobby of the hotel, and Paul slid onto the bench and began to play what I didn't recognize at the time as "Imagine." The mellifluous sound emanated from the piano like scent from a rose, filling the space with beauty. I begged my mother for lessons afterward, but she told me in no uncertain terms that we didn't have money for frivolity.

To this day, the tambourine is the extent of my musical ability.

Outside I hear a peal of laughter accompanied by a splash in the pool. Someone begins plucking the opening notes of "Blackbird," and I turn to see Lucas on the floor with one of the guitars, his eyes closed as he strums it with practiced fingers while a pretty girl with cascading dark locks plays with his hair. She looks vaguely familiar, and I briefly wonder whether she was an actress in her prior life.

It once again strikes me how comfortable he seems in his own skin, playing for a group of strangers, his sonorous voice rising and falling with the music. He opens his eyes and before I can look away, his gaze locks on mine. Caught red-handed, I feel the heat creep into my cheeks, but he doesn't flinch, studying me unhurriedly as he continues to play.

I shift my gaze to Kali, reposed on the couch while Aguilar gives her a sensuous foot massage. She also has her gray eyes fixed on Lucas, watching him with an expression I can't quite read. Is it desire I see flickering across her flawless face, or distrust? She must feel me looking at her because she turns her head ever so slightly to meet my eye, her faint smile enigmatic, her stare so sharp it stings. Covering my unease, I recast my gaze to Ruby, reclining in Rex's lap, his hand beneath her dress, stroking her breast.

I think it's about time for me to go to bed.

I rise from the love seat with a fake yawn and make my way through the candlelit room toward the foyer.

My limbs seem to grow softer as I climb the stairs and move down the dark hallway through the weak rectangles of light that shine from each open doorway. By the time I reach my own darkened room, I'm so sapped, it's all I can do to drag myself into the bathroom in hopes of finding some way to brush my teeth. To my amazement, there on the marble counter is my toothbrush, next to what I figure is Lucas's. Too glad to question it, I brush with the charcoal toothpaste I find in the drawer and wash my face with the lavender-scented face scrub sitting beside the sink. Through the door to the adjoining bedroom I hear the movement and unmistakable muffled groans of a couple in the throes of passion.

Stifling a smile, I tiptoe from the bathroom to my bed, where I flip on the small bedside lamp. In the soft light, I see a folded yellow notecard on my pillow. I open it and read the message scrawled in black ink, in all capital letters:

GO HOME NOW

I drop the notecard onto the bed as though it's on fire and spin around, expecting to see some malevolent force behind me. But there is none. Heart thumping, I move quietly to the door and peek into the hallway, but it's deserted, the only sounds those of the couple next door.

I sit on my bed with the note in my hand, willing my heart to slow. Who would want me to go home? Regardless, I have no plans to stay; my flight home is tomorrow, which only makes the note stranger. Why scare me like that?

I hear footsteps in the hallway and burrow into bed in my dress, pulling the covers up over my head like a toddler afraid of the dark.

Through a gap in the sheets I see Lucas come in, trying unsuccessfully to be quiet.

I throw back the covers and sit up, quietly beckoning to him. He lowers himself onto my bed, and I thrust the note into his hands. "This was on my pillow."

He swallows as he reads the card, his mouth in a hard line. "Okay. No big deal." His words are calming, but I can tell he's as unsettled by it as I am. "It's probably nothing. We're out of here tomorrow." He places a calming hand on my back. "Breathe."

I do as instructed, but it doesn't really help.

"It's okay," he says. "I'm here. You're not alone."

"Thanks." I give him a weak smile. "Why are you up here with me, anyway? I noticed you made a friend down there."

He disregards my question, rising to his feet. "I'm gonna brush my teeth. You'll be okay here while I'm gone? I can leave the door open."

"It's fine—I'm fine," I say, feeling stupid for mentioning the girl.

I turn off the light and lie down on the bed as he shuts the bathroom door behind him.

GO HOME NOW.

Oh, I want nothing more.

I breathe through the fear tightening my muscles, suppressing the unanswerable questions about who left the card on my pillow and why they want me to *GO HOME NOW*, to place my focus on the other question the note raises: *Where will I go when I leave here tomorrow?*

The loft I share with Chase is technically my home, though it was his place first and never really felt like mine. Anyway, I don't think I'm ready to go back there, back to the status quo of trying to fit into his life. My whole adult life I've felt like an outsider—an impostor, like it would be five minutes before someone discovered I didn't belong and threw me out into the snow—and I'm sick of it.

In the beginning, Chase swept me off my feet, and for a while, I felt like I was living in a fairy tale. But the fantasy grew cumbersome with the constraints of real life. And rather than running like I should have when his mother gripped me by the elbow out of his earshot and asked me about my intentions with her son, I dug in, determined to prove I wasn't the gold digger she clearly believed me to be.

Over the past three years, he's endured his family's disapproval of me while I've tried to become someone they approve of without giving up too much of myself, a constant battle that's exhausted me and left me more self-doubting than ever. I thought the engagement would end all the back-and-forth, but the opposite has happened. The things that define me have evaporated—first my spontaneity, then my friends, my apartment, my career—and I've become all the more dependent on him. Surrounded as I am by people who reinforce my insecurities, it's no wonder I'm so unsure of myself.

I know he really does believe he's making my life better, though. I have to stop blaming him for everything and stop trying to fit myself into a space where I'm not comfortable, or I'll never be happy. I need to create a home that works for *me*. Even if that means facing the hard truth about my relationship with Chase.

It's like what my uncle wrote: *It's up to you whether you live a life of bliss or sorrow.*

I hear the bathroom door open, bringing me back to this strange villa in the deepest jungle. As Lucas settles into the bed across from mine, a female moan of pleasure filters through the wall. The banging of the headboard next door morphs into the sound of drums as I drift off to dreams of Kali prowling through the villa in the body of a jaguar while breathless strangers ravage me in the dark.

FOURTEEN

Day Two

A terrible, guttural howling awakens me. Unnerved, I sit up to see Lucas standing at the window shirtless in rumpled linen pants, holding aside the gauzy curtains.

"What's going on?" I blurt.

"Howler monkeys," he says, scanning the misty trees. "One of the loudest animals in the world, but they're only about fifteen pounds."

"They sound angry," I comment, rubbing my eyes. "Do you see them?"

He shakes his head, squinting out at the dreary morning. "It's pretty foggy, though. They live in the canopy and their howls can carry for miles, so they could be anywhere."

I notice neatly folded piles of burnt-orange linen clothes at the end of each of our beds. "I guess that's what we're supposed to wear today," I say.

He unfolds his, which are similar in style to scrubs. "A little creepy someone was in here while we were sleeping."

I pick mine up—drawstring shorts and a sleeveless tunic. "At least they're clean," I say. In the space between the yowls I can make out the light tapping of rain on the roof. I yawn. "What time is it?"

"I don't know. I heard people leaving about an hour ago, just before sunrise."

"Somebody said something last night about sunrise meditation," I say, remembering. "Guess we missed that."

My head is hazy, the memory of last night a mirage shimmering in the distance. My gaze lands on the notecard on the bedside table, and a jolt of unease shoots through me.

He sits on the edge of my bed, lowering his voice. "Did you notice anything . . . strange last night?"

"Besides the threatening note on my pillow?"

"I mean did you feel anything—out of the ordinary?"

I try to remember specifics, but the fog in my brain is as thick as the one outside. "I felt pretty good, actually, all things considered."

He nods. "Me, too. Too good. And this morning everything's really fuzzy."

"But we didn't even drink," I say. "Or anything. It was a stone-cold-sober evening."

"Did you feel sober? Because I sure didn't. And I was definitely catching a vibe by the time I came upstairs."

"What kind of vibe?" I ask, remembering Rex's hand beneath Ruby's dress, the moans of pleasure penetrating the walls.

He levels his gaze at me, confirming we are thinking of the same definition of vibe.

"Right." I recall my near-religious experience during the chanting, the sensation of levity. "Are you saying you think they drugged us?"

He shrugs. "That tea we toasted with was pretty rank."

I can almost taste the thick medicinal flavor now. "I mean, I know some spiritual traditions use herbal medicine in their ceremonies . . . but surely they'd say something?"

"Kali isn't . . . she doesn't strike me as the type of person to stress about informed consent."

Regardless of the implications of that, I'm glad there might be a reason for the attraction I felt toward him last night.

He stands and stretches. "Good news is, we're out of here in a matter of hours. I just need to have a conversation with Kali about the contents of the will—which you don't have to be present for—then our boat pickup is at noon, to get us back to the airport in time for our four P.M. flight."

I nod, remembering my inclination to stay. This morning it seems like a silly notion, especially in light of the warning note and what Lucas has just suggested.

"What?" he asks, watching me.

I throw back the covers and swing my feet down to the floor. "I want to be there when you talk to her about the will," I say. "Smooth things over, you know. Make sure she's okay with it."

I grab my orange linen and start for the bathroom. "Sveta . . ." I turn as he approaches, his voice barely audible, his face suddenly dead serious. "You have to be prepared that she may fight the will. Not just the corporate holdings, but all of it."

"I know."

"But it's my job to protect Paul's wishes," he says darkly, "which were that you should inherit the estate."

"Should I, though?" I ask. "Sure, the money sounds great, but I know nothing about his business or this organization, and . . . I just don't understand why he would give it to me. I mean, we were close when I was young, but I'd seen him one time since I was eleven."

"I know, but . . ." He bites his lip, reluctant to say whatever's on the tip of his tongue.

"What?"

He draws me to him, his breath hot on my ear, his chest so close I can smell his skin. "He didn't trust Kali anymore."

I look up at him, thrown.

"He told me he wanted to shut Xanadu down," he confides.

"And you didn't think that was something you should share with me?" I demand, pulling away. "You promised me you weren't withholding information. That you'd told me all there was to tell."

"I'm sorry," he says. "I didn't want to freak you out."

"You lied to me." I stare daggers at him. "When did he tell you this? Did you see him?"

He shakes his head. "It was over the phone . . . a week ago, or so."

"What else did he say? And don't leave things out. I want all of it."

He sighs. "He wanted to be sure that if anything were to happen to him before he was able to shut it down, I would ensure it was closed."

"What the hell, Lucas?" I want to punch him. "You should have told me that from the get-go." Realizing my volume is rising with my anger, I lower my voice. "Why the hell did you bring me down here if you knew he didn't trust her?"

"I wanted to see it for myself," he admits. "To see what we were up against and figure out the best way to close it."

"And you couldn't come down here without the excuse of escorting me." I narrow my eyes at him. "You used me."

"I'm sorry."

"I should have known better than to trust you."

I spin on my heel, slamming the bathroom door behind me.

"Sveta—"

But I don't respond, my hands shaking with anger as I change clothes. He lied to me, the asshole. It's my fault, though, blindly trusting a guy who'd already burned me once. I never should have believed a single word he said. My head spins with questions, each leading to another. Can I believe him now? Or is he trying to manipulate me into turning against Kali? And if he is, then why?

A rapping on the bathroom door cuts into my swirling thoughts. "What?" I snap.

"Kali's ready," Lucas says, "if you want to come with me."

I compose myself and swing open the door to find Aguilar hovering behind a repentant Lucas.

"She's waiting in her quarters," Aguilar says.

"Thank you, Aguilar."

I can feel Lucas looking at me, but refuse to meet his eye as we follow Aguilar into the quiet hallway.

FIFTEEN

At the top of the second set of stairs, the entry to Kali's chamber is closed. Aguilar raps softly and Hikari answers, closing the elaborate doors behind us when we're inside.

Kali's lair smells of incense and rain. The French doors on the jungle side of the room are open to the covered porch and constant light patter, the forest beyond obscured by mist.

Hikari leads us beneath the archway on the left, into an informal dining room featuring a gold Sputnik chandelier over a large oak table where Rex and Ruby are seated, typing away on matching laptops.

So I guess the tech regulations don't apply up here.

Across the room, Kali stands before a picture window in a white dress, looking out at the steam rising off the lake while sipping a mug of tea, Ix-Chel curled at her feet, square head resting on her giant paws.

I stiffen.

"Did you get that?" Kali calls over her shoulder to Ruby and Rex. "It's important not just to face suffering but to embrace suffering."

Hikari clears his throat and she turns, her eyes lighting on us. "That's all for this morning," she says to Ruby and Rex, who obediently close their laptops and rise. "Namaste."

"Namaste." They both bow and exit the suite, leaving their laptops on the table.

Ix-Chel raises her head, following Kali with golden eyes as she settles

into a cream bouclé dining chair at the head of the table, before a manila
envelope that I assume contains the will.

"Help yourselves." She gestures to a bowl of cut fruit and a basket
of muffins in the center of the table. "The muffins are papaya, fresh this
morning."

But Lucas and I are still rooted to the spot, watching the jaguar. Lucas
clears his throat and gestures to Ix-Chel. "Please."

"Aguilar," Kali says with a hint of exasperation.

Once Aguilar has removed the jaguar from the room, I take a seat
next to Kali, plucking a pinkish-tinted muffin from the basket.

"We need to discuss the will." Lucas cuts to the chase, taking a seat
on my other side.

"Yes." Her serene face is inscrutable. "As you know, Hikari is our
resident attorney, so I'll let him speak on this."

"The document you provided is invalid," Hikari says flatly as he lowers
himself into the chair next to Kali.

Lucas narrows his eyes. "How do you figure?"

Hikari extracts a printed document from the manila folder in front
of him and slides it across the table to Lucas.

"What's this?" Lucas asks, scanning it.

"Shiva's mind cleared in the days before his death, and knowing he
would soon transcend, he instructed me to type up a new will. As you
can see, he wished to revoke the will favoring Svetlana and leave his
entire estate, including the Mandala Corporation, to Kali."

My stomach drops. I peer over at the paperwork to see that the typed
legal document dated three days ago does indeed say what Hikari claims,
and is signed by my uncle, in addition to multiple witnesses.

Dread settles over me as Lucas scrutinizes Hikari, dubious. "Why
didn't you mention this when we spoke on the phone?" Lucas asks.

"I wanted to tell Sveta in person," Kali says, "that I intend to take care
of her."

"And why didn't Paul call me about this?" Lucas presses, dismissing her.

"He didn't trust you," Hikari says.

Lucas's words ring in my ears. *He didn't trust Kali anymore.*

"Right," Lucas returns dryly. "How can I be sure this is even a valid document? I have no way of knowing whether this will was made under duress, or whether this is even his signature."

"You can compare it to his certified signature and you'll see it matches," Hikari says. "Of course, he was weak, so if the signature appears different in any way, that is why."

"Convenient," Lucas says. He's right: all of this sounds incredibly convenient. "As an attorney, Hikari, I'm sure you have looked into the differences in US and Mexico law regarding wills, so you know that for a will to be legal in Mexico it needs to be notarized, which this is not."

"It will be filed in California," Hikari says.

I watch their exchange like a tennis match, my heart in my throat.

"You're certain that jurisdiction will apply to a will signed in Mexico?" Lucas challenges. "Because it's murky territory, which we will dispute. I'm sure you recognize that a dispute will tie up the assets in probate for years, and that if we succeed, the rules of intestacy will be applied. As Sveta is the only living descendant of the deceased, his estate will go to her."

"Kali was his wife."

"Not legally," Lucas returns.

"And she is offering," Hikari continues, "out of the goodness of her heart, to give Svetlana five percent of Shiva's net personal estate—excluding the Mandala Corporation—once the taxes and debts have been settled. A very generous offer, under the circumstances."

"Like I said," Kali interjects, looking at me, "I want to take care of you."

Lucas fixes his searing gaze on Kali. "I'd say our nuisance value is a bit higher than five percent," he challenges.

"Look." Kali holds up her hands, unfazed. "It's nothing personal. It's simply what my husband wanted. I know how much he cared for Sveta, even though they were estranged for some time, so I'm happy to share with her some of the proceeds from our life work. But Xanadu was Shiva's heart and soul, and I am the only person capable of ensuring the survival of it."

I can see it's on the tip of Lucas's tongue to challenge this, but he holds back.

"The offer only stands as long as you're here," Hikari adds. "Once you leave, it's withdrawn."

"We're leaving at noon." Lucas exhales, frustrated. "You've just ambushed us with this, and you know there's no way it's going to be worked out today. I can't let you put pressure on Sveta to make hasty decisions, the ramifications of which she hasn't had time to properly understand."

"That's her choice, not yours. We believe it's best for Svetlana to make her own decisions based on her own beliefs, not the beliefs of someone else who may not have her best interests at heart."

"I stand to gain nothing from this," Lucas says. "My only goal is to fulfill Paul's wishes."

"It's true," I say as gently as possible, feeling a need to have a voice in all of this. "I can't make a decision without understanding what I'm making a decision about. But I hope we can come to a mutual agreement."

Kali turns to me. "I'm so sorry this has come between us. I care deeply about you. I hope you know that."

"Thank you," I say with what I hope is a genuine-looking smile. While I'm wary of her intentions, as she surely is of mine, I do recognize it's best to remain friendly with her, now more than ever.

"Gentlemen, can you leave us?" she asks.

Lucas looks to me, his eyes begging me to refuse, but he lost his right to ask anything of me when he lied to me. Anyway, I'm curious to hear whatever Kali has to say. "I'll see you in a bit," I say.

Kali rolls her eyes conspiratorially as Hikari and Lucas exit in opposite directions. "Men."

"Worse," I commiserate. "Lawyers."

She rises and tops off her tea, then pours a cup for me, which I accept, though I have no intention of drinking it. As I follow her through the door and across the expansive covered back porch, I'm again struck by the enormity of the villa—closer in size to a hotel than a home, really. The rain has stopped, but the fog is still so dense that the forest is barely visible on the other side of the pool deck.

Kali leads me to the near end of the porch, where a daybed is suspended from the ceiling by chains to hover a foot off the ground. "My favorite place to think," she says, sinking into the pillows that line the sides.

Butterflies flutter in my chest as I settle against the opposite end of the bed and take a tentative whiff of my tea. It smells like jasmine and oranges, and . . . what the hell, I might as well ask her point-blank. "What kind of tea was it that we drank last night?"

She seems unbothered by the question. "The afternoon tea was for rejuvenation after your long journey—mainly a mixture of Saint-John's-wort, skullcap, poppy, and—"

"Poppy?" I ask, recognizing the plant that opioids are made from.

She smiles at my alarm. "A very small amount, just enough to relax the body. This one is similar, with orange blossoms and jasmine added as well. The one in the evening was . . . let me see . . ." She stares into her tea, thinking, as birds call to one another in the misty treetops. "Poppy, ginseng, gingko, muira puama . . . and a few other things I can't remember. But it was more of a celebratory tonic."

I recognize gingko and ginseng, both noted to have a stimulant effect, and Saint-John's-wort is meant to make you happy. All are commonly used. But I'm still stuck on poppy, no matter what she says.

"Why? What did you feel?" she asks.

"Just . . . light." I don't want her to think I'm accusing her of anything. "I mean, it was good. I felt super in tune with everyone, very . . . sensitive, physically."

She laughs. "Everyone calls the tea we had last night the sex bomb, because it does have an arousing effect. But that's a good thing. Sex is beautiful when done properly. Orgasm is an opening to God consciousness."

I nod, recalling the rumors of free love associated with the Mandala that I'd always turned a deaf ear to, not wanting to think of my uncle that way. I'm tempted to ask about it now, but we're meeting the boat soon, and Kali and I have more pressing things to discuss.

The mist is tinted yellow with the rays of the sun, quickly evaporating as the day warms. In the brighter light, I notice Kali's gray eyes are tired, and for the first time I see the toll all this is taking on her. "I'm sorry about the mess with the will," I say, gently swaying the bed swing with my foot. "I had no idea."

"No, I'm so sorry for springing that on you," she apologizes, her face radiating sincerity. "I invited you to Xanadu because I know Shiva would have wanted you here, but I also thought it would be better if we spoke of these matters face-to-face. I thought we could work together to honor Shiva's wishes, as family. I didn't realize that Lucas would follow you down here."

But her idea of Paul's wishes seems to be diametrically opposed to Lucas's. "Lucas said my uncle intended to close Xanadu," I venture, trying to sound diplomatic.

Her face darkens. "That's a lie. This place was his life work. Our work, together—"

"But why would Lucas lie to me about that?" I ask. "It doesn't make any sense."

"I assume he hasn't mentioned my history with his father?"

Feeling more in the dark than ever, I shake my head, wondering exactly how many things Lucas has neglected to mention to me.

"He was a conformist who never understood Shiva's calling—he could only see it as a slave to the capitalist machine would, in terms of monetary gain. I was the antithesis of that, and he always resented me for it. When Shiva and I met, he had more money than he knew what to do with, but he was burnt out and losing his way spiritually. I helped him expand the scope of his teachings beyond the realm of self-help and into the spiritual."

I nod, registering Kali's outsize portrayal of her role in the evolution of Shiva's career. "And Lucas's father didn't like your influence on him?" I ask.

She shakes her head. "He wanted Shiva to grow his business like a good capitalist. He thought it was a mistake to sell the nutrition company and buy this place, and he was convinced it was my idea."

She points to the canopy of trees a stone's throw from the porch, and I see a shaggy brown monkey with a black face, about the size of a cocker spaniel. He's swinging from tree to tree, stuffing his mouth with green leaves. "Howler monkey," she says.

The monkey stares at us blankly as he shoves fistfuls of leaves into his wide mouth. He's quite a sight, but I'm not about to be diverted by a monkey. "I don't understand. Was Lucas's dad profiting off of Shiva in other ways than being his attorney?" I ask.

She nods. "He was a silent partner in VitaLife. He made a ton of money off the sale but wasn't happy because it was nothing compared to what he could have made if we'd kept the company. But we preferred to have the money from the sale in hand to run the Mandala without having to worry about income."

I frown. "Lucas didn't mention his dad was business partners with Shiva."

"Lucas is clearly charming, and not bad looking, either, right?" She gives me a knowing smile. "But how well do you really know him?"

I bite my lip, feeling stupid.

"Look." She lowers her soft voice so much, I have to lean closer to hear her. "I know you're not sure who to trust right now. But Shiva loved you, so I feel it's my duty to take care of you." Her mesmerizing eyes are unclouded, entreating me to trust her. "If Lucas convinces you to challenge Shiva's will in court, he's right: it could take years for either of us to see anything, but that will affect you more than it will me. Xanadu is run by the corporation and will continue to operate in the interim as it had before. But when the new will is verified—and it will be, it's completely valid—you'll be left with nothing but mountains of legal fees. If you accept our offer, you walk away a multimillionaire and don't have to deal with court or probate or any of the other complications that will certainly arise."

When she puts it like that, the answer seems clear. And perhaps her offer would be better for me regardless of whether or not the new will is valid. I don't know anything about this business, and if they're drugging people, the liabilities far outweigh the benefits. But if it's true my uncle didn't trust her . . . "I see your point," I say carefully. "But I need to think about it. Can you give me a little more time?"

"I wish I could," she says. "But once the negotiation leaves here, it's outside the circle of trust." She sighs. "My personal feelings about the will aside, I'd be careful with the Baranquillas. In my experience, they're only interested in their own needs."

Her warning is so spot-on it's unsettling, as though she heard our exchange this morning. "You think Lucas is using me?"

She evaluates me. "Just because he's trying to doesn't mean he'll be successful."

Little does she know how successful he's already been.

"Shiva's estate is a lot of money," she continues, her eyes serious. "And money does strange things to people." She gently places her hand above my heart and gazes into my eyes as if she can see into my soul. "But you are stronger than most. On the inside. I saw it the moment I met you. You just need to tap into your power."

"I don't know that I'm all that strong," I demur, thinking of my inability to stand up to Chase's family.

"The Divine resides inside you," she says, stroking my cheek before dropping her hand. "The power of the entire universe is within you."

I laugh nervously. "That's not intimidating or anything."

"I know," she says. "I felt that way too. Like I told you in New York, I fought the call tooth and nail. But once I surrendered"—she laughs— "everything became so easy."

I nod, but I'm still stuck on what she said about Lucas. "I don't understand what Lucas stands to gain from all this," I say. "My legal fees wouldn't exactly change his life."

"It's personal with the Baranquillas." She rises and goes to the railing, looking up at the clearing sky, then turns back to me, thoughtful.

"But at the end of the day, you're in control. Don't forget that. Your happiness is up to you."

If the Divine really does send messages, clearly this is the one I need to hear right now.

"Thank you," I say, rising to leave.

She takes my hands in hers. "Shiva lost connection with the Divine once he became sick. It made me incredibly sad. But he was clear that last day, and that's why he changed his will." Her luminous eyes burn as she continues, "The Divine has called me to lead the Mandala, and that is what I must do."

It's clear that regardless of what Lucas or anyone else thinks, Kali fervently believes in what she espouses.

"You say you want to fulfill your uncle's wishes," she continues. "That's what I want, too. We're on the same team."

I nod, at a loss for words, and she envelops me in a musky sweet-scented hug.

PART THREE

CHALLENGES

The challenges put in front of us are opportunities
for spiritual growth, for the Divine gives us what we
need to make positive change in our lives. But most of
us keep doing what we're doing, even if it's painful,
because we are afraid of change. We are blinded by
fear of the unknown, conditioned to believe that we
hold far less power over our lives than we truly do.

—Paul Bentzen, *Surrender*

SIXTEEN

When I return from Kali's quarters, I find Lucas pacing the red rug in our room, agitated.

His head snaps up as I enter. "Everything okay?"

I nod.

"What did she want?"

"Nothing, really." I shrug. "Just to talk civilly, without male egos present."

He frowns. "Sveta, I'm sorry I wasn't forthcoming with you—"

"You didn't mention your dad knew Kali," I challenge.

"Of course he knew Kali, he was Paul's attorney," Lucas returns. "I don't think he knew her well—"

"And they didn't get along?" I cut him off.

He shrugs. "I honestly don't know. He never talked about her. The first I heard about anyone not trusting Kali was when Paul called last week. Okay?"

I nod, replaying Kali's words of warning in my mind as I twist my engagement ring on my finger.

He lowers his voice. "That new will is bullshit."

"I realize it seems convenient," I admit. "But there were multiple witnesses, and—"

"Oh, come on. Like the people here wouldn't do whatever Kali asked of them, regardless of the legality of it?" He pops his knuckles. "If Paul wanted to change his will, he would have called me."

"It is strange," I return, "but it was also strange he would give me everything in the first place. It makes far more sense for his wife, who has been running his business for years, to inherit it."

"She's not his wife and he wanted to shut it down." He scrutinizes me. "You know she's trying to manipulate you, right?"

I narrow my eyes at him. "Funny, she said the same thing about you."

"Of course she did."

I wonder what Chase would do in this situation. *Hire the most expensive attorney he could find.* And that's what I should do, too, once I get back. Someone I can trust.

Or I take Kali's offer and walk away from this mess with several million dollars in my pocket and no court battle. As incredible as it would be, I don't *need* $180 million—if that's really what's at stake. The idea of that much money and the responsibility that comes along with it is daunting, to say the least. Nine million would be more than enough to change my life.

"Why didn't you tell me your dad was involved with VitaLife?" I ask.

He sighs, frustrated. "Because that was a hundred years ago and has nothing to do with this."

"How much did he make in the sale?" I ask.

"His share was about thirteen million."

"Which you inherited?"

He nods. "If anything, that should make you trust me more. I don't need the money. I'm doing this because I care."

His countenance is clear, his eyes begging me to believe him, but I can't trust him. Not anymore. No need to let him know that, though.

"Regardless of the politics, maybe this new will is actually a godsend," I volunteer, softening my tone. "She's offering me a generous sum, and I won't have to deal with any of this." I wave my hand to signify Xanadu. "I know nothing about the Mandala. Zero. Zilch. Let alone how to run it, and honestly it seems like a liability. I mean, free love? Now? This isn't the sixties. It's a miracle they were only sued once."

"You're right about that," he admits. "Look, I believe this new will is a play by Kali to grab what should be yours. Ultimately, though, it's up to you whether you want to fight it or take the nuisance payment—which I doubt she'd be offering if she thought her claim would hold up in court."

"What are my options?" I ask.

"Accept, negotiate, or take it to court."

I go to the open window and stare out at the fathomless forest, turning everything over in my mind. "Our boat pickup's at noon, right?"

He crosses his arms, his face dark. "About that . . ."

"What?"

"Blaze just stopped by to say he'd been informed there's a problem with the helicopter. They're ostensibly trying to fix it now, but it may not be ready today."

I gape at him. "Are you serious?"

"Deadly."

"Shit." I let my forehead fall against the glass. "But our plane's at—"

"Believe me, I know." He sighs. "And there's only one a day."

"Aren't there other helicopters that could pick us up?"

"I asked the same thing. Supposedly not that will land where ours needs to land. Something about it being a difficult angle."

My mind reels. "What about . . ." But I don't have any suggestions, and I know Lucas is as in the dark as I am. "Whoever wants me to go home isn't going to be happy." I laugh nervously.

His eyes are more serious than I'd like them to be. "No. But it seems like someone else wants you to stay."

"What do you mean?"

He lowers his voice, joining me at the window. "I don't buy this broken helicopter crap. Like the new will, it's too convenient."

My chest tightens. "You think someone's trying to trap me here?"

He points a finger up toward Kali's lair.

I evaluate him. Kali seemed so kind just now, so uninterested in material gain. But of course she would.

"Where is Blaze?" I ask.

He jerks his thumb at the door. "Down by the water, cleaning up the pyre."

The last place I want to be. "Okay." I press the heels of my hands into my eyes. "Let's go."

"Hey." I feel his hand on my arm and open my eyes to see him looking at me with such convincing tenderness, I swear he should have been an actor. "We're gonna figure this out, okay?"

I nod and turn quickly away, lest I fall for his act.

Outside, the clouds have melted into the milky blue sky, turning the day from warm to torrid. I squint against the sun as we descend the dazzling white marble steps into the Technicolor morning, like Dorothy waking in Oz to see color for the first time: golden jaguars glint in the aquamarine fountain, red flowers pop against the verdant green of the surrounding forest, the lake sparkles in the sunlight. The hues are almost garish, as though deliberately brightened to draw the eye away from the shadows at the edges of the picture, saturated to mask the darkness lurking beneath.

The howler monkeys are at it again, their whooping barks drowning out the hum of the insects. Weren't there monkeys in Oz? And poppies . . . if only this were no more than a strange dream. We troop down the wide stone path toward the water, past the terraced grounds sprinkled with burnt-orange-clad gardeners wearing wide-brimmed straw hats, weeding, harvesting, and planting.

Closer to the funeral pyre, the smell of stale campfire lingers in the humid air. As I near the ashes, I shade my eyes against the reflective glare from the water, scanning the handful of men picking through the gray-and-black rubble. They all wear construction face masks, heavy rubber boots, and gloves with their orange linen, but it doesn't take me long to spot Blaze's rangy form.

"Blaze," I call, waving.

Blaze pulls down his face mask as he approaches, bucket in hand.

"Lucas told me about the helicopter," I say. "Any word?"

He shakes his head. "I've been working down here, though. Rex might know something. He takes care of the boats and coordinates with the pilot." Blaze points in the direction of the large boathouse at the far perimeter of the clearing. "He should be in there."

"Thanks." I can't stop myself from sneaking a glance into the bucket as I turn away. It's full of bones.

Nauseated, I walk quickly along the water toward the boathouse, as though putting distance between myself and the bucket of jumbled bones stained with ash will erase the image from my mind, but it's no use. All I see are bones. Were they fingers? Toes? A femur? The ulna or radius? Were they all cleaned by the fire or did some retain bits of muscle and flesh? What of the skull? The teeth? What will they do with the bones once they've gathered them?

My uncle's laugh echoes in my mind, his smile skeletal. His long, tapered pianist's hands fly across the keys, fingers rendered fleshless by the fire. The memory of Lenten ashes on my forehead as a child.

You are dust, and to dust you shall return.

"Hey." Lucas hastens to catch up with me. "Are you okay?"

"Just very ready to go home."

"Me, too," he agrees, falling into step with me.

I appraise the ornate two-story boathouse as we approach, wondering what type of boats are inside and whether we might be able to borrow one to sail out of here. The stone structure is obviously built to echo the villa, perched on the shore and extending into the water, with enclosed boat slips downstairs and what appears to be living space upstairs. The fact that I didn't register its considerable size before now speaks not to its substantial proportions, but to the tremendous height and vast expanse of the surrounding rain forest. As we draw closer, I notice a tall wire fence extending from the far wall into the forest and see it prowling the edge of the enclosure: a muscular spotted cat bigger than Ix-Chel, kohl-rimmed golden eyes trained on us. I freeze, watching the black rosettes on its tawny coat ripple as it moves.

"That must be the one she warned us about," Lucas muses, his voice low.

"Xibalbá." A woman's voice.

We turn to see two petite brunettes kneeling in the garden nearby, watching us with sharp features so similar they must be sisters. I smile. "Ix-Chel's mate?"

My smile goes unreturned. The older one, who can't be more than twenty-two, straightens up, a tomato in her hand, her eyes guarded. "Right." She seems to want to say something else, but evidently thinks better of it.

"They're beautiful," I say.

She tosses the tomato into the basket at her side and resumes weeding, turning her back to us.

"They weren't very friendly," I whisper when I'm sure we're out of earshot.

A barely audible rumbling vibration emanating from the jaguars' cage draws my attention to Xibalbá, pacing the perimeter, regarding us like prey, fangs bared. Kali was right: I can tell the difference between a purr and a growl. My knees shake as we ascend the two steps to the boathouse entrance.

Lucas pushes open the door, and we enter a cavernous room with slips and pulleys for three large watercraft beneath a high beamed ceiling. The garage doors that open to the lake are all up, allowing in light that bounces off the water, throwing rippling reflections across the stone walls.

Two of the slips are occupied, one by a pontoon boat and the other by a small deck boat that hovers above the water. On second glance I notice that the same wire barrier used outside runs the length of the interior, cordoning off a third of the boathouse, including the empty boat slip closest to the jaguars and a staircase that leads to the upstairs. As if on cue, Xibalbá slinks through the doorframe in the far wall and over to the water, where he drinks deeply and then stretches out and rests his head on his crossed paws, his eyes still fixed on us.

Rex comes out of a small office to our right, wiping his hands on a towel. He looks at us inquisitively.

"The jaguars live in here?" I ask.

He nods. "We weren't utilizing the whole space, so we customized it as a shelter for them. Enclosed the slip and installed a step down so they can fish or cool off in the water. They seem to like it."

"Where did they come from?" I ask.

"Their mother was killed by a poacher when they were just cubs, so we rescued them and raised them," he says. "Kali's got a soft spot for animals."

"Do you know what's up with the helicopter?" Lucas cuts to the chase.

"It's the rotor mast," Rex says. "The crew at the airport in Palenque has been trying to fix it, but it looks like they're going to need a new one."

"How long will it take to fix it?" I ask.

He shrugs. "Hard to know. They have to order the part. It could be a few days to a few weeks."

"A few weeks?" I exclaim.

"Shit," Lucas mutters. "What about other helicopters?"

"Anything owned by a rental company can't utilize our landing for insurance reasons," he says apologetically. "We're searching for something privately owned, but there's not a lot of available inventory down here."

"Okay, what about one of these boats?" Lucas asks.

"There's a waterfall just upriver from the landing pad, so you can't go any farther that way," he says. "And downriver is all national parkland, all the way to the ocean." Catching my look, he shakes his head. "It's hundreds of miles. You could never get through."

"But the guy that picked us up—" I protest.

"Miguel?" Rex dips a rag in the wax and rubs the underside of the bow. "He lives upriver near the landing site with his family. Has all his life. They know the area better than anyone and keep an eye on the perimeter for us in exchange for supplies. But it's at least a full day's hike to get to the nearest usable road from there."

"I don't understand. How was this place built, and remodeled?" I ask, incredulous. "There must be an access road."

He nods. "There was, and we were able to secure the use of it for the remodel through the local workers, who had connections. But it's no longer accessible to us."

"How do you get supplies if no one can get in or out?" I press, still not convinced.

"We're pretty self-sufficient. We grow everything here," Rex says. "The other stuff comes every few months. We're always way ahead of our needs."

"So, what would you say are our chances of getting out of here today?" Lucas asks, frustrated.

"Not gonna happen," Rex replies. "Sorry, man."

"We can pay to expedite the process of getting the part or borrowing a helicopter," Lucas says.

Rex chuckles. "So can we. Don't worry, we'll get this taken care of as soon as possible. But for now, you'll want to suspend your flight. There should be someone in the tech center who can help you get online."

Lucas and I exchange a dubious glance, resigned. "Okay," I say, at a loss for what else to say, what else to do.

"If I hear anything, I'll let you know," Rex assures us.

Xibalbá lifts his head to watch us exit with wary golden eyes. But it's not just his growl that makes me uneasy. As much as I don't want to admit it, Lucas is right. All of this is awfully convenient. We're utterly helpless here, at the mercy of Kali and her loyal followers. She's the queen, and we're nothing but pawns, a long way from home.

Pawns that stand between the queen and her fortune.

Outside, the stream gurgles and the birds warble in the treetops, but the vivid day feels glaring, and the forest seems more impenetrable than ever.

SEVENTEEN

We find the tech room at the end of the long marble hallway on the first floor. Light filters through a wide window that overlooks the pool, reflecting off the teal rug to give the space an eerie glow. A wood table with two desktops on it stands in the center, and against the wall to our right, a curvy ginger-haired girl who looks to be in her early twenties sits cross-legged on a Danish-style navy couch with wood legs.

She looks up from the Chromebook in her lap with a smile that crinkles her light brown eyes. "Hi, I'm Amber. You guys need to visit the twenty-first century?"

Over the sound of dual vacuum cleaners in the hallway, Lucas and I introduce ourselves, explaining our need to postpone our flights and check email. "You can use a laptop or a desktop," she says, "but the laptops are faster."

"Great. Laptops it is," I say.

She sets us each up with a laptop on the matching couch opposite hers. "If you need to use the phone, it's there." She points to a side table between the two armchairs in front of the window, on which rests a red rotary phone that looks straight out of the 1950s. "I know it looks old but it's actually digital, connected through the satellite."

"Do you have our cell phones and laptops?" I ask. Lucas's phone is still under his mattress, useless without a signal, but she doesn't need to know that.

She wrinkles her nose. "Um, no?"

"Oh," I say, exchanging a glance with Lucas.

"We were told they'd be here if we needed them," Lucas says.

A wave of confusion crosses her face. "I'm sorry," she says. "I'm just doing my hours here. We rotate, so, um, I don't know about that kind of thing."

"Aren't there lockers or cubbies where people keep their devices?" Lucas asks.

She points at a wall of shelves stacked with laptops and tablets, next to the couch where we found her. "We all share. There's plenty to go around and they're always up to date. We don't need cell phones, there's no service. It's hard enough to get internet," she confides. "When it's cloudy the speed is soooo slow, and sometimes the satellite gets off course."

"Off course?" I ask, doubtful.

"I don't, like, understand it or anything," she says, shrugging. "It just doesn't work sometimes, you know? We're in the jungle, so."

Feeling increasingly claustrophobic, I open the web browser and put my flight on hold, then check my email to find a message from Chase informing me Brock has invited us to join him in his company's box for the Knicks game next week. Finding a silver lining in the fact that I at least have a perfectly good excuse not to spend unnecessary time in tight quarters with Brock, I quickly reply, letting Chase know I'm staying for a bit. I wrestle with whether to mention the broken helicopter, but in the end decide against it, instead blaming my decision to delay my return on the arduous journey and the desire to "be there for Paul's widow." I don't want him to worry, nor do I need a lecture on how dangerous it is here and that I shouldn't have come.

Once I've sent my email, I have the urge to check my voice mail, but I don't remember how. It's been ages since I had to call in to check it. I consider phoning my mom, but the conversation we need to have isn't one I want to have in front of Amber—or Lucas, for that matter. Instead, I do an online search for helicopter rentals in Palenque, coming up with nothing but a link for the rudimentary website of the airport. "We should call the airport," I say to Lucas, who is typing away on a laptop on the couch next to me.

"On it," he agrees, moving to one of the chairs by the phone, his computer in his lap. He picks up the handset and dials a number, referencing the computer screen.

Lucas speaks into the phone in Spanish too rapid for me to catch the details, but I recognize the word "*helicóptero*." I glance at Amber to see if she understands or cares, but she's engrossed in something on her laptop.

Hoping to turn up anything that might give me some sense of who to trust, I take the opportunity to google "Paul Bentzen VitaLife sale," but the articles that pop up contain no juicy details or hints of scandal. I search for information on Kali, but strangely, can't come up with anything—not even a last name. The Mandala website makes no mention of her, and as I scroll through the videos I watched at Tara and Roz's, I realize she's conspicuously absent from those as well. It's as though the web has been scrubbed clean of her presence, which I find more ominous than any dirt I might have turned up on her.

Before I can search for anything else, a bell tolls somewhere in the house. "Lunch," Amber announces, taking off her headphones. "We can walk up together."

Lucas holds up a finger to signal he needs a minute as he wraps up his conversation. "They're working on finding another helicopter," he says when he hangs up.

Amber holds out her hands for the computers, and Lucas and I reluctantly hand them over, watching as she stores them on the shelf before we exit.

"Why do you lock it?" I ask as Amber bolts the door behind us. My voice echoes so loudly in the stone corridor that I lower it. "I assume nobody around here steals?"

"Of course not." She laughs, twisting a strand of hair around her finger. "But technology is a drug worse than pharmaceuticals, and too much of it is bad for your energy field. Locking the door takes away the temptation to plug in."

Yesterday I was grateful for the excuse to unplug. Today I just feel trapped.

THE NOISY DINING HALL IS a sea of orange when we arrive. "Do you guys usually wear orange?" I ask Amber as we attach ourselves to the back of the buffet line.

"We rotate the colors of the chakras with the days of the week, so we cycle through each chakra every week," she replies. "Like, Saturday is red for root chakra, today is Sunday so it's orange for the sacral chakra, tomorrow will be yellow for the solar plexus, like that. All the yoga and chanting and Reiki or whatever we do that day is focused on purifying the chakra of the day."

"That's a lot," Lucas comments.

"It serves the dual purpose of delineating time," she explains cheerfully, oblivious to his laconic tone. "We don't have the traditional work-week structure out here, so it's important to keep up with what day it is so we don't go loco." She draws a loop in the air near her ear with her finger and crosses her eyes. "White's for special ceremonies, and Kali," she adds.

"Who makes the clothes?" I ask as we inch closer to the serving table.

"We do," she says proudly. "There's a sewing room across the hall from the tech room." She passes me a plate from the end of the long table and grins. "We do literally everything ourselves here. It's kinda wild. I had no idea how to cook or sew or clean or garden or anything before I came here. And now I can do all of it. Makes you realize that you really can do whatever you put your mind to."

"Where were you before?" I ask.

"Rhode Island. But I had shitty parents so I ran away when I was sixteen."

"I'm sorry," I say. "What brought you here?"

"Aguilar. He found me on the Venice boardwalk in California. I was in a bad place, he totally saved my ass."

The pesto penne smells delicious, though the knowledge that we're stuck dampens my appetite. Clearly Amber doesn't have much of one, either; she takes only the salad, skipping the dressing. Noticing my glance, she confides, "I struggle with my weight."

I gaze at her, perplexed. "But you're in great shape."

"That's because I work so hard at it. Your body is your temple," she says. "The external reflects the internal. Some of us just have to work a little harder to get the external into a shape that glorifies God."

A shape that glorifies God? No wonder everyone here is so fit. Thrown, I look for Lucas to corroborate the craziness of this theory, but he's already seated at a long table at the front of the room. "Is that . . . part of the belief system here?" I ask.

"It's the truth," she says, her tone matter-of-fact.

I don't quite know what to say to that, but after years of counting calories and eating salad with the dressing on the side while trying (in vain, mostly) to help friends wasting away from actual eating disorders, I have to say *something*. "I'm sure God finds all bodies equally glorious."

She laughs and looks me up and down. "Easy for you to say. Aren't you, like, a model or something?"

"I was," I admit. "And I can tell you, I've worked with some of the most externally attractive people in the world, and their insides generally do not match their outsides."

Her head shake says I simply haven't seen the light. "Beauty is the mark of God's favor."

Wow. "And all bodies are beautiful," I demur, anger swelling inside me.

"One day you'll understand," she says with a placating smile.

"Actually, I'm way ahead of you on this one," I return, not about to let her have the last word. "I spent my entire career practically starving myself, taking diet pills, trying every fad that came along to make my body skinnier than God ever intended it to be. I didn't have a period for years. You think God intended that?"

Amber stares at me, clearly stunned anyone would challenge what she believes to be the Word of God.

"God created your body," I go on, turning her own logic against her. "Therefore, it's already perfect."

Before she can respond, I turn, my blood pumping, and thread my way to the table where Lucas is seated. I take deep breaths to calm down as I slide onto the bench next to him, across from a tattooed rocker-looking guy and a beautiful older woman.

"I hear you're staying," the woman says amiably.

"We are," I confirm, focusing on her. "The helicopter needs a part, apparently."

"That's great," says the rocker guy. "Cheers." He raises his glass of water to us. "I'm Clef, and this is Smoke," he says, gesturing toward the older woman.

For all its emphasis on nomenclature, the Mandala naming system seems to be almost laughably lazy. After watching him on the bongos the other night I can say with confidence that Clef is a musician; Smoke has long silver-gray hair reminiscent of smoke; and Amber has eyes of amber.

Luna plops down next to me, securing her long chestnut hair with a ponytail holder. "Sveta, I promised Kali I'd take good care of you today, so I'm taking you to yoga," she says with an air of finality that makes me doubt whether I have any choice in the matter. "It's a ladies-only class," she clarifies. "Sometimes we need to tend to our feminine energy."

I force a smile. "Sure."

"Don't worry, I showered." Blaze's voice precedes him. He takes the seat across from us, no longer covered in ash, his wet hair pulled back in a bun. "I'd love to show you around the property this afternoon," he offers to Lucas and me.

"That would be great," Lucas and I both say at once.

"Not a good idea," Rex interjects, throwing Blaze a look of disapproval as he takes the seat next to him. "The last thing we need is you getting lost or kidnapped."

"Kidnapped?" I ask warily.

Luna turns and hits Rex hard in the shoulder. "Don't scare them." She turns back to us. "It's nothing."

"Just the cartel," Rex fires back. "No big deal."

The *cartel*? My unease deepens.

"They don't bother us if we don't bother them," Luna says with a roll of her eyes. "Anyway, Sveta, you're with me. Yoga will be way more fun than tromping around the jungle."

I think I see just a flicker of rancor in the glance Blaze gives the two of them before he turns his attention to Lucas. "Anyway," Blaze says, "I'd be glad to show you around."

"I'll come along, make sure you don't get into any trouble." Rex says it as though it's a joke, but his tone is barbed.

Is he really worried about our safety, or is there something in the woods he doesn't want us to see? Either way, I'm quickly getting the feeling the big happy family on display yesterday isn't quite as perfect as Kali would like us to believe.

EIGHTEEN

I lie in shivasana atop a yoga mat on the wood floor of the open-air yoga studio, my body completely wrung out from an hour and a half of Ruby's inspired instruction. My limbs are loose, my skin glistening, my mind sharper than it's been in weeks. But the sense of foreboding still lingers deep within me.

"Listen to the sound of the rain forest," Ruby directs in a soothing voice. "What do you hear?"

I count three, no . . . four, five different species of birds chattering before I recognize the humming of something that sounds like a cicada, a rustling in the trees, the gurgling of water rushing over rocks. It would all be very peaceful if my brain weren't racked with anxiety.

When Lucas and I managed to snag a moment alone by the pool after lunch, he told me the operator he'd spoken to at the Palenque airport hadn't received any requests for helicopter transport from our location or heard anything about a helicopter needing a part.

"She said today was unlikely for pickup, but it shouldn't be a problem to arrange for tomorrow," he whispered, shading his eyes against the sun. "She knew the landing point and there are no flight restrictions for it that she's heard of. I'm supposed to call her back at four."

"So Rex lied."

"Or was lied to," he confirmed. "I'm telling you, Kali's trying to keep you here to influence you."

"But why give me *more* time to come to a decision about the nuisance payment?" I argued.

"Because she's desperate for you to take it, and if you leave now, you won't. Her claim won't stand up in court and she knows it, so she's trying to intimidate you into complying."

I didn't want it to be true, but it did seem increasingly likely. I kicked off my sandals and dipped my toes in the pool. "Amber was telling me at lunch about how she had to keep her weight down to make sure her shape 'glorifies God.'"

He gave me a quizzical look.

"They believe the external reflects the internal," I clarified. "I've been noticing a pretty serious obsession with beauty. I guess that's where it stems from."

He frowned, scanning side to side to confirm we were alone. "You realize this is a cult, right?"

"I don't know." I bristled, unable to process the idea of my kindhearted uncle as a cult leader, but I did see his point. "I mean, every different part of society is kind of a cult, right? Like, my fiancé's family are all about wealth and status, and everyone they're surrounded by at their country club and in their tony neighborhood reinforces that's what's important."

"I don't think—"

"And my friends Tara and Roz," I went on. "They're total bleeding-heart liberals and so are all their friends. They don't hang out with anyone conservative. My point is, who you're surrounded by influences who you are and what you think is normal. People want to belong. Like your yoga instructor girlfriend who wanted you to go vegan and stop wearing deodorant—I bet that's what most of her friends do. I'm sure your point of view is influenced by being a surfer."

"Oh, but I snowboard, too."

"Ha ha," I returned dryly. "You get my point. There's cultlike behavior everywhere."

"Okay, first of all, no offense, but your fiancé's family sounds like assholes."

"You're not wrong," I admitted.

"Seriously, though, I get what you're trying to say," he said earnestly. "And it's a great observation. But this"—he waved his hand at the hulking villa behind us—"isn't cult*like*. It's an actual cult. It isn't choosing not to hang out with someone who has different political views from you, it's isolating people and convincing them if they don't follow a strict set of beliefs, God—and all their friends—will turn their backs on them, or worse." He lowered his voice even further. "One of the girls last night told me her father is dying, but she can't go to visit him because he's a 'censor,' which is their word for a person who gets between them and the Mandala. Apparently he tried to get her to leave this place, and now if she goes to see him, she's 'choosing' him and can't come back here."

"So she chooses the Mandala over her own family," I said.

"Yeah. She thinks this is her 'true' family, that spiritual ties are stronger than blood ones." He caught my gaze and held it, his dark eyes serious. "I've seen it before—the group I was in with my mom used the same kind of tactics," he divulged, without elaborating further. "So go to yoga, play along, but please, please don't buy any of the bullshit they're trying to sell you."

Now, lying on the floor of the yoga studio with twenty other women, listening to the birds chirping and Ruby's haunting voice rising and falling with ancient mantras that hang in the heavy air, I measure Lucas's words against Kali's. Both of them are so convincing, and neither of them is trustworthy. But it's Amber's unquestioning adherence to the Mandala's unhealthy belief about her weight that tips the scales in Lucas's favor. That, and the protective expression I catch on his face when he looks at me sometimes.

Once the chanting has ended, we wipe our mats down and return them to the cubbyholes along the back wall.

"We're going to the hot springs," Ruby says. "If you want to join."

I check the clock on the wall. Three thirty. Lucas isn't talking to the airport until four, and even if he can secure a helicopter for us, it won't be until tomorrow. I might as well get a sense of the place. "Sure," I say.

"You're an awesome teacher. I've done a lot of yoga in my life, and that was the best class I've ever taken."

"Thank you," she says sincerely.

"Seriously, if you ever get sick of the jungle, my friend has a yoga studio in New York. He'd hire you in a heartbeat, then I could take your class every day."

She laughs. "Thanks, maybe someday."

We follow the others out the door and down the stairs, onto the soft-packed black dirt of the forest floor. Sinuous vines curl snakelike around exposed tangled tree roots, and thick green moss carpets the space not covered by ferns. The canopy above is so dense that scant light reaches the path, leaving me with the strange sensation that I'm under emerald water, walking along the ocean floor.

"How did you end up here?" I ask.

Ruby sighs, looking off into the forest. "It's a long, pathetic story."

"I'm sorry," I say. "I don't mean to pry."

"No, it's fine," she returns, refocusing on me. She has that same grounded energy that Kali has, accentuated by large, expressive eyes that exude warmth. "I made a dumb mistake, it seems like a lifetime ago now. I was in grad school for psychology in Chicago, and I had an affair with my married professor. His wife found out and told the university. He was fired, I was expelled. And he'd also been a student at the yoga studio where I taught, so I lost my teaching job there as well. My whole life disintegrated, just poof!

"After, I was barely making ends meet working in a café when Shiva came in one night. We got to talking while I was closing up. He could see I was struggling, so he offered to fly me to Palm Desert and comp a Mandala super-starter seminar he was teaching there the following week. He convinced me it would change my life. He was right."

"Were you close with him?" I ask.

She nods, tears welling in her eyes. "Very. After a year of working at the Sonoma retreat center, I became his personal assistant, so we spent a lot of time together." Her lip trembles. "He knew everything about me, every secret I ever had, and he loved me just as I was."

"I'm so sorry." I reach out and squeeze her hand.

She pats her eyes with her tunic and takes a deep breath. "I heard there's a problem with your helicopter?"

I nod. "Hopefully we'll be able to find another one," I say, watching for her reaction.

Ruby sweeps her braids over her shoulder, avoiding meeting my eye. "Yeah."

"Does this kind of thing happen often?" I ask.

"People used to come and go a lot more," she says, slowing her pace so that we fall farther behind the rest of the group. "But that ended a while ago, and since Shiva left, no one comes or goes anymore."

I cock my head. "What do you mean, Shiva left?"

She pauses, putting more space between us and the rest of the women. "He's been gone. For the past two years. He was back for a month last spring, then left again. He returned the night he died."

I stare at her in amazement, wondering if Lucas knew this—if it's yet another thing he neglected to mention. "Where was he?"

Ruby lowers her voice. "The official line is that he was doing book promotion stuff in the US. But he confided in me that he had cancer and was receiving treatment that Kali didn't approve of."

I have so many questions, it's hard to know where to start.

She wipes her cheeks with the tips of her fingers. "Sorry. It's hard to talk about."

"No, of course," I say. "I don't want to upset you. I'm just curious. Did the treatment work?" I ask.

"For a while." She watches a lizard with an iridescent blue under-side scurry up a moss-covered rock, stopping at the top to stare at us. "It seemed to be working the first time he came back to visit a year ago. I was hopeful. But he wasn't well when he returned this time. He was weak, really skinny. He thought he might only have a few months left."

"But he didn't. He died the night he arrived." I watch her carefully. "It seems strange."

She makes air quotes with her fingers. *"Left his body."*

"Right. But you don't believe that." I focus on her until she finally gives a slight shake of her head.

"Hey, slowpokes!" We spin to see Luna walking toward us on the path. "You coming?"

Damn it. Just when I was getting somewhere with Ruby.

"Yeah, sorry," I reply, covering my irritation at the interruption. My questions about whether Paul mentioned changing his will are going to have to wait.

"What were you two whispering about?" Luna asks.

"Just talking yoga stuff," I fib.

Luna bisects us, linking an arm through each of ours to stroll toward the springs arm in arm. I'm once again reminded of *The Wizard of Oz*. *Follow the yellow brick road.* If only I could click my heels and declare "There's no place like home."

"Snake!" Luna points gleefully at a tree branch that hangs over the path just above head level, where a large green snake is coiled, watching us lazily.

I flinch and stop dead in my tracks, but Luna pulls me forward. "It's just a rat snake," she says. "He's not interested in you."

Still, I shiver as we pass beneath.

"Snakes are powerful omens of transformation," she goes on. "Seeing one means it's time to shed beliefs that no longer suit you, like they shed their skin. A rebirth, which is of course also linked to sexuality. Maybe you need a new sexual partner."

"You think everything is about sex," Ruby goads.

"It's true," Luna says lightly. "But orgasm brings you closer to the Divine, so I'm vibrating at a very high level. And I do love to vibrate." She shivers dramatically and turns her flashing eyes on me. "Have you had an orgasm since you got here?"

"Uh, no."

"Oh, you have to," she exclaims with the same enthusiasm my New York friends might exude when talking about a new restaurant. We crest a hill and the path grows rockier as we descend the other side. I hear water rushing somewhere down below, but the palms are so close-packed I can't see the source of it. "Orgasms here are way more powerful because of the clarity of the energy field. Right, Ruby?"

Ruby nods, but I detect an uneasiness as she observes Luna. Luna, however, doesn't seem to notice.

"It's really transformative," Luna continues brightly. "I mean technically none of us can have sex with you because you're not initiated—not that it would stop everyone, between you and me—but there's no reason you can't give yourself one. Or Lucas could give you one," she suggests.

Thrown by the thought of that, I nearly lose my footing on a mossy rock and Ruby catches me by the elbow. Her brief glance tells me she's about had enough of Luna. "I'm good," I say with as much nonchalance as I can muster. "I'm actually engaged, so."

"The Divine didn't create us to be monogamous," says Luna. "You can't own another person. We do this incredible love ceremony here, where we use the rhythm of the drums to all orgasm at the same time. It takes intense training to master the beat patterns, but it's life changing."

"Cool," I say, at a loss for what else to say to that.

We step over the roots of a gargantuan tree and come around its wide trunk to see the riverbanks scattered with piles of orange clothes. Below, our group skinny-dips in a handful of steaming pools of varying sizes carved into the rocks, beyond which a river rushes past. The space created by the river is wide enough that sunlight filters through the trees to bounce off the rippling water, throwing bright flares of reflective light that give the scene an otherworldly glow.

"Is this the same river we came down to reach Xanadu?" I ask, turned around.

"No," Ruby says. "That one's much bigger. This is really just a tribu-tary. There's a beautiful waterfall farther up that way, too." She indicates upriver with her elbow as she secures her hair atop her head. "Water temperature in the hot springs hovers around a hundred."

I gladly shed my clothes and step into the nearest pool, realizing too late that the three women already occupying it seem to be in the midst of a heated discussion. A blonde with dreadlocks is turned away from us, speaking vehemently to the scowling brunette sisters Lucas and I met earlier on the way to the boathouse. I startle when I see that the blonde's back is scarred with raised red diagonal stripes, as though she's been whipped—from the looks of it, somewhat recently. "I know be-cause he didn't ask for it," she's insisting, her Nordic accent apparent. "If he wanted it, he would have asked for it." She pauses when she notices Luna, Ruby, and me. I quickly avert my gaze from her bumpy back, but too late. The guarded, almost defiant intensity in her pale blue eyes tells me she's seen me looking.

"Don't let us interrupt," Luna says, catching their glances as she splashes into the pool. "We share everything here."

The sisters cut their beady eyes toward me as I sink into the sublimely warm yet somehow invigorating water, suddenly self-conscious. "We were just reminding Sunshine," says one of them, "that Kali knows bet-ter than any of us what Shiva wanted."

So Sunshine is the blonde—named, I'm sure, for her yellow hair, because her disposition is anything but sunny.

"Kali's our guru now," Luna agrees. "We have to stop thinking about what Shiva would have wanted. We have to let him go. His spirit will not be able to be free if we hold him here."

Sunshine drops her gaze to the water, frustrated. "Right," she mum-bles. But whatever she was upset about is still obviously not resolved.

Ruby abruptly changes the subject to the new vegetables and herbs planted in the garden this morning, and we spend the rest of the time at the hot springs discussing what plants grow best in a tropical jungle environment and which time of year is best for planting. But the tension between the sisters—Karma and Karuna—and Sunshine never completely dissolves, leaving me curious about what they were arguing about so intensely.

And I can't help but notice as the women move between the spas, their nude and invariably toned bodies glistening in the afternoon sun, that Sunshine is not the only one with scars on her back.

NINETEEN

It's nearly dinnertime when I return from the hot springs. Eager to know whether Lucas had any success securing a helicopter for us, I immediately head up the double marble staircase to our room, but he's not there. I tread back downstairs to the tech room looking for him, but the room is locked and dark inside. In the kitchen, the night's dinner prep is well underway, but he's not among the aproned chefs, nor is he in the first- or second-level lounges.

Off the hallway on the first floor, I find the stairs down to the basement. The hardwood stairwell doubles back on itself, leading down to a brightly lit open space with a brushed concrete floor and mirrored walls. It's freezing cold, and the treadmills, ellipticals, and weight-lifting machinery are all unoccupied. At the far end of the room, a light shines beyond an open door leading to a hallway that extends along the back wall of the house. Curious, I cut across the gym to the hallway.

"Hello?" I call out. "Lucas? Anybody down here?" My voice bounces off the white concrete block walls, but no one answers.

I peer into the first open door to see a large, windowless storage room full of gym equipment and various items of furniture. Across the hall are three empty doorframes leading to three identical rooms. Each has the same concrete floor as the rest of the basement and a high window with a view of the tree house; the only furniture is simple cots without sheets.

A prickling sensation creeps up my spine. If it weren't for the lack of doors, I'd swear these rooms were jail cells, and the security camera mounted in a high corner of each room only serves to reinforce this speculation.

Unnerved, I hasten down the hallway back to the gym, where I nearly collide with Hikari, striding toward me. "What are you doing down here?" he asks, his tone accusatory.

"Looking for Lucas," I sputter, covering. "I'm sorry, am I not supposed to be down here? No one told me."

"This is the infirmary," he explains, taking a key from his pocket and securing the door to the hallway behind us. "We normally keep this door locked."

The infirmary. It makes logical sense but rings false, especially with all Kali's assertions that no one ever gets sick.

"Dinner's ready, we should head up." He places a hand on my back, guiding me toward the stairwell. "In the future, when you want to explore, come get one of us. We'd be more than happy to show you around."

"Sure," I say, attempting to sound nonchalant. "Of course."

But as I ascend the stairs, my knees are shaking, and I'm relieved when Hikari leaves me at the back of the line in the dining room.

Kali spots me immediately and waves me over to the head table, where she sits with Rex, Aguilar, and Ruby.

Aguilar and Rex are deep in whispered conversation but stop abruptly when I approach. Aguilar eyes me warily, while Rex's gaze is more . . . flirtatious? Maybe Luna told him I needed an orgasm. But he's not supposed to give me one, is he?

"Sit here," Kali says, patting the seat between her and Rex. "We made you a plate."

Indeed, a delicious-looking plate of artichoke cakes over a bed of kale with what looks like a lemon poppy dressing waits on the table in front of the empty chair. My stomach growls, my hunger overthrowing my unease. I wanted to talk to Lucas, and I'm not totally sure I trust Kali anymore not to drug me, but I also can't see any tactful way to turn her down, so I slide in next to her. "Thanks."

"I'm so sorry about your helicopter," she says with an apologetic smile, "but I have to admit I'm glad you're here."

I arrange my face into what I hope is a friendly expression. "Hopefully they'll get it fixed soon," I say.

I take a bite of the artichoke cake, racking my brain for how to get more information out of Kali without eroding the increasingly tenuous goodwill between us.

"I'm just curious," I venture, "because I want to be respectful, as your guest—are there things we shouldn't do or rules we should be following?"

She graces me with a warm smile. "We live by Divine Will here, but we want you to enjoy yourself while you're with us."

That doesn't really answer my question, but I don't know how to phrase it better without getting specific, so I change tactics. "I didn't realize Shiva was out of town before he died," I say carefully. "That must've been so hard for you."

She pauses, studying my face with her all-knowing gaze, and I again have the unnerving sensation that she can read my mind. "It was," she says. "But it was necessary."

"Where was he?" I ask, my breath shallow.

She lowers her voice, her face placid but her gray eyes intense. "You remember what we discussed yesterday." I assume she's referring to the unnamed cancer that ostensibly killed him, that no one is supposed to know about, but everyone seems to be fully aware of. "We can talk further later, if you like."

"That would be great," I say. I'm terribly thirsty now, but the only offering on the table is tea, which I've resolved not to drink.

I look around and finally spot Lucas sitting across the room between Blaze and the girl who was playing with his hair last night, listening intently as she talks. He's a good listener, I've noticed, always fully invested in whoever he's conversing with, never looking over his shoulder for someone better to talk to. I wrest my focus back to the task at hand.

"I'd love to check out the tree house," I say.

"I'm afraid that won't be possible," Kali replies with an air of finality.

"Oh?" I ask. "Why's that?"

"It's where Shiva's spirit left his body. We have to hold that space for him until his spirit has been released, so that he can leave in peace."

O-kay. That sounds like a load of crap, but I have no way of knowing whether it's actually something she believes or something she's making up to keep me out of the tree house—which would raise the question, what's in there she doesn't want me to see?

"Are there other places we're not supposed to go?" I ask lightly.

"It's not like that," she demurs. "As long as you stay on the property, you're safe."

"Safe from what?" I ask.

"There are poppy and marijuana fields in the mountains, and the people who operate them prefer to be left alone," she says diplomatically.

"Drug runners?" I ask, thinking of Rex's mention of the cartel earlier.

She shrugs. "It's common in this area, not much we can do about it. But here on the property, you're perfectly safe."

Perfectly confined, is more like it.

"So, Sveta," Rex pipes up from the other side of me. I swivel around, having practically forgotten he was there. He fixes his midnight-blue eyes on me. "Kali says you're a model?"

Yep, he's hitting on me—I'm guessing at Kali's behest, as he's shown no interest until now. With his square jaw and muscular physique, I'm sure he's used to his targets swooning under his spell, but it's not going to work with me. I do recognize that he could be useful, though, and I also know how to turn on the charm, so I smile and allow him to pepper me with questions, feigning flattery at his attention.

After dinner, we troop quietly through the dark forest to the meditation and yoga studio for candlelit meditation—or, I should say, ninety minutes of the terrifying night sounds of the jungle duking it out with my clamorous thoughts while I wait with growing impatience to speak to Lucas. But Rex sticks so close to me that it's impossible to get a moment alone with him.

Once the session is over, Kali asks one of the kulas—the Mandala's word for the groups they're divided into—to stay, and I hustle out of the meditation studio with the rest of the crowd, turning down Rex's not-so-subtle offer to "look at the stars" down by the lake, which I'm sure is the Xanadu version of "Netflix and chill." I keep my head down as I follow the forest path back to the villa and climb the stairs to my room. The lamps on our bedside tables burn low, dim light reflecting off the swirling scarlet rug to lend the white walls and bedclothes a reddish tint. Tomorrow's mustard-colored linen outfits are set out on each of our beds, but Lucas isn't there.

Still thirsty, I gratefully chug the glass of water I find on my bedside table. The thought that it might be drugged does flash through my mind, but I dismiss it. No one is secretly drugging us, I reason. Kali was up-front about the herbs in the tea, which were well intentioned, even though she didn't warn us of any side effects they might have.

Once I'm finished brushing my teeth, I linger by the sink listening to the sound of Luna's and Blaze's voices rising and falling through the closed door to their room. They sound like they're arguing, but I can't make out what about.

When I come out of the bathroom, I'm relieved to find Lucas lying on his bed, his arm over his eyes. "I was starting to think you'd stayed at the meditation studio," I say.

"God, no," he says without moving.

"Why, what's going on back there?" I ask, intrigued.

"Fuckfest," he mutters.

I guffaw. "What?"

He sits up, making air quotes. "'Love ceremony.'"

"Ah." I nod. "Luna mentioned something about group orgasm to me this afternoon."

"Fun," he says flatly.

"Did you talk to the airport?" I ask.

He nods and flips off his bedside lamp, indicating for me to do the same, then beckons me over to his bed. "So we're out of the line of sight of the door," he murmurs.

I can barely make out his eyes glistening in the gloom as I perch next to him, close enough that my knee touches his thigh when I pull my feet up to sit cross-legged.

"The airport changed their tune," he says. "Told me there were no helicopters available. I pressed, but came up against a brick wall. So I told them whatever they'd been paid, I'd double it."

"That was bold," I say, impressed.

"It was obvious," he says. "The woman paused for long enough I thought it might work, but then she just said she was sorry and hung up."

"You think someone here paid her off not to rent us a helicopter?"

"Yes," he says. "And the internet mysteriously went out directly after my phone call, so I couldn't research further. But it's okay. I have someone working on it—"

"Who?" I ask.

He runs his hand through his hair. "My assistant. Anyway, there may be another way out. I saw tire tracks today in the forest, near the hot springs." His voice is so low I have to lean in closer to listen, catching a trace of his woodsy, masculine scent. "I went up there with Blaze and Rex while you were at yoga, and when I wandered into the woods to take a leak, I saw tire tracks in the mud. I asked them about it, and Rex said the cartel has poppy fields somewhere nearby, that it was probably theirs."

"Kali told me something similar," I say. "You think it's an access road?"

"That's the hope."

"Okay," I say, considering. "But I think we're probably safer here, waiting for your assistant to figure something out, than wandering into cartel territory."

"If they're telling the truth," he says. "Regardless, if we can find the access road, it has to lead to a main road. I want to go back tomorrow to see if I can follow the tracks."

It does make me feel marginally better that Lucas is so damn capable. Of all the people I could have been stuck with in the jungle, I'm beginning to realize he's not a bad choice, and as much as I didn't want him coming with me, I'm glad he's here now.

"Did Blaze or Rex say anything else?" I ask.

"I got the sense Blaze wanted to, but Rex stuck so close to us that he couldn't. That guy's a damn barnacle." He shifts to take something from his pocket, the moonlight through the window glancing off his cheekbones and the slight bump in his nose. "But Blaze did slip me this."

His fingers brush mine as he hands me what looks like a dirty grayish-white piece of jagged rock about two inches in diameter.

"What is it?" I ask, running my thumb over the porous surface.

He points at the back of his neck. "Spinal cord, from the neck."

"Oh God!" Horrified, I dump it into his lap and wipe my hands on my shirt. "Why did he give you that?"

"To prove death, if we can't get the death certificate. It has Shiva's DNA, and it's a bone a person can't live without."

I shiver. "Because without a body or a death certificate, Shiva's only missing, and his will can't be executed."

"For seven years," he confirms, slipping the piece of spinal cord back into his pocket. "Five if you're lucky."

"During which time the Mandala stays open and Kali's in charge, regardless of which will is right."

His eyes catch mine. "Do you see now why I'm so wary of what's going on down here?"

"I admit it looks like there's a darker side to this place," I acknowledge with a sigh. "You knew Paul hadn't lived here for two years?"

"Yeah. He told me at my dad's funeral."

I bristle. "You didn't want to maybe share that information with me?"

He furrows his brow. "I didn't tell you?"

"No," I say, dubious of his lapse in memory.

"I'm sorry—"

"Anything else you might have forgotten to mention?" I ask sharply.

"I don't know," he says. "I don't think so."

"What else did you and Paul talk about?"

He bites his lip, thinking. "He mentioned he'd been less and less involved since they moved down here from California; that Kali had taken the Mandala in a direction that wasn't in line with his principles. I don't know how the shift happened, but I definitely got the impression she was running Xanadu."

"But if he didn't agree with what she was doing, why not shut it down back then?" I ask.

"Seemed like he planned to, but his health got in the way. Regardless, he intended to when he came down a few days ago." He catches my gaze and holds it. "Which is what makes me so suspicious about the fact that he happened to die as soon as he got here."

A current of dread runs through me. "You think Kali found out he was going to end it, and killed him," I surmise.

He clenches his jaw, his expression grave. "I wouldn't put it past her."

Goose bumps prickle my skin. It doesn't take much of a leap in logic to figure out that if she did in fact kill her husband, doing the same to me would be no problem. But this is all conjecture. "That's quite an accusation, with no evidence, of someone you've known a day," I venture.

"I recognize the pattern." He pauses, staring down at his hands. When he continues, his voice is halting. "The group I was in with my mother, the leader was charismatic, beloved—the Kavi, we called him, the 'chosen one.' His word was God's word, literally—the group believed God spoke through him and they would do whatever he told them, no matter how crazy it was."

"Like what?"

"Penance in the form of self-harm, sexual favors—both men and women were encouraged to use sex as a way of luring others to the group—'love trapping,' they called it." He hesitates, grimacing. "Adolescents were encouraged to discover their sexuality with older 'guides.'"

Adolescents like him. It hits me like a ton of bricks why he seemed so experienced in bed at twenty, why he's so brooding all the time, so guarded about his past. I can't even comprehend what he must have been through. And my heart breaks for him. "I'm so sorry, Lucas," I say quietly.

"It was really fucked up. And it fucked me up for a long time. When we first met, I was going through some shit—trying to work through it all. It was a really rough time in my life. It's why I put off college for two years—why I didn't call you after I got back to California," he admits, his eyes locking on mine. "I wish I had been in a better place then, but it was just . . . very bad timing."

I nod, at a loss for words. There it is, the explanation I've wanted all these years. I suppose it should make me feel better that his ghosting me wasn't ever about anything I did or didn't do—wasn't about me at all. But it just makes me sad, to think he was even more messed up than I was.

"It's okay," I finally say, swallowing the knot in my throat. "I did wonder . . . back then. But I understand. I mean, I'm really sorry that happened to you."

His gaze slides down my face. "I should have told you a long time ago, but once I'd had enough therapy to realize it, so much time had passed I figured you might be weirded out some guy you spent one night with was still thinking about you after all these years."

"I wouldn't have been weirded out," I say too quickly. Heat spreads through my chest as I try not to think about what might have happened if he'd called before I met Chase. I tuck a strand of hair behind my ear, forcing myself to break eye contact. "So the leader of your group, he was like Kali?"

"Basically, yeah." He clears his throat. "But toward the end, a faction of members began to doubt him and tried to overthrow him." He sighs. "Until the head of the resistance 'committed suicide,' and the rest were accused of rape and child abuse."

"That's vicious." I breathe. "Where is he now, the leader of your group?"

"Serving a life sentence."

"How old were you when all this happened?" I ask.

"I was sixteen when the group was disbanded." He finally turns to me, his dark eyes the most vulnerable I've seen them. "I mention it because of the similarities between him and Kali. He would have done anything to maintain control, and I see the same hard-line resolution in her. She . . ."

It seems like he's about to go on, to tell me more, but then he stops. "She's dangerous, Sveta. I know she is."

With his background, it's no wonder he finds her so intolerable. I can understand how, after going through what he did, a place like this could be triggering. How he might be primed to see the absolute worst-case scenario. And he could be right. But he could also be wrong, his personal experiences clouding his vision.

Instinctively I lay a hand on his knee. He covers it with his. Suddenly the warmth of his skin against mine is all I can feel. I want to hug him, but I don't think that's a good idea.

"Okay then," I say, taking my hand back. "Tomorrow we find the road."

I cross to my bed and slip under the covers, rolling to face the wall, my skin still buzzing from his touch.

TWENTY

Day Three

I awake the following morning to Lucas gently shaking my shoulder. The light through the gauzy curtains is muted, the sun just beginning to rise.

"Morning," he says, brushing my tangled hair from my face. He seems to recognize the intimacy of the gesture after his fingers have left my cheek, and stands quickly, going to the window.

Something's shifted between us after he opened up to me last night. I wouldn't go so far as to say I fully trust him, but I understand him a lot better now, and I have confidence that while some of his actions may be misguided, his intentions are good.

"What time is it?" I ask, dazed.

"Early," he says. He's already dressed for the day in his mustard clothes, his five o'clock shadow deepened, making his face only more ruggedly handsome. "Everyone's just left for morning meditation. This is our chance if we want to try to find the road without an escort."

I sit up, rubbing the sleep from my eyes. "Okay. Can we get coffee first?"

"Unless someone's down there."

I wrench myself out of bed and stumble to the bathroom, where I change, brush my teeth, and gather my tangled hair into a ponytail, attempting to sweep away the tender feelings toward Lucas suddenly muddling my mind. But I can't quite forget the way he looked at me last night, or the sound of his voice, unsure with the admission that he'd thought of me for years after our brief encounter in New York.

And neither of us had drunk any tea.

I wash my face, scrubbing the thought away. In the gray morning light, I see my eyes are clouded with worry. We're actually stuck here, and Lucas thinks Kali killed my uncle. *Are we being held hostage?* I'm sobered by the reality of exactly how isolated and at the mercy of this group we are.

No, this is no time to indulge in hypothetical romantic fantasies.

"Okay," I say as I emerge from the bathroom, a tight knot of apprehension in my stomach. Lucas turns from his post at the window and nods, his eyes just as uneasy as mine. "Is there another staircase?" I ask.

"There's one at the far end of the hall that leads to the butler's pantry, off the kitchen. We'll still have to pass the landing."

My gaze lands on a piece of paper on his pillow that reads "Gone to waterfall, back soon."

"They'll look for us," he says. "But this way hopefully they'll think we're just out exploring, and with the head start we'll have, we should be able to reach the road before they find us."

"What are we going to do when we reach the road?" I ask. "We don't have any money or ID or anything."

"I just want to confirm there is a road, maybe follow it to see where it might go. If it seems like a viable option, then we'll make a better plan."

"Bring your phone, maybe we'll find reception."

He reaches under the mattress and pockets his phone before we step quietly into the passageway. We steal past the empty bedrooms, pausing to listen inside the archway that opens to the soaring entrance hall below, but the silence of the villa is interrupted only by the incessant calling of the birds outside.

At the far end of the hallway, a narrow set of stairs disappears into the depths of the building, growing darker as we descend what feels like much farther than only one story, thanks to the height of the ceilings in the monstrous villa. I follow Lucas, gripping the wall to steady myself as we zigzag downward, the creaking wooden stairs doubling back every few steps. Suddenly he stops, catching me softly when I crash into him in the pitch-black.

"You hear that?" he whispers. "Voices."

He creeps down the stairs toward the door that leads to the pantry, its edges dimly illuminated by light from the other side.

I can make out muffled voices on the other side of the door. A woman and a man. Lucas presses his ear to the door, and I follow suit. The voices are still muted, like hearing someone talk while submerged in a pool, but I can pretty clearly understand the words.

"No, you didn't," the man is saying.

"I was there," the woman returns in a slight, familiar accent. "In solitary, my window faced the front of the tree house. I saw with my own eyes."

Solitary. Lucas gives me a weighted glance as I recall the rooms Hikari claimed were the infirmary.

"It's not possible because it didn't happen," the man insists. His voice is familiar, too. "You probably had too much tea."

"There's no tea in solitary," she snaps. "Do whatever you want to me, but I'm not going to shut up and pretend I don't see what's going on here."

I'm nearly certain that she's the Nordic girl from the hot springs yesterday. She was arguing with Karma and Karuna, and now she's arguing with—Hikari?

"What do you want?" he growls.

Lucas turns to me, mouthing *Hikari*. I nod.

"Destroy the videos, or I tell everyone what I saw," the woman demands.

"You think the people in the outside world are going to believe a woman who paralyzed a man while driving drunk, then fled the scene of the accident?" Hikari mocks her. "We took you in when no one else wanted you, and you repay us by spreading lies. God will not look kindly on you. If you leave here, your life will become such a living hell that you'll welcome death with open arms when it comes. And it will come."

Jesus.

"I'm here of my own free will," she returns, her voice shaky. "I can leave anytime I please."

I hear footsteps as she storms away, directly toward the door we're pressed against. Lucas wraps his arm around my waist and jerks me backward, thrusting us both into the space behind the hinges of the door in one swift movement, just as it flies open and Sunshine storms up the stairs.

She's so upset that she doesn't notice the door is unable to slam into the wall behind it. Neither of us breathes until we hear her footfalls exit the staircase on the floor above.

Luckily, Hikari doesn't follow, and the spring on the door pulls it closed behind her.

"I met that woman in the hot springs yesterday," I hiss as we unwedge ourselves from the small space. "Sunshine. She was arguing with the sisters we met by the boathouse, Karma and Karuna, I don't know what about."

Lucas casts a glance down the stairwell that continues to the basement, but I shake my head, getting down on all fours to press an eye to the crack at the bottom of the door. I can see the tiled floor of the butler's pantry, and on the other side of the small room, the door that leads outside to the grill area. "No one's in the pantry," I say quietly as I rise. "But the door to the kitchen is open."

Lucas silently turns the doorknob and pulls the stairwell door open an inch, then another inch. The back door is maybe ten feet away, but if Hikari is still in the kitchen and happens to be facing this direction, we're screwed.

Lucas steals into the pantry and stops, listening. All is quiet. I slip out to join him among the shelves full of giant bags of dried beans and rice, again holding my breath.

From the kitchen comes the sound of a plate scraping the countertop. Lucas and I freeze.

A man's voice calls out from the direction of the dining hall. "They're still not up?"

"If they are, they haven't come down," Hikari answers, the sound of his voice moving away from us, toward the other man. "We have a problem with Sunshine."

Their voices become more indistinct as their footsteps grow quieter, then fade away completely.

After a moment, I slink toward the back door, glancing quickly over my shoulder into the empty kitchen. The giant coffee maker taunts me from the counter, but it's not worth the risk.

OUTSIDE, I'M GRATEFUL FOR THE low cloud cover as we hustle over the espresso-colored dirt and viridescent moss, tripping over exposed roots and slipping on rocks slick with moisture in our flimsy huarache sandals. Soon panting and wet with the dew that drips from palm fronds, I follow Lucas at least a half mile up a path that leads in the opposite direction from the meditation studio, down a ravine, up a steep hill, and into a clearing. At the far edge of the glade I'm shocked to see a worn stone pyramid nearly the height of the trees standing sentinel.

"Holy shit," I say, resting with my hands on my knees to catch my breath as I stare up at the towering structure. "What is that?"

"It's a Mayan temple," he says. "Blaze pointed it out to me yesterday. Apparently it's one of the reasons Paul and Kali wanted this land. It's an 'energy vortex.'"

It's nowhere near the size of the famous pyramids at Chíchen Itzá, and parts of it have been reclaimed by the vines and shrubs of the ever-ravenous jungle, but the temple is still awe-inspiring. Up the center of each of the four sides runs a climbable stairwell that leads to a largely intact square stone structure at the top, with columns framing a gaping portal that reveals nothing of the dark inside.

"Have you been up there?" I ask.

He shakes his head.

I start for the pyramid. "Up top is probably our best chance for cell service. And if there's a road, we should be able to see it."

We fight our way through the encroaching undergrowth to circle around to the back of the temple so that we'll be out of sight in case anyone comes along the path we just took, and ascend the fragmented stairs, carefully navigating the worn rocks in our thin sandals. When we reach the top Lucas turns to check out the view, and I step through the doorway into the cool, dusky interior of the temple, allowing my eyes to adjust to the dark.

At first all I can see is the dense greenish black produced by the sudden change in light exposure, but after a moment, shapes begin to take form. The room is perhaps fifteen by fifteen feet and mostly empty, save a large stone altar in the center. The opening on the side of the temple that faces the clearing is wider than the one on the back, and through it, down the slope of the hill that leads to Xanadu, I can make out a sliver of the lake beyond the trees, glinting in the morning sun.

I join Lucas in the doorway, where he stands with his phone raised to the sky. With no clearing on this side, it's more difficult to make out the lay of the land through the widespread leafy branches and unbroken jungle in every direction.

"Okay, maybe I was wrong about being able to see the road," I admit.

"No service, either." I feel guilty about dragging us up here for no reason when we're on borrowed time, but he shows no resentment. "Good ideas, though. And the spot where I saw the tracks isn't far."

He moves past me into the temple, trailing his hand along the altar. "What do you think this was used for?"

He stops and stares, and I step closer to see what he's focused on.

The center of the stone slab is stained dark red.

A chill runs through me, Kali's offhand comment about virgin sacrifice echoing in my mind.

"Human sacrifice ended, like, five hundred years ago, right?" he asks, his voice hollow.

"If you're wondering whether bloodstains last that long, I don't know," I say, studying the thick sanguine blotch. "But if they do, I'd expect them to be more faded." Our eyes meet, both our expressions grave. "Just because there's blood doesn't mean it's human," I point out unconvincingly. "And just because it's not five hundred years faded doesn't mean it's recent. This could be left over from when the cartel had this place. A vicious punishment for traitors."

"True." He moves to the front of the pyramid, where he again holds his phone to the sky.

"We should get out of here," I suggest. "Morning meditation is probably over."

We scramble down the back of the pyramid as quickly as we can and head deeper into the untamed forest along a narrow footpath, in places indistinguishable from the forest floor. The call of what turns out to be a brightly colored jungle turkey makes me just about jump out of my skin, and with every movement in the brush I envision an anaconda, its long body poised to squeeze the life out of me. I realize I'm being ridiculous—it's likely the humans around here I should be most afraid of—but that doesn't make me any less edgy.

As the path slopes downhill, I stop, scanning the woods. "I feel like we're going the wrong way," I say.

He shakes his head. "You're thinking of the big river we came down. The waterfall we're headed to is off a tributary that feeds into that river. It's this way, I promise."

WHEN LUCAS AND I FINALLY reach the waterfall, I register the twenty-foot cascade into the deep blue pool below, the mist forming rainbows in the light that filters through the leaves, and I wish we really were just taking a leisurely hike to appreciate this place. Regardless of the circumstances, I've enjoyed our morning together. I feel like I can be myself with him, without worrying about his judging me or wanting me to be someone else.

"This is incredible," I breathe, crouching at the river's edge to trail my fingers through the cool, clear water. "I wish we could stay and enjoy it."

I take in the natural stone grottoes, struck by how incredibly romantic the setting is, nearly overcome by the reckless desire to shed my clothes and dive into the tranquil lagoon. I splash my face with water, and when I rise, I find Lucas contemplating me, his gaze soft. His lips part as his dark eyes meet mine, and suddenly the world drops away and all the feelings I bridled this morning come rushing back. Not for the first time this week, there's something protective about the way he's looking at me. But there's something else, too. Something new. Something raw, that lights a fire inside me.

Every nerve in my body tingles as we stand frozen at arm's length, staring at each other wordlessly.

His gaze drops to my lips, and I'm almost certain he's about to reach for me—when instead he breaks eye contact with a slight shake of his head. "We should go," he says, turning away to scale the rocks next to the waterfall. "We don't want to get caught before we discover anything."

After the moment it takes to remember how to walk, I follow in a daze, my heart strangely swollen in my chest. What was that?

I know I didn't imagine the tenderness in his gaze. And I also know I wouldn't have turned him down if he had reached for me. But he didn't.

Wait a second. What the hell is wrong with me? I'm engaged to someone else! Albeit someone who I haven't exactly missed since I got here. But now I'm ready to just jump into Lucas's arms at the first opportunity? Is Luna right about this place being some kind of sexual vortex? Or is this a sign I need to end things with Chase?

I struggle fruitlessly to untangle my feelings as I follow Lucas silently up the embankment and upstream along the water's edge until we reach a large, jagged rock nearly swallowed by a white-blossomed crawler. I'm so agitated, I would probably miss one of the jaguars standing right in front of me right now, but he's completely focused as he surveys the forest, no hint that anything just transpired between us, which leaves me even more confused.

"There." Lucas indicates two ropelike vines that crisscross above the carcass of a fallen tree. I trail him past the tree's jagged trunk, crawling with dime-sized ants, between a clump of palms shot through with yellow orchids, until he pulls up short, looking at the cocoa-colored ground. "It was here."

Regaining my bearings, I train my eyes on the ground to scrutinize the sinuous roots, fallen leaves, decaying branches, moss, rocks, dirt, until . . . "I see it." I point.

A wad of forest-floor detritus is clumped together, ridged at one side, and there at the far edge in the mud is the unmistakable impression of a tire tread. Lucas claps me on the back as he rushes past, following the intermittent tire marks beneath a pair of little black monkeys chasing each other through the trees. Suddenly he stops dead in his tracks, holding his arm out to stop me. He turns with his finger to his lips, then points down a ravine.

About fifty yards below us, a muddy, overgrown road cuts through the jungle, winding up the ridge. And there, tromping along the road with his back to us, is a man dressed in camouflage with a giant automatic rifle slung over his shoulder. Acutely aware we're wearing yellow, I sink to the forest floor, pulling Lucas with me. We squat behind a fallen tree watching the man's unhurried gait, listening to the sound of his boots crunching over fallen leaves as he troops down the road, until he disappears from view.

Lucas rises as though to follow him, but I stop him. "You don't sneak up on someone with an automatic weapon," I caution.

"But how are we going to find out who he is if we don't follow?"

I shake my head. "He could shoot you."

Our argument is interrupted by Hikari and Aguilar running toward us through the woods, scuttling over roots and dodging palm fronds, their faces apprehensive. "Where are you going?" Aguilar hisses as they approach.

"It's not safe out here," Hikari adds, panting.

"We were just exploring," I say as innocently as I can muster.

Lucas looks over his shoulder toward the road, his vexed gaze catching on mine as he turns back to Aguilar and Hikari. "Where does that road go?" he asks, pointing in the direction of the road.

Hikari and Aguilar exchange a weighted glance. "The poppy fields," Hikari says. "It's not ours. This is the property line."

"I told you, man," Aguilar chimes in, his voice low. "This is cartel territory. They don't bother us if we don't bother them, but if you get up in their shit, all bets are off."

Hikari waves for us to follow him back in the direction we came. "They patrol this area with guns," he says as we start back up the ridge. "We found a body last year, right around here. They hadn't even bothered to bury it."

I stare at him, chilled.

"Kali wants to see you when we get back," Hikari says as we descend the rocks that rim the waterfall.

My heart races even faster at the thought of another tête-à-tête with Kali. I can't let her manipulate me this time. I have to be the one to manipulate her into allowing us to leave—without, of course, letting on that I think she's keeping us here against our will.

Hikari suddenly freezes, throwing his arm out to stop the rest of us. "Back up slowly," he instructs, moving backward. "Pit viper."

I peer over his shoulder to see a yellowish-green snake dangling from a low branch across our path, pale pink mouth open to display long sharp fangs jutting from the pronounced triangular jaw indicative of venom. My skin crawls as I back away slowly with legs of jelly, barely able to contain my urge to run.

Luna would see the snake as a symbol of rebirth and sexuality, I rationalize, trying to slow my racing pulse. But everything inside me is screaming for me to heed the warning of danger ahead.

TWENTY-ONE

Kali strokes the long furry tail of the little monkey on her shoulder, allowing it to nibble on her finger. "Most people's lives are ruled by fear of pain, which makes them no more evolved than Buddhi here." She calmly withdraws her finger from Buddhi's mouth, revealing a red dot of blood blooming from a puncture on her fingertip. Thoughts of terrible diseases flash through my mind, but she's unfazed.

At least her familiar is a monkey today, not a jaguar.

Untouched porcelain cup of tea in hand, I watch from one of her green velvet couches as she paces before the oil painting featuring gods and goddesses fornicating graphically, while on the couch opposite me, Rex and Ruby catch her words as they drop from her lips, pouring them into the computers balanced in their laps.

"Pain stimulates spiritual growth, and anything that stimulates spiritual growth is positive, a gift from God," Kali continues.

Behind me, the water trickles over the rippled glass wall, a tinkling liquid sound barely audible above the constant drone of insects and warble of birds through the open windows.

"That's all for today, thank you." And with that, Kali sweeps out of the room, her white dress billowing behind her. "Sveta," she calls, beckoning to me.

I follow her out the French doors onto the front balcony, joining her at the balustrade overlooking the flourishing terraced gardens that spill down to the shimmering lake. Puffy cumulus clouds cast shadows on the tufted blanket of knobby green on the far side of the water, and a gentle breeze cools my sunburned shoulders.

She rests her back against the parapet, evaluating me. "I hear you and Lucas went exploring today."

I nod slightly, keeping my gaze trained on the reflection of the blue sky in the lake. "I saw the Mayan temple," I say, thinking of the red-stained altar. "Do you still use it?"

"On occasion," Kali says. "It's sacred ground, only used for certain ceremonies." Before I can question her further, she goes on. "Sveta, I know you're anxious to get back to your life, but the road through the jungle belongs to the cartel." For the first time I detect the hint of threat in her voice, like a smooth piece of metal pressed to the skin that when turned reveals itself to be a knife. Not yet drawing blood but angled to do so, should I make a wrong move.

"What's the deal with them, anyway?" I ask, trying to sound casual. But it comes out *too* casual, like I'm a valley girl asking about a group of skater boys, which only shows my hand.

I can feel the pull of her steel eyes on me, but I don't turn. "I didn't want to have to tell you any of this," she says, stroking Buddhi's little head, "because it's not totally legal. And once I tell you—well, there's no plausible deniability. So if you want to stay out of it—and I strongly believe you should—you'll accept Shiva's latest will, take your five percent, and stop asking questions."

"I want to know about the cartel," I say.

"Your choice." Her luminous eyes cloud. "When the government seized this place after the raid that killed Menendez, the poppy and marijuana fields in the mountains were taken over by another cartel who paid the local authorities to look the other way and continued to use the river and the dirt road in the years this place sat empty. When we bought the property, we had no idea. But we didn't have much of a choice but to allow it once we found out."

"So they still use the road and the river?"

"Yes." She sits on a cushioned deck chair, tucking her feet beneath her. "We found a body on our property last year. As disturbed as I was, I thought we should look the other way—we were in no position to argue with them. But Shiva refused. He was hardheaded that way. He told them they could no longer use our property, and they threatened to kill him. He left shortly after, and they continued using the road and the boathouse just as though nothing had ever happened. And then, on the night he came back, they killed him."

I freeze. "I'm sorry, what?"

"The cartel killed Shiva because he refused to continue to let them use the property," she confirms, resigned. "But if the authorities find out we've allowed them access, we're complicit in their crimes."

I stare at her, my brain struggling to make sense of what she's just said. Whatever I'd thought she was going to tell me, this was not it. And yet . . . and yet. It would explain the mystery surrounding Shiva's death and the armed man in the jungle. Though the fact that he changed his will the morning he was murdered still seems awfully coincidental.

Could it be true? She's convincing, but then she's always convincing. Seductive. That's how she has seventy-five people here bowing down to her as though she's a deity.

"How did they kill him?" I manage.

She draws a finger across her throat. "In his sleep. Well, I can't be sure he was asleep, but I hope he was."

"Jesus, that's . . . *so* awful," I say, contorting my face into a mask of dismay. But what I really feel is a lot closer to disbelief. It's just too far-fetched.

Isn't it? The oppressive heat and the constant hum of insects make it hard to think.

She passes a hand over her face as if to wipe away invisible tears. "I begged him to sleep in the house with me, but he refused. Said he wouldn't live in fear. He recognized he wasn't long for this Earth and felt if his time to transcend came sooner rather than later, he was ready."

"And you're sure it was the cartel?" I ask.

She nods. "Aguilar was standing guard at his door. He had only a knife and there were four of them with machine guns." I notice her hands are trembling as she strokes Buddhi's tail. "They gagged and bound poor Aguilar under the tree house and told him the only reason they let him live was so he could deliver the message that if anyone got in their way, they would be killed. Rex and Hikari found him unconscious the next morning shortly before we discovered Shiva. We couldn't let anyone know the truth about what happened, of course. We didn't want to scare them."

I knit my brow. "But how did the cartel know Shiva was back?"

"It could be someone at the airport recognized him, though he was a ghost of his former self, or . . ." She glances over her shoulder and, though there's no one around, lowers her voice. "Someone here could have told them."

"Who?"

"I don't know." She bites her lip and studies me as though debating whether to tell me what's on her mind. A baritone roar suddenly cuts through the noise of the jungle, a reminder of the power she wields.

"You know something," I encourage her.

"Blaze has been the one who communicated with them." She sighs. "He was the contractor when we rebuilt this place, so he was here before any of us, though I always thought he was loyal to Shiva. He's grown secretive lately, but . . . I don't know." She dismisses the thought with a wave of her hand. "Rex runs the boathouse, so he's had some contact with them. Aguilar has as well, as a native Spanish speaker. I know he wasn't happy when we told him exclusivity wasn't permitted here. But he got past it and has been a valuable member of our leadership for years now."

"Exclusivity?" I ask.

"Sexually," she clarifies. "He and Amber were a couple when they came here. But for there to be true equality among a group, we have to love one another equally. A couple can't have an exclusive sexual relationship and be expected not to favor their partner above all others."

"Speaking of Amber," I say, remembering our conversation, "she mentioned to me that she struggles with her weight." I eye her for a response, but her countenance remains placid. "It worried me."

"You don't need to worry," she says. "We make sure everyone here is healthy."

"It's just working in the fashion industry, I had a number of friends who struggled with eating disorders. Some of the things she was saying sounded familiar."

"Thank you for bringing it up, that's very considerate of you. I'll talk to her and make sure she's okay," she assures me.

I nod, unconvinced. "About Shiva—are you sure Aguilar didn't stage the whole thing?" I ask. It sounds implausible, but then, all of this sounds implausible. "Did anyone else see the cartel members?"

"He's the only one who saw them," she admits. "But he had no reason to murder Shiva. I just don't see it."

"Who else knows about this?" I ask.

"No one," she says. "And I'd like to keep it that way." She rises to her feet. "You don't want any part of this. Please, consider my offer. It's for your own good more than anything."

TWENTY-TWO

I peer out the window of the gold-trimmed bathroom to watch a trail of people moving silently into the dense green forest.

"Are we supposed to be going somewhere?" I whisper. "It looks like they're all headed to the meditation studio."

"I'm sure they'll round us up once they realize we're missing," Lucas says.

"Maybe they're doing another love ceremony," I suggest.

He shakes his head. "That's a twenty-four-person thing."

"How do you know that?"

"One of the girls mentioned it."

"I wonder if the love ceremonies were Paul's idea, or Kali's?" I muse.

"Hers. Definitely hers." I peer at him quizzically, and he shrugs. "From knowing him, and what I read of his books, most of this stuff is hers."

In my mind, I replay my conversation with Kali. "I know I'm maybe not as familiar with my uncle's work as I should be, but I get the feeling that on every level, she's distorted his words so much, it's like a game of telephone. And everybody just follows what she says like she has a direct line to God."

"It's what the fanatic fringes of every religion have done with their sacred texts," he says. "Prioritizing obedience to the leader and their interpretation of the text over the text itself and punishing anyone who dares to ask questions."

"This has always been my problem with organized religion," I whisper. "Not the religion itself but the humans organizing it, who turn it into a power thing."

"What better way to control people than with the fear of God?" He leans over to peer out the window, his chest grazing mine as he does.

The nearness of him makes me suddenly light-headed, and I chide myself. But he must sense it, too, because I swear he lingers there for a moment longer than necessary, and when he rocks back to where he'd been standing before, he seems to have forgotten what he was going to say, his dark eyes flickering over my face with something indecipherable.

This time I'm the one to break eye contact. "I thought at first this place might be different," I say, looking out the window at the emerald forest. "From what I'd read of my uncle's books, I figured maybe I'd find something that would make me feel the way my mom feels about church. I always thought that would be nice." I sigh. "But it isn't what I thought it would be."

"Nothing ever is." I can feel his eyes still on me, melting my resolve. "You said that to me, the first time we met. Do you remember?"

I nod, afraid to meet his gaze for fear he'll see all the other things I remember.

His vulnerability with me last night combined with our moment in the woods earlier has smashed the wall I'd built between us, and now, regardless of the logic that says I need to rebuild it immediately, when he looks at me the way he is at the moment, I can't seem to stop myself from imagining what it would be like to . . .

The grating screech of some unknown animal in the forest brings the awareness of our circumstances crashing back to me with the force of a tidal wave. "We need to get out of here," I say, moving away from him.

He crosses his arms and leans against the sink. "You know she's not going to let us leave until she gets what she wants, right?"

"So maybe I should just take my five percent and call it a day," I say. "Let her keep this place and all its problems."

He studies me with that penetrating gaze. "That's the last resort, Sveta. I don't believe for a minute Paul changed his will. Don't let her play you. He wanted you to have this place, not her."

"But I don't know that I want it," I say earnestly. "Outside of the orgies, raids, and murders—*cartels*? Seriously. What the hell."

"That's why he left it to you—so that you would shut it down."

"I didn't make this mess, why do I have to clean it up?" I hiss, a flame of resentment flickering inside me. "Sorry." I take a deep breath and let it out. "I know, he was sick. It's just . . . it's a lot."

"I know." He places a comforting hand on my shoulder. "I hear you. And I'll support you in whatever you want to do. Just at least sleep on it tonight before you agree to anything."

There's a knocking at the bathroom door, and we both freeze. I motion for him to move out of sight, arranging my face into a calm expression as I open the door a crack to find Ruby on the other side. "Hi, Ruby," I say. "What's up?"

"Everyone is heading down to meditation in the kuti," she says. "Kali told me to let you guys know you can sit this one out. Just relax here in your room, or take the opportunity to use the gym or sauna downstairs."

I evaluate her, puzzled by her unnatural cadence and the slight shake of her head as she speaks. "She doesn't want us to come?" I ask.

"No," Ruby says definitively. "You should not come." But there's something in her unblinking eyes, in her forced cheerfulness, that says the opposite. "I'll be here, arranging flowers in the foyer, if you need me. Just make sure you don't go down the back stairs or you'll miss me. Okay?" Her gaze is sharp as she waits for me to nod. "Enjoy your rest."

She abruptly turns to go, but I call out to her. "Ruby—"

"See you soon," she says over her shoulder. And she's gone.

I turn to Lucas, who looks just as mystified as I feel. "I know you couldn't see her eyes, but I swear she was telling us to take the back stairs and go to the meditation studio," I say.

He nods. "I heard it in her voice."

"But why not just say it? No one is around."

"The walls obviously have ears in this place," he says. "And she's supposed to be babysitting us."

I CAN HEAR RUBY HUMMING to herself in the foyer below as we discreetly cross the landing and hasten down the hall to the back stairs. Adrenaline pumping through my veins, I follow Lucas out the door off the pantry, around the pool, and into the forest, careful to travel in the shadows. We pause at the bottom of the stairs to the meditation studio, listening.

A male voice announces something I can't make out, followed by a chorus chanting, "Your body is the temple of the Divine."

Lucas and I strain to hear more, but the voices inside are drowned out by the sounds of a family of monkeys who have decided to have a whooping match just above our heads. Applause erupts, and Lucas and I ascend the stairs as quietly as possible, pausing in the shadowy anteroom with our backs pressed to the wall of cubbyholes.

Through the doorway I can see the open-air studio washed in the green of the forest, the majority of the group seated on meditation cushions facing the platform, where Kali and Hikari stand before three naked women: Amber, Sunshine, and a short, curvy, dark-haired woman about my age whom I haven't met. All their eyes are downcast, their body language apprehensive. In front of them, a naked man I don't recognize descends the stage and begins to dress, next to another woman in the process of dressing. What the hell?

Breathing shallowly, I press my back farther into the wall behind me and exchange an uneasy glance with Lucas, terrified we're going to be caught. *What would they do if they caught us?*

"Amber," Hikari reads from a clipboard in his hand.

Sweeping her auburn hair over her shoulder, Amber steps forward between Kali and Hikari and stands on what I recognize is a scale, her gaze fixed on the back wall. My stomach drops.

"Your body is the temple of the Divine," everyone chants in unison.

"One hundred twenty-six point four," Hikari reads from the scale's digital display. "Down from one hundred twenty-eight point two."

Everyone claps, and Amber beams. I look to Lucas, disturbed.

Once the applause dies down, Kali smiles at Amber warmly, laying her hands on her shoulders and kissing her on each cheek. "Congratulations, Amber. Your hard work is paying off. Not only is your body improving, your aura has never been so bright."

Amber gathers her clothes from the platform and quickly dresses, then returns to her spot on the floor, where those seated around her pat her on the back and congratulate her as Hikari calls the next name. "Blanca."

Blanca's wavy dark hair falls in front of her face as she steps onto the scale, her shoulders rounded and gaze fixed on the floor. I guess she's somewhat voluptuous, but fit and healthy looking—not remotely overweight. None of these people are.

Again everyone chants in unison. "Your body is the temple of the Divine."

"One hundred thirty-five," Hikari announces. Blanca winces and her hand flies to cover her eyes; rage churns in my chest. "Up from one hundred thirty-two point three."

The group is silent as Blanca stands crying, mortified, in a scene reminiscent of sorority hazing from a horror film. But no one pulls out a black marker to circle her fat; instead Kali approaches and helps her off the scale, gently removing Blanca's hand from her eyes and forcing her to meet her gaze. "God gave you this body, Blanca," Kali says, her face sympathetic. "Are you not grateful?"

"I am grateful," Blanca whimpers.

"Then why do you disrespect Her gift to you?"

"I tried," she pleads. "I did my exercise. Maybe I'm just not made to be skinny."

"Are you saying that God made a mistake?" Kali asks. "That the Divine failed to create you in Her image?"

I feel nauseated watching as Blanca shakes her head, fighting back tears.

"That's right. God does not make mistakes. We make mistakes." She turns to the group. "Who do you think knows what is best, you or God?"

"God," everyone replies.

"That's right. Do you want to disappoint God?"

"No," everyone answers.

Tears flow freely down Blanca's cheeks. "God has asked you to keep your body as a temple for Her," Kali goes on. "We are all here to support you." She turns to the group. "Aren't we?"

The crowd nods their heads and murmurs agreement. I hold my breath as Hikari scans the studio, praying we're hidden deep enough in the shadowy anteroom that he doesn't see us.

"You're better than this, Blanca. And I know that next week, your numbers will be down." Kali pats her on the back, sending her scrambling off the stage.

As Blanca hurriedly dresses, Sunshine stands still as a statue at the back of the platform, her vitriolic gaze fixed laserlike on the back of Kali's head. A hush falls over the crowd as Sunshine begins to stalk slowly to the front of the platform, her jaw set. The roots of her blond dreadlocks are frizzed, her light eyes rimmed by dark circles. Rex and Aguilar rise warily from their seats on the floor, approaching the stage as she steps onto the scale. "One hundred thirty-three," she announces, an edge in her voice.

"Down from one hundred forty," Hikari reads from his clipboard. "A loss of seven pounds."

"Congratulations, Sunshine," Kali says. "Your hard work is paying off. I know it's been difficult, but we all support you on your spiritual journey."

Sunshine stares daggers at Kali. "Oh, you support us?" She turns to show her scarred back. "Are these support? Are days of sleeping on a concrete floor and shitting in a bucket support?"

Hikari, Rex, and Aguilar trade weighted looks, closing in on Sunshine, but Kali remains unfazed.

"We did not do that to you, Sunshine. You did it to yourself. You chose to spend time alone cleansing to atone for your sins, and we simply supported you in that choice. You are here of your own free will. You can leave at any time."

Sunshine lets out a high-pitched peal of laughter. "Sure. I'll call a helicopter, like our guests." She points at Hikari. "What was it you said this morning, Hikari? *If I leave here my life will become such hell that I'll welcome death with open arms.*"

Hikari moves another step closer to her, but his face remains stone.

"Hell is a prison of your own making, Sunshine," Kali says. "There is no doubt that if you turn your back on the Divine, your life will become a living hell."

"It's not Divine Will, it's your will!" Sunshine aims a shaking finger at her, clearly coming unhinged. "The Divine doesn't need videos of us bringing ourselves to orgasm to prove our commitment, and neither did Shiva. You do! I know what you did, all of you." She sweeps her pointing finger across Kali, Rex, Hikari, and Aguilar. "The windows in solitary have a view, you know." She turns to the group, her eyes wild. "They killed him. I saw it."

I grip Lucas's elbow, watching in shock as a collective gasp goes up from the crowd, but the outrage seems directed at Sunshine, not at Kali or her men.

"They killed Shiva!" Sunshine shouts, her face red with rage. "Murdered him!"

"Enough!" Kali roars, the strength of her normally light voice jarring. "We'll hear no more lies from you, Sunshine."

It's like watching a car accident in slow motion; I'm so thrown by the sudden aggressive turn of events that I don't notice Rex striding toward Lucas and me until he's halfway across the room.

"Rex," I gasp, grabbing Lucas's hand and pulling him with me out of the anteroom and down the steps.

I sprint off the footpath and into the dense forest as fast as I can fly, with Lucas right behind me. Palm fronds slap my face and branches scratch my skin as we hurtle over twisted roots, trampling ground cover that hides God only knows what. I glance over my shoulder, looking past Lucas toward the meditation studio, now hidden by the trees, scanning the woods for Rex. I don't see him, but that doesn't mean he's not there; I'm well aware how much better he knows these woods than we do—he could easily have taken a shorter path to cut us off up ahead.

Through the foliage, the tree house comes into view, the pylons that hold it hovering above the forest almost mistakable for trees. I make a mad dash around the side of it and up the stairs that lead to the front door, Lucas hot on my heels.

From the deck, I desperately survey the forest looking for Rex, but the woods are still.

"Come on," Lucas hisses.

He holds the door open, beckoning to me. I cast one last glance over my shoulder and duck inside the tree house.

TWENTY-THREE

My pulse racing, I turn to lock the tree house door behind us with shaking hands, but unsurprisingly, there is no lock.

"Hello?" Lucas calls out.

No one answers. I lean my back against the door, taking deep breaths in an attempt to slow my pounding heart.

The space has a soaring thatched roof and smells faintly of teakwood and sage. Before us is a rustic kitchen with a dining table, past which is a staircase up to a loft above. Under the staircase is a door that presumably leads to the bedroom, and at the far end of the room is a simple couch and two chairs atop a colorful tribal-looking rug, facing a wall of windows that overlook the lake.

"What happened back there?" Lucas asks.

"Rex saw us." I cross to the window, looking out toward the path that leads from the meditation studio to the house, but it's deserted. "I was so focused on Sunshine that I didn't notice until he was halfway across the room coming toward us."

"Are you sure?"

I close my eyes, picturing him striding toward me. Could it have been possible he was simply striding in my direction, unaware I was watching him from the shadows?

"You didn't see him?" I ask.

He shakes his head. "I mean, we were in the trees by the time I looked back, but no."

I sigh. "Maybe I'm wrong."

"Let's hope so." He looks as disturbed as I feel. "That was fucked up."

I shudder. "Do you think she really saw them murder Paul?"

"I don't know. She's obviously got some mental stuff going on, but at the same time it sort of makes sense."

The pit in my stomach deepens. "If it's true, we're seriously fucked. What do we do? Should we—I don't know, try to call someone to get us out of here? The authorities?"

He chews his lip, thinking. "I don't even know if we'd be able to reach anyone without cell service or access to the tech room. Plus, I don't know what they could do for us at this point. We haven't been threatened, we're not injured or being kept against our will—as far as we know, anyway."

"Not yet." I grimace. "But it's not exactly like we can leave, either."

"Regardless of whatever happened with your uncle, it would be deeply stupid of Kali to do anything to us. One very ill man dying on his own property is far less suspicious than two healthy visitors, one of whom just inherited the estate."

The fact that he's right doesn't make me any less eager to leave. "Have you heard from your assistant?" I ask.

"My assistant?" He shakes his head. "No, no I haven't. I haven't had a chance to visit the tech room since we spoke yesterday."

"Okay, so that's priority number one," I say, pacing back and forth in front of the window. Having some semblance of a plan does make me feel slightly better, though just the memory of the look in Sunshine's eyes is enough to send chills down my spine. "What was it that Sunshine said about masturbation videos? It sounds like they're being blackmailed."

"These groups always have some kind of blackmail to keep people from leaving or spilling secrets."

The way he says it, I know he's speaking from experience.

"But why do they comply?" I ask, bewildered. "Why do these people stay here, starving themselves, recording videos that'll obviously be used against them if they ever want to leave? I don't get it."

He sinks into a chair, the slanted light through the windows turning his dark eyes bronze as he watches me pace. "They've restructured their whole belief system to conform to this ideology, so even when cracks appear in the foundation, they'll perform Jedi mind tricks not to see them. They want desperately to believe."

"Like confirmation bias with conspiracy groups," I offer.

He nods. "As you said earlier, it's human nature to want to belong. This is an extreme case of it, clearly, but these people have given up everything—their families and friends, their money, their careers—to be here, and this place has become their entire world. Without it, they have nothing. I mean shit, why does anybody stay in a bad relationship? They're afraid to leave."

His words hit me like a bucket of cold water. *But I'm not like these people,* I rationalize. Yes, perhaps I'm afraid to leave Chase, but our relationship isn't bad—it's just . . . complicated. Right?

I go to the window, gazing out over the grounds. The sun is low over the lake, the trees on the far side casting long shadows on the luminous water, the varied flora and fauna that overflow the flower beds glowing purple and red and orange in the evening blush. But under the circumstances, I can't drum up any appreciation for the beauty of the sunset.

Lucas's comment makes me wonder—not for the first time this week— if I'm in denial about my relationship with Chase. And that weigh-in ceremony has unearthed feelings I thought I'd long since laid to rest. Anger at the perpetrators, obviously, but also, strangely, the impulse to comply. The voice that taunted me throughout my modeling days, whispering I wasn't thin or pretty or exciting enough, now asks how I would fare on that scale.

When I started modeling at fourteen, I couldn't believe my luck at being plucked from a cattle call at the mall and was thrilled to be in the big city, treated like an adult. But looking back, I realize a teenager shouldn't be treated like an adult. It's hard enough to be a teenager without weathering ten rejections a week, without being told by the adults who are supposed to have your best interests at heart that you'd book a lot more jobs if you lost ten pounds, got a nose job, and did something about your chin.

Even once I booked a job, I was often treated like an inanimate object—poked and prodded, talked about as though I wasn't standing right there.

"No, use the other one, this one isn't interesting enough."

"Her eyes are too flat."

"She's not sexy enough."

"She's too sexy."

"Try pinching the fabric so her thighs don't look so thick."

When I was twenty-three, I booked my biggest job, a yearlong contract for a well-known luxury brand, only to be sent home because the client decided I wasn't "aspirational" enough. Whatever the hell that means.

I was never *enough*.

It strikes me like a bolt of lightning that even now, I've chosen a relationship that reinforces this feeling of never-enoughness, though in a different form.

"You okay?" Lucas asks.

I look over at him, returning to the present. "The body shaming really triggered me," I admit. "Maybe I was wrong about wanting to walk away. Maybe I should fight for control of this place so I can shut it down."

"You know my feelings." He rises to stand next to me. "But I think it's best we keep our plans to ourselves until we're out of here. Especially after what Sunshine said."

"I thought you weren't afraid of Kali," I say.

"Just because I don't think she'll kill us doesn't mean I'm not afraid of her," he returns.

I look up at him, shaken. "We're gonna get out of here, right?"

And then he's hugging me, his strong arms encircling my shoulders, and I'm returning the embrace, my body pressed to his, my head resting against his chest, gently rising and falling beneath my cheek. I close my eyes, breathing in his scent, the pressure we're under momentarily diminished by the nearness of him.

I'm in trouble.

I pull away without meeting his eye. "We should check out the rest of this space before they miss us," I mumble, moving across the room to push open the door beneath the stairs.

I'm relieved to find there's no blood or any other sign of a murder in the bedroom, but I can't think straight, the feeling of Lucas's body against mine still blinding the rest of my senses.

Focus, Sveta.

A large window looks into the jungle on the far wall, opposite a stripped king-size platform bed with a mosquito net suspended above it. The walls are empty except for a large wooden Buddha carving to one side of the window and a mandala above the dresser.

"Come here," he says from the open door of the walk-in closet.

I flip on the light, illuminating built-ins featuring rows of expensive-looking men's suits, dress shirts, sweaters, and jeans. Shelves of organized shoes that range from sneakers to leather oxfords line the far wall, and the drawers are full of T-shirts and underwear. All the cosmopolitan clothing makes me feel like I've teleported back to New York. "It looks like he wore regular clothes," I say. "And underwear."

I slide out the top drawer in the built-in, revealing a handful of watches, a passport, and a wallet. I go for the wallet as Lucas pulls out a beautiful watch with a brown leather band and a white face and slides it around his wrist. "Patek Philippe," he says, admiring it before carefully placing it back in the drawer.

"It's weird, isn't it? That he had all this normal stuff."

"I wouldn't say a Patek Philippe is normal," Lucas counters. "But I know what you mean."

My arm brushes his, leaving my skin tingling as I open the wallet to see a current California driver's license for Paul M. Bentzen, listing an address in Berkeley, alongside credit cards, receipts, and a couple hundred American dollars.

Lucas fishes out a white envelope from the back of the drawer and extracts a stack of pictures. I look over his shoulder as he flips through them: a younger Paul alongside a guide in Tibet; with a man I don't recognize in front of a prop plane; with his arm around my father, dressed in his fatigues; with a dogsled team in the snow; as a baby in his mother's arms. The final picture shows a grinning blond girl of about eight, sitting in the lap of a slender brunette at an outdoor restaurant. Involuntarily, I reach for the picture.

"What is it?" Lucas asks.

"It's me," I say. "And my mom."

"She's beautiful," he says, studying the photograph. "You look like her."

I manage only a nod as I run my finger over her face. My mother is still beautiful, though she's thinner now, her body hardened by years of back-breaking work, her face lined with worry. "I remember that afternoon," I say. "He played 'Imagine' on the piano in the lobby of his hotel."

Lucas replaces the photos in the envelope and thumbs through the receipts in the wallet. "Looks like he was in South Florida recently," he says. "Palm Beach, Miami . . ."

Something catches in my brain. "Weird. You know that's where my mom lives. But they haven't spoken in years."

He furrows his brow. "When was the last time you talked to her?"

"Christmas." I recall our conversation three weeks ago, distressed to realize we talked mostly about me.

I'd just returned home from Chase's family's Christmas brunch, and was upset that even with our engagement, they'd persisted in treating me like an outsider. But Chase was in such a good mood, and we'd already fought so much about his family in recent months, that instead of confessing my feelings to him, I'd told him I needed to run to the bodega on the corner and huddled in a doorway down the street, crying into the phone to my mom. She was on her way to dinner with a friend's family, then was taking an unprecedented vacation to the Florida Keys, so we didn't chat long, planning to catch up in the new year. But I'd avoided calling after

Chase and I decided to take some space, knowing it would worry her. And then of course I hadn't reached her before I came down here.

I'd never realized just how worried my mom had been about me until I first introduced her to Chase and saw the relief wash over her face. She adored him (all mothers did) and couldn't understand my frustration with his family treating me like I was less-than, because as she saw it, I was. They were blue-blooded American royalty, and we were blue-collared immigrants. She took the long view. By marrying Chase, I would be taken care of and my children would never want for anything. I called her whenever I had a problem with him because I knew she would talk me out of doing anything rash.

But she isn't here now, and from ten thousand feet I recognize that while well intentioned, her assumption that I need a savior is not only archaic but a little insulting. And it only speaks to the depth of my insecurity that I've played into it.

"Hey." His fingers on my shoulder are light, raising goose bumps down my arm. "You okay?"

I sigh. "I'm just having an existential crisis, no big deal."

He gently strokes my forehead, smoothing my wrinkled brow. "How so?"

I know that answering that question will make me completely vulnerable in front of him, but what does it matter? I've been trying for half my life to be someone else—cooler, skinnier, richer, deeper, more interesting, more educated—and suddenly I no longer want to keep up the charade. "I don't think I've ever truly believed in myself," I confess.

I look up at him, his face so close in the tight space that I can feel his breath on my cheek, his eyes like two dark pools. "You could have fooled me," he says quietly. "From the first time I met you, I was in awe of your confidence."

"It's all a front," I admit. "I've never felt like I was enough. And I just . . . I don't want to feel that way anymore."

He takes me by the shoulders and looks into my eyes. "You are enough," he says, and his eyes tell me he means it. "You are more than enough. You're incredible, I'm—" He stops and reaches out to tuck a loose strand of hair behind my ear.

Before I realize what I'm doing, I'm leaning into his hand. Both of us still. My breath grows shallow as he traces his thumb over my cheek and across my lips, studying my face with that penetrating gaze. A small voice in the back of my head shouts that I should stop this immediately, but it's inconsequential in juxtaposition to the magnitude of my attraction to him. I can't pull away.

"Sveta," he says, his voice husky.

He leans in closer, his mouth tantalizingly close, hovering there for a maddening moment before closing the gap. At the touch of his lips, my whole body lights up. I reach for him, my hands in his thick hair, his arms around my waist, our bodies pressed together like magnets.

Tangled up in each other, we plow into a row of hanging suits, sending jackets and shirts tumbling to the floor. The taste of him only makes me hungry for more, his touch igniting sparks inside me like the disco ball that showered us in light the first time we kissed, so long ago.

When I felt this exact same way, before he ghosted me.

And now I have a lot more to lose.

But it feels so good.

His lips are on my neck now, the firmness of him against me an invitation I want nothing more than to accept.

But I can't.

It takes every ounce of willpower I can summon to pull away, the feeling of his body leaving mine like my heart being ripped out of my chest. "Lucas," I say desperately. "I can't. I'm engaged."

"I'm sorry," he says, cradling his head in his hands. "Shit."

"It's okay," I say.

"I'm so sorry," he repeats.

"It wasn't just you, it was me, too."

Our eyes meet. There's no denying how much I want him, but today has only confirmed for me that even if I weren't engaged, I could not have casual sex with Lucas Baranquilla.

Why do you assume it would be casual? The little voice in my head prods.

The way he's looking at me right now definitely doesn't seem casual. *And he thought about me over the years.* When I don't look away, he reaches for my hand and I let him have it, the brush of his thumb over my palm like the strike of a match.

I close my eyes and take a deep breath. "The office must be upstairs," I say.

"We should check it out," he says without releasing my hand.

I open my eyes to find his dark gaze still fixed on me. The pull toward him is so strong I have to turn away.

I can hardly feel my feet for the tornado swirling inside me as we mount the steep stairs to the platform office perched above the bedroom. A maroon rug is centered on the wood floor, and half-walls lined with bookshelves full of spiritual titles are open to the great room below. On the back wall is a desk positioned beneath a window that looks into the forest.

Trying to focus, I slide open the desk drawer, only to find a collection of pens, Post-its, and paper clips. A filing cabinet stands next to it, but it's empty as well.

"If there was anything here, it's gone now," Lucas says.

Our eyes meet, the space between us dense with the residual energy of what just happened. I can still feel him against me, taste him on my lips.

Outside, a bell clangs. Thank God.

"Dinner," I say gratefully, rushing back down the stairs. "We should head back before Ruby gets in trouble for letting us out of her sight. Unless Rex has already said something."

"I guess we'll find out," he says dryly, hurrying to catch up with me.

I do my best to regain my composure as we slip out of the tree house and steal through the verdant woods around the side of the villa, but I'm drowning in a sea of mixed emotions.

We enter through the butler's pantry to find the kitchen bustling with dinner prep, everyone too busy to notice us quietly scamper up the service stairs to the mercifully empty second-floor hallway.

Through the open doorways I can hear murmured conversation as we make our way down the hall. A man's voice rises above the rest: ". . . don't know if more solitary's gonna fix the problem. She's obviously losing it."

This, at least, draws my attention away from my own inner turmoil. But before he can say more, someone shushes him.

"There you are!" We turn to see Luna at the far end of the hall, coming out of our room. "I've been looking for you," she says. "Dinner's ready."

"Thanks," I say. "We were just headed down."

She eyes us with a hint of wariness. "Where were you?"

I glance at Lucas, scrambling for an answer. "In there," I say, gesturing to the sitting room.

She narrows her eyes. "I was just there, and I didn't see you."

"So weird," I say with a smile, looping my arm through hers. "Shall we?" I can tell she's dubious, but she's not sure enough of herself to challenge me.

The slanted evening light through the windows reflects on the frescoes on the ceiling above, bringing them to life as we descend the grand staircase toward the crowd filing into the dining room. "How was meditation?" I ask.

"Sunshine—" she starts, then stops herself.

"What about her?" I ask.

"She—" I think she's about to spill it, but she catches herself. "She's turned her back on the Divine and is suffering because of it. Don't say anything," she adds quickly.

"Did something happen?" I ask, feigning ignorance.

But she shushes me as we near the bottom of the stairs.

I want to press further, to dig up her feelings about what happened, but the foyer is swarming with people and Luna's clammed up.

"Hey, do you think I could get a key to the tech room?" Lucas asks. "I need to check in with work."

Luna's face contorts into a mask of feigned sympathy. "Not today," she says. "Kali asked not to be disturbed the rest of the evening."

"Does no one else have a key?" he asks.

"It's not gonna happen tonight," she says definitively. "But I'm sure someone can help you in the morning."

Kali and her inner circle are absent from the dining hall, as is Sunshine, not surprisingly. Over dinner of chickpea stew flavored with turmeric and coconut, I catch whispered snippets about her from the tables abutting ours, but everyone around us is mum on the subject, causing me to wonder whether Kali told them specifically not to mention it, or if they instinctually know to close ranks.

When the group decides to go skinny-dipping in the pool afterward, Lucas and I easily slip away in the gathering darkness, ascending the stairs to the relative sanctuary of our room, illuminated only by the dying light through the window.

I head to the bathroom to brush my teeth, and when I return, I find Lucas at the window. I can hear squeals and splashing coming from the pool below. "How's the party?" I ask.

"Pretty wild."

Curiosity calls me to join him. Our shoulders brush as we peer down at the glowing blue pool, full of naked revelers. The daybeds and loungers in the shadows at the edge of the deck are littered with intertwined bodies, writhing together in the dark. "Free love," I comment.

"Nothing here is free," he mutters.

After a moment, I feel his eyes on me and turn. "What?"

He shakes his head, his gaze once more swirling with something indecipherable. And there it is again, the heat I've barely kept at bay all day, buzzing beneath my skin.

I force myself to look away. Out the window, bodies glow in the moonlight, slipping and thrusting.

He moves closer, his chest grazing mine, his proximity dizzying.

Now is the time to go to bed. Alone.

Want builds like a volcano inside me. I can't help myself, he's like gravity, pulling everything inside me toward him with a force I can't resist.

When I turn to face him, I find his look no longer indecipherable. My entire body hums with desire.

I don't know which of us leans in first, but in an instant, his mouth is on mine. The softness of his lips, the rough bristle of his scruff against my face, the strength of his arms around me are intoxicating.

He kisses me more slowly than he did this afternoon, more deliberately. I slip my arms around his neck, breathing his breath, feeling the warmth of his body through the thin linen of our clothes as I press into him. Every inch of me wants more, the weight of him against me at once new and yet strangely comfortable. Our lips locked, one of his hands finds its way up my shirt while the other slides down the back of my drawstring shorts. He groans and kisses me harder as I loosen the knot in his drawstring pants with my free hand.

He pulls away and finds my eyes in the gloom. "Is this what you want?" he asks, lacing his fingers through mine.

I answer without hesitation. "Yes."

His mouth is on mine again, hot and urgent now. The moonlight filters through the window as we tumble onto his bed, shedding clothes as we fall, all tongues and skin and breath. And this time neither of us is stopping it.

LIBERATION

Eternal life is a liberation only attainable by the spirit when it has been freed from the bondage of the human body. Once the state of Divine Purity has been attained, the soul can evacuate the body and, no longer burdened by physical or temporal limitations, cross the Divine Portal into the spiritual plane. To cross the threshold of the Divine Portal before Divine Purity has been attained requires the Divine Sacrifice of physical death.

—Kali, *Manifesto*, January 11, 2022

TWENTY-FOUR

Day Four

I awaken in Lucas's bed, our limbs tangled, to find a bleary-eyed Luna shaking my shoulder. I can hear the jungle stirring with birdsong and distant howls as I blink at her, pulling the sheet up to cover myself.

She smiles, her long hair falling in waves around her soft face in the muted morning light. "How was it?" she asks.

Last night comes rushing back to me in flashes that raise the color in my cheeks. She laughs. "I told you so." She drinks in Lucas's sleeping form, barely covered by the sheet, and drops our olive-green clothing on the foot of his bed. "I'm jealous. But we have to get up. Sunshine is missing."

I prop up on my elbows. "Missing?"

"She was supposed to sleep in the infirmary last night but was gone this morning."

I assume that by "infirmary," she means the solitary confinement rooms I saw in the basement. Ice wraps around my heart. After Sunshine's accusations yesterday, I have a sinking feeling that her disappearance isn't coincidental.

"Wake up." I jostle Lucas's shoulder. "Sunshine's missing."

"What?" He rubs his eyes. "When was she last seen?"

"Yesterday afternoon," Luna answers. "She might have just left, but . . ."

In light of how difficult it's been for us to depart, the idea of Sunshine leaving seems far-fetched, unless she knows some escape route that we don't. Regardless, my intuition tells me she didn't simply decamp.

"But what?" I ask.

Luna's muddy green eyes grow solemn. "Well, last year this girl Ivy ate poison berries, so—"

"Intentionally?" I ask.

She nods. "We found her body in the woods the next day."

"Damn," I mutter, disturbed. "That's awful."

Lucas glances at me, and I know he's thinking the same thing I'm thinking. "Has anyone else died here?" he asks.

"Ivy's best friend slit her wrists in the hot springs right after. And there was a guy, Guna, who drowned a couple of weeks ago," she says. "But that was an accident."

I gape at her, horrified. "What happened?"

"We were doing a ceremony to communicate with our higher selves and he ate too much jimsonweed, then went swimming. At least we think that's what happened."

I frown. "So, in addition to Shiva, three people died here in the past year?"

"It happens," she says, seemingly undisturbed. "The work we do is rigorous. We know that going in, but some people still aren't ready for it."

An image of Sunshine's scarred back flashes before my eyes. "What work?" I ask.

"Ridding the soul of impurities is no joke," she says sincerely. "You know, like, in the military during basic training they break recruits down to rebuild them as soldiers? We do that, but with the spirit. We go through all kinds of therapy—"

"Who's the therapist?" Lucas demands.

"We're all each other's therapists."

There's pride in her voice, but what I hear is a dangerous social experiment with as many ways to go wrong as there are participants. A bunch of untrained spiritual fanatics cut off from society, regulating one another? No wonder it's not going well. "And this therapy," I say, still trying to wrap my head around her laissez-faire attitude toward the deaths that have occurred here, "can make people suicidal?"

"Not in the way you think." She sighs, at a loss for how to explain it to a couple of simpletons. "Sometimes people have so many blockages that they hit a real roadblock to healing. They've been broken down but can't seem to put themselves back together in the right way. They see death as a way to clean the slate and start over."

All the rage I felt yesterday comes rushing back. "Maybe people shouldn't be broken down so far that they might become suicidal," I snap. I have far more to say on the subject, but recognize I can't blow my lid right now. I cross my arms and breathe, forcing myself to calm down.

Lucas notices my fury and holds my gaze, checking that I'm okay, but Luna is oblivious. "I know it's hard to understand out of context," she says. "But physical death is inevitable. The spirit goes on. The body has to die so that the soul can be reborn."

I clench my jaw. Organized religion may have its faults, but all the prophets I'm aware of viewed life as a gift and encouraged believers to use all the pain and joy of existence as opportunities for spiritual growth. The only group I know of that uses suicide as a shortcut to heaven are the jihadis, and I think it's safe to say they got it twisted.

"What about Shiva's death?" I ask.

"The illness that killed Shiva was a catalyst," she says. "It freed him from his physical form so that he could continue his evolution as a spirit."

I recognize there could be something beautiful about looking at death this way, but with the frame of reference Luna's just provided, it skews very dark. I can see quite plainly how if someone truly believed this, they might be compelled to commit suicide . . . or murder.

She rises and starts for the door. "We should go downstairs, everybody's waiting."

"Hey," Lucas calls. "I really need to check in with work. Can I get a key to the tech room?"

"I don't know that it's gonna happen this morning with the search and everything," she says apologetically. "But you can ask Rex."

Once she's left, he brushes my hair from my shoulder and kisses it. "You okay?" he asks.

I nod, the moon rock of guilt in my stomach outweighed by the feeling of his scruff against my skin.

"I'll ask Rex," I volunteer. "I think I'll have a better chance than you, as long as he didn't see us yesterday."

"Definitely." His face grows serious. "Let's find some time to talk later, okay?"

My stomach turns, anticipating how he's going to let me down, but he gently kisses my forehead as he rises, and for once I check my insecurity. Regardless of what does or doesn't happen between us, I don't regret last night. Even though I realize it means I'm going to have to come clean with Chase, and his family will be proved right about me.

IN THE DINING HALL, WE find the army-green-clad group gathered beneath the ornate crystal chandeliers, drinking coffee and talking in hushed tones. Kali is again nowhere to be seen.

I grab a mug and approach Rex and Ruby, standing before the vaulted windows watching the mist drift across the glassy surface of the lake. Saying a silent prayer that Rex did not in fact see us in the meditation studio yesterday, I flash a tentative smile. "You guys wouldn't happen to know how I could get a key to the tech room, would you?"

For a split second they both look at me like I'm speaking Dutch, before they remember to don their smiles. "I don't know if anyone will be here to run the tech room today," Rex says.

If he did see us, he's not letting on, and Ruby's certainly not giving away the fact that she all but directed us to sneak over there—a risk I've yet to have the opportunity to ask her about. I fire up my most apologetic smile. "I could let myself in." I bat my eyes shamelessly. "I just need to send a quick email. It's my mom's birthday. Oh!" I snap, lighting up as though remembering. "Better yet, I could use my own computer, if that's easier. I brought it with me, but someone stowed it away, and I'm not sure where."

Rex nods. "I'll see what I can do."

"Thank you." I give his biceps a quick, flirtatious squeeze.

Once we've all downed enough coffee to fuel our search, Hikari breaks us into groups of roughly ten and sends us off in different directions. Lucas and I are split up, with him in a group led by Blaze, headed toward the waterfall. I'm initially placed in Rex's group, slated for the upriver section of the jungle, until Ruby steps in, claiming me for herself.

Our group will be searching the forested area that stretches from the meditation studio to the river, so we head toward the laundry room exit with Blaze's group. As we move down the cool dusky hallway that leads to the back door, Lucas throws an arm around my shoulders. "I'm gonna try to slip away and follow the road," he whispers into my hair. "See if I can find a way out of here."

I nod, cold at the idea of being separated from him. "If I get the key, do you want me to call your assistant?"

"No, just hold on to it. I'll call when I get back with more information."

Once we've rubbed our arms and legs with a mixture of rosemary and citronella meant to ward off bugs, we set off into the balmy morning. The sun is just beginning to burn through the haze, glinting off the dew-covered plants of the bountiful garden that tumbles down to the lake. Across the footbridge over the trickling stream at the jungle's edge, the groups part ways. Amber is the only person I know in my group, so I fall into step with her as we follow Ruby up the path to the meditation studio. The shady forest smells of rain and soil and resonates with birdsong.

"What do you think happened to Sunshine?" I whisper to Amber.

She shrugs uncomfortably, unable to meet my gaze. "I don't know." Her eyes flick from side to side as if afraid someone might be watching before she rushes ahead, inserting herself between two women. I trail behind, feeling more and more unwanted here.

At the base of the steps to the meditation studio, Ruby gathers us around her. "We'll spread out and walk directly toward the lake," she says. "Then back this way, moving downriver."

Everyone talks in low tones as they tramp through the moss and leaves covering the forest floor to take up their positions. Ruby beckons to me, turning her back to the others as I approach, motioning for me to do the same. When we're shoulder to shoulder, she transfers something from her pocket to mine. "Lucas wanted this," she whispers as my fingers trace the jagged edges of the key in my pocket. "I figured you might be able to use it, too. If anyone catches you, say the door was open."

"Thank you," I say.

"I'll tell the others you're sick to your stomach. And this," she says, taking an envelope from the waistband of her pants and slipping it into mine, "is from your uncle."

My eyes widen in surprise, but she waves me on without further explanation, turning her back to join the rest of the group.

TWENTY-FIVE

My stomach is in knots as I hike back down the path toward the house, praying no one stops me. But no one is around. Seemingly everyone besides Kali is in the forest searching for Sunshine. I scurry past the garden and around the pool, entering quietly through the back door.

My ears are strained for any signs of life as I steal up the deserted stone corridor, but the villa is completely still. I insert the key in the lock of the tech room, silently slip inside, and, breathing a sigh of relief, bolt the door behind me. The gauzy curtains that hang in front of the window overlooking the pool are far from opaque, but I'm relatively certain that no one who happens to pass by will be able to see me in the shadowy room.

As curious as I am about what's in the letter, my first instinct is to call Lucas's assistant. That was our plan. I know he said he'd do it, but he's not here, and who knows what the rest of the day will hold. I take a laptop from the shelving unit and google his office phone number.

A woman answers, her voice perky. "Baranquilla Hall Webster."

"Hi," I say. "I'm looking for Lucas Baranquilla's assistant. It's an emergency."

"That's me," she says. "Nina." I can hear her nails clacking over a keyboard. "How can I help you?"

"This is Sveta Bentzen. I'm here in Mexico with him. I know he called you about our helicopter being stuck—"

The clacking stops. "I'm sorry?"

"Our helicopter is broken? Or at least they say it is, that's why we're stuck here. He said you were working on finding us an alternate way home. I was curious if—"

"Svetlana," she says, as if finally placing me. "I remember speaking to you on the phone last week."

"That's right," I say.

"What's this about a helicopter?"

"It's broken," I reiterate, confused. "Lucas said you were finding us another way home?"

"I'm so sorry," she says. "I haven't spoken to Lucas since he left."

This stops me. "No email or anything, either?"

"No," she says, just as baffled as I am.

There has to be some mistake. Surely Lucas didn't lie to me. "Does he have another assistant, someone else he might've reached out to?"

"Just me," she says. "We're a small office, so."

"Okay," I say slowly, dizzy from the number of somersaults my mind is doing.

"Can I help you with something?"

"We're in Palenque, in the state of Chiapas, Mexico. We need a helicopter that can fly to Xanadu, as soon as possible. We're stuck here and there's no other way to leave." My words tumble out like rushing water over stones. "It's on the river in the jungle, they should all know it. It's going to be hard to contact us, so please, if you can find one, just send it. There's a man named Miguel who lives near the landing site and can boat downstream to pick us up. I'll pay for it. We need to get out of here. Please," I beg.

"Are you okay?" she asks, alarmed.

"For now," I say, afraid to reveal more for fear someone might be listening in. "But we need to get home as soon as possible. Please."

"Okay," she says. "I've written it down. I'll see what I can do."

"Thank you," I say.

Unnerved, I hang up, my hand shaking as I replace the handset in the cradle.

Lucas said he'd called his assistant, that she was finding us an alternate way out.

Didn't he?

Maybe he'd said he meant to call her. Or he'd left her a voice mail she didn't get. Or his message was intercepted—not unlikely around here, especially if it was email. I could've sworn he said he'd spoken to her, but I've had so much on my mind, I could be wrong.

I have to be wrong. The possibility that Lucas lied to me isn't one I can process right now.

But if he did lie to me, did he also lie about calling the airport?

I google the number and dial, praying the person on the other end at least speaks more English than I do Spanish.

"Hola," I say when the man answers. "Do you speak English?"

"Un poco," he answers.

"I need a helicopter. Helicóptero? To Xanadu, on the river."

"Lo siento, no," he replies.

"Por favor," I plead. "I'll pay. Mucho dinero."

"Lo siento," he says, and hangs up the phone.

So at least I'm pretty sure he didn't lie about that. I stare at the phone. I should call my mom. I'm about to pick up the receiver again, but then I remember the letter.

I take it from my waistband and settle onto the couch, praying there's something helpful in it. I turn it over to see *Irina Bentzen* and my mother's address scrawled across the front.

What the hell?

Perplexed, I unseal the envelope and take out two sheets of plain white paper lined in black ink front and back with slanted, neat handwriting. The letter itself is addressed not to my mom but to me, signed by my uncle and dated the day of his death:

Dear Sveta,

By the time you read this I'll be gone. The body I've occupied on this trip has been fighting illness for many

years, and the illness has finally won. I'm not afraid of
physical death; I see my imminent demise only as the end
of this chapter, the passing of my spirit from one form to
another. But there are many things I want to tell you before
I depart, things I wish I could have told you years ago.

This letter should be coming from your mother—we have
discussed the contents and she has given me her blessing,
though she asked to speak to you first. Some of the things
here she may already have told you, some she may have left
for me to tell.

I first met Irina two years after she married Hank. I'd
seen pictures of her, but had been unable to visit, as I was
living in India at the time. She was a vision: jet-black hair
and ice-blue eyes, delicate as a bird with the strength of an
ox. And she was miserable. Hank didn't speak any Russian,
and she was working to learn English, but they had a hard
time communicating, made no better by his struggle with
what at the time was undiagnosed depression and PTSD,
combined with his deployment schedule. She'd tried since
they married to get pregnant, but had been unsuccessful,
and was worried your father was going to send her back to
Russia if she didn't produce a baby soon.

I don't know if you remember this, but I lived in Moscow
for a time, and speak Russian. Irina was overjoyed to have
someone to talk to, and we became fast friends—or I should
say, I immediately fell in love with her, and she was kind
to me but loyal to my brother. When Hank began his next
deployment the following month, I offered to stay with her to
keep her company.

We spent the summer going to the beach, to the
mountains, eating ice cream and arguing over Dostoevsky.
She tried to convince me of the merits of Russian Orthodoxy
while I introduced her to meditation. She cooked the

traditional Russian dishes your father disliked, and I took her to tango lessons. By the end of the summer, I was not the only one in love.

Please don't hate her for this; she wanted to be true to your father, but the heart is defiant and neither of us had ever felt the way we did for each other.

We decided to tell him upon his return, convincing ourselves that he would understand: they had not married for love, had no children, and while they cared for each other, she was certain he was as unhappy as she was in the relationship. But when he came back, he was in the throes of a down cycle, more desolate than we'd ever seen him, so we decided to wait.

Six weeks later, she was working in the garden on a hot day when she fainted. He took her to the hospital, where they found out she was pregnant with you. Hank turned on a dime with renewed purpose in life, telling everyone in the hospital he was going to be a father. It was all that mattered to him.

That night she called me, and we made the decision that she should stay with him. We loved each other, but we loved him, too. We knew we had to sacrifice our relationship to save his life.

I know you're wondering if you're biologically my child or his, and I can't tell you definitively. There is a possibility you're his. There is a larger possibility you're mine.

Your mother asked me to stay out of your life so as not to complicate things, and I'll allow her to share with you her reasons for keeping it that way after your father's death. I made mistakes along the way that I take full responsibility for, but please know my heart was always in the right place. I never stopped loving her, and I want you to know that I'm sorry for any hurt I caused you two. I wish I could have been there to see you grow up.

As you'll be receiving this letter after my death, you may have already learned that I've left my entire estate to you.

My former partner Kali has taken over the operation of xanadu while I've been gone the past two years, and I must warn you: she will not be happy when she learns she is not my heir.

I hope that I will have time to disband the Mandala and right the wrongs done in my absence before my time comes, but I fear that it will fall to you.

xanadu was a fever dream, just like the poem: "A savage place! as holy and enchanted as e'er beneath a waning moon," but dreams are inherently ephemeral. How egotistical of me to believe that I could bend the laws of human nature to create a lasting utopia, when no one else before me had been able to do so. I should have ended the experiment when it began to fail; instead I walked away, leaving it in the hands of the "woman wailing for her demon-lover!" I was that lover, turned demon by neglect, and she was drunk on the milk of paradise, her disciples made supple with heaping servings of honey-dew. The shepherd left the flock, and driven by the need to belong, the sheep followed the wolf, believing her to be the God she claims to be.

"And all who heard should see them there, and all should cry, Beware! Beware!"

Kali is no God, but the taste of power is a compulsive nectar. I've sampled it myself and was afraid of my appetite.

xanadu must end. But the monster I created has matured into a savage beast that will not meet its demise without a fight. I am prepared to lay down my life to finish what I began. If I fail, I give you full rein to destroy everything in order to end it.

I wish that we'd had more time together. Please know

that I've watched you from afar all these years, and I am so proud of you.

I love you always,
Paul

I stare at the page in shock, the tendrils of fear spreading through my body like creeping vines, intertwining with the heaping pile of burning ash that is everything I believed about my past.

My mother and my uncle?

There is a larger possibility you're mine.

But I don't have time to untangle that bombshell for the other, more pressing issue: Paul didn't change his will to favor Kali and he almost certainly wasn't killed by the cartel. He came down here to end this place knowing he was walking into the hornet's nest, and Kali killed him for it. I know it more clearly than I know who I am—which, to be fair, is murky at the moment. I'm trapped here in the jungle with a wolf, drunk on the milk of paradise, and everything I thought I knew about my history is a lie.

My head is spinning so fast, I think I might be sick.

How long had my uncle known Kali was dangerous? What of our scheduled lunch in New York? It seems increasingly likely that he never emailed me to begin with; that it was Kali all along, aiming to create some sort of alliance with me. She had to know he didn't agree with the direction she was taking things and must have at least had an idea that she might be cut out of the will.

Then why kill him?

The answer is as ugly as it is clear: she assumed I'd be more controllable than he was. When she learned I'd inherited the estate, she drafted the new will and invited me down here to manipulate me out of my inheritance, supposing I'd either be naïve enough to fall under her spell or intimidated enough to give her what she wants.

But she underestimated me. For all my insecurities, I am both sharper and more courageous than she gives me credit for being. Of that, I am sure.

Outside I hear voices and peer through the sheer curtains to see what must be the lunch service crew filtering in from the forest, shading their eyes against the noonday sun. Their voices don't sound excited or urgent, which leads me to believe they haven't found any sign of Sunshine.

I stuff the letter inside the waistband of my shorts, waiting for the noise to be contained inside the kitchen before I slip into the hallway, quietly locking the door behind me. I creep down the corridor and ascend the stairs like the wind, two at a time. A peal of laughter from the kitchen pushes me even faster. As I race down the hallway that leads to my room, an unmistakable voice stops me in my tracks.

"Sveta."

TWENTY-SIX

Kali stands on the landing in her usual long white dress, illuminated from above by the skylight in the cupola so that she glows like an angel.

"I'd like a word," she says calmly. "In your room."

"Sure!" I respond, my voice too high.

I'm panicking inside as she follows me down the hall. I'm no longer fooled by Kali. But if I want to get out of here alive, I can't let her know that.

"Everything okay?" I ask once we're in my room.

"Ruby told me you weren't feeling well," she says. She's backlit by the window, the swirling scarlet rug casting a red glow on her white dress and reflecting in her eyes so that they sparkle like rubies. The effect is unnerving. "I expected to find you in bed."

"I've been resting in the lounge downstairs," I quickly lie. "Hoping to feel better so I can rejoin the search party."

"Your aura is muddy." She leans against the windowsill, studying me. "You really should drink the tea," she suggests. "There are all kinds of bacteria and insects down here that your body is unfamiliar with, that can cause inflammation and indigestion. The tea is designed to combat that."

And make us easier to control, I think. But I simply nod. "Okay, thanks."

"I notice you haven't been drinking it," she presses.

"I'm just not much of a tea person, to be honest," I say, sitting on my bed. "But I'll give it a try if it'll help my stomach."

Her gaze is steady. "You told Lucas about how Shiva died?"

You killed him, you psycho bitch. "The cartel, yeah."

"And what did he say?"

"I mean, he thought it was pretty crazy," I answer, picking at what remains of my chipped gold nail polish from New Year's Eve, two weeks and a lifetime ago. "He's anxious to get back to San Francisco. Have you heard anything about our helicopter?"

"They've located the part in Mexico City," she says without missing a beat. "They're shipping it to Palenque, then will install it. A few days, no more."

"That's good to hear," I say. "Any news about Sunshine?"

Her face darkens. "That's what I came to talk to you about. I had a phone call just now, from a man who identified himself as part of the cartel. He said they picked up Sunshine last night on their property and are demanding a ransom for her release."

I stare at her, processing. The truth? Or another lie? The web she's spun is so thick, I have no idea what I should believe. "I thought you had an understanding with them," I venture.

"An understanding that includes staying off their property," she returns.

"How much do they want?" I ask, dubious.

"One million US dollars, transferred to a numbered account."

"Did they give you proof of life?" I ask.

She nods. "I spoke to her. She didn't sound like she was in good shape, but she was alive. We're lucky they didn't kill her. Yet."

This all seems incredibly far-fetched, but I'm in no position to confront her. "Do you have access to that kind of money?" I ask. "With Shiva deceased?"

"In the business account," she says. "Hikari assures me that during probate I'm authorized to make any transactions to keep the business running, regardless of which will prevails in the event of a challenge. But I wanted you to be aware of it, before Lucas objects, and understand that this is a necessary transaction to preserve her life."

Even if she's lying, I don't see that there's much I can do about it. "Of course."

Her gray eyes are steely. "So you'll ensure he doesn't interfere."

"I don't know where he is right now," I say, trying to keep my voice as calm as hers, though my heart is beating so loudly, I'm surprised she can't hear it.

"He'll be on his way back to the house with Blaze."

Sure enough, outside I register the voices of everyone returning from the jungle. "They all know?" I ask.

She nods.

"Can I ask you something?"

"Of course," she replies with a phlegmatic smile. "Ask me anything."

"Why stay here?" I ask. "You have to allow the cartel that killed your husband to use your land, you're so cut off from society that if there's something wrong with the helicopter, you could be stuck for weeks . . . I don't get it."

She sweeps the curtains aside and peers out at the treetops. "This place is special. It's one of the most sacred places on earth." When she turns back to me, her eyes are feverish. "The world as we know it is ending—climate change, pandemics, famine, weapons of mass destruction—and this place—*right here*—is where the human race will be reborn."

"How do you know that?" I ask.

"The Divine guided Shiva to this place, and now that same Divinity speaks to me," she says, her face enraptured. "The work we're doing here is so important to the future of mankind. We are evolving to the next plane, eliminating the flaws in our human form to merge with Spirit and become enlightened beings who can lead the evolution of the world to a place of peace and love, completing the circle of life."

I swallow, hoping my wide-eyed nods sufficiently cover my incredulity. But Kali's blind to my skepticism, her vision obscured by the blaze of belief.

"The energy field here creates a vortex that vibrates at a level so close to the Divine, it's possible to close the gap," she continues. "The temple you saw is a portal. The Mayans before us knew it, and I know it now." I can nearly feel the heat from the blaze that burns inside her, rising in waves off her flawless bronze skin. "Shiva wasn't ready. He was overwhelmed by it, and his human doubts festered and turned into illness. Divine Will brought us together, so that I could learn from him and take over the leadership of his flock. He is my guru, and I will be forever in debt to him, but it's up to me to lead these souls through the portal. I resisted the call at first, but I know now that I am the chosen one. *I* am the Kavi."

The Kavi. Why does that sound so familiar? I can't quite place it. But I'm certain I've heard it before, though not from her. Maybe it was from someone here, speaking of her?

What's startlingly clear is that, as Lucas suspected and Paul confirmed in his letter, Kali is not the consort, she's the queen.

I think of a documentary series I binge-watched a couple of years ago, about a cult from the seventies and eighties where the deified leader was always sequestered, leaving the woman who was his second-in-command to call the shots, which she attributed to him. It was ingenious, really, shifting authority and blame onto a rarely seen entity, made only more venerated by his absence. It allowed the "second-in-command" to remain beloved by the people, untouched by the disciplinary measures ostensibly doled out by the leader. After all, everyone knows not to shoot the messenger. It seems as though Kali has taken a page from her book.

"I'm sorry to interrupt." Aguilar bows slightly from the doorway, his eyes trained on Kali. "You're needed upstairs."

She turns her magnetic gaze back on me, her geniality restored. "Thank you for being so understanding," she says, squeezing my hand affectionately. "We'll chat after the ransom has been paid and Sunshine has been safely returned. Stick around the house this afternoon."

As pleasantly as she says it, I recognize an order when I hear one.

After she departs, I rise and go to the window, pushing aside the curtains to watch the olive-clad group trickle in from the dense forest, talking among themselves as they trek across the pool deck through dappled light. The trees at the edge of the wilderness cast shadows that merge with the shade of the villa, creating the illusion that the jungle is closing in, the branches reaching, grasping, constantly encroaching like strangler figs. I get the feeling if I stand still for too long, vines will wrap around my legs and keep me here forever.

TWENTY-SEVEN

In the dining hall, nearly everyone is wet, having hit the hot springs to wash off the jungle. Lucas, however, is missing.

I fill my plate with some concoction of quinoa, peppers, and jackfruit, and take the chair next to Ruby, across from Blaze. I want to ask Blaze about Lucas, but don't want to alert him to the fact that Lucas is missing if he slipped away without telling him, so I don't say anything. Instead, I listen to the gossip from neighboring tables as everyone discusses Sunshine's kidnapping.

". . . because she was upset," a girl behind me is saying.

"Try wacko," a second girl declares. "That stunt yesterday was nuts."

"Maybe she wanted to be kidnapped," a male voice suggests. "We all know not to go into cartel territory."

Blaze catches my eye across the table. His energy is subdued today, his twinkling eyes flat. "He'll be back soon," he says quietly. It takes me a moment to register that he's talking about Lucas.

I nod, relieved that Blaze knows what Lucas is up to, and is supportive. Maybe we have more allies here than we realize. God, I hope so.

Ruby gives me a half-hearted smile. "Wanna go for a walk after lunch?" she asks.

Beneath the table, I finger the key to the tech room in my pocket, wondering if she wants it back. "Kali asked me to stick around the house," I say.

"We won't go far," she promises, pushing the food around on her plate. "We could go now. Jackfruit isn't really my thing."

"Mine, either." Stringy and pungent, it's my least favorite meal yet. I scan the room to confirm Kali hasn't turned up.

Ruby rises from the table with her plate in hand, looking at me pointedly. "Shall we?"

I trail her through the swinging door to the cavernous kitchen, where we scrape our food into the mulch bin and deposit our dishes in the hands of the guys on dishwashing duty, then exit by the back door off the butler's pantry.

The second I step outside, the heat hits me like walking into a sauna. "Wow," I say.

"It's a hot one," Ruby agrees, sweeping her braids off her neck and tying them back with a strip of fabric she unwinds from around her wrist.

Instead of going straight into the forest toward the temple or to the right, in the direction of the pool, she turns left and follows a packed dirt path between raised wooden planting beds baking in the noonday sun. A handful of gardeners in straw hats work in the oppressive heat, pruning and picking beans.

"This is where we grow most of our edibles," she says, sweeping her hand out at rows of full-to-bursting raised and in-ground beds that occupy what must be at least a half acre of tilled ground between the side of the house and the forest.

I gaze longingly at the gloriously shaded forest as she calls out the names of the plants we pass. It's so sweltering I can hardly breathe, and my mind is jam-packed with so much anxiety that it's impossible to focus on what she's saying, let alone retain any information. Nor can I ask her the questions on the tip of my tongue in the presence of the gardeners among the rows.

"Arugula, kale . . ." Both are leafy and healthy, not a bug in sight. "Thyme, rosemary, mint . . ." She picks a mint leaf and places it on her tongue. I do the same, plastering the rough leaf to the top of my mouth and running my tongue over it, savoring the cooling taste. "Basil, to-matoes . . ." The tomatoes are fire-engine red, juicy enough to be eaten straight off the vine. "Snap beans, kidney beans—we have a lot of differ-ent beans, they're a big part of our diet . . ."

"Everything looks so healthy." I feign interest, caressing a wide leaf of purple and green amaranth. "How do you keep the bugs away?"

"We have a whole row devoted to bug deterrents," she says. "Some we grind into a powder, others we press into oil and mix into a spray. The earth provides and protects."

Ruby turns left again, moving along the path at the garden's edge that slopes gradually down toward the sparkling lake. The row closest to the water is surrounded by a chain-link fence with a padlocked gate. Ruby glances over her shoulder before taking a key from her pocket and open-ing the lock.

"Why's this row locked?" I ask.

"This is where we keep the good stuff," she says with a wink.

The gardener picking tomatoes one row over looks up as Ruby latches the gate behind us and points to a group of small trees with dark green leaves and furry yellowish buds. "Muira puama," she says. "Native to the Amazon, but we haven't had any trouble getting it to grow here."

"It's an aphrodisiac, right?" I ask, wondering whether she's really dragged me out here simply to show me the garden.

She nods. "The bark and roots are used as a sexual tonic and are also good for treating menstrual cramps and upset stomach."

She wanders over to a raised bed, where she points out a row of low, frilly, fernlike bright green plants. "Shatavari," she says, loud enough the gardener can hear. "Usable as an immunity and mood booster, mainly. The roots grow in this crazy-looking bunch bigger than the top." She indicates a minty-looking plant with small tubular blue flowers. "Skull-cap. Antibacterial, antiviral, anti-inflammatory, and anti-anxiety."

"How'd you learn all this?"

She picks a leaf and pops it in her mouth. "Kali taught me. She trained under a master herbalist."

A bell rings. Out of the corner of my eye, I see the tomato picker gathering his things.

"What's this?" I ask, squatting next to a low-lying hedge covered in sweet-smelling yellow flowers.

"Saint-John's-wort. It's an antidepressant, and also good for treating wounds and bruises. Most of these plants have multiple uses."

"Do you guys ever use, like, Tylenol? Or antibiotics?" I ask.

She shakes her head. "We believe healing should only come directly from God, in the form of plants and natural remedies such as cleansing, meditation, and orgasm."

She pulls me into the shade of the muira puama trees, her eyes fixed on the gardeners as they move up the hill toward the house. "Paul had changed his mind about medicine, though."

"You call him Paul," I note.

"He asked me to, the last time I saw him." She carefully gauges my reaction as she speaks, her forehead knit with anxiety. "He said he was just a man and no longer wanted to be called by the name of a god."

"He gave you the letter?"

She nods. "The day he died."

"Did you read it?"

She shakes her head. "It wasn't my business. He told me to get it to your mother, but I thought, with everything going on, I should give it to you."

"Thank you," I say.

"I told you I was his personal assistant until he left two years ago?"

I nod.

"We were . . . close," she says haltingly. "He told me things . . ." Her pleading eyes meet mine. "Kali can't ever know, or she would—" She breaks off, her eyes searching mine. "I wouldn't be safe."

A brew of excitement and fear swirls inside me. "Why are you still here?" I ask, hoping my face telegraphs my sympathy.

She sighs. "Until recently, I was as under her control as everyone else here."

"What changed?" I ask.

She moves to a raised bed that holds low, weedy plants with wide ragged leaves, white trumpet flowers, and spiky seedpods. "Datura stramonium," she says. "Jimsonweed. Hallucinogenic deliriant that produces strong spiritual visions."

I wipe a bead of sweat from my cheek, not following.

"A few weeks ago, Kali asked us to add it to a tonic for use in a ceremony communicating with our higher selves, and I refused. Jimsonweed can be dangerous even in a supervised environment, but seventy-five people taking uncontrolled amounts without supervision is a recipe for disaster. She berated me, said I was enslaved to worry and that my fear was a cancer that would spread if I were in the community, so she sent me to solitary for five days of fasting to cleanse my mind, body, and spirit. My first night there, Guna drowned in the lake."

I look out toward the dark water, shimmering in the midday sun. "I heard about that."

"They blamed it on him, said he'd taken too much—but in this group where we were supposed to be a family, no one was looking out for him. Something snapped inside me while I was in solitary. I'd been trapped in this prison of belief, and suddenly the door flew open and I saw Kali for what she was."

"Which is what?" I ask.

She glances around to confirm we're completely alone, but there's no need to worry: the gardeners have all returned to the house, leaving the day deathly still. The trees don't even rustle; the only movement is that of a solitary fish, jumping out in the lake.

"A megalomaniac. She really believes she's a god, sent here to save us from ourselves. Since Paul left two years ago, she's become obsessed with this idea of transcending the mortal plane through energetic cleansing and surrender to Divine Will, and she has everyone here believing that if we follow her faithfully, she'll lead us through the portal and we'll become immortal."

I tilt my head, trying to understand. "You mean, like, immortal in the sense of the spirit lives on after the body dies? Like heaven?"

She shakes her head. "More like celestial beings or angels, gods on Earth."

"And all the herbs and cleansing and weight stuff, it's all part of this?" I ask.

She nods. "None of that was a part of the program when Paul was in charge."

I slap a mosquito that's settled on my arm, wiping the carcass on my shirt. "Why didn't he do something to stop her sooner?"

"I don't know." Ruby sighs, her eyes sad. "He wasn't perfect. Far from it. And he definitely had a blind spot where Kali was concerned. But he was a good man, who genuinely wanted to make this world a better place. You've heard he was sued a few years ago?"

I nod.

"He wasn't even there the weekend it happened," she continues, "but he blamed himself for it—as did the media. He lost his zest for teaching after that, and Kali started taking on more of the guru role—even though the whole mess was her fault."

"How so?" I ask.

"The love ceremony is her thing, not his. She's the one who oversaw it and decided to open it to non-initiates back in Sonoma. He was skeptical, but she was so passionate about sharing the healing power of orgasm and he was so passionate about her that he allowed it to go on. Afterward, he moved down here with us, but he wasn't around much even from the beginning, spending most of his time in meditation or traveling alone. By the time he left two years ago to seek cancer treatment in the US, Kali was already the de facto leader, and the people here were her people, not his."

Growing faint in the sweltering heat, I sit on the lip of the wooden planter box in the dappled shade. "But if you were so close with him, why did you stay here with Kali?"

She perches next to me, her face full of regret. "After he retreated from community life, Kali took me under her wing and elevated me to her kula, and I fell under her spell like everyone else. You have to understand, the change in ideology didn't happen overnight. It was gradual—

and thrilling, the idea of becoming one with Spirit. I believed as much as everyone that we were doing God's work.

"When Paul came back to visit last spring after being gone for over a year, he quizzed me about what had been going on in his absence, but I was so blinded by faith that I defended Kali and assured him everything was well—which I believed it was. It wasn't until after he left that the solitary confinement and self-flagellation started. And still, at that time I was so indoctrinated that I saw it as a necessary part of the process." I picture Sunshine's scarred back, Amber's empty plate. "The pledge wasn't instituted until after Guna died, a month ago, and by that time I'd lost faith."

"The pledge?" I ask.

"We each had to submit a video, bringing ourselves to orgasm. To prove our devotion."

I nod, remembering Sunshine's unhinged display.

"So, what happened after Guna died?" I press.

"I had no choice but to pretend everything was fine and wait for an opportunity to leave. As you've seen, it's not easy. And like everyone, I'd turned over all my money to the Mandala when I moved down here, which makes it that much harder."

I raise my brows, incredulous.

"I know, I know," she concedes. "But it was a 'pay-what-you-can,' donation-based gesture of gratitude' that made sense at the time—all my needs are met here. Regardless, I knew I needed to get in touch with Paul, but all our communication is monitored, so I really couldn't. Someone must have somehow, though, because the night he died he told me he'd come back with a plan to shut down Xanadu."

"How do you think he died?"

"Not by natural causes, I can tell you that much." She trails her fingers through the skullcap. "He was frail, but not deathly ill. We didn't speak for long, but he must've had some idea what might be coming, because he asked me to make sure your mother got the letter in the event anything happened to him. I left that note on your pillow the first night, too," she confesses. "I was afraid for you."

The more she talks, the more afraid for myself I'm becoming. "Kali told me the cartel killed him, for reneging on his agreement to let them use the property as a cut-through to their poppy fields," I say.

"I don't believe that. It's too convenient." Ruby glances up at the hulking villa, backlit by the sun. "Kali killed him, Sveta. I know she did or had someone do it. Sunshine found out, so they killed her, too. Just watch. She won't turn up. This whole ransom thing is a red herring."

As much as I don't want it to, it makes total sense. "And Kali gets a million dollars," I add. "In case I fight her on the will."

"The will?" she asks.

"I'm the sole beneficiary of the will Paul filed with Lucas's father. But Kali says he wrote a new one the day he died that gave everything to her. It's signed by multiple witnesses."

"'Witnesses.'" Ruby makes air quotes with her fingers. "Ha. Most of the people here would follow her into a fire, no questions asked."

The image of Kali circling the crackling funeral pyre in her white dress materializes before me. "But why?" I ask.

She shakes her head, apprehensive. "They believe she's a goddess, the embodiment of the Divine, that she's guiding them to immortality. The Kavi."

There's that word again. My inability to place where I've heard it chafes like an itch I can't quite scratch.

"Stealing your inheritance is the least of it," Ruby continues. "I'm afraid for your life. And not just yours. I worry, if she doesn't get what she wants, what she'll do to the rest of us."

The fear in her eyes sends a shard of ice into my heart. "What do you mean?" I ask.

She rises, gesturing for me to follow. "Let me show you."

Just outside the gated garden, she pulls me close enough that I can smell the rosemary and citronella bug deterrent on her skin. With our lines of vision in sync, she points in the direction of the stepped flowering garden that spills from the villa down to the lake. "You see those pretty purplish cone-shaped flowers?" I spot a row of stalks whose multiple pale lavender to plum-colored bell-shaped flowers form a cone shape. "Fox-glove." She taps her heart. "Stops the heart. And there"—she points up the hill at a row of tall, pink-flowering shrubs along the side of the house—"oleander. Very pretty. Very toxic. We can turn both into serums."

Before I can respond, she turns and marches around the enclosed garden toward the forest, where she points in the direction of the water. "See there, in the shady, marshy area where the water meets the edge of the forest, the lacy white flowers that look like tiny Queen Anne's lace? Poison hemlock. The same hemlock Socrates drank when he was forced to commit suicide. Looks like it just sprung up there, right? And if we were somewhere else, it might have, but it doesn't naturally grow here. It was planted."

Nauseated, I stare at the delicate, harmless-looking flowers as she tramps up a narrow path into the woods, beckoning me to follow. The shadowy forest is wonderfully dark and cool after the roasting sun, and smells of rich earth and vegetation, but I'm jumpy after our run-in with the viper yesterday. Not fifty feet into the woods, she points at a thick vine growing between two trees. "Ayahuasca. Native to the Amazon but replanted here. We use it for ceremonies. Not toxic, but definitely mind-altering, and can be dangerous when taken in the wrong dosage or circumstances."

I feel a tickle on my shin and slap a bug I can't identify. Ruby certainly seems truthful, but a voice in the back of my mind wonders whether she's really sincere. Is she showing me all this because she's genuinely concerned, or is she manipulating me at Kali's request, scaring me into compliance with her wishes?

"Are you saying you think she'll poison me if I don't give her what she wants?" I ask, imagining my slow, painful death as poison eats its way through me before stopping my heart.

But she shakes her head. "No. I think she'd kill you more quickly and effectively." This does little to diminish my trepidation. "The poison is for the rest of us."

"But you're her flock," I protest. "Why would she want to kill you?"

"She doesn't see death as permanent; she sees it as a bridge to the next life. All that stuff about transcending to the next plane to merge with Spirit and achieve immortality? There are two ways to go through the portal. The first is by cleansing and raising our vibration enough that it's possible to transcend. The second is through physical death." She kicks a nearby log, then, satisfied there's nothing hiding inside it, sits on it. "You remember Jonestown?"

I dredge up a hazy recollection as I lower myself next to her. "Wasn't that the cult in the seventies that committed mass suicide?"

She nods. "If you want to call it that. Some of the members were willing, others were convinced at gunpoint or after their children were shot in front of them." My hand flies to my mouth. I did not remember that detail. "Jim Jones had moved the cult to Guyana because he was getting too much pressure in the US. But when a congressman came to visit with a group of concerned family members, Jones saw the gig was up. He was convinced if they couldn't live the way they wanted, it wasn't worth living. So, nearly a thousand people poisoned themselves like they'd rehearsed."

"Oh my God," I say, so horrified I'm barely able to formulate words. "Has she had you rehearse suicide?"

"No," she says. "But she talks about the evolution of the spiritual self through death and takes her responsibility to lead the people to God seriously. She doesn't believe our vibration is high enough yet to go through the portal bodied, so she might very well turn to death as a way of completing the mission, if her hand is forced. You have to understand, she doesn't see it as murder, she sees it as a way of freeing the souls of her people."

I study her regal face, looking for any sign of trickery, but I find none. Her eyes are clear, her face etched with worry. If she's telling the truth, she's taking a very real risk by talking to me. "What do you think I should do?" I ask, taking her words seriously.

"Let her think she's getting whatever she wants from you," she says. "Leave as soon as you can, then find a way to get us out and shut this place down."

"How?" I ask, bewildered. I'm about as far from civilization as I can get, in a foreign country known for its corruption. Not to mention, stuck here myself.

I notice a flash of movement at the edge of the woods up near the house and grip her shoulder, putting a finger to my lips then pointing. We strain to see the tall, dark-haired man moving down the path from the back of the house into the jungle. I can't make out his face for all the foliage between us, but there's something familiar about the slope of his shoulders, his long, ambling gait. I rise quietly to my feet, watching as he moves deeper into the woods.

My trepidation turns to relief when he swivels his head and I recognize his profile. I whisper to Ruby, "Lucas."

Afraid to call out for fear someone might hear, I evaluate the forest between us for the best path toward him. Before I can move, Ruby grabs my arm, jerking me down behind the log we were just sitting on. She points, and I see another figure enter the woods.

A figure in a white dress.

Lucas stands in a clearing not fifty yards from where we crouch, his arms crossed, waiting as Kali steals toward him, glancing quickly over her shoulder.

He must be meeting with her to try to negotiate our way home. But why do it out here?

They exchange words as she approaches, but we're not close enough to make out what they're saying.

As she draws nearer, she reaches for him.

I blink, unable to process what I'm seeing as she slips her arms around his neck, pressing her cheek to his chest.

The air goes out of me.

He embraces her, his hand big on her delicate back, just like the first time they met.

Only, I realize with a jolt, it wasn't the first time they met. It couldn't have been, the way they're talking now, their intimacy apparent in their body language.

I feel as though I've been punched in the gut, unable to breathe as I watch them converse with the familiarity of lovers.

But he hates her! my brain cries out.

Just like my mother hated my uncle.

No, he lied to me, played me. Brought me down here to what, convince me to turn over my inheritance to her? To them?

But he hasn't. The opposite, in fact.

Perhaps they'd had a tiff of some sort, were angry with each other, and now they've made up.

Only, as I watch, his face twists with fury, his voice growing louder as he pulls away from her. She grips his arm, vehement, but he's not having whatever she's dishing.

A lovers' spat? I strain to hear, but they are still too far away for their words to be discernible.

I glance over at Ruby, who meets my glance wide-eyed, fear written across her face.

That's when it strikes me, where I've heard of the Kavi before.

Lucas.

TWENTY-EIGHT

He's thirty-two, so it would have been about sixteen years ago," I say, climbing onto a massage bed next to Ruby, a laptop between us.

Ruby does the math in her head and types the date into the search bar of the computer she smuggled out of the tech room. It was occupied, but the Wi-Fi stretches easily down the hall to this empty massage room, which mercifully has a door, though no lock.

I don't know what transpired at the villa in the time since lunch; the place was eerily deserted when we returned from the forest, after allowing Kali and Lucas the time to arrive first. They never kissed and made up—in fact, my brain keeps reminding me, I never saw them kiss at all—and they didn't seem to be on good terms when they parted ways. Not that it matters. It makes no difference what terms they're on; Lucas lied to me, again. Slept with me under false pretenses. I'm horribly angry with myself for falling for it, for falling for his sob story about the cult he was in—with her, if I'm right. I want nothing more than to feed him alive to piranhas, but at this point I'll settle for getting out of here in one piece.

"This has to be it," Ruby says. "'July 21, 2006, former missionary-turned-cult-leader Alan Garcia was arrested on charges of sex trafficking, child pornography, and sexual exploitation.'" She shows me a picture of a handsome long-haired man in a white tunic who looks startlingly like Kali. "Does this sound right?"

I nod.

She continues reading, "'He led a group called The Circle on a five-hundred-acre farm donated by one of his wealthy followers, located in the foothills of the Sierras, in northeastern California. His followers called him the Kavi, or the enlightened one, the son of the Divine. They believed that by purifying the body through exercise, fasting, orgasm, and herbs, they might become immortal.'" She looks up at me, her eyes wide. "It's exactly the same." She continues to scour the article. "It looks like they believed orgasm was sacred and didn't believe in monogamy. He had sex with everyone, they all had sex with each other—just like us—Oh." She stops. "They had sex with minors. Shit. 'At thirteen, children were initiated into the cult by sex with an adult mentor, who groomed them until they were considered ready to join the group at large.'"

I shake my head, disturbed. "Lucas told me some of this," I say. "It's beyond fucked up."

"Kali doesn't allow children here," Ruby says. "All the women have IUDs. If it fails, you're expected to abort. She says children can't come through the portal because their vibration hasn't matured enough." She reads further. "But here it says The Circle believed children would lead them through the portal."

"I feel like I remember something about this in the news," I say.

"I don't," she says. "Though this article says that some of the members were from prominent families who sued to protect the privacy of the minors involved, so maybe that slowed the reporting on it."

I reach for the computer. "Can I see that?"

She hands it to me, and I rake through the article, stopping on a picture of a circle tattoo just like Lucas's, described as the mark members were given upon initiation. "Lucas has this tattoo," I say, showing her. "Below his navel."

Her eyes meet mine, disturbed. "So does Kali."

"Mandala," I say. "In Sanskrit, it means circle, right?"

She nods. "What does it say happened to the group, after Garcia was arrested?"

I return to the article, scrolling to the bottom. "Seems like a lot of them were arrested on the same charges he was. They had made video-tapes having sex with minors as assurance of their loyalty to the group, which were later used to convict them." I shudder. "Some ran before they could be arrested, though. And the minors underwent deprograming and therapy."

"But what brought it all to a head?" she asks. "Why did it all come down in 2006, not before or after?"

"This article doesn't say." I pull up the search bar and enter that specific question, then click on the first link. "Here it is: 'A group of concerned family members had been complaining to the authorities for years and had finally garnered enough evidence that the FBI implanted an operative in the cult. When Garcia learned he was being investigated, he realized the end was near and decided to lead his followers through the portal, located in a cave on their property that had been used for Native American buri-als. He and his inner circle prepared a tea of poison but were never able to serve it because the commune was raided that afternoon.'"

Chills run through me. "I worry if I don't sign over my inheritance, Kali will think the end is near and decide to lead you all through the portal."

Ruby nods.

"If I cooperate, then maybe she'll let me return to the US and I can go to the authorities there," I say, chewing my lip. "I'll say you convinced me of it. Increase your value to her so maybe she'll listen to you if . . ."

"She won't listen to me," Ruby says. "She doesn't listen to anyone. And I worry, after Sunshine's meltdown yesterday accusing her of killing Paul, that she may already be making plans."

We exchange a look of dread.

"I think I'll be most useful in the herbarium," she says, "keeping an eye on what's going in the tea."

"Where is that?"

"Under the kitchen, down the stairs in the butler's pantry."

"Okay." I hop down to the floor. "You want to take me to Kali?"

She shakes her head. "If she sees me, she might assign me something that will keep me out of the herbarium."

So I'm on my own.

MY HEART IS BANGING AGAINST my chest wall like it wants out, my breath so shallow I feel faint as I raise a hand to rap at Kali's closed chamber doors. I steel my nerves, rehearsing my speech in my mind with my knuckles poised just above the carved wood. Before I can knock, Aguilar swings open the door, as though expecting me.

"Is Kali here?" I ask. "I need to talk to her."

Unsmiling, he beckons me into the deserted living room. We follow the sound of low voices into the dining room, where Kali is seated at the head of the table, flanked by Hikari and Rex. She looks up and gives me a mournful smile, gesturing to the seat next to Hikari.

"Any news about Sunshine?" I ask, sitting.

"We've just wired the money," she says. "We expect her back within the hour."

"That's a relief," I reply, masking my skepticism. "Any news of what happened to her?"

"She was caught on their property," she returns. "You wanted to see me?"

"Yes," I say, doing my best to sound normal. "I've been thinking about your offer."

She raises her brows.

"You're right. I mean, I don't know anything about Xanadu, and you've done such a wonderful job of running it." Suddenly I worry I've gone too far. No sane person could possibly believe she's done a wonderful job of running it, with three followers and my uncle dead in the past year, and now Sunshine ostensibly kidnapped. But she's nodding as though I've finally seen the light. "Everybody here clearly loves you," I add, for good measure. "I think my uncle must have seen that when he came down here before he died, and I respect his decision to change his will to favor you."

Behind the serenity of Kali's steady gray gaze, I detect a hint of triumph. "Yes," she says. "That's right. You're so perceptive, Sveta."

"So, I'd like to take you up on your offer of five percent of my uncle's estate," I conclude, my heart in my throat.

Kali nods. "I know this decision couldn't have been easy for you."

"In return, you'll agree not to challenge the will." Hikari steps in.

"Of course." I smile.

"We'll need you to sign something to that effect," Hikari says.

I nod as Kali reaches past Hikari to take my hand in hers. "I knew you'd make the right choice." She flashes her enigmatic smile, but the warmth doesn't quite reach her eyes.

"I'll draw something up," Hikari says. "I'll have it ready this—"

He's cut off by a sudden, forceful beating on the door to the suite in the adjoining room. "Are we expecting someone?" Kali asks Aguilar.

He shakes his head as the sound continues, insistent.

"Answer it," Hikari snaps.

I watch through the archway as Aguilar rushes to open the door to a soaking wet, mud-flecked Clef, and another guy I don't recognize. I can't quite hear what they're saying but can tell from their cadence and urgency that they're upset.

"Rex, please get them towels," Kali requests.

Rex hurries down the hallway that extends from the kitchen, reappearing with towels over his arm, which he hastens to present to the shivering men.

Aguilar's brow is pinched, his shoulders tense. I can tell he wants to speak, but doesn't want to do so in front of me. Finally he leans in and whispers something in Hikari's ear.

Hikari gives a slight nod, his face blank, then turns to me, standing abruptly. "You'll have to excuse us," he says. "We have some unexpected business to attend to."

"Has something happened?" I ask.

"I'll draw up the document, and we'll fetch you when it's ready," Hikari says, sweeping his arm toward the door. "Please."

Not wanting to rock the boat, I reluctantly stand.

Kali grips me gently by the shoulders and looks into my eyes. "You were put in a very difficult position and you showed your strength, you listened to the Divine. Shiva would be proud," she says, kissing me on the forehead.

But I can't shake the feeling that something is off.

As I pass beneath the archway and cross the sitting room, I focus on the men in the doorway, whispering urgently. They stop talking as I draw closer, nodding at me uneasily.

On the way back to my bedroom, I notice the mood in the villa has shifted in the short time I've been in Kali's quarters. A small group is huddled together talking intently in the second-floor lounge and the faces I pass in the hall appear anxious. Luna exits her room and nearly plows into me, avoiding meeting my eye as she hurries down the corridor.

"What's happened?" I call out after her.

But she doesn't stop.

I look up to see Blaze standing just inside the doorway to his room, a finger to his lips. He's disheveled and sweating, his clothes splotched and streaked with dirt, his hair wet. I follow him into the bathroom between our rooms, where he closes the door and turns on the faucet to drown out his voice.

"Sunshine's dead," he says, his voice so low it's barely audible over the sound of the water.

My eyebrows shoot up. "What happened?"

"She was stabbed, multiple times."

"Shit." I stare at him, unnerved.

"A couple of the guys found her body caught in some rocks downstream," he continues. "There was a rope around her waist that had probably been tied to something heavy to make her sink, but it looked like it had been chewed in half."

"God, that's awful," I whisper. The image of Sunshine's lifeless body flashes through my mind. "You saw her?"

He nods. "I helped bring her in. Her body was pretty waterlogged, so she must have been dead awhile."

"What about the ransom?" I ask. "Kali says she paid it this afternoon."

He peers at me from beneath a knitted brow. "There was no kidnapping," he says flatly. He shakes his head and exhales. "There's no cartel."

I stare at him, trying to piece together the reality he's just shredded. "But the men with guns—"

"Park rangers. There hasn't been any cartel around here for a long time. I was the contractor when this place was rebuilt, I know the area well. It's just a control tactic."

I don't know why I'm surprised. Everything else Kali has said is a lie. "Why didn't you say something?"

"Kali had me convinced it was for the greater good." He sighs heavily. "She's very persuasive, as you've seen."

"Then who killed Sunshine?" I ask. But I have a bad feeling I know, and the look Blaze gives me says I'm right. "The ones she accused of murder yesterday," I answer my own question.

"That'd be my guess," he confirms.

"But—why are you still here?" I ask. "At Xanadu, I mean. You don't seem to see Kali the way the rest of them do."

He gazes out the small window above the toilet at the light bleeding from the sky, resigned. "I believed in her, for a long time. I thought Shiva did, too. She told us he did, she gave us messages from him regularly. I didn't realize how much of it was a lie until he told me the day he died." He shakes his head. "I'm an idiot."

"What did he say, the day he died?"

"That it was all bullshit, that she was delusional and drunk on power. He showed me an article about this cult, The Circle, that she'd been part—"

"I know," I say.

"How?" he asks.

"Lucas was in it, too."

He stares at me. "Lucas?"

"His mother took him there when he was young. He and Kali have the same tattoo. I only just made the connection today."

He frowns, discomfited. "I told Lucas this morning, about the cartel. I showed him the road and how to get to the park rangers' station. I'd intended to show him the other day, but Rex stuck so close to us, I didn't have the chance." He leans against the marble countertop, his deeply tanned arms crossed. "Where is he now?"

"I don't know. I don't care. He's been lying to me this whole time." I catch and hold his gaze. "Blaze, has Kali mentioned anything about leading everyone through the portal?"

"Of course. She talks about it constantly."

"Not through raising your vibration or whatever, but through . . . physical death," I specify.

"She calls it the rip cord," he confirms. "In case anything happens before we're pure enough to go through in our human form. What are you—"

"Did Paul mention that the leader of The Circle had the same plan? The day he was arrested, he intended to poison his flock to lead them through the portal on their property."

He nods slowly, beginning to understand.

"I worry Kali's feeling threatened now," I go on. "I worry—"

"She might poison everyone the way her father tried to." He finishes my thought.

"Her father?"

"Alan Garcia, their leader. He had a lot of children by a lot of different women, but Kali was one of them."

Well, that makes perfect sense. "Ruby and I read an article today about him."

"Ruby," he repeats, surprised. "I thought I was the only one—besides Sunshine," he adds darkly. "Most people here are true believers who think it's their duty to out anyone who expresses doubt. The last person who started questioning Kali ended up dead, too."

My eyes go wide. "The guy who drowned high on jimsonweed?"

He nods. "But knowing Ruby feels the same is promising. She's done a good job of hiding it." The muted sound of the dinner bell downstairs echoes through the hallway. "I hope you're wrong," he says. "But . . ." He pauses, thinking. "The park ranger station is about five miles down the road. I'm gonna head down there, try and get some help. Just in case."

"I hope I'm wrong, too," I say. "But regardless, I'm signing the document rejecting my inheritance. Giving Kali what she wants is the best thing I can do right now."

He nods. "I'll be back as soon as I can."

TWENTY-NINE

I descend the grand staircase in the dwindling evening light, scanning the room below for Lucas. But he is still nowhere to be seen, and Kali and her inner circle are missing as well, as is Ruby, who I assume is still in the herbarium. The crystal chandeliers in the dining room are dimly lit, residents hunched over their plates at the wood tables, talking in somber tones and exchanging furtive glances. Outside the big bay windows, night is rapidly closing in, the trees on the far side of the lake jet black against the lavender sky, the enormous moon rising like a golden dinner plate.

The meal is the simplest I've seen, with no sides, salad, or even bread to complement the main dish, a linguine with a fragrant mushroom sauce that would definitely make me ravenous if my stomach weren't tied in knots. I load my plate, forgoing the dubious tea in favor of ice water, and take a seat next to Amber, who I notice has no pasta on her plate, only a dollop of mushroom sauce. Across the table, Smoke, the woman with the wild gray hair, looks up at me, tears brimming in her eyes.

"You heard about Sunshine?" she asks quietly, her voice trembling.

I nod. "Were you close?"

A tear spills down her cheek, and she quickly wipes it away. "She was my roommate."

"I'm so sorry," I say, reaching across the table to squeeze her hand.

Amber toys with her silverware with a slightly sour expression on her face, like she's just smelled something foul.

"What are they saying happened?" I ask.

For a moment, no one speaks. I take a tentative bite of my mushroom pasta, earthy and rich on my tongue. The sauce is so velvety and perfectly salted, it draws my attention away from the awful circumstances for a fleeting moment, regardless of my churning stomach.

Finally Amber drops her fork to her plate with a clatter and looks up at Smoke, the corner of her mouth down-turned. "I'm sorry, I know you guys were friends, but it was her fault," she pronounces. "Everybody knows not to leave the property. She tried to leave, she got herself kidnapped and killed."

Smoke eyes her. "That's what they're saying."

But I can tell she doesn't believe it.

The grasp Kali has on her group is slipping, their unity fracturing before our eyes. And that only makes me more uneasy about what drastic measures she might take to preserve her power. You don't have to be familiar with the animal world to know a beast is most dangerous when threatened.

Through the archway in the foyer, the giant chandelier flickers to dazzling life at the same time a fork dings against a glass, and we all turn to see the beast herself, flanked by Rex and Aguilar, dressed in spotless white that contrasts with the dull green of the rest of the group.

Kali certainly doesn't appear to be afraid. Everyone quiets down as she sweeps the room with her hypnotic gaze. "My family," she begins, bringing a hand to her breast. "Our hearts are broken for a second time this week, with the departure of our dear Sunshine." She floats between the tables, squeezing hands and patting shoulders as she moves. "I know this is hard, and that many of you are blaming yourselves for her death, but I am here to remind you that she is closer to the Divine now than any of us, her spirit joined with Shiva's on the other side. So we will not mourn her, but celebrate her transcendence of the mortal plane."

I take another bite of pasta, watching warily as she drifts from table to table.

"I encourage you all to drink the special soothing tea we have tonight to lift your spirits," she continues, "and please, eat. Your bodies need nourishment."

I immediately stop chewing, staring dubiously at the delicious mushrooms on my plate. I've avoided the tea, but didn't think about the fact that she could spike our food. How could I be so stupid, especially after the plants Ruby showed me this afternoon? These mushrooms could very easily be poisonous. I raise my napkin as casually as I can and, when I'm sure no one's looking, spit my half-chewed bite into it.

"The alignment of the stars tonight is auspicious," Kali continues. "We will honor Sunshine's memory with a pyre and ritual at the temple. And I have a special treat for all of you. So please, after dinner, go wash up and change into your ceremonial whites, then we'll walk over together. I love you."

A special treat. That doesn't sound good. The buzz of subdued chatter resumes as Kali glides out of the room. I feel a tap on my shoulder and turn to see Rex towering over me, his wolflike grin out of place in the sea of fretful faces. "We've got that paperwork drawn up," he says. "No rush, finish your food, I'll wait."

Again with the food. Something's definitely not right. "I'm good," I say, pushing my plate away. "This is my second plate."

"Okay," he says. "Come this way."

I can feel the eyes on us as I follow him through the tables into the foyer, where Aguilar waits for us. Kali has once again evaporated.

"I just need to run to the restroom first," I say, darting past the restroom under the stairs to the more private one in the hallway before anyone can protest.

I lock the door behind me and flip on the water in the sink, then kneel before the toilet and jam my finger down my throat. My esophagus burns as I retch, hoping against hope that the bite I took was too small—and the ten minutes since not long enough—for whatever may have been in the food to seep into my system.

When there's nothing left in my convulsing stomach, I wash my mouth out as best I can and splash my face with water, then rejoin the others in the foyer expecting to be led once more up the two flights of stairs to Kali's lair, but instead Rex heads for the front door.

"Where are we going?" I ask.

"The boathouse," he replies without turning around.

"Why?" I ask, alarmed.

"Hikari's office is there," Aguilar explains, casually waving me through the open door. "This won't take long."

The knot of foreboding in my stomach tightens. But I don't see that there's much I can do other than follow. Does it matter, anyway, whether I'm in the villa or the boathouse? I'm greatly outnumbered, either way, and Ruby and Blaze aren't here to help me.

Kali believes I've agreed to her terms, I rationalize; she has no reason to harm me. And once I've signed this document, I have to imagine she'll be far less likely to harm anyone else. I steel my nerves and follow them into the night.

The path down to the water is damp, the air cooler after the rain, scented sweet with blooms concealed by the darkness. Offset by myriad twinkling stars, the nearly full moon is the crown jewel in the night sky, bathing the scene in pale silver light that reflects off the rippling surface of the lake.

I turn to look back at the hulking villa, a phantom in the moonlight against the pitch-black forest, and spy two backlit figures silently watching us through the dining room window. I flinch as Aguilar takes my elbow and ushers me down the path.

Heightened with apprehension, my senses are in overdrive. At least I hope it's just apprehension and not the result of whatever was in the food. The slight breeze is like ice on my skin, the chorus of humming insects and croaking frogs as loud as a jet engine. I scan the cascading flower beds, registering every fluttering petal, every scuttling lizard. Near the water I spy lights moving at the edge of the forest down by the lakeshore, way up-river past the charred ring of the pyre, and strain to see what they're doing.

I count three figures that appear to be wearing the same sort of protective gear Blaze and the others wore while cleaning up Paul's pyre. They're probably fifty yards away, but with the aid of the moon, I can make out one of them holding a light steady while a second crouches and gathers something from the ground, then stuffs it into a large bag held by the third. My immediate impression is that they're cleaning up trash or weeding. But at night, down by the water? It doesn't make sense.

Could they be disposing of something? The specter of Sunshine's waterlogged corpse appears in my mind, but Kali mentioned a funeral pyre tonight. I cast one last glance over my shoulder as we turn toward the boathouse, trying to imagine what they might be doing, dragging my memory for anything of interest I noticed when I was in that area earlier today with Ruby.

Suddenly it hits me: *deadly hemlock.*

I'm nearly sure it was right there. Tiny lacelike white flowers that can easily fell a horse, much less a human. My chest constricts as if in the grip of a boa constrictor, my mind racing. Could Ruby be right about Kali possibly poisoning everyone?

But why now, when I've promised her what she wants?

Maybe I'm being paranoid. Maybe those people at the water's edge are simply cleaning up the deadly hemlock so that it *doesn't* poison anyone. Or maybe they're doing something else entirely.

As we near the boathouse, I hear—no, feel—a deep rumbling emanating from the jaguars' cage that I'm certain is a growl, not a purr. Both animals appear to be riled up, stalking back and forth along the nearest perimeter of the fence, periodically baring their sharp teeth and casting menacing glances in our direction, their eyes reflecting yellow in the porch light.

"The jaguars don't look happy," I comment nervously.

"They're hungry," Rex grunts. He ascends the two steps and pushes in the door.

The interior of the boathouse is brightly lit but empty, the boats bobbing in their slips, the lakeside roller doors closed. To our right is a small office built into the corner of the building, but that's not the direction Rex heads in. I gasp as he strides directly through the open gate to the jaguars' pen.

"It's okay," Aguilar says, pulling the boathouse door closed behind me. "The gate to outside is shut."

Inside the fence, Rex mounts the stairs to the second story. "This way," he calls over his shoulder.

But my feet have turned to stone. Something about this just doesn't feel right.

"You know, I'm not feeling well," I say, my voice quivering. I bend over, gripping my stomach. "My stomach . . . it must be something I ate."

I can hear the eye roll in Rex's exhale. "Okay, let's just get this taken care of, then you can go lie down."

"I think I need to lie down now," I say, wincing as though my stomach has cramped.

"This will only take a minute," Aguilar chimes in.

The door at the top of the stairs swings open. Hikari. "Is something wrong?" he asks.

"She doesn't feel well," Rex says flatly.

Hikari smiles at me, for the first time since I've been here. It's an unnatural, thin-lipped smile that looks all wrong on his stern face. "Come up and have some water," he says. "There's a comfortable couch you can lie down on up here, too."

"I need a bathroom," I say, feigning embarrassment as I back for the boathouse door.

"There's one upstairs," Rex says.

Aguilar blocks my path, his hands behind his back. A heavy dread settles over me.

I see his eyes flick up to Rex and Hikari for just a moment before he pulls the knife from his waistband. I freeze. I can feel my blood pumping in my veins as time seems to slow down.

In a flash Rex is at my side gripping my arm, and I see he and Hikari also have knives in their free hands. All the air goes out of me.

"Upstairs," Aguilar says, prodding me forward with the tip of his blade.

Rex's fingers dig into my skin as I slowly walk toward Hikari, who watches from the stairs like a predator observing wounded prey.

"What is this about?" I ask when I can speak again, trying and failing to keep the tremble out of my voice as I climb the steps. "I agreed not to challenge the will. Kali's getting everything she wants." My heart is galloping like a racehorse, and I think I might faint.

Aguilar and Rex herd me to the top of the stairs, where we follow Hikari through the door to the second story. The musty open space is airless and stiflingly hot, the walls lined with shelving units full of supplies: dried beans and rice, giant canisters of sugar and flour, canned goods, and gardening supplies. The middle of the room is crowded with random bits of unused or damaged furniture: extra mattresses and bed frames, stacks of worn-looking dining chairs, a desk with a broken leg.

Rex points from me to the base of one of the metal shelving units. "Sit on the floor."

I comply, lowering myself to the floor. "I don't know what's going on," I say with as much bravado as I can muster, "but I'll give you whatever you want."

"It's too late for that," Hikari says.

I can smell Rex's pungent sweat as he squats next to me, roughly securing my hands behind me and around the vertical metal shaft between the bottom and second shelves with a piece of rope while Hikari and Aguilar hover above, their knives glinting in the scant light that filters through the open door.

"Why?" I ask desperately. "What did I do? I don't understand. Don't you want me to sign the papers?" When Rex is finished with me, the ropes are tied so tightly I feel like the blood supply to my hands is cut off. "This is really tight."

"The door has a dead bolt," Hikari says, going to the door, "and we're letting the jaguars back into the boathouse as soon as we leave. They have not eaten today."

Despair takes root in me. "Wait! This is crazy! Can I please talk to Kali?" I ask, frantic. "Please?"

But the three men turn their backs and depart, shutting and locking the door behind them.

I listen to the sound of Rex, Hikari, and Aguilar's feet tromping down the stairs, hardly able to breathe for the spiraling horror twisting through me. How stupid of me to follow them here.

I wiggle my wrists against the rope securing them together, but it's tied tight. My panic morphs into anger that erupts in a scream as I struggle fruitlessly against my bindings. She's going to kill them all, I'm feeling surer of it by the minute. I pray Ruby has had more success with executing her plan than I have, but at this point, I'm not optimistic.

I have to get out of here and stop Kali.

Straining my neck to see the shelf behind me, I see I'm tied to a shelf of gardening supplies. I swing a foot at the shelf, knocking off a bag of fertilizer, then again, sending a shovel flying out of my reach. Realizing I need to get my hands in front of me, I scramble from sitting to a squatting position and, fighting against the rope lashing my wrists together, use all my might to wiggle my butt between my elbows. Straining every tendon in my arms, I straighten my legs so that I'm standing in a forward bend with my wrists still locked around the pole behind me. Thanking my stars for all those years of yoga, I step backward through my arms, ending up with my hands in front of me, though twisted.

I lean into the shelf, my left arm over my right at an odd angle, and grab a clay pot from a stack. I smash it on the floor, shattering it, kick off one shoe, and use my toes to pick up the largest shard and bring it to my hands. It's not easy to get into a position where I can angle the piece of clay in such a way that it will loosen the rope, but now that I can see it, I notice the knots aren't tied as securely as I'd feared. Rex used simple square knots, and the rope is stiff enough that they shouldn't be impossible to undo. I set the shard down on the shelf and bite the rope, using my teeth to loosen the top knot. Relief cascades over me as I run my tongue around my mouth, spitting the stray rope hairs onto the floor.

I undo the second knot and then the third with my teeth, finally pulling my hands free and letting out a big breath of relief.

I quickly cross to the door and try the handle, but as promised, it's locked—with hungry jaguars keeping guard below. Not an inviting option. I survey the room, unnerved by the ominous shadows, overwhelmed by the mass of objects preventing me from discerning any logical exit strategy. I scan the walls, looking for windows. There are two above the jaguars' cage, one on the wall opposite, and two that face the lake, all of them at least partially blocked.

I push aside a box blocking the window opposite the one over the jaguar enclosure and lift the weather-beaten blackout shade to peer out. I can see the villa illuminated on the hill, a handful of white-clad figures gathered on the steps out front. Too much exposure, and so close to the shore that I can't be sure how deep the water is beneath.

I sidestep a stack of chairs and climb over a pile of mattresses to reach the windows on the lake side. It's probably a fifteen-foot drop to the water below, but the lake must be deeper here, to allow for boat access.

As desperate as I am to escape immediately, I realize I've got to time it right to avoid being caught again, so I take up a post in front of the window with a view of the house, keeping watch until the figures filter inside and the lights dim. Once I feel certain there's no one around to hear my splash, I return to the lake side, steeling my nerves.

I lift the sash and lean out into the moonlight, the cool night air refreshing after the stifling heat of the boathouse. As I peer out at the lake, shimmering like liquid platinum in the moonlight, I can't help but wonder what terrifying animals call its depths home.

I climb onto the ledge, shaking away the thought. *It's my only way out.*

Before I can chicken out, I take a deep breath and jump, the wind on my skin like flying as I plummet into the lake.

THIRTY

I swim up to the surface of the inky water and brush my hair from my face. The villa is deserted, as far as I can tell. I've lost a shoe, so I kick the other one off, and as I do, something below the surface tickles my ankle. I nearly jump out of my skin, terrified it must be a snake or some other horrifying river creature, a crocodile or piranha.

Something splashes behind me, and I swim for shore like I'm being chased, staying as close to the surface as I can.

When I near the edge of the lake, my feet strike soft, slimy mud that squelches between my toes as I scramble up the embankment onto the grass, wringing out my hair and clothes. Moonlight bathes the gardens in a lustrous glow, casting deep shadows at the edge of the tree line that merge into the formless, yawning black of the forbidding forest. Ducking low, I sprint as noiselessly as I can across the open space between the lake and the garden, the slight breeze raising goose bumps over my wet skin.

A low growl draws my attention to Ix-Chel, her yellow eyes reflecting in the moonlight as she paces along the fence closest to me, staring me down with hungry eyes. I pause, looking back at the cage, scanning for the other one, the big one, the one Kali warned us about, Xibalbá. God of the underworld.

But I don't see him. I rationalize that he must be inside, but the image of the bloodstained altar flashes before my eyes, and it's impossible not to think of Kali's assertion that the Mayans sacrificed virgins to the jaguar gods.

I can say with near certainty that there are no virgins here. But Kali's bastardized so many spiritual traditions, I can't see that stopping her.

No, it's too far, even for Kali. Surely she doesn't intend to feed the beating heart of one of her followers to Xibalbá.

Surely he's just inside.

With a shiver, I turn my back on Ix-Chel and swiftly ascend the path along the forest's edge in the shadows cast by the trees. Adrenaline pumping through my veins, I traverse the footbridge over the stream and move furtively along the top row of the moon-swept gardens toward the eerily still house. What will I find once I reach the temple? The thought makes me queasy.

I consider the villa. As much as I don't want to have to use a weapon against anyone, it would definitely be wise to have protection, *just in case.* After all, I'm alone now.

The thought of Lucas's betrayal raises a blister of rage inside me. It's his fault I'm in this position, his fault I'm here at all. Yet I still wish he were here right now. Wish he were who I thought he was, that I wasn't alone in this nightmare.

But there's no time to dwell on that now. In the unearthly blue glow of the pool, I press open the door to the mudroom, saying a prayer it's vacant.

Inside, the house is quiet, the room lit only by the light from the hall-way beyond. I grab a dress off a rolling rack of white linen garments and shimmy out of my wet clothes, slipping the dress over my head. Once I'm clothed, I snatch a pair of sandals from the shelf and steal into the corridor, shoes in hand.

I turn off the hall light and creep along the darkened passage to the lounge that opens onto the pool. It's deserted. I pass through the foyer, glancing into the living room before crossing the dining hall and exit-ing through the swinging door to the cavernous kitchen, lit only by the under-cabinet lights.

I see a knife block on the counter and pull the first curved black handle, exposing a meat cleaver. Not right. The handle next to it belongs to a thin blade so long it would be cumbersome; the one beneath reveals a deadly-looking chef's knife with a palm-length blade. The light caresses the sharp edge as I turn it in my hands, then lay it on the granite. A good option. I extract a smaller paring knife from the block. An even better option.

I move it around, getting used to the feel of it in my hand.

A thump comes from somewhere in the house, and I drop to my knees, crouching behind the island, listening intently as another thump breaks the silence. This time I realize it's coming from somewhere below me. Wasn't that where Ruby said the herbarium was located?

I hear a muffled cry.

Gripping the chef's knife in one hand and the paring knife in the other, I skid into the butler's pantry and swing open the door to the stairs, feeling my way downward in the dark. The cries get louder as I approach, feeling along the wall for a light switch. At the bottom of the stairs, my fingers catch on something bumpy and plastic, and the blackness is suddenly blown away by dazzling light.

Before me is a room about half the size of the kitchen, the walls covered with built-in shelves lined with jars of every size and shape, holding all manner of indiscernible substances, above wide counters with two sinks and a cooktop. In the center of the room, beneath an abundance of hanging dry herbs, is Ruby, bound to a chair and gagged.

I rush over to her, quickly ripping the duct tape from over her mouth. She draws in a grateful breath. "Are you okay?" I ask, slicing the bindings from her wrists and ankles.

"I think so," she says, rubbing her chafed wrists.

"What happened?" I ask.

"I failed," she says, distraught. "After I left you, I waited down here until Karma and Karuna came down to make tonight's elixir. They were suspicious because I haven't been on herb duty since the jimsonweed incident, but I convinced them Kali had asked me to help since tonight was special." She fingers the bump on her forehead. "At first everything seemed normal, we made a celebratory tonic—but then Hikari and Aguilar came down carrying these big bags."

"Of what?" I ask.

Her lip trembles. "Hemlock."

My blood runs cold. "Oh God."

"They had us put on masks and gloves to handle it. Karma and Karuna were so calm, so focused. I kept waiting for Aguilar and Hikari to leave, thinking I'm stronger than Karma and Karuna, I could probably fight them off if I had to—but they didn't leave. I knew I had to speak up. I started by invoking Shiva, telling them this wasn't what he would have wanted. But they didn't listen. I quoted him, I quoted scripture, and they called me a censor, a traitor. I begged them, told them to at least give everyone a choice—then they were on me. I managed to grab a lighter and tried to light the pile of hemlock, but it was so wet, it didn't burn. Then—" She breaks off, at a loss. "That's the last thing I remember. They must have knocked me out."

"It's a miracle they didn't kill you."

She shakes her head. "They wouldn't unless they felt they had no choice—like with Sunshine making noise about Paul's murder. They see death as a privilege."

So that's why they'd left me alive.

"They threatened me with knives," I divulge. "Locked me in the boathouse—I'm guessing right before they came here."

"We have to go to the temple," she urges. "We have to stop her."

I press the paring knife into her hand, bracing myself for whatever lies ahead. "Was the poison in some kind of container?" I ask.

She nods. "One of the giant drink dispensers they use."

"We have to get rid of it before anyone drinks it."

She levels her gaze at me. "If we're not too late."

Wasting no time, we run up the stairs and out through the back of the villa.

Outside, Ruby's olive green provides greater camouflage than my white dress, which turns me spectral in the light of the moon. We hasten along the path that leads into the woods and make our way through the pitch-black forest supporting each other, feeling our way along the trail. I have the sensation of being in a dream, so terrified by what we're doing that the normally hair-raising snaps and slithers and shrieks of the jungle at night are only background noise; the branches and vines that scratch my arms and catch in my tangled hair barely register.

After a while, my eyes adjust to the dark enough that I'm able to make out the varying shades of black that indicate ferns and trees, and we pick up our speed, catching each other when we stumble. When we're about halfway to the temple, Ruby stops abruptly, listening. "Do you hear that?"

Without the noise of our feet on the forest floor, I can make out the faint sound of drums and chanting echoing through the ravines. "We're not too late," I say, hurrying forward.

We scramble as quickly as we can down the side of a gully, across a creek, and up the other side, the tribal sounds growing louder the closer we get to the ruins. Near the top of the hill, I notice the forest ahead of us beginning to lighten, a faint flicker of orange sending shadows leaping between the trees.

Gathering my dress in the fist that doesn't hold the knife, I steal along the trail toward the light with Ruby on my heels. As the glare grows stronger, we move into the woods around the side of the clearing, using the tree trunks and underbrush as cover. Drawing closer, I can feel the odd rhythm of the drumbeats reverberating in my chest, drowning out my heartbeat and vibrating beneath my skin. The chanting is discordant and raw, sending prickles up my spine.

When the clearing finally comes into view at the edge of the forest, I draw my breath. After the dark of the jungle, the otherworldly glow of the moon is like daylight on the glade, its pale luster punctuated by the flickering light of countless torches arranged in a semicircle at the base of the looming temple. At the bottom of the stairs that ascend the pyramid, Sunshine's shrouded corpse rests atop the funeral pyre while ghostly figures gyrate around it.

Kali presides over her flock from the lowest of the stone shelves that encircle the monument, her flowing white dress illuminated by torch-light. Hikari and Rex stand sentinel on either side of her. Next to them, three men beat giant taiko drums.

The sight of the frenzied forms swaying and spinning like phantoms on the grass reminds me they've all had far more of whatever was in the food—and, likely, the tea—than I have.

"No one seems to be drinking anything," Ruby notes.

She's right. I don't see anyone holding a cup, nor do I see any sort of drink dispenser, and if they'd already drunk poison, surely they wouldn't be dancing so exuberantly.

I allow my gaze to rove over the frenetic crowd, searching for anything out of place in the Dionysian tableau. A pile of sandals discarded near the trailhead; two men lying on their backs at the side of the clearing closest to us, one of them pointing at the heavens; three women dancing naked in a circle, their fingers intertwined; a man waving a torch around as though it's a sword.

"They don't look like they're preparing to die tonight," I comment, uncertain.

"They don't know."

A series of short, guttural barks rises above the din and I turn my head toward the noise, my gaze landing on Xibalbá, chained to a ring halfway up the temple. I gasp, pointing.

"He's a representative of the gods," Ruby says darkly. "Part of the ritual includes a sacrifice to allow passage through the portal."

The hair stands up on my scalp, all my worst fears converging in my mind. "Of who?"

"I don't know." She shakes her head. "An animal, I hope. Though I wouldn't be surprised if Karma or Karuna volunteered. They see it as an honor."

Suddenly the crowd around the man with the sword torch thins as he swings it in dangerously wide circles near the base of the shelf where Kali's perched, and I notice Karma, Karuna, and Aguilar leaning against the base of the pyramid, a giant orange-and-white barrel-shaped drink dispenser resting on a log between them.

I elbow Ruby. "Just beneath Kali. Orange cooler," I whisper urgently.

Her eyes dart to it, and she nods confirmation.

"We have to knock it over," I say, as I watch the man wave his torch erratically. "The torches. We'll join the dancing with our backs to Kali, then we can grab torches and charge."

"Then what?"

"Then we run like hell into the forest."

I watch as Aguilar fills a blue Solo cup and passes it to Karma or Karuna—it's so dark I can't be sure which. The sister glances down at it with what looks like a grimace before handing it to a passing woman while Aguilar fills another cup. My stomach clenches with apprehension, and I look back at Ruby.

Her face is resolute. "Okay. Let's do this."

"If they catch me, you keep running."

"Same."

I turn my attention to Kali, huddled in conversation with Rex and Hikari. "Now, while they're not looking. Ready?"

She inhales deeply and nods.

I grab her hand and leap into the clearing in imitation of the frenzied throng. We cavort across the open space, careful to shield our faces from Kali as we merge into the crowd, though Ruby's green clothes make it harder for her to blend in with all the white attire. I see Clef holding a blue cup and spin into him, knocking it from his hand onto the ground. His eyes are so glazed, he barely notices.

As Ruby and I back toward the orange container, I notice Amber in the center of the mob loosely holding a cup, swaying to the beat of the drums with her eyes closed as she absently raises it to her mouth. I beeline for her, swatting the cup from her hand a moment before it reaches her lips.

She stares down at the spilled drink, then up at me, her pupils wide as saucers as she reaches out and caresses my face. "So pretty," she mumbles.

"Don't drink the tea," I hiss. She closes her eyes and rolls her head around her neck. "It could kill you, do you hear me?" I shake her, trying to get her to look at me, but it's useless. "Don't drink anything."

I feel a hand on my shoulder and my heart leaps to my throat. But when I turn, it's only Ruby. "Come on," she says with an urgent nod toward Kali's pedestal. They've noticed us. "Now!"

I rush toward the closest torch and yank it out of the ground, the herd scattering as I haphazardly swing the flaming six-foot pole around, clenching my knife flush against the rod. Ruby is faster than me, already wielding her torch like a battering ram as she charges toward the drink dispenser. Chaos erupts as drugged-out disciples dive out of our path. From the corner of my eye I can see Hikari and Rex racing down the temple stairs toward us.

Karma, Karuna, and Aguilar lunge out of the way as Ruby brings her torch down on the drink dispenser, knocking it off the log. Through the black smoke billowing from my torch I watch it crash to the ground, but not a drop spills on the packed dirt.

"Cover me," I holler, casting aside my torch and tucking my knife beneath my arm to attack the top of the drink dispenser.

"Out of the way," I hear Hikari yell as I struggle with the tightly fastened top.

Ruby swings her torch wildly, blocking his way. "Right it so it doesn't spill on you," she hollers over her shoulder at me.

I finish unscrewing the top, wincing at the acrid smell that rises from the murky liquid within but careful not to breathe it in. With my burning torch, I push over the container, sending odious brown fluid sloshing onto the ground.

I hear a crackle as the pyre catches fire. It must have been doused with gasoline, because it suddenly bursts into flame with a whoosh, belching an extraordinary amount of heat and light that only stokes the bedlam further. At the top of the temple, Xibalbá lets out a thundering roar.

The scene before me is total pandemonium. People are screaming and running, some of them wielding torches of their own. Ruby and

I are hemmed in by ancient stone and a mass of keyed-up bodies, our backs to the pyramid, Rex and Hikari blocking our path to the forest. I pray they no longer have knives. Rex now brandishes a torch, which he uses to keep us from advancing toward him; above us, Kali shouts for everyone to calm down, her voice drowned out by the clamor.

"Drop the torches," Hikari says.

Somewhere in the ruckus, a woman's bloodcurdling scream cuts into the thick night air. I quickly scan the crowd for the source until I see a man drop to his knees next to the howling woman, his twitching body silhouetted by the light of the pyre as he keels face forward onto the ground. My heart sinks like lead with the realization that we were too late to save him. How many others might have already drunk the poison?

"Don't drink the tea!" I shout, but my voice is devoured by the commotion.

I glance up at Kali, who seems to have given up on calming the crowd and now stands on the steps of the temple with her arms raised to the heavens, chanting. A smattering of followers hold hands a few stairs beneath her, swaying to the sound of her voice, which I can hardly hear over the ruckus.

I turn to see Hikari and Rex closing in on us.

I sneak a fast glance at Ruby, who desperately cuts her eyes to the woods.

As the crowd swarms around their fallen comrade, Ruby and I bolt for the jungle, Rex and Hikari on our heels. The unwieldy torch sways and catches on branches, throwing me off balance as I careen around the side of the temple.

"Toss it!" Ruby yells over her shoulder, throwing her own flaming stake onto the stone steps of the monument.

I do the same, but a glance over my shoulder reveals Hikari and Rex still gaining on us. I push myself faster, the smooth bottoms of my thin sandals sliding on the damp ground.

"This way," Ruby pants as she rounds the back corner of the temple, into the dark shadow cast by the towering structure.

I can see her searching the edge of the woods for a trail, but it's so dark it's difficult to make out any break in the underbrush. "There." I point ten yards ahead on the far side of a fallen tree, where the trailhead is barely visible.

We cut into the woods and immediately slow down, unable to see five feet in front of us in the inky darkness. The only light is the flame from Rex's torch behind us, casting dimly flickering shadows that pervert the placement of trees and turn the vines to slithering snakes. I stumble over a root and roll my ankle. Sharp pain shoots up my calf and down into my foot, but I don't have time to stop. I grip the knife tightly in my hand as we blunder blindly through the forest, fear coursing through my veins.

I can feel them gaining on us. There are two of them and two of us; we're smaller, but we have knives, which levels the playing field— assuming we're the only ones with weapons. Tearing through underbrush, I struggle to remember what I learned in the self-defense classes my mom insisted I take when I first moved to New York. Vulnerable points: eyes, neck, balls. Aim to stop the attacker at any cost.

Suddenly something whacks violently into my lower back and I'm engulfed by a searing pain. I scream in agony, stumbling to my knees, my skin on fire. The pain is so horrific I lose my breath and vision for a moment; when my sight returns, Rex towers above me with the torch.

He burned me.

Immediately Ruby knocks into him from the side and they tumble to the ground as Hikari pounces on me. Where the torch hit my back, my skin feels like it's being ripped off by sandpaper and doused in salt. Panicked, I bite back the exquisite pain and wiggle my hand beneath my leg, fumbling as Hikari pins me to the dirt, his hands around my neck, cutting off my breath. My chest burns and my vision goes black around the edges as I fight for air, desperately groping the ground for the knife as my body grows weaker. My hand strikes something hard, sending adrenaline surging through me. The knife.

With numb fingers, I blindly swing the blade with every ounce of energy I have left, connecting with soft flesh. Hikari emits a terrible noise somewhere between a moan and a choke, and immediately the pressure on my windpipe lessens. As my lungs fill with blessed air, my vision returns and I see the knife sticking out of his neck, just above the collarbone. Now he's the one gasping, his eyes wide in shock. I grip the shaft, horrified, unsure whether to pull the blade out or leave it in. Blood blooms from the entry point, a trickle quickly turning to a river of red. He gurgles as I feel his weight go slack on top of me.

The knife seems to be the only thing holding back a torrent of blood, so I leave it embedded in his neck in the hope I haven't killed him as I push him off and crawl out from beneath him, trembling with shock. I rip my eyes from the ghastly sight of his twitching body, turning my attention to the snarled mass of thrashing arms and legs.

A torch rests in the crook of a nearby tree, illuminating the deep darkness in flickering firelight. Rex has Ruby on her back, one of her hands pinned to the ground as they scrabble. I desperately scan the area for her knife, but before I can find it, Rex raises his arm to hit her. I throw a powerful kick to his ribs before he can connect, knocking him sideways. Ruby takes the opportunity to pounce on him but doesn't weigh enough to keep him down, and he throws her off, locking his maniacal eyes on me as he springs to his feet like he's possessed.

I don't have time to think. I stoop and yank the knife from Hikari's neck as Rex advances toward me, spinning to face him with the bloody blade raised. He draws nearer, unfazed, his fists clenched and ready. Out of the corner of my eye, I see Ruby rise quietly to her feet behind him. When Rex is nearly upon me, Ruby seizes him around the waist and pulls him backward, kicking the back of his knees to make him collapse.

I spring toward them as they tumble to the forest floor and dive at Rex, sinking the blade into his thigh and immediately pulling it back out again, then plunging it in once more. He howls in pain and throws Ruby off him. I grab her arm and snatch up Rex's torch as we back away from him, bleeding and writhing on the forest floor next to Hikari's slumped body.

Ruby and I begin running through the woods again, the faint sound of shouting coming from the direction of the temple, somewhere behind us.

Both of us are too traumatized and shocked to speak as we climb the ridge, slogging through ferns and vines and clambering over rocks as unseen animals howl and jabber in the dense black forest around us. A twig snaps close by and I start, tripping over the hem of my dress. I swing the torch in a circle around us, revealing nothing but thick greenery and dancing shadows. We continue on, my knees wobbling and my back stinging like someone's holding a giant cigarette to my skin.

Over the top of the ridge, we come upon a fallen tree, and Ruby slows. "Let's stop a minute," she says. "Rex isn't going anywhere—you got him pretty good."

I gladly sink onto the horizontal trunk, exhausted, Hikari's bloody neck swimming before my eyes. I can still hear the terrible sucking noise as he tried to breathe. "And Hikari? Do you think he's dead?" I ask.

She contorts her face into a mask of sympathy that tells me all I need to know.

"Oh God." I cover my face with my hands, shaking.

She wraps an arm around my shoulders and squeezes. "You did what you had to do. It was him or you."

"Are you okay?" I manage. We're both so filthy, covered in sweat, blood, and dirt, it's difficult to tell how damaged we are.

"I'll live," she says.

I turn, positioning my back toward her. "How's my back look?"

She draws in air through her teeth. "It's not good. But it could be a lot worse, and your tiger is intact. How's it feel?"

It hurts like hell, and just thinking of the night we have ahead of us is enough to make me want to curl up right here on this log and sleep for a thousand years. "I'll live," I echo her. We share a look of solidarity. "What happened to your knife?"

"I don't know. I lost it in the scuffle."

She watches as I lift the hem of my dress and stab the fabric with my bloody blade. "I'm sick of tripping," I mutter as I rip off the bottom of the dress, leaving it a good two feet shorter and much more manageable than it was. We rise and begin moving slowly through the thicket, down the far side of the ravine, Ruby now leading the way with the torch while I follow closely behind. I'm light-headed and clumsy, drained but buzzing with residual adrenaline. When she stops abruptly, I blunder into her back.

She whips around with her finger to her lips, pointing. Down the hill, obstructed by the trees, I see pinpricks of light moving through the forest. The first three turn into five, then I lose track as the group multiplies to probably ten or fifteen—coming from the opposite direction of the temple.

A glimmer of hope flares inside me. "Blaze," I say.

THIRTY-ONE

The line of flashlights moves through the forest toward the temple with a speed Ruby and I are unable to match cutting through the jungle. By the time we reach the trail, we're probably a city block behind them. Torch extended to light the way, we race down the muddy hill, leaves slapping our faces as we hurtle over rocks and roots.

When the group finally comes into view, I see they're dressed in camouflage and carrying automatic rifles that seem excessive for park rangers, though the one we came across the other day did have a similar weapon.

"Wait," I call out.

My breath quickens as the two well-built men at the back turn, taking in our disheveled appearance, then holler to the others in Spanish. Slowly the band comes to a halt and reverses direction to gather around us.

"Sveta!" Lucas pushes through the pack of camouflage toward me, his arms outstretched.

What the fuck?

I stare at him in shock, my mind doing somersaults as he grips my shoulders, scanning me for injuries, his face a mask of concern. "Thank God," he says. "Are you okay?"

I wrench away from him. "Don't touch me," I spit.

He draws back, thrown, as Blaze appears beside him. "We were worried we weren't in time," Blaze says.

"Where'd you find him?" I ask, throwing a venomous look at Lucas.

"At the ranger station," Blaze answers.

"I went to get help," Lucas jumps in. "Did you not get the note I—"

"There was no note." I cut him off, my eyes hard.

"Okay, okay," Blaze says urgently. "Do you guys know what's happening now? Where everyone is?"

"They're all at the temple, high out of their minds on whatever was in the food," Ruby says. "But we managed to destroy the poison before—"

"Good," Blaze interjects, visibly relieved. "Let's go. The guys are going to surround the field. Ruby, will you speak to everyone with me? It'll be stronger coming from both of us."

"I'll do whatever it takes."

Blaze scuttles toward the front to lead the way while Ruby and I follow behind. "Once we've rounded everyone up," he says as he jogs toward the temple, "we'll lead them down this path to the road. About three miles out, there's a wider fire road where we have trucks waiting to take them to a shelter in the nearest town."

"What if they don't want to go?" I ask.

"We may have to take Kali forcibly, but we're not going to hurt anyone," Blaze says, picking up the pace.

The pack of men moves ahead of me as my legs slow, unable to keep up. I feel Lucas's eyes on me as he falls in beside me, but I refuse to look at him.

"Sveta," he whispers.

"I know, Lucas," I snap. "I saw you and Kali in the woods."

"I can explain—"

"I'm not buying your lies anymore," I return. "I'm done."

"I'm so sorry, Sveta. But you have to let me—"

"I don't have to do anything," I say forcefully.

"Please—"

"This is not the time." Ruby cuts him off. "We need to focus. Please, save it for later."

He looks at her, stricken, then nods and hurries ahead.

As we get closer, a fluttering amber glow dimly illuminates the woods, accompanied by the noxious odor of the funeral pyre. Swallowing the bile that rises in my throat, I cover my mouth and nose with my hand as we near the edge of the forest. In the clearing, a handful of backlit figures sway before the intense crackling blaze that belches black smoke into the thick night air. Half the torches around the base of the temple have been knocked over or appropriated, and I can make out bodies lying on the ground here and there, but I can't tell whether they're dead or merely passed out. I pray the latter.

The rest of the crowd is gathered around the base of the temple, listening raptly to Kali, who stands on the stone shelf above them, seemingly preaching.

Everyone is so high that none of them notice the militiamen stealthily fan out around the perimeter of the knoll with their weapons raised. Staying out of sight as much as possible, Lucas and I follow Ruby and Blaze along the fringe of the moonlit clearing. As we near the pyramid, I watch Kali through the shimmering waves of heat from the pyre, seemingly praying while a chained Xibalbá prowls the temple stairs above her, agitated. I lose sight of Ruby and Blaze for a moment as they cross behind the inferno, and while I'm looking for them, a shout goes up from the field. Someone has spotted the men with the guns.

A ripple of confusion and alarm passes through the herd as they swarm up the base of the temple, away from the militiamen, surely thinking they're members of the cartel they've been conditioned to fear. Holding my breath, I scurry past the raging pyre to the corner of the structure, where I have a clear view of Ruby and Blaze clambering up the crumbling stones on the side of the temple, onto the ledge.

Kali's disciples form a wall around her so that I lose sight of her as Blaze ascends the steps behind them, waving his hands above his head. "You're safe," he shouts over the crackling fire. "No one is going to hurt you. These men are here to help you."

A murmur sweeps through the crowd as they move closer to hear what he's saying.

"Everybody stay calm," Blaze orders.

"What's going on?" someone yells.

"Who are they?" another overlaps.

"Why do they have guns?"

"It's okay!" Blaze motions with his hands for them to simmer down. "Everything is okay. They are not going to hurt you."

Kali pushes through those gathered around her to address the rest. "Don't listen to him, he's a censor!" she shouts fiercely.

The park ranger closest to us calls out to Lucas in Spanish, and Lucas approaches him, straining to understand what he's saying over all the commotion. As they converse, I return my eyes to the spectacle unfolding on the platform. Ruby stands to the side with her back to us while Blaze continues trying to pacify the shaken crowd.

A flicker of movement in the shadow of the temple draws my eye, and I gasp. There on the ledge around the corner from Ruby, hidden by the dark silhouette of the pyramid, is Rex. She's completely unaware, all of her attention focused on Blaze as Rex hobbles stealthily toward her, the knife she dropped clenched tightly in his fist. It seems no one else sees him.

There's no time to deliberate. If I call out to Lucas or the rangers, I'll risk drawing Rex's attention, and if I don't move immediately, he'll be on Ruby in seconds. I scramble up the mossy gray rocks like a lizard, never taking my eyes off Rex, now within striking distance of Ruby. "Ruby! Move!" I yell, hurtling onto the ledge.

Rex's gaze flicks to me as I lunge toward him, my foot aimed directly at the wounds I gave him earlier. The knife comes down as I connect, slicing into my upper chest with a searing pain, and we both tumble to the slab, his shoulder breaking my fall. I try to rise but I'm woozy and weak, every nerve in my body screaming in agony as I attempt to locate the entry point of the knife, now gone. My entire torso is exploding with pain, but the worst of the torture is localized somewhere between my neck and shoulder, high enough, I pray, that it hasn't hit any organs.

I see blurred movement above, feel the cushion of Rex's body ripped from beneath me by more than one set of hands, hear grunting and flesh hitting stone. Chaos has erupted again, this time the screaming punctuated by rapid gunfire shot into the sky, the stone beneath me reverberating with footsteps as the park rangers scurry up the temple, yelling to one another in Spanish, fighting to contain the situation. I roll my head to find blood from my wound pooling on the stone next to me. A few feet beyond, the knife that did the damage rests abandoned on the ledge, tapered blade glinting in the firelight.

Summoning all the energy I have left, I roll over my undamaged arm and onto my stomach. I can see nothing but shadows and movement beyond the leaping flames of the pyre as I drag my exhausted body toward the weapon.

A sudden rush of singed white linen, and the knife is gone before I can even process what's happened. I look up to see Kali standing above me, backlit by the raging blaze, bloody blade in hand. Her black hair is wild around her face, her gaze eerily serene.

Weakened by my injuries and loss of blood, I struggle to stand, but it's no use. I'm no match for her in my condition. I look for help, but our group is sorely outnumbered, struggling to control the keyed-up crowd without hurting anyone.

Kali raises the knife.

"Please," I whisper.

But her attention has drifted from me, her eyes glazed and dreamy, a hint of a smile playing around her lips, forming words I can't make out. An incantation, perhaps.

Time warps and stretches, images from my life swirling like sparks from the fire before my eyes. At once I'm a child again at the beach, my uncle and father swinging me squealing up over a wave; I'm a teenager walking my first catwalk, my heart in my throat, the spotlight so bright I can barely make out the edge of the platform; holding hands with my mother at my father's funeral, her face multicolored in the light through a stained-glass window depicting Jesus on the cross, a sword in his side.

The vision fades, the knife in Kali's hand coming into sharp relief as I realize she's not going to use it on me. Jesus offered himself so that his people might have eternal life, and she believes she is doing the same.

She is the sacrifice, her own life the key to lead her people through the portal into eternity. She's deified herself and now the time has come for martyrdom.

Above me, she tosses her head back and closes her eyes, enraptured, her lips moving in prayer. I watch in horror as she holds the knife to her skin and abruptly draws the blade across her own throat.

The line across her neck ruptures, turning the top of her white dress deep red. She wavers, gurgling, then sinks to her knees and keels forward, her forehead striking the unforgiving surface with a dull thunk.

I collapse next to her, our blood mingling on the ancient stone as the life drains from her.

PART FIVE

TRUST

Everything you need is within you, for the Divine
resides inside of you. The infinite power of the universe
is at your fingertips, if only you will believe in yourself.
Once you realize that, truly anything is possible.

—Paul Bentzen, *Surrender*

THIRTY-TWO

I awake to jostling darkness and crushing pain. For a brief moment I'm confused, my mind a black hole. Fear stiffens my spine; I don't dare move. And then it all comes rushing back. The fire, the blood, the knife in my chest.

I work out that I'm in the back of a vehicle—on a dirt road, I guess, from the bumping and the lack of light. My head rests on something warm and firm. A leg. I'm in someone's lap. I wiggle my ankles and wrists ever so slightly, relieved to find they're free of bindings. I struggle to lift my head, but it weighs a million pounds.

A rough hand sweeps my hair out of my eyes. Lucas. I know I'm supposed to be angry with him but can't remember why.

"You're awake."

His touch is gentle, his voice kind. I let go of trying to remember the source of my anger. "Where are we?" I mumble, my voice hoarse.

"In a jeep on our way to a hospital. You lost a lot of blood, but we've got you patched up now. You're gonna be okay. Just don't move too much."

The events of the evening rush back to me with the force of a tidal wave, the gash in Kali's neck flashing before my eyes like something from a horror movie. "Kali . . ."

"She's dead," he confirms.

I see her dress turn red, hear the sickening crack of her skull on the stone. "Where's Ruby?"

"In a car behind us. She's fine."

"Rex?" I ask.

"I don't know. He wasn't in good shape after Blaze and I finished with him."

I shift, gasping as the pain sends shooting stars across my vision.

"Don't move." He strokes my head. "Just rest."

WHEN I AWAKE AGAIN, I'M dying of thirst, my throat so dry I can hardly swallow. It takes every ounce of effort I can muster to open my eyes.

Fluorescent lights come into focus, mounted on a ceiling made of perforated tiles. I'm lying in a hospital bed in a small room, facing a clock on the dull green wall that reads 3:20. A plastic bag of something is hooked up to one of my arms, another attached to my hand.

Light bleeds around the edges of the blackout shades. A man in jeans is curled uncomfortably on the thin cushion atop the window seat, asleep. I look down and see a call button on the side of my bed, but when I try to raise my hand to reach it, I can't. My fingers won't move at all, like the signal from my brain simply doesn't reach them.

I begin to panic. Am I paralyzed? I wiggle my toes, confirming I can feel both feet, and the fingers on my other hand. But I have no sensation in my right arm. Did the knife sever something? Anxiety pumping through me, I reach over with my functioning hand and press the call button.

After a long moment, a nurse wearing scrubs with dolphins on them bustles in, speaking in rapid Spanish.

"No Español," I say, my stomach in knots. "Inglese?"

"Lo siento," she replies with a smile, then goes on to say something else I can't understand.

Why, oh why, did I never learn Spanish?

The man on the window seat uncurls and sits up.

"Chase?" I stare at him, confounded. "What are you doing here?"

He's bleary eyed but put-together for someone sleeping in a hospital room, his Prada trainers and robin's-egg cashmere hoodie incongruous in the threadbare room.

"Your mom called me," he says, dragging a mauve chair across the worn linoleum to the edge of my bed.

"My mom?"

"Yeah, I guess your attorney called her last night? I was able to get an earlier flight than she was, but she should be here in a few hours." He takes my hand in his, but I can't feel a thing. "There's something wrong with my arm," I say, alarmed.

"You were stabbed," he says.

"I can't feel my fingers."

He frowns, directing his voice at the nurse and pointing at my limp arm. "She can't feel her arm."

The nurse replies in a torrent of Spanish, and I instinctively wish Lucas were here, before I remember I shouldn't. "Where's Lucas?" I ask.

"He went back to the hotel."

"No Español," I tell the nurse again.

She holds up a finger and fishes her phone from her pocket, then types something into it. "Nerve block," she translates, pointing at my arm. "Para el dolor." She taps at the phone again. "For pain." She smiles. "Estás bien."

"Gracias." I lie my head back on the pillows and let the tsunami of relief wash over me as the nurse checks my vitals and makes a few notations, then leaves.

"How are you feeling, besides the arm?" Chase asks. His concerned face makes me wish I were happier to see him.

"Like I got hit by a truck," I say, forcing a smile. "Thanks for being here. I'm sorry you had to come all this way."

"Of course." He lifts my hand and kisses it. "I came as soon as I heard. What happened?"

I cheated on you.

"It's a long story." I sigh, what little energy I had upon waking already drained. "I'm too tired to get into it right now. Can we talk about it later?"

"Yeah, of course," he says.

"Has anyone mentioned how long I have to stay in here?" I ask.

"I think they'll let you out in the morning. It sounds like they want you to stick around down here a few days to give statements and deal with paperwork, but I'm gonna see what I can do to get you on a plane home as soon as possible."

I close my eyes and sigh. The thought of going back to New York with him and returning to the status quo makes me feel like I might suffocate. But I can't exactly break up with him from this hospital bed, when he's dropped everything and flown down here to be with me.

He stands and kisses me on the forehead. "I'm going to go get us something to eat. What do you want?"

"I'm mostly thirsty," I say. "But I'll take whatever looks good."

"I don't know that good is going to be an option," he says. "But I'll try to find something edible."

THE NEXT TIME I ROUSE, I know where I am. A machine is beeping, my fingers are still numb, and the clock on the wall now reads 6:10. I must've drifted off while Chase went to get our food. I turn my head to look for him, and instead find my mother seated in his chair.

As usual, she's wearing a sundress, this one a dusty pink that makes her appear even paler than normal, a lilac sweater wrapped around her thin shoulders. Her long, nearly black hair hangs limp, her indigo eyes rimmed by dark circles.

"Solnyshka," she says, taking my hand in hers. Her voice is hoarse, as though she's been crying.

"I'm okay, Mom. Just a flesh wound," I reassure her, my own voice barely a croak. She hands me the bottle of water on the bedside table and I drink the entire thing down in one gulp. "Where's Chase?"

"At the hotel, sleeping."

I can feel her cold hand trembling in mine. "I tried to call you to let you know I was coming down here," I offer. "But it felt wrong to leave the news of Paul's death on your voice mail."

She bites her lip, tears pooling in her eyes. "I haven't been honest with you." She pulls a tissue from the box beside my bed and dabs at her eyes.

"I got Paul's letter," I offer.

She lowers the tissue from her face, her shoulders quivering.

"I know you were supposed to get the chance to talk to me first," I say, "but with everything that was going on at Xanadu, the woman he gave it to thought I should read it."

She takes a deep breath and wipes her nose, attempting to pull herself together.

"I know I may be his daughter," I continue.

She reaches for my hand, keeping her gaze trained on my fingers. "I wanted to talk to you before—"

"I know," I say. "Did you know I was Paul's beneficiary?"

She nods. "I was going to tell you. When I told you about the rest of it."

"How long have you known?"

"Since your eighteenth birthday. When Lucas's father met with me in New York."

"All this time . . ." I shake my head, incredulous. "And were you ever planning to tell me Dad wasn't killed at war?"

Her face crumples. "I'm so sorry, solnyshka." She drops her head to her hands. "Hank was in the military, before. But he suffered from mental illness. PTSD and depression, and eventually schizophrenia. He was in and out of hospitals and halfway houses for most of your childhood. I told you he was fighting overseas because you were so little . . . I wanted to protect you."

"But why didn't you tell me all this when I got older?"

"I wanted to." She exhales, studying our intertwined hands. "But it was never the right time."

I quell my annoyance, trying to see it from her point of view. "It must have been very hard for you."

A tear slips from her tightly closed eyes and rolls down her cheek. "I felt so much guilt, about Paul. But after all the bad things, to find something so good . . ." She grabs another tissue and sobs into it. I reach out and stroke her arm.

"Dad had brown eyes," I say, the fact that I'm a dead ringer for my blond, blue-eyed uncle hanging between us in the Lysol-scented room. "And nearly black hair."

She looks at me, her eyes full of regret. "But they were brothers and sometimes family genes . . ." She shrugs. "Paul believed you were his. But your father believed you were his, too." She dabs beneath her eyes with the tissue and takes a deep breath. "They both loved you so much."

I can see that she's emotionally exhausted, but I need to know the rest of it. "So why didn't you let Paul back into our lives after Dad died?" I ask.

"Oh, solnyshka, it's complicated," she says shakily. "The schizophrenia—it made your father think crazy things."

"Like what?" I ask.

"Oh . . ." Her eyes grow far-off, remembering. "That there were microphones in our house—the government was listening, or they had tested something on him. That I was a Russian spy . . . He also thought some not so crazy things. Like that you were his brother's baby."

My chest grows tight with sympathy. "Oh, Mom, I'm so sorry."

"At the hospital, they tried so many medicines—some helped a little, but never for long. He tried to kill himself many times. He believed God talked to him, he saw angels. He started to pray and read books about religion—all religions, not just Christianity—all the time. He wrote pages and pages of the things God told him and mailed them to me weekly. I thought it was good because for two years, he never tried to kill himself. He went to live in a halfway house, and I thought he was getting better. Then one day I got a call he was gone."

She takes a sip of water, twisting her long hair over her shoulder. "There was no note. But when I went to clean out his room at the halfway house, I found a letter postmarked the week before he killed himself. It was from the man who had married my friend from Russia. He wrote about how his wife had left him for another man. He was angry at"—she grimaces—"'these Russian whores.' He wanted Hank to know he saw Paul and me together, a long time ago."

Realizing my jaw is hanging open, I close my mouth and swallow.

"His wife hadn't let him say anything at the time, but . . ." Her voice cracks. "It's all my fault," she says, tears once again sliding down her cheeks.

My heart breaks for her. "It's not your fault, Mom. He was sick. He tried many times before that."

She reaches for another tissue but the box is empty, so she wipes away her tears with the back of her trembling hand. "It was too much for me. I sent all his things, his religion books, all his crazy writing about God, to Paul. He wanted to be with me then, but I felt so guilty about your father, it didn't feel right to be happy, and I told him I wasn't ready. So he left again. Said he was working on a book and would come back in a year, when he was finished. I agreed that was good. After a year I was ready, but he didn't come—he said he was working with a guru now. It was not until another year later—when his book was published—that I learned the real reason why he stayed away." She takes another swallow of water. "The book—*Surrender*—was all your father's crazy writing about God."

I stare at her. "What?"

"He stole the ideas from your father," she says. "Paul wrote better, made it all sound not so crazy. But the ideas were the same. I was so angry. He promised he'd done it for me and you, that he wanted to give us all the money from the book. He said he didn't tell me about it before because he knew I would ask him not to publish it. That just made me angrier. I told him I didn't want his money and I never wanted to see him again."

"And he agreed?" I ask.

"Oh, no, no, no, he never agreed." She throws her hands up. "He sent checks that I destroyed. One time he sent a car."

"The Mustang?" I ask.

She nods. "I tried to send it back, but it was in my name, so I had to keep it. He wanted to see you. He promised to keep the secret you were maybe his daughter. But I didn't trust him anymore. I didn't want a life built on a lie."

I furrow my brow, trying to see it from her perspective. I can understand not wanting a life built on a lie—though it turns out that's what my entire life has been. But when I think of the childhood I could have had, the advantages we might have had with my uncle's money, it's really difficult not to be angry with her. I could've had the opportunity to go to college and get a job without an expiration date, that wouldn't have left me with body dysmorphia. I can't help feeling like she sacrificed me for her pride.

She must see the frustration in my face, because she again reaches out and takes my hand, years of pain in her eyes. "Solnyshka, I have so much guilt."

My immediate reaction is that she deserves guilt for not telling me, for putting me through all I've been through. How could she be so selfish as to not think of what would be right for her daughter?

But she's all I have, and she's been through hell. I don't want to hate her. I close my eyes and try to breathe through it, listening to the beep-beep-beep of the machine as I struggle to defuse my swirling fury.

Then Kali's advice comes back to me, my uncle's—my father's—words, meant to manipulate me at the time, but meaningful regardless: *At the end of the day, you're in control. Your happiness is up to you.*

My mother allowed her guilt to guide her. She was never happy because she believed she had no right to be. But I don't have to live like that, and I don't have to blame her or hold it against her. She was doing the best she could—is still doing the best she can. I know she means well, and that is what I must focus on. The past is over, but the future is before me and it's up to me what path I choose.

When I open my eyes, she's gazing at me from beneath her thin brows like a repentant dog ready for punishment. I squeeze her hand. "I'm sorry you were never happy."

She gives me a sad smile. "Happiness is not everything. I have you. And in the end, this year with him—"

Again my brain snags. "Wait, what?"

"Paul. He came to me a year ago. He was sick, and he apologized again—"

"And you forgave him?" I ask, astonished.

She nods. "I wasn't so angry anymore, and I wanted to spend the time he had left with him."

"But Kali—"

"She didn't want him to get treatment, she claimed because she didn't believe in treatment—but I think she wanted him to die. Paul wanted to end Xanadu, but Kali knew he stole your father's words, and she knew you might be his daughter, so she held him prisoner."

"How did she know?" I ask, surprised.

"He told her," my mother admits. "They were together a long time and he trusted her—in the beginning, anyway."

So that was why he left Xanadu and turned a blind eye for as long as he did. I feel a gnawing sense of guilt that I was a part of the reason, but there was nothing I could have done. I didn't know.

"Why did she change?" I ask, trying to wrap my head around Kali's motives, who she really was behind the façade.

"I think she always liked power, but at first she was okay to be beside him. Then, around the time he got sick, she had a vision that she was the chosen one. She decided she knew better than him what was right. She believed that God spoke to her, and she should be the leader." My mother pulls her sweater closer around her shoulders. "When he came to stay with me, he and Kali weren't together anymore. He decided he would close Xanadu when he finished treatment, no matter the consequence, and we would tell you the truth. I wanted to tell you face-to-face, but then his health became so poor, I had to cancel my visits to take care of him."

I nod, remembering her canceled visit for my birthday, and again for Thanksgiving.

"After Christmas, when he found out what was going on—that people had died—we knew he had to close it immediately."

"How did he find out?" I ask.

"Someone told him, I don't know who. We were on vacation in the Florida Keys, it was a phone call. I felt Paul was too sick to travel that far, but he thought Kali might listen to him if he came in person."

"Mom, I'm pretty sure Kali killed him," I say. "Or had him killed. Though I don't know that I'll ever be able to prove it."

She sighs. "I believe you."

I lay my head back and close my eyes, exhausted. It's a lot to process, and I'm bone tired.

"You should rest," she says. "I'll be right here."

"I'm fine," I protest. "Go to the hotel where you can really sleep. I know you're tired, too."

But she's still holding my hand when I drift off to sleep.

THIRTY-THREE

The following afternoon, the hospital releases me. My nerve block has worn off and my shoulder and back hurt like hell in spite of the painkillers they've given me, but I'm glad to be out of there, regardless. I'm also glad to be wearing my own clothes again, thanks to Lucas, who was able to recover our bags from Xanadu. I've yet to see him, though I'm told he stayed by my side in the hospital until Chase arrived, refusing to sleep until he knew I'd be okay.

"Lucas is bringing the car around," Chase says, and for a moment I worry he senses my mixed feelings. But when I glance at him, all I see is concern for me—which makes me feel like a total asshole.

With my shoulder in a sling and my greasy hair hidden by my Yankees cap, I shuffle into the warm day on Chase's arm, and turn my face up to the sun.

"There he is." My mom points at a mud-splattered jeep as it turns into the parking lot, and my heart clenches when I spot Lucas behind the wheel.

Conscious of Chase beside me, I try to act nonchalant as Lucas hops down to the pavement, but by the time he reaches me, I'm so overwhelmed by the sight of him that I'm hardly able to breathe.

"Glad to see you looking better," he says, giving me an awkward half hug.

He has a welt on his cheekbone and a bandage on one of his arms, and I can make out what looks like a black eye behind his sunglasses, but otherwise he seems to be in one piece.

"Are you okay?" I ask, shading my eyes against the sun with my good arm to study the welt on his cheekbone.

"Yeah. Rex," he says in reference to his face. "That guy's a machine."

"Is he . . ."

"Alive? Yeah. Somewhere in there." He gestures to the hospital.

"And everyone else?" I ask. "How are Blaze and Ruby? What's happening?"

"They're okay. Right now, everyone's being put up in a church and interviewed by the authorities. Once they've all given statements, they'll be moved to hotels until they can get their papers in order, then will be repatriated to whatever countries they came from."

"Are any of them going to be prosecuted?" I ask.

"Maybe Rex and Aguilar? I don't know. It's tough to prove anything, and they were all under Kali's influence. She left a manifesto that outlined her intentions to escort her flock through the Divine Portal."

"Wow," Chase says. I look over at him, and he raises his brows. "Crazy."

"How many died?" I ask.

"Four—that I know of." Lucas runs his fingers through his hair. "Kali, Hikari, the man we saw go down in the field, a girl who intentionally drank what was left in the dispenser—"

"Who?"

He cracks his knuckles. "One of the sisters—Karma or Karuna? The older one."

"God, that's awful."

Lucas notices my mom fanning herself and opens the car door for her, handing her up into the front seat. Chase helps me into the back and slides in next to me, and we pull away from the curb, Lucas driving as carefully as he can over the uneven roads toward our hotel.

On the outskirts of town, colorful well-worn buildings with rusting corrugated roofs give way to thicker vegetation and taller trees, past which I can see the mountains in the distance. At a hand-painted sign that reads "Villas Las Palmas," we turn down a winding dirt driveway that leads through the dense green forest to a collection of wooden bungalows with tile roofs scattered along a rushing river.

Lucas parks in the shade behind the next-to-farthest bungalow and helps my mom down from the jeep, while Chase helps me. "This is you guys," he says, indicating the bungalow in front of us. "I'm on the end, and Irina is next to you."

It hits me then that I'm sharing a room with Chase, that I'll finally have the opportunity to come clean with him, and I'm overcome with the desire to run back to the dingy hospital.

"I have to give a statement this afternoon," Lucas says. "Then I'm going to check on Blaze and Ruby and the rest. But Irina has my phone number if you need me."

I don't look at him as he leaves, swallowing the lump in my throat as my mother and I follow Chase up the walkway to our bungalow.

"You feeling okay?" Chase asks, unlocking the door to our room. "You look pale."

"My shoulder hurts." I manage a weak smile.

Inside, the bungalow has high beamed ceilings and terra-cotta tile floors, with abundant windows open to the breeze and a porch with a hammock overlooking the river at the front. A white bed is centered against the back wall with a mosquito net draped over it, facing the small sitting area with a matching turquoise-and-red-patterned love seat and chair. "This is beautiful," I say, looking around.

"It's kind of a shithole," Chase says. "But there's not exactly a Four Seasons close by, and we won't be here long. I've gotta get back for the Knicks game tomorrow, and you can leave as soon as you've given your statement."

And just like that, the differences between us are once again in sharp relief. "Hey, Mom," I say, suddenly ready for what I have to do next. "Can we have a sec?"

"Of course," she says.

"Thank you," I say. "I'll come by a little later."

Once the door has closed behind her, I turn to Chase, steeling my nerves. "We need to talk," I say gently.

"Okay." He perches on the arm of the chair and looks at me.

Guilt weighs heavy on me as I force myself to meet his eye. "I haven't been faithful."

Anger flashes across his face; his eyes harden.

"I'm sorry." I pause, struggling with what to say, how much to say.

He crosses his arms, then pinches the bridge of his nose. "I haven't, either," he says.

I draw back, stung. The image of the lipstick on the coffee cup in his loft materializes before my eyes. My impulse is to ask when, with who? But I gave up that privilege when I slept with Lucas. Anyway, it doesn't matter now.

We stare at each other, our relationship disintegrating between us.

"So I guess we're even," he says.

"Yeah." I sigh, wishing I'd planned this better. "I love you, Chase. And I care about you deeply. But I think we both know we're not compatible. We've known for a while."

He nods curtly. "I tried."

"I know. We both did. I'm sorry it had to end this way."

He doesn't meet my eye. "Yeah."

"I really wanted this to work," I say. I reach for his hand, but he grabs his messenger bag instead, and slings it over his shoulder. "I'm sorry," I repeat.

He pauses for a long moment, and when he finally meets my gaze, I see that the anger in his eyes has been replaced by resignation. "Me, too."

I twist the ring off my finger and place it in his hand. He pockets it.

"Something happened to you down here." He says it not as an accusation but an observation.

"A lot happened to me," I agree.

"Not just the physical stuff." He evaluates me. "You're different. I could tell the minute you woke up. It's like you're more—I don't know, stronger, or something."

"Thank you," I say.

"I mean you've always been strong. But you had that look, like you did on the catwalk the night we met, when you were the cockatoo. Like nothing was going to get in your way. I hadn't seen that in a long time. And I realized, maybe I'd clipped your wings."

I stare at him, stunned by his perception.

"I'm sorry," he says. "That was never my intention."

"It's not your fault," I say finally. "It was us, together."

He nods. "What are you gonna do?"

"I don't know," I say. "I was thinking about getting some information on classes at CUNY. Maybe I'll finally find my calling, figure out something positive to do with this estate."

One hundred eighty million dollars. The amount hangs in the silence between us. I haven't had time to fully absorb the meaning of it, the changes it will bring to my life. I recognize I'll have to work to remain grounded with that kind of insulation, and I know finding the right purpose for it will be key to that.

After a moment, he grabs his duffel bag. "You will."

Once he leaves for the airport, I sit on the bed for a long time, allowing myself the space to find closure. A relationship doesn't have to last forever to be successful, I realize. I learned a lot about love and myself, about what I do and don't want, and I'll carry that knowledge with me going forward. I have no ill will toward Chase—the opposite, in fact; I really do wish him all the best—but I also feel no regret for letting him go.

Which I take as confirmation that I've made the right choice.

I FIND LUCAS IN THE hammock on his porch, tapping away at his phone. He puts it down when he sees me. "Hey," he says.

"Hey," I say.

I sit in one of the wicker chairs, looking out over the river.

"Where's Chase?" he asks.

"On his way to the airport."

He glances down at my bare ring finger and nods, understanding. I keep my eyes trained on the forest as his gaze settles on me, the thing we're not talking about heavy between us. "Sveta—"

"Were you involved with Kali?" I cut him off.

He measures his words before he speaks. "Not for a long time."

I let that double-edged sword sink in.

"I owe you an explanation," he continues, moving from the hammock to the chair next to mine.

"And an apology," I say.

He nods. "I'm sorry, Sveta. I'm so sorry. I want you to know, everything between us was real. I'm so angry with myself that I fucked it up by not telling you the whole truth."

I evaluate him. "What is the whole truth?"

He meets my gaze. "Kali was my mentor in The Circle. We were matched when I was thirteen and she was nineteen."

I feel a stab of fury at the confirmation of what I had assumed. "That's statutory rape."

"Yeah." His stoicism speaks to the heat of the rage he once felt and the work he's done to quell it. "They saw sex as a sacrament." He runs his fingers through his hair. "My father was one of the people responsible for getting the FBI to break up the cult, when I was sixteen. I went through deprograming therapy, then to live with him, and never spoke of it again."

"What happened to your mom?" I ask.

"She went through deprograming, too. Remarried and lives in Canada now. I've forgiven her, but we'll never be close."

"And Kali?"

"She left the country," he says. "Changed her identity and used sex, the way she'd been taught in The Circle, to get what she wanted."

"So she was, what, a call girl?"

He shrugs. "The way she saw it, she brought beauty and spiritual depth to the people she had relationships with, and in return they supported her. But she always stayed in touch with me. And we'd see each other when she was in town."

"Why?" I ask.

"Abuse messes with your head." He sighs. "Kali and I shared something that no one else would ever understand; she was the only one I could talk to about this huge part of my life that cast a shadow across everything else. It bonded us, and I couldn't escape it. Not for a long, long time."

I let my gaze drift past the trees to the river, reflecting the blue sky as it meanders through the jungle. "So how did Kali end up with Paul?" I ask.

"I introduced them," he admits. "I took Kali out to his retreat center in Sonoma—showing off to her, really, that I knew this famous self-help guru. No one, not even my dad, knew my relationship with her—we let them think we'd met only recently, randomly. She charmed Paul, and before I knew it, they were together."

"Did you keep seeing her?"

He nods. "In the beginning. But as I got older and spent more time in therapy and less time with her, I wanted less and less to do with her. I didn't want my time in The Circle to determine the rest of my life. I wanted to be normal, have real girlfriends, maybe even my own family someday. So we grew apart.

"After they moved down here, I hardly heard from her. Until I got this crazy email from her about two weeks ago. She was claiming to be the Kavi, just like her father had, spouting the same BS about leading her flock through the portal. It was The Circle all over again, and it scared the shit out of me."

"What did you do?" I ask.

"I called Paul and confessed everything to him," he answers. "I also reached out to the FBI agent who had been assigned to my case sixteen years ago and showed the message to him. He was sympathetic, but there was very little he could do about consenting adults in a foreign country, without any evidence of wrongdoing."

"Damn," I say.

"Yeah." He sighs. "That's when Paul decided to come down here and close Xanadu. So of course when Hikari called me last week to inform me of his death, I immediately had this terrible feeling Kali had done something. I went to the FBI again to ask them to investigate, but they told me the same thing."

I frown, considering him. "Why the hell didn't you tell me?"

"The agent advised me not to say anything to you, for your own safety." His voice is heavy with the implications of what he walked us into. "I'm sorry."

"Right. And they couldn't help when Kali trapped us down here?"

He shook his head. "Not in any official capacity. I think after Sunshine died, they would have been able to do something. But by then it was too late."

"So, the assistant you called—?"

"Was my FBI contact. A call I later found out Kali heard every word of. That's the argument you saw us having in the woods."

Beyond the lush greenery, the river gurgles. "But I don't understand—you introduced Kali to Paul, so why pretend not to know her here?"

"No one here knows that. It would have complicated things, brought up questions about our past that we didn't have easy answers for."

"Did she know you were coming down here?"

"No. And she was not happy about it," he admits. "She was so angry yesterday that I'd betrayed her by calling the FBI. She thought she could convince me to come over to her side, and when she realized she couldn't, she saw the end of her reign was near—which I knew would make her more dangerous than ever. Blaze had told me in the morning about the park rangers, so I went for help. I hated leaving you, but I couldn't find you and I didn't think I should wait a minute longer. I left you a note—"

"That I didn't get."

"I'm sorry."

"So, Kali killed Paul before he could shut down Xanadu," I say, putting it all together, "then, when we got in the way of her plans to take over, and she found out the FBI was involved, she decided as a last resort to pull the rip cord and lead everyone through the portal?"

"Like her father." He grimaces. "I'm so sorry I brought you down here, got you involved in this." His dark eyes rove over my face. "I wish that . . ." He bites his lip, searching for the right words. "I know I shouldn't have slept with you without telling you the truth first. I knew it when I was doing it. But I . . ." His gaze locks on mine and a flame flickers inside me.

It's too much, the way he's looking at me right now. I stand and go to the railing, putting more space between us. The river gurgles as I stare unseeing at the jungle, my emotions swirling. "You said you're going to see Ruby and the others later?"

"Yeah."

"I want to come," I say. "I want to help them. Put them through deprograming, like you went through. Give them some money to get started. I told Ruby I'd connect her with my friend in New York who has a yoga studio . . ."

He joins me at the railing. "I can help you with all that, if you want me to."

The question hangs between us as I wrestle with myself.

The truth is, I do want his help. He knows better than anyone what someone coming out of a cult needs. And no other attorney is going to take as good care of me during probate as he will. "I'd appreciate that, thank you," I say.

"Sveta . . ." The brush of his fingers against my arm sets a humming-bird loose in my chest. "I know I screwed up. And as much as I want it, I know I don't deserve another chance with you. But if you can ever forgive me, I hope we can at least be friends."

Friends. Could we be just friends?

"Lucas . . ." I gather my willpower, choosing my words carefully. "I forgive you. And I can't say you'll never have another chance with me." This elicits a small smile. "But I need some time to myself to figure things out. Figure out who I am and what I want."

He pauses, considering me. "I respect that," he says, wrapping me in a hug that very nearly weakens my resolve.

"And it's not like we're not gonna talk during probate," I add.

"If conversations about trust accounts and revenue shares is all I can get, I'll take it," he murmurs into my hair.

I allow myself to enjoy the warmth of his strong arms around me for just a moment longer, knowing it may be a while before I'm this close to him again.

I don't know what will happen between us, I have no expectations. I won't cut him out of my life, though. He's made mistakes, but he's been through a lot, and I understand now that he was never out to take advantage of me. I don't care if some people think that makes me a pushover. Life isn't black and white. If I've learned anything in the past year, it's to be true to myself. I'm more determined than ever to do the work to make myself whole. And I trust myself to make the right decisions for me.

After all, it's my choice whether I lead a life of bliss or sorrow. And I choose bliss.

ACKNOWLEDGMENTS

So much goes into writing a book, from the creative process right down through production, and I am so fortunate to have had such wonderful support along this journey. First and always, I am grateful for my most favorite people in the whole wide world, my family. My little girls, my biggest fans even though they aren't yet allowed to read my work, who take every opportunity to shamelessly market my books to anyone who will listen (no matter how inappropriate the circumstance) and (mostly) allow Mommy to work when she needs to; my husband, Alex, who is mercifully a far better cook than I am and patiently pretends to listen while I drone on and on about ever-changing plot points and character arcs, always ready with a bear hug when I need one; my parents, Celia and Frank, who have always believed in me and encouraged me.

This book was written during the pandemic, which I would not have made it through without the support of some very special friends who kept me sane with the aid of strong margaritas, lively discourse, and hearty laughter: Ashleigh and Manish, bubble family forever! If the past couple of years have taught me anything, it's just how important friends are, and I am so grateful for beach outings with Lance and Vanessa, hikes with Lawren, golf course shenanigans with Dina, and the open arms of my husband's family, who took such good care of us, allowing me to actually finish this book. Charise, you have a heart of gold and I am so thankful you are my mother-in-law!

I am always and forever grateful to my superb agent, Sarah Bedingfield, who is my rock, my net, my champion, and above all else my friend. To Stephanie Rostan, for taking such good care of me, and the entire team at Levine, Greenberg, Rostan, my literary family. To my fabulous film agent Hilary Zaitz Michael and the team at William Morris Endeavor, thank you for your tireless work on the Hollywood side of things.

I feel so fortunate to have connected with my incredible editor, Liz Stein, who pushed me to make this book the best it could be and made the process enjoyable along the way! I am also grateful for the support of the outstanding team at William Morrow: Francie Crawford in marketing, Holly Rice in publicity, assistant editor Ariana Sinclair, production editor Michelle Meredith, copyeditor Greg Villepique, and cover designer Mumtaz Mustafa.

Last, but certainly not least, I am grateful for you, reader. Thank you for reading.

ABOUT THE AUTHOR

Katherine St. John is a native of Mississippi, a graduate of the University of Southern California, and the author of *The Lion's Den* and *The Siren*. When she's not writing, she can be found hiking or on the beach with a good book. Katherine lives in Atlanta with her husband and two children.